Church Ladies' QUILTS

a novel by

Ann Hazelwood

American Quilter's Society

www.AmericanQuilter.com

Located in Paducah, Kentucky, the American Quilter's Society (AQS) is dedicated to promoting the accomplishments of today's quilters. Through its publications and events, AQS strives to honor today's quiltmakers and their work and to inspire future creativity and innovation in quiltmaking.

Executive Book Editor: Elaine H. Brelsford
Copy Editor: Julie Schroeder
Graphic Design: Lynda Smith
Cover Design: Michael Buckingham

This book is a work of fiction. The people, places, and events described in it are either imaginary or fictitiously presented. Any resemblance they bear to reality is entirely coincidental.

PO Box 3290
Paducah, KY 42002-3290
americanquilter.com

Additional copies of this book may be ordered from the American Quilter's Society, PO Box 3290, Paducah, KY 42002-3290, or online at www.AmericanQuilter.com.

Library of Congress Cataloging-in-Publication Data

Names: Hazelwood, Ann Watkins, author.
Title: Church ladies' quilts : a novel / by Ann Hazelwood.
Description: Paducah, KY : American Quilter's Society, [2017]
Identifiers: LCCN 2017031134 | ISBN 9781604603941 (pbk.)
Classification: LCC PS3608.A98846 C48 2017 | DDC 813/.6--dc23
LC record available at https://lccn.loc.gov/2017031134

Cover quilt: Bow Tie Quilt by Martha Dellasega Gray (2007). 62" x 78". Hand pieced and hand quilted.

Dedication

I dedicate this book to all the wonderful ladies who quilt for their churches and other worthy causes. I've gotten to know so many of them through the years. I admire their stitches, their stories, and their continuous dedication. Thank you!

To all the residents and businesses in beautiful East Perry County, I thank you for setting the stage for this fictional series.
Ann Hazelwood

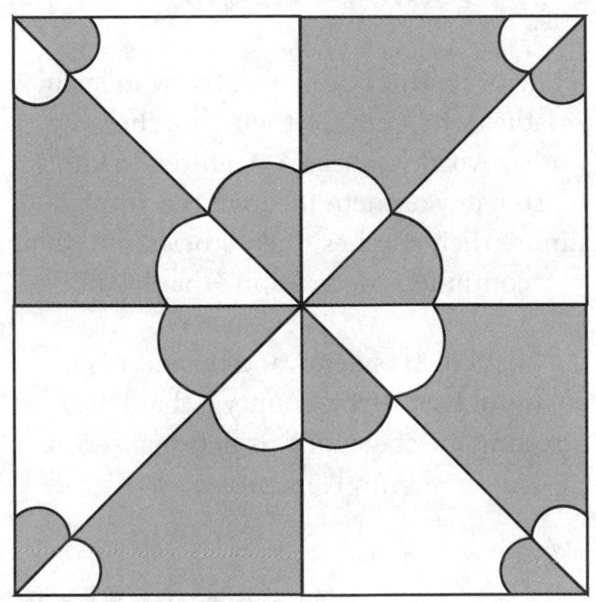

Hearts and Gizzards block

Chapter 1

"Drive safely, Miss Kate," Cotton said as he tapped the hood of my red Jeep.

"I think Red is up to the challenge!" I flashed him a confident smile. "It's the perfect trip to break him in."

Cotton laughed and waved as I backed out of my driveway at 6229 Main Street in Borna, Missouri. It was clear, cold, and sunny as I headed to my hometown in South Haven, Michigan, for the Thanksgiving holiday. It had been quite some time since I had been back to visit, but with the insistence of my best friend, Maggie, and my condo neighbor, John, I had agreed to return.

It had been a couple of years since I had moved from South Haven following my husband's fatal car accident. In Clay's will, he left me property in Borna, which I had never seen. After traveling there and working to get it ready to put on the market, I not only fell in love with the house, but with the whole community of East Perry County.

There, I found many new friends and male companionship that I never would have experienced if I had stayed in South Haven. Shortly after my husband's death, I also discovered that he had been involved in a longtime affair. Not being able to confront a dead man, I left my life in South Haven behind and started a new life in Borna.

As I drove along, I reminded myself of what a good idea it had been to invest in a condo on Lake Michigan so that my son and I would have a place to stay when visiting. Jack had found success in the advertising business in New York City. He was engaged to Jill Malone, Maggie's daughter. That was a miraculous dream that Maggie and I still couldn't believe! Jill was very independent and wanted to plan her own wedding, which was driving Maggie crazy.

As I left the scenic countryside of East Perry, I tried to think of the joyous days ahead. Even though it was only the beginning of winter, the red barns and white fences provided a striking contrast to the dull colors appearing on the grass and trees. I had much to accomplish on this visit. One of the Beach Quilter's members was seriously ill with ovarian cancer. I wanted to be sure to see her. She had visited my guest house with a few others not that long ago.

I also kept an ongoing relationship with my former housekeeper, Carla. She looked after my condo, and had graciously adopted Clay's dog, Roxy, whom I could muster no affection for after I learned that Clay had been unfaithful to me. Carla had successfully survived breast cancer. On my last visit to South Haven, I had accompanied her to her surgery and tried to be helpful to her since she lived alone.

There was no avoiding John at my condo. He was a successful writer whose company I enjoyed very much. He had tried to make our relationship romantic, but we finally came to the conclusion that it was best to just be friends. I'll admit that I was flattered that a younger man had pursued me and had taken enough interest in me to visit Borna, but eventually, my common sense prevailed. He wrote an article about Borna, which delighted the whole community when it was published in a travel magazine. Of course, I wanted to spend time with him at some point on this visit, but it would be brief.

Thanksgiving Day meant Jack would be home. As was our tradition, we would be going to the South Haven Country Club, as we had done for so much of my married life. Clay had been big on being anywhere that he could be social and promote his company, Meyr Lumber Company. When Clay died, James, his brother, took over as president and later pressured me to give him the property in Borna. When I didn't give in, he took me to court, leaving bad feelings between me and the Meyrs. Sadly, his wife committed suicide after she and James divorced. So, the only family member I continued to have contact with was James's daughter, Emily.

Chapter 2

When I arrived in South Haven, I was welcomed by the charming drawbridge that brought back so many memories of events and festivals here. South Haven is the blueberry capital of the world and its summer blueberry festival is not to be missed! As one of its former blueberry muffin contest winners, I often made muffins at my guest house in Borna for my guests to enjoy. My friends in Borna also looked forward to the blueberry treats I would bring them from the Blueberry Store downtown.

Rather than turning onto my street, I drove a few blocks further to see the famous red lighthouse perched out on Lake Michigan. It was the icon of South Haven and was featured on every postcard and advertisement. Visitors could walk onto the pier where they could see its majesty. It was also a perfect place to see the sunset, something I had enjoyed many times while living here. All of these memories made me feel anxious to settle into my condo once again.

Light snow was scattered on the parking lot as I pulled into my assigned space. John's space was empty, indicating that he wasn't home. He knew I was coming, so I was sure we would catch up.

After I made several trips from my car to unload, I gazed at my little home away from home. It was painted in cool colors and featured beach house décor. In contrast, my 1920s guest house in Borna was filled with antiques that I also dearly loved. It was fitting décor for the former home and office of Dr. Paulson and his wife, Josephine. As I had learned more and more about the life of Josephine, I had eventually decided to name my guest house after her.

It was now six o'clock and I was very hungry. The refrigerator was bare, with the exception of wine and beer left from Jack's last visit. I helped myself to a glass of merlot and ordered a pizza. I was happy to be back in a place that had pizza delivery! When I sat down to relax, I wanted to open the doors to the deck to get a view of the lake, but decided otherwise due to the current temperature. Within a short period of time, a knock at the door meant my pizza had arrived. I opened the door. To my surprise, it was John with a pizza box in hand!

"I thought I'd make a personal delivery," John said. "I took care of the charge, thinking it would get me a free pass to come in."

"John, you are something!" I said with a chuckle in my voice. "Please come in and join me." I was happy to see him again because I truly enjoyed his company.

"I might be talked into a slice or two, if you insist. When did you arrive?"

"About an hour or so ago. I lucked out with the weather."

"You certainly did! There is a storm coming in tomorrow."

I poured John a glass of wine and we sat on the couch to

enjoy our pizza. He wanted an update on everyone in Borna and I wanted to know how Carla was doing. Besides keeping an eye on my place, she had begun cleaning John's condo. I also loved hearing about what he was currently writing. He told me that his quilt article, which I had helped with, had been a big hit. His publisher encouraged him to write about quilts again in the future. Two glasses of wine and an empty pizza box later, the clock on the mantel struck midnight.

"It's so good to have you here," John said as he got up to leave. "Once you know your schedule, I'd love to take you to dinner."

"I can't promise anything, but I'm glad we had this unexpected visit."

I walked him to the door. When he came closer, he only pecked me on the cheek, which took me by surprise. Had we finally reached the point of just being neighbors again? I hoped so. I smiled with satisfaction as I closed the door. There was no question that John's earlier flirtations had elevated my self-esteem. I was so glad I had not succumbed to his suggestions that we take it to a deeper level.

My bed was already made, thanks to Carla, so I eagerly undressed and slipped into the comfy warmth of my flannel sheets. It had been a long day!

Chapter 3

The next morning, like clockwork, I knew to meet Maggie at the Golden Bakery for the best blueberry scones known to man. It was our ritual when I came back to visit. I was hoping she would bring Carla with her as she sometimes did.

The familiar aroma was so inviting. Before I placed my order, I saw that Maggie and Carla were already seated in our favorite corner booth. Happy cheers and hugs greeted me.

"I took the liberty in ordering you a scone," Maggie said as I sat down to join them.

"Thanks, girlfriend," I said, beaming at the large delight. "Okay, so fill me in on everything."

Their faces suddenly turned somber.

"It's Marilee," Maggie said in a soft voice. "I'm afraid she is much worse. They stopped her treatments and are just trying to make her comfortable."

"Comfortable until what?" I said in disbelief. "You don't mean it's that far along! Can she have visitors?"

Maggie shook her head. "Family only."

"Does she know she's going to die?"

Maggie nodded.

"How sad for all of you not to be able to say good-bye," Carla soothed.

"She's pretty sedated," Maggie said.

"I just can't get over how quickly her disease progressed," I said, holding back tears. "Life is just not fair."

"Look, Kate, it's Thanksgiving," Maggie said firmly. "We have a lot to be thankful for. We will get to see Jill and Jack and we have a wedding to look forward to."

"That seems rather insensitive," I responded, looking into her eyes.

"What I meant is that we have to make the most of our lives right now," Maggie explained. "We can't do anything to help Marilee. Let's change the subject."

I paused, feeling the sadness, but also sensing that what Maggie suggested was correct. "Carla, what are your plans for tomorrow?" I asked, since we were almost ignoring her.

She blushed. "I have an invitation from a friend, so I'm taken care of," Carla said with a smile.

"Now, tell Kate that it's just not any friend," Maggie coached.

"Really?"

"Oh, it's just a man that I met at the post office one day," she admitted shyly. "I asked him some questions and we started a conversation. Come to find out, he's a widower and lives in my neighborhood. He said he loves to cook. He invited me over and I've been spending some time with him."

"Carla, that's wonderful!" I said, touching her hand.

"How about more coffee?" the waitress asked.

"Yes, please, but could you box up six blueberry scones that I could take home with me?" Turning to my friends,

I remarked, "I think Jack thinks these scones just appear automatically when he's home."

"Certainly," the waitress responded. "I remember you always coming in, Mrs. Meyr."

"Jill loves their cheesecake, so I made sure I picked one up when I arrived," said Maggie.

"I take it that we're all set to go to the country club tomorrow?" I asked Maggie.

"I hope so, because I haven't cooked on Thanksgiving in many years," Maggie confessed with a chuckle.

"Carla, you made us so many wonderful dinners through the years," I said. I turned to Maggie. "Jack would always request his favorite dishes, which melted Carla's heart."

Carla blushed and nodded in agreement.

"Kate, we can come pick you up," Maggie offered. "Jill and Jack will have their own plans, I'm sure."

"No thanks," I answered quickly. "I'll just meet you there at noon."

I left the girls and decided to head to the Bayberry Cottage and the Blueberry Store, which were just across the street from one another. I was always in awe when I walked into the Bayberry Cottage. Their home accessories were classic in taste and they stocked interesting area rugs like the one I had purchased when I bought the condo. As I browsed, I was attracted to a narrow, contemporary table that would look grand behind my couch. It had the perfect lamp sitting on it, which I could also picture in my living room. I made an impulse decision to buy both pieces, hoping they would fit in the Jeep. The clerks assured me that it was no problem because they offered same-day delivery on any merchandise purchased. I was pleased.

After successfully getting the items tucked in my Jeep, I went to the Blueberry Store to pick up all the goodies I knew my crew in Borna would be expecting. On every visit, this store seemed to have more and more product to tempt me. I could order online, but it wasn't the same as holding things in my hands and taking them home with me.

It was nine that evening before Jack finally arrived from the airport in his rental car. He looked fatigued, but was as handsome as ever. It was hard not to think of his father when seeing Jack. They favored one another so much. After he helped himself to a beer, we talked for awhile before he wanted to crash for the night. I was feeling very blessed to be under the same roof as my son once again.

Chapter 4

When I awoke on Thanksgiving morning, I knew it would fall to me to make the coffee. Jack would be thrilled to see the scones, but I knew he'd be sleeping in. I waited until ten to call Aunt Mandy in Borna to wish her a happy Thanksgiving. It was so grand having her move to Borna from Florida. She'd had a clever home built behind my wooded property so we could be close to one another. I was pleased to see Jack getting up so he could say hello to her as well.

"Happy Thanksgiving, Auntie!" I greeted her cheerfully.

"Oh, how nice of you to call," she answered in a crackly voice.

"How could I not think of you after your visiting me last year in Borna for Thanksgiving?"

"It was splendid. This year, I'll be joining Wilson at his daughter's house. I'm looking forward to that."

"I'm pleased to know that. Tell them all hello for me," I added. "Here is Jack. He wants to say hello." I handed the phone to Jack and he and Aunt Mandy began a cheerful conversation.

I was pleased that she and her architect had remained an

item. Jack and Aunt Mandy talked longer than I expected. I could tell she was pressing him for wedding information. Better her than me! After a sweet good-bye, he handed me the phone so I could say good-bye.

"Are you going to miss Borna today?" Jack asked as he devoured his scone.

I nodded. "It's my home now, Jack. I have put my heart and soul into that house and community."

"I know. I'm happy for you," Jack said as he put his arm around me. "I worried about your making that decision until I met your friends and saw what you created with that guest house. You made the right decision."

"I'm afraid I have not been the most successful businesswoman. I had no idea how few guests I would have."

"Well, excuse me, but how many folks want to travel to Borna to spend the night?" Jack teased.

"We have some lovely tourist spots to visit," I countered.

"How is the restoration coming along with some of those vacant buildings I saw? I know you were concerned about the county not having any guidelines to protect some of the historic buildings."

"I haven't seen much movement on the subject. I know the topic is controversial, but my friend just opened up a cute little coffee shop in the old bank in Dresden."

"Wow, a coffee shop! You are getting big time!" He snickered. "I wish it had been there when I visited."

"We'd better get dressed, Jack. You don't want to keep your future bride waiting."

My phone showed that I had gotten a text from John.

Happy Thanksgiving! Free for dinner? J

I was tempted to say yes, but I knew my day was devoted to being with Jack and the Malone family.

Thanks. Too busy. See you before I leave. K

I showered and changed into a fall colored outfit with dress boots. The forecast of more snow did not present an opportunity to be a fashion plate. Jack looked handsome in his sport coat. He asked if he could drive my new Jeep. It made me happy to have his approval. I told him that I had purchased it from a very nice man by the name of Cole Alexander. The more I described him, the more Jack grinned. I knew what he was thinking.

"Does this mean that Mr. Alexander is the new hottie in town? What happened to Clark McFadden?"

He loved to tease me. "Stop it, Jack! Don't be smart. Clark and I never had a commitment, even though everyone thinks we did."

"Why not?"

I paused. "We are both too independent. Clark is a good friend, but he wants a lot of freedom. Most of the time, I never know if he's in town or not. He is not a good communicator. By the way, he just learned that he has a daughter. It's a long story, but he's quite excited about it."

"You're kidding me! He must have had a more adventurous background than I would have guessed. I'd like to hear that story sometime."

We arrived at the country club as the snowflakes were getting heavier and heavier. Mark, Maggie, and Jill were already seated at a round table in one of the dining rooms. It was touching to see Jack and Jill embrace like two lovebirds. I felt like the fifth wheel in the midst of two happy couples.

Chapter 5

Mark was about to make a toast when I asked to say a prayer of thanksgiving. Jack reached for a hand on either side of him, like we had in Borna, which made me proud. Jill, Mark, and Maggie were a bit taken aback, but seemed genuinely touched by the moment. We then toasted the engaged couple and Maggie gave a special thank-you toast to me for coming back to visit.

As always, the country club outdid itself. It offered a beautiful array of food that was fit for a king. The conversation quickly turned to the big wedding. Maggie and Mark once again expressed their disappointment that the reception would be at Hawk's Head rather than at the club. Jill continued to stand up to her parents. My Jack fell in line like a good future husband. I couldn't help asking Jill how she felt about moving to New York City.

"I look at it as an adventure. It will likely help my career, too," she answered.

"Jill says you spotted a larger apartment for the two of you, Jack," Mark stated. "I can't believe the outrageous rents they are getting!"

"Hey, Jack!" Former schoolmate Ed Spencer approached our table. "I hear congratulations are in order."

Jack got up to address him. "Good to see you, Ed," Jack responded, shaking his hand. "You are correct!"

"I got hitched last year to Courtney Wallace," Ed volunteered. "Do you remember her?"

"Why, yes! Congrats! Is she here?"

"Yes, we're in the other dining room. Come by and say hello before you leave. Sorry to interrupt your dinner."

"Good to see you, Ed," I said, shaking his hand. "How are your parents?"

"They got divorced a couple of years ago," Ed said quietly. "We're with my dad."

"I'm sorry to hear that," I said, feeling badly for him.

"Funny you should ask, because he asked if I knew whether you were still single!"

I blushed.

"Tell your dad my mom can't handle another suitor," Jack teased. "He'd have to get in line."

"Jack!" I corrected, feeling embarrassed.

"Okay, I get it!" Ed said with a chuckle. "Here's my card, Jack. Give us a call."

After he left, I tried to imagine Ed's father. He was certainly not someone I would be interested in. Thank goodness I was away from this country club scene.

"Does anyone want to visit the dessert table?" Jack asked.

Everyone responded positively except Jill. She said that she was watching her weight. When I walked to the dessert table, I was sorry I had agreed to check out the delicacies because there stood James and his new wife.

"Hello, James," I said calmly while passing by. I did not give him a chance to engage me in conversation. I chose a slice of blueberry pie and went back to our table. I wondered if James had cornered Jack to say hello, but then I noticed that Jack and Jill were off to see Ed and his wife. I remained for a while with Maggie and Mark.

"Please remember to come to lunch at Taste tomorrow," Maggie reminded me. "I don't know who will be there from our group."

"Sure. Maggie and Mark, thanks so much for treating me to dinner," I said, giving them both a peck on the cheek.

"Will we see you at Christmas?" Mark asked quickly.

"Sorry, not likely," I responded.

I couldn't leave the club fast enough. It would be nice to visit just once without a reminder of the country club and the Meyr family. It only brought me unhappy memories. When I arrived at the condo, John was coming out of his door.

"Well, I see you survived the club," John teased.

"Just barely, and I'm exhausted. I ate too much and I need a nap."

John laughed. "I'm off to run an errand, but perhaps later we can share a cocktail if you don't want to commit to dinner."

"Maybe. We'll see," I said. I had little interest at the moment.

"See you later," John said as he made his way to the parking lot.

Chapter 6

When I kicked off my shoes, I became homesick for Borna. I called Ellie."Happy Thanksgiving!"

"The same to you! Wish you were here. How are things going?"

"Nothing has changed. I wish I were there too! I loved seeing Jack, of course, but the usual run-in with James at the country club is getting old. Are you at the winery?"

"Yes. Everyone has pretty much left. Now it's time to clean up. I think everyone enjoyed themselves."

"Of course they did. You do such a nice job. I was so impressed with your dinner my first year in Borna. Did Clark show up?"

"No. Trout thinks he's out of town. We did have a quick stop from another friend of yours, however."

"Who?"

"Cole Alexander. I think Cole and Trout are lining up another fishing trip. He asked whether I knew if you and Red made the trip to South Haven okay. I said I hadn't heard from you. I think he's a bit smitten with you."

"He's just being nice, but at least he asked about my trip. That's more than I hear from Clark. Tell him Red did fine. Why wasn't he with family today?"

"He was on his way to Perry to be with his daughter for dinner. When are you getting back?"

"It will likely be the day after tomorrow. We have snow now and maybe more coming."

"Well, don't bring it with you," Ellie teased. "Say, you haven't mentioned John."

"He's fine. We may have a drink later."

"You sound kind of down, girlfriend," Ellie observed.

"You may be right. I'll text you when I leave South Haven, okay?"

Talking with Ellie made me feel a little bit better. Perhaps my friendship with Maggie had changed over the years. She was living in the old world that I was trying to forget. Perhaps seeing my other quilter friends tomorrow at lunch would perk me up.

Jack called as I was changing clothes. He told me that he and Jill were meeting up with friends. It made me feel good that he hadn't lost touch with the friends he grew up with.

I heard classical music coming from downstairs, which meant that John was home. It did bring a smile to my face as I remembered the night we both were out on our decks. My complimenting his music started our first conversation.

Minutes later, my cell phone rang and it was John.

"Are you up for some company and a drink? I have a nice bottle of Cab to share."

"Sure, for a bit," I said with a smile. "I must caution you about my somber mood."

"That's what the Cab is for," he teased.

I did a quick check in the mirror and then put my shoes back on before he knocked at the door.

"I can't believe I have you to myself tonight!" John bragged.

"Lucky you!" I said, giving him a wink.

"Did you see how heavily the snow is coming down? What are your plans tomorrow?"

"Just lunch with the Beach Quilters. I'm afraid we're about to lose one of them to cancer. It just breaks my heart."

"No wonder you're down. Any news about the wedding? That should make you happy."

"I just have to turn in my guest list and I am done. How about that?" My cell phone rang and it was Maggie, which surprised me.

"It's Maggie," she said. It was uncharacteristic of her to introduce herself when she called.

"What's wrong?"

"It's Marilee. She passed away this afternoon." She broke into a sob.

"That's awful," I finally responded. "She died on Thanksgiving? Was her family with her?"

"Yes," Maggie mumbled. "The poor girl was only fifty-one, Kate," Maggie said with an angry tone.

"Has Betsy been told?"

"She's the one who called me. She's beside herself. They have been inseparable for years."

I took a deep breath to get past crying on the phone as John watched me react. "What about tomorrow?"

"I will meet you there. I don't know about the others."

We quietly said good-bye. I felt like I was in shock. I sat down as tears rolled down my face.

"How awful for you, Kate. What can I do?" John asked, looking helpless.

I shook my head. "She was so carefree and happy the last time I saw her in Borna. I keep thinking about how they joked around with an Ouija board when they were there. They asked the board if there was anyone else in the room—like a ghost. The answer was cancer. Can you imagine how scary that was?"

"Now, Kate, did you really believe it?"

I couldn't answer.

"Look, I'm here to listen if you want to talk. If you want to be left alone, I understand."

"That might be a good idea, John. This is so hard to absorb. I would like to have some time alone."

"Say no more. Drink some of this wine and try to get a good night's rest. Remember, she is in a better place and isn't suffering."

I nodded. He was right. "Thanks for the wine. I will see you before I leave."

He gave me a peck on the cheek and went out the door.

Chapter 7

There wasn't much sleep to be had. I kept thinking of Marilee. Jack didn't return home until one in the morning. My visit sure wasn't going very well so far.

I got up early and checked the accumulated snow. There wouldn't be my friend Cotton to come clear my car, but I had to remind myself that I had a healthy son who hopefully would help me out. I got coffee and sat down to strategize about my trip home to Borna. I wondered about Marilee and when her funeral would be held. I finally called Maggie to see how she made it through the night. She said Betsy told her Marilee was going to be cremated and that a memorial service wouldn't be held for a couple of weeks.

Maggie said, "Cornelia said we should all still meet today to decide what to do about a memorial."

"I agree. When Emma from our Friendship Circle died, we all just wanted to be together and remember her. I will plan to leave tomorrow."

"I'm sorry your visit has been disappointing. I hope you'll return in the spring when there is a wedding shower scheduled for Jill."

"I wouldn't miss it. I'll see you at lunch."

Jack was up and getting his coffee as I told him about Marilee. He didn't remember her, but he felt truly sorry for me. It was times like this that it was natural to bring up plans for when we pass. I told Jack I wanted to be buried in Borna and not in the empty plot next to his father. I could tell he was taken aback, but he nodded his head in agreement. A space on the cemetery hill at Concordia would be fitting for me.

I dressed in layers to keep me warm as Jack went out to clear off the car. I had to admit that the parking lot and streets had been attended to quickly, unlike the roads in East Perry County when it snowed there.

"Be careful out there, Mom," Jack cautioned when he came in. "I'm sure glad you have this Jeep instead of your Mercedes."

"I am too! Thanks for clearing the car. Do you still plan to leave in the morning?"

"Yes, I have to. Today, Jill and I are meeting with Hawk's Head to finish up some details on the reception."

"Great. Remember, if there's anything I can do, just let me know."

"Well, I guess I'll drop a hint since you're asking. Jill asked if I thought you would make us a quilt."

"She did? Well that's great! Just give me a hint about what kind of quilt you would like. I'd love to. I'll still contribute to your honeymoon, of course."

"I showed her a photo of the lighthouse quilt you made, so something personal like that would be great."

"I know you both are more contemporary, but I'll think

about it. I've never made a king-size quilt before, but I have quilting friends that can help me."

Jack grinned and I was pleased that they both liked quilts.

I bundled up and drove slowly to the downtown area near the harbor where the restaurant was located. When I went in, it was just Maggie and Cornelia sitting at the table. They both looked so sad.

"I was hoping Betsy would come," I said as I joined them.

"She's a wreck," Cornelia said.

We ordered lunch and then I pressed them about coming up with a memorial for Marilee.

"I'm so glad we made that quilt for her when she was going through treatment," Cornelia added.

"Did Marilee have any special interests or organizations she belonged to?" I asked as I picked at my chicken salad sandwich.

"Yes," Cornelia quickly responded. "She had two dogs and she served on the board at the humane society. She always had a heart for rescue dogs."

"Perfect! There you have it," I pointed out. "A nice donation in her name would be very fitting."

"Consider it done!" Maggie said with a nod.

Chapter 6

We were all thinking about sharing a dessert when my cell phone rang. I didn't recognize the number.

"Hey, Kate. It's Cole." His voice sounded upbeat.

"Well, this is quite a surprise," I responded. The call from Cole caught me completely off guard.

"Am I interrupting anything?"

"No, it's fine. Is everything okay?" I left the table to walk closer to the window for privacy.

"Oh, sure," he said. "I was just curious to know if you and Red got there okay. I heard you had a lot of snow."

"Red and I did just fine," I assured him. "I was glad I didn't have my Mercedes."

"That is a stroke of luck. When are you returning?"

"Tomorrow. I hear the snow should let up soon."

"Be sure to check out the road conditions before you go. It's fine here, but very cold."

"I'll be fine. I'm anxious to get home. It has not been a jolly visit."

"I'm sorry to hear that. I'd like to take you to dinner

when you get back, if you think it possible."

I wasn't expecting an invitation. "Why, that would be nice," I agreed, surprising myself.

"Would Saturday around six be okay?"

"I think that can work," I said, still feeling surprised to hear from him.

"Well, I'll look forward to that. Be safe coming home," Cole said before he hung up.

I stood there for a moment in shock. Someone had formally asked me to dinner, which was rare and nice. I was taken aback. I walked back to the table. I'm sure I looked like I had seen a ghost.

"Is everything okay?" Maggie asked, concerned.

I nodded. "Cole Alexander sold me my red Jeep. He wanted to know if I made it here okay," I explained.

"He couldn't wait until you got home?" Cornelia wondered aloud.

"Then he asked me to go to dinner with him when I get back," I added. "I can't believe I said yes."

The girls chuckled.

"Okay, so where is that handsome hunk, Clark, in all of this?" Maggie asked, clearly happy to tease me.

"I don't know," I answered truthfully. "I don't even know where he is. We just sort of do our own thing, you could say."

"What's Cole like?" Cornelia asked.

"He's just a nice man who sold me his Jeep," I said, shrugging my shoulders. "He is recently divorced and is a real estate developer. When I test drove the Jeep, I had to take him home and it was a very nice house on a great piece of property. He has one married daughter who lives in Perry."

"Is he handsome?" Cornelia asked, leaning forward.

"I guess so," I said, picturing him. "He has salt-and-pepper hair and has a good build. No potbelly."

We erupted into laughter.

"Sounds like Cary Grant, if you ask me," Maggie added with a smile. "How come you didn't share more about him earlier?"

"Because there was nothing to tell," I explained.

"Well, it sounds like this Clark had better pay attention," Cornelia warned. "If you snooze, you lose!"

I had to snicker, but she wasn't wrong. "Cornelia, I want to know a little bit more about what will happen to your quilt shop," I asked, eager to change the subject. "Is there still no one interested in buying it?"

She shook her head. "I'm working on your best friend," she said, looking directly at Maggie.

"I told her absolutely N-O!" Maggie stated emphatically.

"I think Maggie really means that, Cornelia," I said in a serious tone. "Maggie would never want to be tied down by anything like that."

"Thanks, girlfriend," Maggie said, giving me an enthusiastic high five.

"I have some interested folks, but none of them really can afford it. I don't want to give it away. One of them is Penny. She has worked for me for years. I suggested that Maggie become an investor and then let Penny run the business."

I looked back at Maggie.

"You know me. I would meddle until it drove them crazy," Maggie said, joking.

We continued pursuing the topic, but Maggie dug in her heels, and properly so, I think.

Chapter 9

It was late afternoon when I got back to my condo. I couldn't help but think about how quickly I had responded to Cole's dinner invitation. That was not like me. I should have checked with Ellie first because she knew him probably as well as she knew Clark.

Perhaps I felt close to Cole because of our secret. Cole was the first to find me after an intruder tied me up. Cole was so caring, but then who wouldn't help a woman in distress? He had respected my request to only call the detectives involved and not 911. He knew I was serious about keeping the incident quiet because I didn't want bad publicity for my guest house.

What would Clark think? We had become close when he came to work at my guest house each day. He witnessed my struggles to fit in and was always there to take my side, including rescuing me from an attack from a belligerent realtor. Our physical attraction grew, but we knew it could not be more than that. We both wanted to be independent. I knew that if I wanted more, Clark would not be able to supply my needs. My biggest complaint about Clark was unreliable communication.

Since I had eaten a late lunch, I didn't need to think about dinner. I would use the time to pack so I could leave first thing in the morning. I had just arrived in my parking spot when my I received a text.

> Still in Holland. Traffic not moving. Sorry I cannot say good-bye in person. Safe travels, beautiful. J

I responded,

> Sorry too. Stay in touch. K

Now I was feeling even sadder. Things just weren't going well. This was just another signal to me that things were changing in South Haven. Getting back to Borna was now my mission.

Jack came home shortly after I did, complaining about stalled traffic in the snow. He looked exhausted. "You know, I'll be glad when this wedding is over," he admitted as he threw his body on the couch.

"I can only imagine. Are you and Jill in agreement on most things?"

"I suppose, but I don't like seeing Jill and her mom go at each other."

I didn't know what to say other than to point out that it wouldn't last forever. "Are you packed?"

"I will be soon. How about you?"

"I'm ready to go, both mentally and physically."

"I'm sorry you had Marilee's death to deal with on this trip."

"It is sad. I'm turning in. I'll see you in the morning. Try not to worry. Everything will be fine."

The alarm went off seemingly right after I drifted off to sleep. To my amazement, I had gotten a good night's sleep. I quickly looked out the window and the weather was clearing. Jack and I had a quick cup of coffee in silence before we hugged and said our good-byes. My baby was grown and experiencing life's stress in real time.

With tears rolling down my cheeks, I drove slowly out of South Haven. The interstate was clear and traffic was moving quickly. My drive would be about eight hours. Time went quickly as I pondered all that had happened during the visit. The next thing you know, it was lunchtime. I pulled over to grab a bite to eat at a small diner. It was the perfect time to call Ellie and let her know that I was on my way home.

"Where are you?"

"About halfway. I'm making good time and the roads are clear."

"That's good. I sure have missed you. I'm anxious to hear about everything."

"You won't believe this one, girlfriend. Cole Alexander called me yesterday to see how Red did on the trip and then asked me to dinner on Saturday night."

"Whoa! Did you accept?"

"I did, and without any hesitation. I managed to even surprise myself! Do you think I should have agreed to go out with him?"

"Only you can answer that question. Cole is a great guy. He's been through a lot with that divorce, but from what I hear from Trout, it's all over. It sounds like he's decided to move on in life, which he deserves."

"Is there still no sign of Clark?"

"Not that we have seen, so he must be gone. When he's in town, he stops by to get food and takes it home. Does it matter, my friend?"

"Right now, I suppose it doesn't. He sure seems to be wrapped up with this new daughter."

"I'll stop by for coffee in the morning. I don't suppose you brought any of those delicious scones with you, did you?"

I had to chuckle. "Of course! My whole back seat is filled with blueberry delights."

When I got back on the road, I felt so much better. When I turned onto Road A, the last leg of the trip, I felt I was already home. The rolling hills soothed my soul. Even though the fall colors were turning brown and gray, the colorful accessories of buildings, fences, and animals made me happy. Finally, coming around the corner, I passed Marv's, Ellie's house, and then the infamous Josephine's Guest House, which is my home.

Chapter 10

I got settled in quickly. I built a fire to take the chill out of the room and sifted through the mail. I wanted to call Aunt Mandy right away because I knew she would worry.

"So good to hear your voice, honey," Aunt Mandy said with a sigh. "You have been on my mind all day."

"I left the bad weather behind and only thought of getting home. I was thinking about how you and I have to plan our Christmas together."

"Heavens, child, we've just had Thanksgiving!" She chuckled.

"How was your day with Wilson and Barbara's family?"

"Splendid. She is such a dear. Her husband's family was there as well, so she had quite a crowd and handled it superbly. Martin, her husband, was also a big help to her. "

"I brought you some goodies from the Blueberry Store."

"I was hoping so. You spoil me. How were Jack, Maggie, and your quilting friends?"

I didn't know where to start. I hated spoiling our happy conversation by telling her about Marilee, but I had no choice. It took me a while to report on everyone. I think she was pleased that I only spent a little time with John. She was sorry to hear that Jack was getting stressed about the wedding, but reminded me that it was normal. When I was about to hang up, I told her about Cole calling me and asking me to dinner.

"He is such a fine-looking man, and if Clark isn't smart enough to know you are getting away from him, he doesn't deserve you."

"I'm beginning to agree with you. I haven't heard from him and I thought he might be a little concerned about me driving to South Haven. I don't think he's insensitive. I just think those things do not occur to him."

"Ellie's coming for coffee in the morning. Would you like to join us? If not, I'll come soon to drop off your goodies."

"Very good. You know I'm not an early riser so I'll pass on the morning coffee, but I'm very pleased that you're back."

I poured myself a glass of wine and sat by the fire to open the mail. I felt as if I had been gone a month. My phone had a text coming in. It was John.

I'm home. How about you? J

Yes. In front of the fire. Thanks for checking. K

It was so sweet of him to check on me. It was nice to know someone was thinking about me. In no time, I had dosed off in front of the fire. I wasn't going anywhere! When I awoke, it was four in the morning. The fire was out, but I was wide awake. I put the coffee on and went upstairs to take a shower.

As I was getting dressed for the day, I grabbed a pair of jeans and a sweatshirt. They felt good. I wondered about Josephine as I looked around the bedroom. Was she glad I was home? I will never forget her appearing at the top of the stairs and scaring my intruder away. She was my protector. I couldn't see what he saw, but from things others had reported, I knew it was her. I was getting the coffee mugs ready for Ellie and me when my cell phone rang.

"Welcome home!" Ellen greeted me.

"Thank you. It's good to be back."

"I'm calling to invite you to quilting this week. Sorry I haven't done it sooner, but I thought I'd wait until you got back from South Haven. We really are behind and can use your help. You're still interested, aren't you?"

"Absolutely. I feel it's a way I can be helpful to the church."

"I think we'll skip their morning coffee break and arrive about ten. They bring a sack lunch, but I have you covered, so don't worry about that since you're coming for the first time."

"That's not necessary, Ellen."

"It won't be fancy."

I knew that everything Ellen was involved in was fancy. "I'll look forward to it." I hung up knowing that Ellen would get me involved in more work, but I so admired the way Ellen and Oscar had their fingerprint on everything in town. It would not be the same community without them.

It was so good to see Ellie again. We hugged like I had been gone forever.

"Kate, these scones are to die for! This is the only good thing about your going back to South Haven."

"There is a bottle of blueberry BBQ sauce for Kelly in

your basket. I know how much he loves it."

"You are so generous with everyone. Okay, now that we can talk, what do you think is really going on with Clark?"

"You tell me! He's one of those weird artists. I'm not calling and chasing him down. He shows up when he feels like it."

"Well, I'm glad you are going to dinner with Cole."

"It's not a big deal, but he's normal."

We both burst into laughter.

"Isn't that crazy?"

"Right on, girlfriend."

"I got a call from Ellen and I'm going church quilting with her."

"I hope you realize what you may be getting yourself into. I know some of those ladies and they are set in their ways. Esther and Ellen might be the only normal ones in the bunch. Esther rarely goes, I think. Emma used to tell stories about them once in a while, God rest her soul."

"Now you're making it sound interesting. I love human interest stories, thanks to John. What kind of stories?"

"They all worship Pastor Hermann, just so you know. They make sure he's fed well, and if he says to worship once a week, they'll go twice. If one day he says he likes sweet potatoes, you can bet on him getting a sweet potato pie the next."

I laughed. "That sounds pretty cute. That's certainly better than the reverse!"

"Emma said that the church really needs the income from the quilting."

"Yes, Ellen said that as well. It's a small congregation, so everyone needs to play a part."

Ellie looked at me strangely.

"I'm just sayin'!"

"I can't wait to hear what you think. I need to be going. Say hello to your Aunt Mandy for me. It's nice to hear that she and Wilson are still an item. Do you think they'll marry?"

"Oh, I never think about that. She's been on her own a long time, so I doubt it."

"Okay, out I go. Everyone would love to see you at the winery, so come on out soon, okay?"

"I will. Please tell Trout I am ever so grateful that he hooked me up with Red."

"And Cole Alexander!" she teased as she went out the door.

I loved that girl. I'll never forget her kindness when I first arrived in Borna. We bonded immediately and she made me feel right at home.

Chapter 11

Who did I find at Aunt Mandy's when I stopped by to drop off her goody bag? Wilson! He and Aunt Mandy were having a bite to eat.

"Please join us, Kate," she suggested. "Wilson brought over some delicious vegetable soup. We have enough to feed an army."

"Wilson, it's good to see you. The soup smells delicious, so a small bowl would be lovely. I am on my way to get groceries."

"Good to see you as well, Kate," Wilson said as he filled my bowl. "I hear your trip to South Haven was rather sad."

"Yes, it was."

"Mandy said you like your red Jeep and it served you well on the trip."

"My Mercedes would have had a problem on this trip," I admitted. "By the way, you have a rather nice Mercedes."

"I'm quite fond of it, but Barbara forbids me to drive it in the snow and ice."

"And that's fine by me," Aunt Mandy added.

"This is delicious soup! Did you make this or did Barbara?"

"Oh, Wilson loves to cook," Aunt Mandy interjected. "He makes wonderful chili as well."

As I watched the two of them, they already looked and acted like a married couple. I finished the soup and then went on my way. After I got home with the groceries, I didn't have much time to change before my big date. I tried on three different outfits before I felt comfortable with my selection. I chose a black sweater and a skirt with heels instead of boots. Not used to wearing heels, it took me by surprise that I had to concentrate to keep my balance. When I looked in the mirror, I was convinced that I had dropped a few pounds and felt proud that I still had some semblance of a figure.

Cole was right on time when he arrived at the back door. He looked very handsome in a black suit and red tie. "Should I have come to the front door?" he asked as I let him in.

"My friends always come to the back door, especially when they come to rescue me."

Early in our friendship, Cole had come by the house one morning to find me bound to my desk chair, unable to free my wrists and ankles. On the previous evening, a murderer had come into the guest house and threatened my life. Thankfully, Josephine frightened him and he fled through the back door. We worked with the authorities to capture the man, but I had sworn Cole to secrecy about the incident because I did not want the community to think that staying at my guest house was unsafe. It did make me feel wonderful to be rescued by Cole, however, and I was truly grateful for his help.

"I am not sure of the right words, Kate, but you look fabulous."

"I like those words, so thank you. I wasn't sure how formal the restaurant would be."

"Forgive me, but I'm probably staring at you. You look very beautiful."

"Well, it's my turn to say that you look very handsome and will make a fine escort this evening."

We laughed at the awkwardness and I asked, "Do we have time for a drink?"

"I think so," he nodded.

"What do you drink?"

"I'm easy, but I'm probably a Jack-Daniels-on-the-rocks kind of guy, if you have it."

"I do! Please sit down. It'll only take me a second."

"No guests tonight?"

I shook my head. "I'm afraid this guest house isn't the most popular place. I need to work on that. I'm sure I'll have some holiday bookings."

"Perhaps I can help with that." He took the drink from my hand and I poured my usual glass of merlot. We talked another fifteen minutes before he suggested that we leave.

The Blue Onion restaurant was an unexpected surprise. I did not know it would be so elegant. It was rather dark with the exception of blue lighting around the statues, some art glass, and a blue water fountain in the center of the dining room. White tablecloths beamed in contrast. Why hadn't Clark ever brought me here? That was a silly question, knowing Clark's log-cabin taste. Cole knew immediately that I was impressed and he couldn't believe I hadn't been there. "For the size of Jacksonville, this is quite stunning," I said, impressed by his choice of restaurants.

Chapter 12

It was obvious that Cole knew some of the servers in the restaurant. He said he knew the owner, but rarely came there to eat. We were ushered to a table near the fountain, which was delightful.

"I think I indicated to you that I really didn't want to date until my divorce was final. I just couldn't afford to complicate things any further."

"That is wise, I think."

He chuckled.

"What's good here?"

"Their seafood is excellent."

We ordered and Cole started what seemed like a list of questions for me. He was baffled by my move from Michigan to Borna, so I answered his questions as simply as I could. I loved seeing him light up when I mentioned his daughter. A certain sadness came over his face when he said that his divorce was the biggest failure of his life. It sounded as if he had done everything he could to keep it from happening. That was respectable! The way he conversed, I had a feeling he hadn't had anyone to talk to for some time. I think he was nervous. My concerns that we may not have anything to talk about went out the door. Hours passed, and instead of dessert, we had an after-dinner drink.

"I haven't stayed out this late in a long time," I foolishly admitted as we began to leave.

"You aren't the only one," Cole said with a snicker. "I apologize for talking so much. It's been a very long time since I've been out on anything that resembles a date."

When we arrived at my back door, I asked him in. He looked genuinely surprised by the request.

"I've kept you up late enough. It's been a wonderful evening. I can't tell you how much appreciation I have for you, especially now that I know more about you."

"I think our little secret of you rescuing me got us off to a pretty personal start. I appreciate you not bringing that up this evening."

He nodded as if he understood. "I hope we can get together again during the holiday season."

"I think that's very possible. The next dinner is on me, how about it?"

"Hold on to that thought," he said, giving me a smile and a wink. He took my cold hands and pulled me close as he gave me a kiss on my cheek.

I responded with a kiss and a slight hug. "Goodnight," I said as he got into his SUV.

I went inside the dark house and turned on the alarm before heading up the stairs. It was a simply wonderful evening and I wanted to cherish the moment. As I got undressed, I realized that my feet didn't hurt from my heels and I was feeling more feminine again. I pulled the covers back and wondered where on earth Clark was this weekend. I thought he would have touched base with me after my trip. What would Ellie think about me having a great time tonight? I wanted to call Maggie, but it was too late to share anything with her.

I fluffed my pillow and started to replay some of our conversations from the evening. He truly listened to every word I said. Women know the difference. Clark used to listen intently to me in the beginning of our friendship. Clay was a good listener in the beginning as well. When I became Jack's mother, it was like I played a different role in his life. How does that happen?

I stayed wide awake until Josephine covered me in her warm light like she had done on so many occasions. It always felt like it was a hug, and off to sleep I'd go. Was she giving me a sign of approval about the evening?

I was in a deep sleep when I heard my cell phone vibrate on the bedside table. I sat up quickly, thinking something may be wrong with Jack or Aunt Mandy.

"Hey, sleepyhead! I'm outside your door and its cold out here," Clark's voice said.

Did he sound drunk? "You're outside my door?" I asked in disbelief.

"See for yourself," he insisted.

I put on a robe, tossed my hair a bit, and ran down the steps to turn off the alarm. Was he in trouble? What was he doing here at this time of night?

"Come in," I said, opening the door.

"I knew this was a friendly place to lay my head if I'd had too much to drink. I'm afraid I've had too many on my way home tonight."

I gave him a weak smile, but nothing about it was happy.

"Do you want coffee?"

"Oh, baby, I would. Thanks."

"Where have you been?" I asked as I made his coffee. It seemed like I was always asking him this question.

"I was on my way home from Springfield and made the mistake of stopping for a few."

"That's never a good idea," I said, handing him a cup of strong coffee.

"You're a good friend, Miss Meyr," he slurred.

I didn't respond.

"I've got something on my mind." He looked down at the floor.

"I figured as much."

He took a deep breath.

Chapter 13

"Discovering that I have a daughter has really messed me up, you might say," he said quietly. "One thing's led to another and I feel that I owe you an explanation."

"About what?" My heart was throbbing.

"About Michelle's mother."

That was not what I was expecting to hear. "What about her?"

"Lucille Kilwin. She was named after the famous Lucille Ball, because of her red hair. She had the reddest hair I'd ever seen." His face was aglow. "It got my attention the first time I met her. She goes by Lucy."

Where was he going with this?

"At my daughter's insistence, I went to see her. Well, I didn't leave her place until a week later."

I wasn't sure I'd heard him correctly. "You stayed at her house the whole time?"

He nodded, not looking at me. This was like a true confession out of a movie.

"Crazy, isn't it? I guess I was caught up with the fact that we had a child together and my life in Borna seemed to fade away."

I cleared my throat and tried hard to contain myself. "That was the last thing I thought I'd hear from you. Why are you here now?" I had to hear something better than my place being a convenient hangover stop.

"I felt guilty as heck coming home. I knew you'd be wondering why you hadn't heard from me."

"So it took a few drinks to get you to come here and tell me, right?" I wanted to slap his face. "Look, I understand if you've fallen for someone else. I'm a big girl. I've had a few knocks in my life. A man doesn't treat a woman he says he loves the way you've been acting. I get it."

He looked at me in shock. "Look, I wish I could explain this better. I didn't mean to hurt you."

"Listen, why don't you catch a few winks in The Study before you go on home? You're in no condition to drive." I got up and took his coffee cup to the kitchen.

"That's all you've got to say?" Clark asked, staring at me.

"I think you said it all. I'm going up to bed. Let yourself out if I'm still asleep."

I headed towards the stairs without looking back. I locked my door in case he wanted to talk some more. I sat on the side of the bed, not knowing whether to laugh or cry. The thought of Clark being shacked up with another woman while I was in South Haven was unbelievable. Clark never showed signs of being a womanizer, so another woman never entered my mind. It appeared that Miss Lucy used her magic touch of being Michelle's mother and rather easily roped him in.

I sank my head onto my pillow, thinking of all the

things that I should have said to him. Maybe I should have said that I'd had a pretty romantic night myself with Mr. Alexander, but I didn't. I had to remind myself that Clark and I weren't engaged or formally committed in any way. I knew Clark would never settle down with anyone, but that always seemed okay with me. Clark had moved on, and that was that.

Chapter 14

I must have fallen asleep for a couple of hours. The light shining in the window suddenly jarred me into reality. Did I dream what had happened in the middle of the night? I got fully dressed in case Clark was still downstairs. I quietly went down to the first floor. When I got to The Study where Clark had been sleeping, I saw that the door was open. He was gone. I thought that maybe he would have left a note behind, but as I looked around, I didn't see one.

I made coffee and tried to think about my day ahead instead of dwelling on last night's event. Ellen would be picking me up around ten to go to quilting at the church. I really wanted to talk to Ellie before she left for work, but didn't think it would be possible. I was anxious to hear her reaction to Clark's confession.

The phone rang. It was Aunt Mandy.

"What are you doing up so early?" I asked.

"Well, I got up to take a pill and couldn't go back to sleep. I was wondering how your dinner date went, too."

"It was wonderful! The restaurant was called the Blue

Onion and the food and atmosphere were awesome. You and Wilson need to go there sometime. Better yet, I will take you there myself!"

"Was Mr. Alexander awesome also?"

"He was a perfect gentleman. I think he was a little nervous because he sure talked a lot. He hasn't taken anyone out since his divorce."

"That's a very nice attribute, I must say. Do you think you'll see him again?"

"I think so, but we'll see. In just a bit, I'm going with Ellen to quilt at the church. She thinks it's a nice way for me to give back, since it generates income for the church."

"She's right, plus we all owe homage to our dear Ellen."

We laughed. I hung up feeling good about not telling Aunt Mandy about my late-night visit from Clark. I had to hurry to change clothes.

Ellen was early when she arrived at the back door. "Say, Kate, if you made muffins this morning, you may want to take some to the ladies. I'm sure they would be a big hit."

"Oh, I'm sorry, Ellen. I didn't have guests, so I didn't bake."

"That's okay. Perhaps another time. If you wouldn't mind driving, I'd love to see what it's like riding in your new Jeep."

"Sure, that's a good idea. It sure did well in the snow at Thanksgiving."

Off we went and it tickled me to see Ellen's response to Red. She was delighted to ride in the Jeep!

We could hear the chatter as we entered the fellowship hall basement door. When Concordia planned the addition, the pastor wanted to make sure the quilters had a nice large room in which to do their quilting.

"Hello, ladies," Ellen greeted everyone. Some of the ladies looked up while some kept on quilting. "Some of you may already know Kate Meyr who owns Josephine's Guest House. She is a quilter and has offered to help us."

"Hello, ladies. It's nice to see you. I hear you do marvelous work and I commend you for that." Some gave me a smile while some did not. I wondered if some of them were hard of hearing.

"Well, we have only a few quilters at this quilt frame, so why don't you and I have a seat here with Ruby and Helen?" Ellen suggested.

There were two opened quilt frames with church folding chairs placed around them. One frame had a pink-and-red cross-stitched quilt attached and the other had a similar one in shades of blue. As the quilt was quilted, the long, wooden slats would be rolled until the quilt was completely done.

After I took off my coat, I slowly walked around the frames where everyone was eagerly quilting away. I was astonished to see such dark quilting lines drawn on the quilts. One quilt's designs were drawn with a blue marking pen, and the other quilt was marked with a dark lead pencil. I quietly asked Ellen why that was and she said some of the ladies preferred one over the other. End of subject. She admitted that some of them had failing eyesight and that the markings needed to be clear, so that was another reason that they were unusually dark.

Chapter 15

"Ladies, I'm going around to introduce you to Kate," Ellen announced rather loudly.

I wondered why the ladies didn't just introduce themselves.

"At our quilt is Ruby," Ellen stated with a smile. "Ruby marks all of our quilts and keeps track of the quilts on the list to be quilted. We are on a first-come-first- served basis. Ruby, by the way, also makes the best chicken and dumplings for our church dinners."

"That's a big job!" I exclaimed. "It's nice to meet you, Ruby."

Ruby nodded, smiled, and proceeded with her quilting.

"Next to her is Helen," Ellen noted. "You may already know Helen for her wonderful homemade coffee cake."

Helen blushed.

"She's also been quilting with us for many, many years."

"I'm familiar with you, Helen," I acknowledged. "I am so glad your daughter decided to open the coffee shop so I can have your coffee cake anytime I want."

"She keeps me busy," Helen shared proudly.

"At this quilt, we'll start with Matilda," Ellen stated. "She keeps us on our toes and is quite a perfectionist, aren't you Matilda?"

"I have to keep after them, and just so you aren't tempted, I prefer to be called Matilda, not Tilly," she responded with a somber look.

"I will remember that, Matilda," I said, smiling.

"Now, Kate, there is an empty chair here for good reason," Ellen explained. "This is where our departed Emma sat to quilt for many years. We keep this empty in her honor."

"Oh, how nice," I responded. "She would be pleased."

"Erna was close to Emma and sat next to her for many years, didn't you?" Ellen asked conversationally. "Erna is our most senior quilter and never misses a quilting. She can tell you many stories."

Erna blushed, but kept quilting.

"That's something, Erna! Good for you. Perhaps I can hear about some of your experiences one day."

"Frieda is our go-getter," Ellen said with a chuckle.

Frieda seemed to like her description. She seemed to be the friendliest so far.

"Frieda brings us a lot of business, you might say."

"We need the money for Pastor," she explained.

"Well, you all seem to be good at that," I said encouragingly.

"Lastly, there's Paula," Ellen pointed out. "She is Milly's sister, whom you know, Kate. She also babysits her grandchildren fairly often, but when she's free, she's always here to help out."

"I come here to rest," she kidded.

"I'll bet you do!" I agreed.

"You already know that Esther comes when she can, and she usually sits here," Ellen explained.

"Well, Kate, let's get started before we break for lunch," Ellen suggested, as she pulled out a chair for me. "Did you bring your thimble? If not, we have extras."

"I'm prepared!" I said, pulling my thimble from my pocket. "Do I just start anywhere in front of me?"

"Sure, but it looks like we're going to have to give it a roll soon," Ellen said as she pulled out the chair next to me and sat down.

Getting serious, I threaded a needle and decided to start on a corner design.

"These embroidered stamped quilts are popular with elderly quilters in the area," Ellen pointed out. They come with the stamped quilting lines on them, which makes it really nice."

I nodded. "I must bring an old quilt top in to have quilted. It dates around the turn of the century, but it's in really good condition. I think the name is OCEAN'S WAVE."

"We don't like those old tops much, Miss Meyr," Ruby said. "They have too many seams and they don't mark very well. I don't know why anyone would want to quilt those."

"Please call me Kate. I'm glad you told me that," I said, wanting to be agreeable.

All of a sudden, Frieda sprang into action and went to the two long tables where we would eat lunch. She set each place setting with napkins, silverware, and a coffee cup. She then went into the kitchen area and carried out a tray containing condiments and two water glasses with fresh mums in them. She placed a glass of flowers in the center of each table. I marveled at the ritual and the special touch the centerpiece added.

"We'll break for lunch now," Ruby instructed us. "Ellen will lead us in prayer."

Ellen stood and prayed, "Heavenly Father, bless this food and our dedicated fingers to support Your ministry. In Your name we pray, Amen."

Everyone said, "Amen." The group rose in an orderly fashion and went to what appeared to be their dedicated chairs for lunch. I waited until everyone was seated before I chose a chair.

"Here's a little lunch for you," Ellen said as she handed me a small paper bag. "It's not much."

Frieda waited until everyone was seated and then poured everyone a cup of coffee. I assumed that was the only option offered as far as beverages went.

"Would you like something else to drink, Kate?" Ellen asked graciously.

"No, coffee is fine." On the other side of me was Paula. She seemed rather friendly. I asked about the ages of her grandchildren. That delighted her.

Ellen's lunch of a chicken salad sandwich and fruit cup was delicious. The ladies did little talking and I wondered if it was because I was there. I would have liked to have been a fly on the wall and heard their conversations when there was not a visitor present.

Frieda knew when to bring dessert from the kitchen. She brought a lemon sheet cake with pieces cut and ready to serve. These gals had it down! Ellen whispered that everyone took turns being the hostess, which meant that you set the table and bring dessert.

Chapter 16

After we got back to the quilting frame, I avoided additional conversation so I could concentrate on my stitches. I hadn't quilted in quite some time, so my consistency was rusty. As I looked across the frame, everyone else's stitches were tiny and perfect.

At two sharp, quilting ceased, much like an alarm had gone off! Ellen thought we should roll the quilt at least one turn so it would be ready for more quilting next week. The clamps at the end were unscrewed and we all turned and held it secure while the screws were tightened again.

I put my thimble away and told Ruby and Helen how much I enjoyed meeting them. Helen smiled and asked if I would be back.

"I will try to," I said, nodding. "How many quilts do you have on your waiting list?

"More than we'll ever get to," Helen said with some frustration.

"Well, you just do what you can. I think you ladies accomplish quite a bit."

Ruby walked away without responding to my compliment, nor telling me good-bye, or inviting me to come back again. For that reason, when Ellen and I got in our car to leave, I told her I wasn't sure I was welcome there.

She laughed. "These ladies are never going to change," Ellen joked. "It's part of the reason we can't get any younger women to join us. It's all business with these quilters. Really, it doesn't have to be that way."

"It seems as if Ruby sets the tone for the whole group," I observed. "Am I right?"

"I'd say both Ruby and Matilda have that influence. They don't like each other, by the way."

"You're kidding! Do you know why?"

"Not exactly, but I'm sure it goes way back in time. They certainly compete over the pastor's attention."

"I heard something to that affect."

"The pastor was out of town today. Otherwise, you would have seen for yourself," Ellen snickered. "He always stops in to say hello. He's usually given at least two food items to take home."

I grinned, picturing the scene. It was a nice gesture. I thanked Ellen and told her I certainly would give it a few more visits before I firmly committed to the group.

I came into the house exhausted. I glanced at Clark's coffee cup sitting in my kitchen sink, which was not a pleasant reminder of last night's exchange. I looked out of the office window to see if Ellie had left for work. Her car was still there, so I picked up the phone and called her.

"Are you about to leave?"

"In just a bit, why?"

"I need to talk to you. Can you stop by on your way? I

promise I won't keep you long."

There was a pause. "Is everything okay?"

"I'll fill you in. Thanks, Ellie."

I hated having to share this with Ellie or anyone that thought so much of Clark. In time, folks would realize that we were no longer a couple.

Ellie arrived at the back door within minutes.

"Come on in!"

She had a serious look on her face as she followed me into the living room. "Did everything go okay with Cole?"

"Oh, sure! It was nice to get dressed up for a change. I think he was a little nervous, but we had great food and good conversation."

"Then, what's on your mind?"

"Well, at three in the morning, Clark showed up at my back door," I said with a deep sigh. "He was drunk."

"Oh, dear," Ellie said, expecting the worst.

I described the chain of events and watched her facial expressions turn from horror to disbelief. She was astounded when I told her I let him sleep it off here at my house.

"You should have made him leave." Ellie said, clearly angry.

"He was too drunk, Ellie."

"How does that make you feel, Kate?"

"Well, we weren't exclusive, but we did have a close friendship. It won't be the same now. I'll truly miss that."

"Trout will be furious when he finds out," Ellie said, pacing the floor.

"Please don't tell him, Ellie," I begged. "Just let things evolve."

"Well, I'm certainly glad you accepted that date with

Cole. It will be interesting when Clark finds out about that."

"I think he'll be glad and will feel less guilty."

"I wonder when we'll see him again at the winery. You're handling this better than I think I would."

"Thanks for keeping this to yourself, Ellie. I wouldn't want to tarnish Clark's reputation in any way."

After she left, I felt much better having shared the experience with someone. I made myself a glass of tea and wrote in my journal. I made sure to include an entry on my church quilting experience and my three-o'clock-in-the-morning visitor.

Chapter 17

I was having breakfast the next morning when Ruth Ann called to invite me to have lunch at her place. She had invited Charlene and Anna to brainstorm about promotions. "I know it's a little late to do much for Christmas, but we have a long winter ahead," Ruth Ann pointed out.

"Count me in!" I said immediately. "I'll see you there." I felt excited about the idea. As I was thinking about the possibilities, the ring of the cell phone made me jump. It was Aunt Mandy.

"Good morning, sweetie. I'm dying to know how your quilting day went."

"It was interesting. I'm not sure they were all that happy to see me."

"Well, when they get to know you, they'll love you. Did you get some quilting done?"

"We did! We even gave it a turn before we left."

"If you don't have plans this evening, come join me for a cocktail. We need to think about Christmas. I sure would like any suggestions from you about what to give Wilson."

"Sure. That sounds great. I'll look forward to it." My day was coming together nicely. I went upstairs to get ready. I had just gotten out of the shower when my phone rang again.

"Cole here."

"Hi, what's up with you?"

"Well, I'm on my way to check out a piece of property and had you on my mind."

"Well, you shouldn't be talking and driving."

"You're right. I'm pulling over as we speak."

"Good. I feel better."

"Are you free for lunch today?"

"Sorry, my calendar is full today, but I'll be happy to take a rain check."

"It's a deal. You have a great day!"

"I will, and you do the same," I said, ending the call.

I hung up. I was keenly aware of the smile on my face. It was nice getting phone calls from a man. John liked to text and Clark wanted no part of either.

The weather was cold, but it was bright and sunny. When I drove past Imy's shop, I could see that she was open for business. I thought I might stop in there to see her after our meeting. When I got to Ruth Ann's, everyone was already there.

"Hey, long time no see," joked Anna. "I had to miss the last Friendship Circle meeting."

"You've been traveling, right?" asked Charlene.

"I have, but now I'm here until spring!"

Ruth Ann had her table set with striking blue and brown stoneware. She even had clever matching water goblets. "I kept our lunch pretty simple," Ruth Ann explained. "I have a cold chicken pasta dish with the cranberry muffins I frequently make. I can't compete with your blueberry ones, Kate, but I love anything cranberry this time of year."

"So do I, Ruth Ann," I agreed. "They look wonderful."

"I brought dessert," Anna volunteered. "Something chocolate always makes the brain sharper, I think."

We chuckled in agreement.

"No one makes this cake better than you, Anna," Charlene bragged.

"How's the coffee business?" I asked Charlene.

"It's not bad, especially with the cooler weather," she reported. "I'm discussing the possibility of providing baked goods for Ruth Ann when she caters an event. I would really like to do wedding cakes, but I just don't have the space."

"That's where I come in," Ruth Ann added. "My commercial kitchen is perfect for her."

"The wedding market is huge," Anna agreed. "I hate that mine can only be seasonal. It would sure be great if all of us could come up with some kind of package that would include everyone. I could certainly offer a free or discounted ticket to our village."

"Ruth Ann and I have talked about that," I said. "Ellie said she would be happy to provide a bottle of wine or a discounted dinner towards the package."

"Of course we need wine," Ruth Ann laughed. "We could have had some with lunch!"

"I'm not Internet savvy, so someone else has to take that on," Anna pointed out.

"I don't mind doing that part," Charlene said graciously. "I have most of my afternoons free."

"I have my Christmas quilts up in the banquet hall, but I have very little booked for the upcoming holidays," Ruth

Ann confessed.

"Neither do I," I offered.

"What about a Christmas tea?" Charlene suggested. "We have the place and the food. We just have to think about how to include Kate's guest house."

"If you really advertise this as a fun girls' event, I could include a night's room with the price of the tea," I said. "Some women may want to make it more of a weekend or overnight trip."

"Great, but it sure wouldn't take many women to fill up your place," Anna mentioned.

"You know, I've collected nutcrackers over the years." Ruth Ann paused as if in deep thought. "We could call it the Nutcracker Tea!"

We looked at one another as if something special had just been discovered.

"I like it," I nodded in agreement. "Let's go for it!"

Chapter 18

It was such a fun, energetic meeting! I wondered why we hadn't thought of doing this sooner. The girls also teased me about becoming a church-lady quilter. I told them that each quilter had such a distinct personality and story that I might report my experiences to John. After all, he may have an interest in writing another article about quilting.

"Is he still pursuing you?" Ruth Ann asked with a grin. "Doesn't he know that Clark has dibs on you?"

"No. He isn't pursuing me. No one has dibs on me."

Ruth Ann looked at me strangely.

"I'm stopping at Imy's afterwards. Is anyone else interested?" I announced.

"I've got to get back to the kids or I'll hear about it," complained Anna.

"I've got a quilt top to complete for Milly," Ruth Ann replied. "She's been kept waiting too long."

"I may stop, but I don't need a darn thing," Charlene said, donning her coat. "I am trying to get rid of things!"

"Imy can probably help you with that," I informed

Charlene.

We thanked Ruth Ann for the wonderful lunch and stimulating ideas.

Imy was glad to see me. We made small talk until Charlene joined us.

"Will you be opening Santa's Workshop this year in your old shed? That was such a nice touch last year." I inquired. "It was so darn cute."

"If I can get my boys to help me," Imy answered with a bit of frustration. "I need to get it open by next weekend."

"Is this stack of fabric all feed sacks?" I asked Imy. There were several tall stacks of them on the counter.

"Yes! Isn't that something?" Imy bragged. "I went to the Hopfer auction in Unionville last weekend and everything went really cheap. There was hardly anyone there. I don't sell these often, but when I get an interested party, they buy a bunch. They are hard to find outside the rural areas."

"I had to wear feed sack clothing growing up," admitted Charlene. "I hated the scratchy old fabric. We even had some underpants made out of them."

"My mom made curtains, aprons, and dish towels out of them," revealed Imy. "I kept a few just as a remembrance. They are too loose of a weave to sew."

"Oh, yes, and Mom would trade with others so she could get enough to make one of us a dress," Charlene added.

"Just look at some of these wild prints!" I said, holding a few up to see. "This purple and red flower print is just plain ugly!"

"It's hard for me to get the ones that have conversation prints," Imy said.

"What's a conversation print?" I asked.

Imy laughed. "Look at this one," she said, holding up one of the sacks. "This has a cowboy scene. It creates an overall, bigger print. Some will have a Mexican or Dutch scene. The conversation term comes from a print that tells a story or theme."

"You sure know your stuff, Imy," I commented. "I think I can pass on purchasing one of these."

"Here's a sack just like the one my mom has an apron out of," Charlene said as she pulled out the bottom stack. "I'll have to take this one. It has too many memories. Mom will get a kick out of seeing this."

"Sold!" Imy declared.

"Have you gotten any quilts in lately?" I had gotten some good deals on antique quilts from Imy in the past.

"This Grandmother's Fan came from the Hopfer sale," Imy pointed out. "When I was looking at its condition, I noticed that it had a lot of feed sack prints in it."

"Really?" I said as I looked closer. "How can you tell which print is which?"

"Well, look here," Imy said. "See the pieces that have a looser, rougher texture than the fabric next to it? They mixed these in with their store-bought calicos."

"I don't think Mom sewed much with store-bought fabric," Charlene said thoughtfully.

"You're right!" I exclaimed as I felt the texture. "It sure is nicely quilted."

"I'll make you a really good deal on it," Imy offered, smiling.

"You don't have to do that," I said, looking closer at it. "I know I don't have this pattern. I like the solid yellow on the back. With all this quilting, it is even beautiful on the back side. I can see it's been washed and it looks really clean."

"How about a hundred dollars?" Imy queried.

"Sold!" I said with a giggle. "Are you sure you are making some money on this sale?"

"I told you everything at the sale went really cheap," Imy reminded me. "I want to see that it gets a good home."

"Quilts are my weakness, Charlene," I confessed.

"I can't think of a better place for them to go," Charlene said with a smile and a nod of approval. Charlene ended up with several feed sacks and I walked out with a Grandmother's Fan quilt. Imy was a good saleswoman!

Chapter 19

The day had slipped by and it was time for cocktails with Aunt Mandy. I grabbed some cheese and crackers and went on my way. Arriving at her door, I once again walked into her unlocked house and once again warned her about being more cautious.

"Now, child, I knew you'd be stopping by. Sometimes I don't hear the door," she said offhandedly. "What's on that plate in your hand?"

"Something that goes well with Merry Merlot," I joked.

"Do you think it's too cool to sit on the porch?"

I nodded. "It is. How about turning on that nice gas fireplace?"

"Oh, very well," Aunt Mandy agreed.

I began our conversation about the inspiring lunch I had with Anna, Charlene, and Ruth Ann. She was delighted to hear that I was doing more to promote the guest house.

"I'll certainly attend that tea! It sounds marvelous. This little community sure has a lot of events at the holidays."

"I was thinking that, because you're in such demand

these days, I should ask you and Wilson to Christmas dinner before anyone else beats me to it."

She smiled. "We haven't talked about it, but I'm certainly willing to commit. It was so wonderful last year. Will you be comfortable asking Clark?"

I knew this was the opportunity I needed to tell her about Clark's visit. "No, there will not be a Clark this year. Rock won't be coming either."

She looked at me, waiting for further information.

I began from the beginning and the look on her face was painful. She thought the world of Clark. I finished by stating that I hadn't heard from him since.

"Well!" She exclaimed in disbelief.

I had to chuckle.

"I guess he prepared you for all this by staying away so long without communicating. That would drive any woman crazy, much less a wife."

"Your point is well taken, I'm afraid. I'm somewhat hurt because I thought we were more than just casual friends. His reaction to this Lucy person just doesn't seem like him."

"It's the male species, my dear," she shrugged. "Who knows why and how they do anything! You're right in that this doesn't sound like the Clark we all know."

"I will miss him, even though he was gone a lot."

"Well, honey, it isn't like you let the grass grow under your feet for too very long. It sounds like Mr. Alexander reminded you of how a real lady should be treated."

I blushed. "I'll have to admit that it was very nice. I'm glad I didn't beat myself up with guilt about going out with him. He called to have lunch today, but I had other plans with the girls."

"Wonderful! Just enjoy whatever comes your way, my dear. That's what life is all about. I feel God has blessed me with Wilson. I just take one day at a time and enjoy what time we have together."

It was great talking to my aunt, despite our age difference. She was a smart, sensible lady who had aged very well.

Chapter 20

It was early the next morning when I got a call from Sharla Lee at the Heritage Museum. "I have you down for decorating a Christmas tree at the museum. You did one last year," she reminded me. "Are you willing to do it again?"

"Oh, I'm afraid it had slipped my mind," I confessed. "Let me think. I purchased an antique feather tree from Imy's shop with all the antique ornaments to go with it. Do you suppose I could put that up for my contribution?"

"If it's in decent condition, I don't know why you couldn't," Sharla Lee reasoned. "Most folks haven't seen one. Can you bring it this Saturday?"

"Sure. First thing." I was relieved I didn't have to think of a new tree theme. Last year, I made hundreds of cookies to hang on the tree. It was a good way for me to advertise the guest house. Now, I should start planning decorations for my own house. I picked up the phone to call Cotton. I hadn't spoken to him since the day I left on my trip to South Haven.

"Well, Miss Kate, we were just mentioning you," Cotton revealed. "Susie was wondering when you'd like her to come and clean again. Did you have a good trip?"

"It was okay, but a quilting friend of mine passed while I was there," I shared. "Is everything okay with your family?"

"Amy Sue's had the flu, but we're hoping the rest of us can avoid it."

"I hope so, too! Tell Susie she can come tomorrow if she wants. The reason I'm calling is to ask you to find me another Christmas tree."

"I've been keeping an eye out and may have one spotted. Does your aunt need one, too?"

"I'll ask her, but she may not want a real tree. She certainly hasn't been used to one."

"Okay, I'll take care of getting one for you."

I don't know what I would do without Cotton and Susie. They had been helping me with things since the first day I arrived in Borna. I tried to support them financially as much as I could. Last Christmas, I helped him buy a new truck and would likely give them money this year. I didn't have plans for the evening, so I toyed with the idea of going to the winery for dinner. It was always fun to visit with Ellie and her staff. I called Aunt Mandy to see if she was up to going with me.

"Aren't you sweet to ask! However, I put a pork roast in the oven in hopes of enticing Wilson over here. He has been hinting about it since I fixed it for him the last time. He has an appointment, but I have an inkling he'll show up eventually. Would you like to join us?"

"Thanks, but Ellie has wanted me to come over to the winery ever since I returned. By the way, Cotton wanted to know if he should cut a real Christmas tree for you."

"I think not, but thank him for asking. I have a white one I've had for a few years."

"He could cut you a nice little real one. They smell so good! I had him cut one for each of my guest rooms last year."

She laughed.

"Well, when in Rome, do as the Romans do. Sure, I'm game."

I had to chuckle at the way she was always a good sport.

A bit later, I checked the computer and was surprised to see I had an online booking for the Wildflower room. It was for a couple that was coming to attend a funeral. I wondered if I knew the deceased person. I sent the couple a confirmation and it made my day!

I got ready for the winery by changing into my better jeans and a cream cable- knit sweater. This was East Perry County as its best, I supposed. Except for church, funerals, or weddings, it was always jeans that arose as the attire of preference.

I was anxious to share our promotional ideas with Ellie. I hoped she wouldn't be too busy to visit with me. The days were getting darker earlier. Before it got completely dark, I hopped into Red and made the short trip. When I pulled up the hill, the parking lot was sparsely filled. Walking in, I saw a couple sitting at thc bar. I joined them.

"Hey, Kate!" Trout smiled. "Good to see you again."

"You, too!" I gave him a big hug. "How have you been?"

"I'm good. I'm getting ready to go hunting for a week. I am so looking forward to that."

"Guess it's that time of year around here. Is Ellie around?"

"She went to get chili out of the kitchen for these guys." Trout nodded toward the couple.

"Hi, I'm Kate Meyr. I'm somewhat of a regular around here."

They laughed.

"Hi!" the girl said. "We've never been here before. A friend of ours told us to check out this place."

"Hey, Kate!" Ellie yelled from behind me. "Glad you made it. What can we get for you tonight?"

"I'll have my usual red. That chili looks pretty darn good," I added. "It's a chili night!"

They laughed.

"Say, Kate, you may want to know that I'm taking a friend of yours hunting with me," Trout said in a teasing manor.

"Oh, who could that be?" I teased back.

"Here you go," Ellie said as she placed the chili in front of me. "Save some room for chocolate pie. When we have chili, I make sure we have a chocolate dessert of some kind."

"It is a good pairing, so yes, save me a piece," I heartily agreed.

Chapter 21

"Kate, I want to warn you about something," Ellie whispered as she sat on the stool next to me.

"What's up?"

"Clark called in an order just a bit ago. He could arrive at any time to pick it up," she revealed. "Trout said he stopped by for a quick beer last night. I was already gone."

"Well, we both have to face each other at some point," I sighed. "I'll just keep eating dinner. If he doesn't want to say hello, that's fine by me."

"He'd better!" Ellie said, her words laced with aggravation. "I sure have mixed feelings about him now."

"Ellie, Kelly needs you in the kitchen," Trout called out.

"Tell Kelly the chili is delicious!" I called after her.

"I will," she said with a big grin.

Running into Clark tonight wasn't what I had planned. Realistically though, it was bound to happen at some point. Borna was not a large area.

Sure enough, minutes later, in walked Clark. I barely glanced at him and he didn't see me at first. Trout had his order ready so he could pay at the end of the counter. That done, I could feel him coming toward me.

"Kate, how are you?" Clark said in a somber voice.

I turned around on the barstool. "Fine. How about you?"

He gave me a sight grin. "Sober," he replied sheepishly.

"That's good," I said and then completely turned around and continued eating my chili.

He stood there. "I don't know how or what to say other than I'm sorry," he mumbled softly.

"Accepted." I nodded without looking at him.

He turned and left.

Ellie was watching from the kitchen door and returned to my side as Clark exited. "Are you okay?" she asked, concerned. "What did he have to say?"

"He said he was sorry and now I've really lost my appetite," I said, looking at the floor. "Forget the pie, I'd better get going."

"Well, at least the first encounter is out of the way. Frankly, I can't think of a better way to move on from this than to spend more time with Cole."

I didn't respond. When I paid my tab, Trout gave me a warm but steady gaze. "Don't waste any tears on Clark McFadden, Kate. Clark only thinks of himself and always has. I can think of a guy who's pretty smitten with you and is the most unselfish guy I know."

"Thanks, but right now, another man is not what I need," I said, smiling. "Thanks for the advice, though."

"Don't go getting weird on us," Trout teased. "There's nothing like having the opposite sex in your life."

I looked at him quizzically. "I don't see a pretty little thing hanging around your neck these days." It felt good to tease him and lighten the moment.

"Trust me, she's there," he grinned. "I just don't want her around the bar scene, that's all."

"Well, I'm happy for you and will think about what you said," I stated as I got my coat and prepared to leave. It had turned out to be a later night than I had planned, but I was glad I had gone to the winery and faced reality. That was some interesting advice coming from Trout. Was he right?

Chapter 22

It was good to see Cotton and Susie again. Cotton said he was keeping fairly busy with various jobs. Susie was just glad to escape the two little ones. I showed them the extra blueberry muffins I had saved for them. They always looked forward to any extras I had left after baking.

"I really missed these muffins, Miss Kate," Cotton exclaimed with a big grin.

"Well, Susie, I'd be happy to give you the recipe, if you'd like it," I offered.

"Thanks, Miss Kate, but Susie could burn water," he teased.

"Cotton, that's a terrible thing to say about your wife!"

Susie just laughed. "Miss Kate, we sure have enjoyed that quilt you gave us that Emma made."

"Good. I hope you won't be afraid to use it. When I went to help the church ladies quilt, they had an empty chair where Emma always sat to quilt."

"That is really special. You're going quilting these days? My grandma used to quilt at her church. Now her arthritis is so bad that she can't anymore."

"I'll bet she misses it!"

"She loved being with her friends more than anything. I can remember playing under the quilting frame."

"Does your mother quilt?"

"No, Miss Kate, but she can cook!" Susie said, laughing.

"I'm heading out to do some cleaning up," Cotton said, heading toward the door. "I'll bring your tree in the next few days. Are you sure it's not too soon? They dry out pretty quickly."

"Next week would be better," I agreed. "Cut a small one for each of my guest rooms and one for Aunt Mandy, if you would."

After Cotton left, I told Susie there was no need to clean the upstairs attic suite. I did let her know that the rest of the house needed her attention.

While Susie cleaned, I put a small beef roast and vegetables in the slow cooker. I had apples that were aging, so I decided to make a quick apple pie. The house would smell great in just a little bit.

"Miss Kate, did you get another quilt?" Susie asked when she saw my fan quilt draped across the banister.

"Yes, I bought that from Imy's shop. It goes upstairs in the Wildflower room if you want to take it on up. It has a lot of feed sack fabric in it."

"I can tell! Our family used to have clothes made from some of those old things. Mama still prefers to sew up dish towels out of those. She said she was embarrassed when she had to wear clothes out of them." Susie carried the quilt upstairs as I thought about how simple feed sacks became so versatile and useful for so many people and spanning so many years.

I called Aunt Mandy and asked her to dinner. She was delighted and said she would bring a salad. The apple pie was done just as Cotton and Susie were leaving. I was delighted to send half of the pie along with them. I was upstairs changing my clothes when a text came from John.

Hey, neighbor! Missing you. Carla is here cleaning and says hello. J

I responded quickly.

Hugs to both of you. K

The message reminded me that Marilee's memorial service was tomorrow. I would look forward to getting a report from Maggie. I ran down the stairs when I heard Aunt Mandy arrive at the back door.

"Brr! The temperatures are dropping again! I think I'm missing Florida."

I laughed. "I made a fire. Go in and warm up while I get you a Merry Merlot."

"Thanks, sweetie. It sure smells good in here! I just made a simple tossed salad for us."

"Great!"

It was a perfect evening with my one and only family member. We drank, ate, laughed, and gossiped before she decided to go on home around ten. I always had her call when she arrived back at her house. She was a brave soul and I could only wish to age as gracefully as sweet Aunt Mandy.

Chapter 23

I picked Aunt Mandy up the next day to take her with me to the Friendship Circle meeting at Charlene's Coffee Haus. After she closed at eleven, Charlene and her mother brought out ham and beans, salad, and corn bread for our lunch. To our delight, there was an assortment of Helen's wonderful coffee cakes. The apricot cheese crumb was one of my favorites.

Charlene called the meeting to order with a long list on her agenda. She brought to our attention that Sharla Lee was hoping we would once again support the needy families in the area with Christmas gifts. Ruth Ann volunteered her place for the wrapping party. Esther reminded everyone about the Christmas caroling schedule as well as the traditional Christmas church tour. This group was so involved that they certainly didn't need to be reminded!

"We need cookies for the church tour, Kate, if you could help us out," Ellen whispered to me.

"Of course, Ellen," I agreed. "Let's hope we don't have a snowstorm like last year!"

"Don't forget the Christmas walk at O'Brazo," Betsy said with excitement. My sister always works so hard on that."

"Several of us are planning a nutcracker-themed tea at Ruth Ann's place to generate a little business," Anna announced. "Charlene has flyers here. Please encourage everyone to buy a ticket."

"Oh, the girls in my family will love that," Ellen commented. "Do you need me to do anything?"

"Just bring everyone you can," Ruth Ann replied.

I was glad to see Ellen embrace the idea. If she was supportive of an event, it would be successful! It was nice to see Aunt Mandy volunteer to make cookies for the church tour. She was truly enjoying all the action.

"I heard you went to quilting last week," Esther said when we broke for lunch.

"Yes. I'm sorry you weren't there, but now I know where you sit!"

She chuckled. "Ruby didn't say anything about what quilt would be next, did she?"

"No, but our quilt should be finished at the next quilting," I mentioned. "Why do you ask?"

"My neighbor is Stella Clifton and she has been waiting for months and months to get her quilt quilted," Esther explained. "She belongs to the St. Joseph Parish Catholic Church, but she doesn't care for their quilting. As an alternative, she has brought us her quilts in the past. Ruby complains that we shouldn't allow quilts from others like that, but money is money and that's why we're quilting. Stella is quite a quilter and always wins ribbons at the county fairs."

"Well, I'll look forward to seeing her quilt," I added.

"Stella said she keeps calling Ruby and never gets a direct

answer about when the quilt will be completed. I guess I'll ask about it at the next quilting," Esther said as she poured my coffee. "Will you be there next time?"

"Yes, I think so," I nodded. "I'm not so sure they'll be glad to see me come back."

"I'm sure you'll be a refreshing addition. We need new blood!"

Chapter 24

The next day, I woke up feeling anxious about the arrival of my guests. I went over the menu and jotted down reminders of what I needed to do. I liked having fresh flowers in the rooms, but my mums were already frozen and the blooms were spent. I was sitting on the sun porch making a grocery list when a call came in from Cole.

"Good morning!" I greeted him happily.

"The same to you! Are you with guests right now?"

"No, but I will be tomorrow."

"Do you have plans for lunch today?"

"No, I do not."

"Well, I have a slightly selfish motive here, but I love Marv's fried chicken and I happen to know it's his special today. It's nothing fancy, but I'll be happy to pick you up. If that doesn't suit, you can meet me there."

"I love his chicken, too! It sounds like a great idea. Why don't I just meet you there at noon?"

"Swell. I'll look forward to it."

I smiled at Cole's impulse invitation. Marv certainly had

many folks hooked on his menu! Cole's invitation reminded me that I had promised to fix him dinner sometime soon. I finished my list and planned to make a grocery run after having lunch with Cole. It was nice to think of a casual get together with him. Why was I smiling inside?

I chose my good jeans and a burgundy sweater that I hadn't worn in a couple of years. I pulled my hair back into a messy ponytail. For some reason, that made me feel sexy. I wondered if Cole would like it. I couldn't help but remember how Clark had been very good about noticing little things when I would make changes. I wondered what Clark was up to.

I decided to walk to Marv's, despite the very cold wind. Once I got started, it was a move I quickly began to regret. I finally reached my destination. I was pleased to see that Cole had already arrived. I knew because I recognized his SUV that was parked out front. When I walked in, our eyes immediately locked.

"Hey, Kate." He flashed me a warm smile and kissed me on the cheek, taking me by surprise. "Let me take your coat."

"Thanks. It feels good in here!"

"You really light up a room when you walk in," Cole flirted, leaning his face close to mine. Situating my coat, he volunteered, "I've already ordered a beer, but I wasn't sure what you wanted."

I gave the waitress my order. I could tell her curiosity about us was aroused. Cole kept smiling at me. We ordered the chicken special with great anticipation.

"Do you know Marv?" I asked.

"Everyone knows Marv," he assured me. "I get dinner from here a lot when I pass by."

"Marv was wonderful to me when I first moved here. I didn't know anyone except Ellie. I didn't have a kitchen set up at first and I would eat at the bar. That's where I met my plumber, electrician, and a heating and cooling guy! That sure made my job a lot easier."

His laughter filled the air. "I can just imagine the stir you caused when they saw a beautiful single lady sitting here with the regulars."

I laughed.

His look became serious. "You are so easy to talk to. I kept replaying some of the conversations we had at dinner."

"I sort of did as well," I admitted. "The entire evening was a real treat."

Chapter 25

Two hearty chicken dinners were placed in front of us. We dove in, fingers first, just like two little kids. We laughed at one another. At one point, Cole took his finger and brushed some crumbs from my cheek. It was something to watch Cole's appetite! I couldn't finish my plate. When I left a piece of chicken, Cole happily agreed to eat it.

"Looks like you folks enjoyed your meal," Marv said as he joined us at the table.

We smiled and nodded.

"Should I send over seconds, or are you ready for some dessert?"

"Not for me!" I said, wiping my mouth. "It was really delicious."

"I don't know how you do it, but I think your chicken was extra good today," Cole remarked.

"I think it's the good company you keep," teased Marv.

"I think you're right!" Cole chuckled. "I'll take the check when it's ready."

"Glad you enjoyed it," Marv said, tapping Cole on the

shoulder like they were good friends.

We cleaned our hands with the wipes provided. Cole gently touched my hand and thanked me for joining him for lunch.

"I haven't forgotten that I owe you a home-cooked dinner," I reminded him. "It won't hold a candle to the Blue Onion."

He smiled in response. Cole's hand was still on mine when Chuck walked in. He spotted us right away. Cole knew I had gotten to know Chuck when he built Aunt Mandy's house. He also knew that Chuck had tried to get me to go out with him. For a moment, it looked like Chuck was going to come our way, but he changed his mind and went straight to the bar.

"Somebody is checking you out again, Cole teased. "How do you manage to hold off all these suitors around here?"

"It's not easy!" I snickered. "It's really not about me. It's about my blueberry muffins!"

He liked that comeback. Then, Cole insisted on walking me back to the house. He took my hand and led me in that direction. As we got close to Ellie's house, I saw Chuck get in his truck and leave. I was certain that he saw us.

"I'd invite you in, but I've got to get to the grocery store this afternoon."

"I have an appointment as well," Cole said when we got to the back door. "I guess there's no harm in kissing you in broad daylight, is there?"

I smiled and looked into his eyes. I let him pull me close for a sweet kiss on the lips.

"Damn, that was good fried chicken," Cole said, smacking his lips.

"Yes, it was. Thanks so much. It was delicious in more ways than one!"

He grinned and walked away looking pretty happy.

Could this guy really be this nice? As I got ready to leave for the store, I wondered what Marv and Chuck thought about us being together. Perhaps everyone else knew Clark and I would never end up together—everyone except me.

On the way to the store, I thought about what my home-cooked dinner would be like with Cole. I wanted to be careful and not rush this relationship. I guess because Clark and I went at a snail's pace, I felt this was happening very quickly. Having Cole's friendship through the coming winter would certainly be a welcome surprise.

Chapter 26

It was late afternoon when Jeanne and Carl Winters arrived. They came in the front door and were immediately enthralled with the house, which they had driven by many times throughout their lives. They had a dinner invitation, so they needed to freshen up before going out.

"I'm glad you liked the Wildflower Room on the website," I said as I was getting them registered.

"I can't wait to see it!" Jeanne said as she signed the guest house quilt. "This is such a clever idea you have here with the quilt."

"Both of our moms made quilts," Carl commented.

"Well, this is quilt country here in East Perry County!"

"Are we the only ones here, Ms. Meyr?" Jeanne asked as she looked around.

"You can call me Kate. You are the only ones," I stated. "What time would you like breakfast tomorrow?"

"We shouldn't leave too late. Would eight be too early?" Carl wondered.

"That sounds fine," I assured them.

When we got to their room, I could tell it pleased them very much.

"Thanks, Kate," Jeanne said. "We won't be too late tonight."

"Just enjoy your evening."

I came downstairs and poured myself a glass of wine and sat by the fire. This was the time of evening that I sometimes felt a little sad. Everyone usually had plans and was excited to be on their way. I seldom had anyone to share dinner with, so my food choices were sometimes as simple as cheese and crackers. My cell rang and it was Maggie. I then remembered why she was calling. Marilee's service was today.

"Maggie, how did it go?"

"Girl, I wish you could have been there. I'm totally exhausted from crying. There were many eulogies, including one from Betsy which just tore me apart. I don't think she was quite finished, but she started sobbing and had to sit down."

"The poor thing."

"You were better off staying where you were. Another reason I'm calling is to make a confession."

"About what, for heaven's sake?"

"I'm financing Penny so she can buy Cornelia's shop."

"How did you come to that decision? Are you going to become part owner?"

"Not at all. I told you that wasn't going to happen! Penny loves the shop and has been so devoted through the years. I have a little money of my own that I really don't have plans for. Our only daughter is doing just fine, so I thought, why not?"

"You are something, girlfriend! What did Mark have to

say?"

"He couldn't say too much! He's been pretty good about it."

"What will Penny name the shop?"

"It will keep the same name so it doesn't confuse anyone. Cornelia has such a following."

"What will Cornelia do with her time?"

"Mostly travel. Her elderly parents are in California and she needs to be spending more time there."

I hung up thinking about all the changes that were happening back home. I was glad I was here in Borna making a new life for myself. It was nine-thirty when the Winters arrived. I was sitting by the fire updating my journal on some of life's changes.

"My aunt was fascinated when I told her where we were staying this evening," Carl shared as he sat down next to me. "She said she remembered Doc Paulson."

"Really? How old is she?"

"In her late eighties, I would say."

"Did she say anything about Doc's wife?"

He paused. "No, she didn't," Carl said, shaking his head. "She asked if your name was Josephine. Why do you ask?"

Chapter 27

It was obvious from the conversation that Josephine had become nearly invisible in people's minds. I suspected that folks thought of her more as a ghost than as a woman who had spent her life in this house. Doc must have had a strong personality. Perhaps no one else could get in the picture! I guess in those days, if you weren't a mother with children, you could easily fade into the woodwork.

The next morning, my guests were at the breakfast table at eight sharp. Carl had a fierce appetite for my menu of bacon-spinach quiche, fruit, and blueberry muffins. Jeanne only picked at her food. She leaned her head on her arm and said she hadn't slept well.

"That's not unusual for Jeanne," Carl explained in a grumpy tone.

Jeanne's head snapped up. "I told Carl that I felt like there was someone in our room."

I stayed silent.

"I said she was nuts and told her to go back to sleep," he said, reaching for another muffin. "At one point, she even turned on the light."

"You didn't see anything, did you?" I asked casually.

She hesitated before she answered. "I thought I did, but maybe I was just dreaming."

"What did you see?" I asked her when Carl went to get the paper.

"It was a woman," Jeanne started. "She wore a black dress and had her hair pulled back. I'm sure it was just the idea of staying here in this old house."

I smiled and nodded. "We all have visions which seem real and then turn out to be unreal."

"We need to get on the road," Carl ordered as he got her coat.

Jeanne hopped into gear and they thanked me for their stay. They didn't say they would return again, which said a little something. As they left, I was sure that Josephine had paid them a visit. The only time she had paid me a visit was to save my life from an intruder. I had never personally seen her. Why was that?

I was on my own to get to quilting today. Part of me wanted to go and part of me said to mind my own business and stay home. I decided to text John before I left to tell him I was going to become a church-lady quilter.

Back to church-lady quilters today. We'll see what happens next. Stay tuned. K

He responded almost immediately.

Hey, beautiful! Go get 'em! Take photos if you can. J

I had some leftover muffins. I decided to take them, even though I knew I would miss their coffee break. I had a good excuse for being late because of the guests in my house.

"Good morning, ladies," I said, entering the room. I saw a few heads look up and smile while some continued quilting. I could see that Ellen was not in her chair. I did notice that Esther was here today.

"Good morning, Kate," Esther greeted me.

"I brought everyone some fresh blueberry muffins I made for my guests this morning," I announced.

"Paula is in charge today," a voice from the group said quickly.

"Thank you, Kate," Paula said, getting up to take them into the kitchen. "I'll put some out for lunch."

"They are really delicious!" Esther exclaimed.

That was nice of her. She sat at the other quilt frame.

"Well, you ladies have sure made some progress," I mentioned as I looked at the quilt.

"If we finish up this row, we can put in a new quilt today," Ruby explained.

I took that as a hint for me to get to work.

"Oh, no! Not again!" Matilda said in disgust. "We can't keep having these blood stains!" She looked accusingly at Paula.

It was clear that Paula wanted to hide. She quickly went into the kitchen to get a cold rag.

"Did she spit on it?" Ruby asked from across the room.

"It's too big for that!" Matilda complained.

"Helen, what did Ruby mean by that?" I whispered.

She smiled. "If you use your own saliva right away when it happens, it will sometimes take it away completely," she explained.

"Really? That's good to know," I whispered back.

Paula tried desperately to get the spot out as everyone at her quilt frame watched. I felt so sorry for her.

"Just go ahead and get the table set for lunch!" ordered Ruby.

It then dawned on me that I hadn't brought lunch. Ellen had brought it for me last week. I decided that I could just eat another muffin. "Ruby, do you make quilts at home for your family?" I really just wanted to lighten the conversation.

"I do and I quilt them myself," she said without looking up at me.

"That's wonderful! What kind do you like to make?"

"Oh, Kate, she makes the most beautiful Double Wedding Ring quilts," Helen interrupted.

"They are hard to do. Good for you, Ruby," I said.

"She pieces them all by hand," Helen added. "I used to do that. It was years ago."

"Helen, do you not quilt at home anymore?" I asked.

"I do a little embroidery. Charlene keeps me busy making those coffee cakes now," she said with pride.

"Yes, I know!" I said with a big smile. "Are you stitching some now?"

"I started stitching some of the stamped state birds," she explained. "I don't know when I'll ever get them done."

"What a treasure that will be," I answered.

"My kids don't want embroidered quilts," said Erna from the other quilt frame.

"What kind do they want, Erna?"

"They like what they call 'modern' designs now," she answered with disgust in her voice. "I'm not even sure what that is about. They take them to be machine quilted until they're as stiff as cardboard."

I was glad Ruth Ann wasn't hearing this.

"Yes, I know," Frieda chimed in. "It's also so expensive! My daughter said she wants one of those big machines in her home! Her husband told her that he could buy them a new car with that kind of money."

Some nodded in agreement.

"Ladies, your hand quilting still seems to be in demand," I remarked.

"Okay, let's break for lunch," Ruby said as she got up.

Everyone marched to their table like little soldiers.

I wanted to sit with Esther at the lunch table. However, I thought I'd better sit where I sat the last time. Everyone brought out their brown bag of lunch. Paula looked at me eating my muffin and offered to share half of her sandwich. I declined, telling her that I had eaten a late breakfast. I watched my muffin basket. Only a couple of the ladies helped themselves. Anyhow, I had the right intentions.

Chapter 28

"Ruby, I'm supposed to check on the progress of Stella Clifton's quilt on our list," Esther mentioned. Everyone waited for a response. "She said it should have come up long before now."

Ruby's face stiffened. "Everyone has to wait their turn," she grumbled. "We don't do special favors."

"Well, she's about to ask for it back now that it has taken so long," Esther added.

"That's nonsense," responded Ruby. "It's probably already marked for quilting."

I went back to the table where Paula was doing clean-up. I told her to take the rest of the muffins home. Then I walked by the other quilt to see their progress. "You do such lovely quilting, Erna. I can tell you've been quilting a long time. Sometime, I'd like to visit with you about Doc Paulson and his wife, Josephine."

She looked at me strangely. I knew she was a little hard of hearing. Perhaps she hadn't heard me correctly.

"Okay, I think we're ready to take this one out," Ruby

announced as she began to unloosen the clamps.

After we folded up the finished quilt, Ruby went over to a wooden padlocked chest to retrieve another quilt, supposedly the next on the list.

"Is Stella's quilt in there?" Esther asked.

It was too late. Ruby rapidly closed the chest and fastened the padlock. I gave Esther a weak smile. It all felt so odd. Ruby had pulled out a plastic bag that contained a pastel-colored embroidered quilt made out of seven-inch blocks containing circles of lazy daisies. It certainly brought back memories of learning to do that stitch as a child.

"This must be for a sweet young lady," I mentioned as I helped unfold it.

Everyone had a complimentary response to its beauty. Ruby and Helen took charge, as I supposed they did with each quilt for this frame. They took the enclosed backing and attached it all around to the ticking which was stapled to the wooden frames. I caught onto the drill as we then dropped in the batting before the quilt top itself. I had to admire how nicely Ruby had prepared the layers. Erna and Esther came to help us hold everything securely as we began to roll and tighten the clamps. Just like that, a new quilt was ready for quilting!

Paula was quiet the rest of the afternoon as she worried about her bloodstain. At two o'clock when everyone prepared to leave, I went over to her and noticed that the stain was still pretty obvious.

"Paula, I think I have just the thing at home to get this out for you," I said on a positive note. "I use it for wine and blood. I will bring it next week."

"Oh, that would be nice of you. I feel so badly. Mrs.

Rector won't take kindly to this."

"It happens to everyone. How are the grandbabies doing, by the way?"

Her face lit up. "We have a new great-grandbaby now!" she said with pride. "It's a girl!"

"Well, congratulations! Do you have a quilt ready for her?"

She nodded. "I just have to bind it off. It's one I bought through the mail order catalog."

"Is it embroidery?"

"It's all cross-stitch. It goes quickly for me while I babysit."

"Did your grandmother and mother quilt?"

"Sure, but their quilts weren't fancy," she explained. "We tied a lot of quilts to get them done quicker. The nicer patterns got quilted. My mom was one of the original quilters here at the church in the 1930s."

"That's wonderful! Do you have a daughter that may want to quilt here someday?"

She snickered. "I brought Marlene with me one day only because she had taken an interest in my quilting. She was still learning, of course."

"Of course."

"When she found out that her stitches had been removed because they weren't good enough, she refused to come back. I felt badly because I think we have to engage beginners when they show some interest."

"Well! Does that happen often?" Naturally, I was thinking of my stitches.

"It's one of the reasons this group is dying off. I was so pleased to see you join us. We need new blood."

"I'm not good like the rest of you. I am hoping to get better with practice."

"There comes a time you have to give it up. We have a reputation for fine hand quilting, which we get paid for. Some of the markings are already getting criticized for being too dark."

We were joined in the room by Pastor Hermann.

"Has everyone gone?" he asked, looking around. "I'm sorry I didn't get here sooner. Kate, this is the first time I've seen you here."

"I started last week and they let me come back!"

He laughed.

"They certainly can use the help," he nodded in approval. "How are you, Paula?"

"Fine. How about you?" Paula blushed.

"I'm pretty busy. We have another funeral scheduled for tomorrow."

"Who passed?" Paula asked, looking concerned.

"Alvin Schuessler," he said. "He had been in the nursing home for quite some time."

Paula nodded like she may have known him.

"Well, ladies, I must move on," he said, shaking our hands. "Please come back, Kate. I hope your guest house business is booming."

"Thanks," I said as he left the room.

Chapter 29

Most of my day was shot at this point. I began a search for the feather tree and ornaments. I had to think about how I was going to get the fully-assembled and delicate tree to the museum. I thought I could definitely use some assistance from Cotton. I called, explained the situation, and he was happy to help.

I was about to text John about my quilting experience when I saw Cole pull into the driveway. I didn't have time to think about how I looked. I went directly to the back door to greet him.

"I hope you don't mind me dropping by like this."

"I just got home. Come on in," I said, giving him a big smile.

"You know, going past your place on my travels is way too tempting," he said, smiling warmly. "Trout said you'd had dinner at the winery. I wish I had known. I would have stopped by."

"Well, I guess I'm a little like you in that I impulsively decided to go."

He blushed.

"I guess you and Trout have a nice hunting trip planned."

"Yes, we're going to try a new hunting lodge in Minnesota."

"Minnesota?"

He nodded and smiled. "You don't think we just hunt on some old man's farm around here, do you?" he teased.

"Excuse me!"

He laughed.

"Well, if you're about to leave town, how about coming over for dinner tomorrow night?"

"Are you sure?"

"Sure! I have to go to the museum in the morning to put up a Christmas tree. That will leave me the afternoon to cook you something wonderful. What would you like?"

"Why don't you surprise me? Please don't go to a lot of trouble."

"Now, you don't mean that."

He burst into laughter.

"Can I get you something to drink?"

"No thanks, it's just good to see you for a bit. Can I bring anything tomorrow night?"

"Not a thing! I owe you for that lovely dinner at the Blue Onion."

"What time tomorrow?"

"How about seven?"

"I'll be there with bells on," he said as he exited.

I watched him leave. I admired his dressy-casual wardrobe. That seemed to be his work attire. I really didn't think this guy knew how handsome he was.

There was no time to waste in planning or shopping for Cole's dinner. He was used to eating at a lot of nice places. What could I fix that would be a nice change for him? Clay traveled a lot and ate out all the time. When I would make him something like meatloaf, he was thrilled. Okay, what man doesn't like meatloaf? I could do mashed potatoes and all the trimmings. I would make a blueberry pie with frozen blueberries from South Haven. I knew he would love that.

The only thing I could do ahead of time was set the table. I proceeded with excitement as I set the table as elegantly as I could. Ivy and berries would be the best I could do for a centerpiece at this time of year. I was pulled from my thoughts by a phone call from Ellen.

"How did your quilting day go without me?"

"They didn't tell me to leave! Paula was even nice enough to tell me how much she appreciated me coming. She also got in big trouble for getting blood on Mrs. Rector's quilt."

"Oh, don't tell me!"

"It's still there, but I'm going to bring something that should take it out."

"Good! I should be there next week."

"I brought muffins, just like you suggested, but they didn't go over that well. These ladies are pros at baking, now that I think about it. They probably wondered what the big deal was."

Ellen laughed. "I hope to bring my granddaughter with me next week. Julie is so interested in quilting right now. I want to encourage her in any way I can."

"That's wonderful! I guess I'll see you in the morning at the tree decorating. I can't wait to see what you've come up with this year."

"Sharla Lee told me about your feather tree and I think that will be a fine addition. Most folks do not know about them."

"That's what I thought. It sure will be easier than baking all those cookies like last year."

"Well, it paid off. You deserved the win! See you tomorrow."

Chapter 30

Cotton was right on time and ready to take my tree to the museum. I drove separately to take the ornaments and accessories. The museum was buzzing with excitement. Sharla Lee was exuding positive energy as she handed me a Josephine's Guest House sign to put by the tree. She showed me a corner area that she thought would be safer for such a delicate tree. Cotton stayed to enjoy all the excitement. Charlene was busy doing an entire tree in cupcake ornaments. It was going to be adorable. She was thrilled to be a first-time participant. I was pleased to accomplish my tasks without breaking even one ornament! Most of them were made of old glass that could shatter even if they fell on a carpeted surface.

"Wow, Kate, this is quite unique," Ellen exclaimed as I was putting on the final touches. "This brings back so many memories of my childhood. I still have some of my mother's and grandmother's glass ornaments."

"I knew that would be the case for many when they saw this tree. That's pretty special. I can't wait to see your tree."

"It's all bells this year," she shared. "I had plenty, but when I knew I was going with bells for the theme of my tree this year, I went crazy!"

"I love bells," I agreed.

"Good morning, ladies," Gerard greeted. "Your tree will certainly bring out the stories, Kate."

I nodded in agreement.

"I'll have to admit that those branches leave a lot to be desired."

We laughed.

"Well, I'm going to take a quick look around and then be on my way," I said, leaving them. I quickly viewed the many trees that had been so carefully set up. I got goose bumps thinking about the anticipation of Christmas. I loved the community spirit this time of year in Borna. I topped off the visit by glancing at all the new additions to the gift shop. I would have to do some shopping here for Christmas gifts, just like I did last year.

When I got home, I decided to check on Aunt Mandy by giving her a call. When I told her that Cole Alexander was coming to my house for dinner, she wanted to know every detail! "I'm making a blueberry pie so I can educate him about South Haven," I joked. We kept our conversation brief and I hung up knowing she would be eager to hear about how the evening turned out.

I looked around and envisioned what I wanted everything to look like and in what lighting. I planned the timing of my pie, bread, and meatloaf so it wouldn't take away from the time we had to visit.

Deciding what to wear was always the challenge. It was getting closer to his arrival time. What could I wear instead of jeans? I showered and chose a long print skirt and a black V-neck sweater. It looked best with long earrings, giving the outfit a gypsy vibe. I felt like a hostess now! When I got downstairs, I put on some light music and put another log on the fire. My cell phone rang and I was surprised to see that it was Jack. "Hey, darling, how are you?"

"Fine, Mom. Am I calling at a good time?"

"It's just perfect. I've started cooking dinner for a friend that's coming over tonight. What can I do for you?"

"Who's coming to dinner?"

"The guy who sold me the Jeep."

"Well, he's certainly made progress since I've talked to you last," he teased.

"He's easy to be with," I explained. "Is everything okay with you?"

"Jill and I have had some pretty stressful conversations lately," he began.

"About the wedding?"

"Everything. It's her work, the wedding, and then the idea of moving to New York."

"That is a lot. I feel for her. Can I do anything?"

"I don't know how concerned I should be. Is this normal?"

"There is no normal," I said to comfort him. "Just be patient and don't lose your temper with her. She just needs to vent." I looked at my watch and once again soothed his worries before we hung up. It did make me feel good that he shared his concerns with me. It honestly felt very good.

Chapter 31

Cole arrived right on time. I was pleased to see him exit from his vehicle holding a bouquet of flowers in one hand.

"Flowers! It has been such a long time since someone brought me flowers."

He looked rather surprised by my comment.

"Where did you get this beautiful assortment?"

"I got them in Jacksonville. I was doing a little business there today."

"They smell wonderful!"

"It smells wonderful in here! Can I help with anything?"

"Sure. You can open this bottle of wine while I put these flowers in water."

"This is real treat, Kate. I've looked forward to this all day."

While I attended to a few finishing details in the kitchen, we sipped on our wine. We shared the activities of the day and I was impressed by how busy Cole's days seemed to be.

We finally settled in at the dinner table. When he saw my home-style meal planned around meatloaf, he was overwhelmed. "My mom used to fix meatloaf like this. How did you know I had a craving for comfort food?"

I smiled with delight. "Just observing your lifestyle, I assumed as much."

"My daughter has turned into a pretty good cook. I'm sorry I can't say the same for my former wife."

"There's been so many times that I wished I had a daughter. I just talked to Jack earlier. We are very close, but he's a son and has many of his father's traits."

He laughed. "It's not easy watching a beautiful girl grow up. The boyfriends!" He chuckled and shook his head.

"I can imagine. I am pleased that Jack will be marrying a girl he grew up with and that she's from a good family. The stress of the wedding is getting to them at this point. I think they'll be glad when it's over."

I watched Cole help himself to seconds. It truly pleased me. The candles were burning down as our conversation continued into the night. I suggested that we have dessert in front of the fire. It was the perfect time to educate him about the history of blueberries in South Haven. I filled him in on some of the better memories I had from that special part of the country.

"Perhaps you can give me a tour of South Haven sometime. You are pretty fortunate to have a condo right on the lake."

"It honestly is so relaxing. I'll remember to invite you."

"I would like that."

Oh dear. What had I done? To break the awkwardness of the moment, I put another log on the fire. When I sat back on the couch, Cole took my hand and kissed it.

"You know, Kate, I don't relish bringing up the incident

of your intruder. However, how are you dealing with all of that?"

I took a deep breath. I really didn't prefer to revisit it all and ruin a good evening. "I'm fine. I try not to think about what could have happened. I often think about Susan's mother and Susan's poor little son. I can't imagine what it's like for a boy to grow up knowing that his father killed his mother. I pray that God will take care of them."

"It's good to hear you say that. My faith has gotten me through a lot."

"Did I share with you that I am now a church-lady quilter?"

"And how is that working out for you?" He visibly stifled a laugh.

"Pretty well! I feel like I'm serving a purpose there. I'm fascinated by these women of German descent. They grew up here and probably are all related in some way. You may even be related to some of them."

He smiled and nodded in agreement.

"If quilts could talk," Cole said, looking deep in thought. "I have quilts in my possession that I know nothing about. We've just always had these quilts and I don't think anyone ever asked who made them. That's rather sad, isn't it?"

"I know. Most of these ladies are over seventy years of age and are very modest about the quilts they make. When I show some interest, they look surprised. I wish they would talk more about their quilts and perhaps a little less about who is sick and who has died."

Cole raised his eyebrows in surprise and laughed aloud.

Chapter 32

The hours flew by. We had covered many topics of conversation. When the hall clock struck midnight, Cole said he should be going. “Your fire is about out. Would you like me to add another log?”

“No, don’t bother.”

“It’s been so comfortable, Kate. I really hate leaving you,” he said, gently putting his arm around me.

“I feel the same, Cole,” I admitted as I snuggled closer.

Cole tilted my chin upward and kissed me on the lips.

I didn’t refuse.

“I don’t want to overstay my welcome. I’m going to pull myself away from this attractive woman and be on my way.”

I smiled as he stood up. “You’ve been easy to please and we’ll do it again soon,” I assured him. “Thanks for the flowers. That was so sweet.” I gave him a hug. It was the kind of hug you would give your brother.

“Thanks for the blueberry pie. That was a real treat for me and I am so happy you are sending me home with the leftovers.” He paused and then asked, “When can I see you again?"

"Anytime you like, Mr. Alexander," I said flirtatiously.

As I watched him leave, I was awash with emotions and questions. Did I have a boyfriend? I went upstairs as if on a cloud. I wouldn't need a warm hug from Josephine tonight! Peaceful sleep came easy.

The Friendship Circle meeting at Ellie's house was the next day. I called her as soon as I got up. I was eager to see if I could bring anything. Her response was what I expected.

"Kelly has everything under control. I asked him to make his chicken and dumplings. I have the rest covered."

"Great! Did you get our list from Sharla Lee?"

"She is actually joining us for lunch. She will bring it."

"Wonderful."

"I wouldn't be a good neighbor if I didn't ask about seeing a black Jeep at your house last night."

"Well, if you aren't the nosey one!" I teased. "I cooked him some comfort food last night and I think he really enjoyed it."

"Girl, you are on it!" she said, laughing. "What did you fix?"

"Meatloaf with all the trimmings. I'll have to admit that it was pretty good."

"The poor guy doesn't have a chance! He'll fall in love with you if you're not careful!"

"He is so nice, Ellie. He is mannerly and very down to earth."

"Well, maybe we need to worry about you falling instead of him!"

We laughed.

"Don't forget I'm well seasoned, girlfriend. Don't worry

about me."

"Ha! Well, I have to get this cake out of the oven. I'll see you later."

Aunt Mandy called to confirm that I was picking her up for the meeting. She was eager to ask me about how dinner went.

"He brought me beautiful flowers and went home with the rest of the blueberry pie. I think we were both pretty happy with how the evening went."

She laughed. "You are spoiling each other!"

"Look who's talking! You and Wilson treat each other pretty well."

"Yes, we do. It's such fun. I have to share with you that he's going to have a knee replaced fairly soon."

"Sorry to hear that. He'll recover a lot quicker if he knows you'll be waiting for him. Will Barbara be able to take care of him?"

"Yes. She assured me that he is in good hands."

"That's good. Keep me posted. I'll send him some flowers."

"Splendid!" she said before hanging up.

I finished my makeup and then proceeded to get chocolate-covered blueberries out of the freezer to take to Ellie's. I knew they would all love them.

Chapter 33

I always loved going to Ellie's house. It was so cute and inviting. It was a tight squeeze for all of us members, but we loved just being there. Aunt Mandy and I arrived at the same time as Charlene and Ruth Ann. Aunt Mandy immediately complimented them on their idea of a nutcracker-themed tea.

"We already have reservations coming in!" Ruth Ann announced.

"You mean other than Ellen's family?" I asked. Everyone laughed, including Ellen.

"Yes, the churches are getting wind of this and there are small groups of ladies signing up at the same time."

"It's a good thing we have a large venue," Charlene pointed out.

"My scrapbook group wants to come. I don't believe they have reserved anything yet," Charlene mentioned.

"I didn't know there was a scrapbook club in town," I said, surprised.

"We've been meeting for a long time. Are you interested?"

I giggled a little and then responded, "Oh, no! I think I have my hands full right now just trying to become a church-lady quilter."

They laughed.

Ellie greeted everyone and started filling bowls with chicken and dumplings and heavenly fresh bread. I'll never forget her making it when I first stayed with her. The desserts of cherry cobbler and pineapple upside-down cake reminded me to go light on the dumplings. Aunt Mandy was focused on the cherry cobbler. She loved cherries in anything.

Sharla Lee enjoyed seeing everyone and took the floor to announce our charity families. "Thank you for participating in this worthwhile cause once again," she began. "Word has gotten out about all you accomplished last year. As a result, we have more requests this year. I will pass around this basket for you to choose a family. If any of you can see your way to take on a family again this year, it would be wonderful. Ruth Ann has once again volunteered to host the wrapping party. If you recall, that makes this fun at the same time! The next day, our staff will pick up all the gifts and see to it that they are delivered. Thanks again for all you do!"

Aunt Mandy picked her family first. "I have a grandmother raising three of her grandchildren," she revealed. "They all seem to be under twelve years old. I'll need your guidance, Kate."

I cautiously opened mine. "I have a mother with three little ones. They are all girls!"

Ellen tapped on the table to get our attention. "I think we've started something here, ladies," she said with a big grin. "My husband said that some of his employees are happy to take a family. How about that?"

Everyone clapped.

"We hope to have a big Christmas cookie bake at Trinity on Saturday," announced Anna. "We plan to package the cookies up so they can go to all these charity families."

There was more applause and it warmed my heart. We left Ellie's feeling very full and very proud. Aunt Mandy was ready to go home and take a nap and I was anxious to go online and start my charity Christmas shopping!

Once home, I got a call from Imy. She said she had purchased a signature quilt that she wanted me to see as soon as I could. I hung up and told her I'd be right there. Once I arrived, I noticed a truck in her parking lot. I assumed that she had a customer.

As I entered, Imy exclaimed, "Well, that was quick!"

"Are you alone? I saw a truck outside."

"Oh, that's my son's truck. He's working in the shed trying to get it ready for Christmas."

Imy turned and opened a lovely patchwork quilt with names embroidered in each block. Some of them had dates and the year 1920 on them. "I know most of these blocks have to be families from here due to the last names," she declared. "I would like to ask a favor of you. Can you take this to the church ladies to see who they know on it and find out why this was made? Typically, these types of quilts were made for events like someone moving away or for a memorial celebration of some kind. I found it quite clever and personal. The pattern is called Album. They used this pattern a lot to make autograph quilts."

"Where did you get it?"

"I got it from a dealer that stops by here on a regular basis. He bought it at an auction here in the county a long time ago. He wanted to unload some things and since this was from this particular area, he showed it to me. I bought it and a couple of other pieces."

"Are you going to sell it?"

"Most likely, but I want to know more about it first. Perhaps someone who's related to one of these folks would like to buy it."

"Sure, I'll be happy to take it to the quilting group for you."

Chapter 34

I left Imy's with the signature quilt. I kept it in the bag and placed it on my sun porch so I would remember to take it to quilting. I was about to go up and change when my cell rang showing Cole's name. "I thought you had gone hunting! Aren't you supposed to be in the woods of Minnesota by now?" I heard him laugh.

"We are here hunting and are currently having a burger at a local diner in town."

"That sounds like you're cheating, all the same. What's the name of the town?"

"You know, I'm not really sure. I just called to see how you are doing."

"I'm just fine. Does Trout know you are calling me?"

He laughed. "No, he doesn't. He's at the gas station filling up right now. My thoughts were on you!"

"Well, that's very sweet. I just got home from a day with the ladies."

"The quilters at church?"

"No, the Friendship Circle met at Ellie's house today. It's a group of ladies here in the county that has been meeting for a very long time."

"What are you doing tonight?"

The question caught me off guard. "I think I have a date with my Merry Merlot in front of the fire. It's quite cold here and there's a fierce wind."

"You're making me homesick. Maybe we should head back."

"You'd better put your hunting cap back on before Trout catches you on the phone!"

"You're right. Have a merlot for me, okay?"

"Sure. Tell Trout hello for me."

"I'll give you a call when we get back," Cole said before hanging up.

Well, that call was a total surprise! I hadn't thought about Cole since he'd left. I didn't think of us as a couple, but it was mighty nice having someone thoughtful enough to call every now and then. I was jarred from my thoughts by another call coming in. It was Mary Catherine. "Well, this is a surprise! We missed you at the Friendship Circle today."

"Peggy was nice enough to choose a family for me in my absence. I had a deadline to finish. It was quite fitting because the paper here at work has heard about the charity work the group did last year and the increased requests we're getting this year. Sharla Lee is giving you all the credit because you went to her and asked what the needs were in the community last year rather than starting a new event. Sometimes it takes fresh eyes to see what a community needs and you have provided that."

"It takes a village! It is amazing how everyone has come through."

Before we finished our conversation, she asked me if I was still looking for information on Josephine Paulson.

"Absolutely!" I answered with excitement.

"Well, it's a long story, but I was talking to Pastor Lohmann at my church and he told me the Paulsons were married there."

"Yes, in 1902," I confirmed.

"Your name came up and we talked about your guest house. He thought your naming the house Josephine's Guest House was very special. Have you ever met him?"

"No, but I will now. I have been concentrating more on Concordia because that's where they went to church and were buried. Did he say anything else?"

"No, but there are church records you may want to look into. By the way, how are you doing with the church quilters?"

"Fine, but I'm on the learning curve."

She laughed. "We have a small group that meets at our church, too. My mother used to quilt with them until her eyes started failing."

"Oh, that must be so hard to accept when you have been quilting for so many years. When does your group meet?"

"Every Tuesday at nine. You may want to meet them if you go see Pastor Lohmann. They are all so sweet. Of course, many of them are related to one another."

That wasn't any news. "I will remember that. Thanks for the tip."

"I have another reason for calling," Mary Catherine said, suddenly timid.

"I just got engaged to Jerry Boschert!"

"Well, that is big news! Congratulations. I don't know Jerry Boschert, but he's a lucky man!"

"Thanks, but he knows I still have to take care of my mom, so we have to work a few things out."

"I am so happy for you, Mary Catherine!"

Chapter 35

Mary Catherine's phone call was informative in many ways. I was anxious to give Pastor Lohmann a call. For Mary Catherine to find a husband in this small community while living at home with her mother was huge. She did her freelance writing from home. That limited her social life even more. I admired her dedication to taking care of her mother. That appeared to be the norm around East Perry County. Ruth Ann had done the same thing until it became too much of a burden.

The hours were passing and I went up to bed. Once settled in, I was wide awake with too much on my mind to sleep. I had my charity family to think about, Cole's attention, Mary Catherine's engagement, and the discovery of a signature quilt from the area. Imagine what a treasure that quilt would be to someone if it had their relatives' names on it from 1920! Too bad I wouldn't have known these folks back then. Thinking back on the day, I should have taken the time to study some of the names.

It didn't take very long for my curiosity to get the best

of me. I went downstairs, turned off the alarm, and retrieved the quilt that I had left on the sun porch. I took it to the living room and spread it on the floor.

Each block was made of tiny pastel prints on a white background. The names on the white fabric were embroidered in black thread. It reminded me of Josephine's quilt that was entirely stitched in black thread.

I got down on my hands and knees so I could read the names. There was no doubt that these folks had to be from the area with a familiar list of last names like Schmidt, Versemann, Winter, Boschert, Hopfer, Grebing, and Petzoldt. I was reading some aloud when I came across a J. Paulson. Interesting! Could it be a member of Doc's family or could it possibly be Josephine? I had to think how old Josephine would have been in 1920. She was born in 1879. That would have made her forty-one when she signed this. Someone had told me that she quilted at church every now and then. Why would she have been a participant making this quilt at this particular church? She wasn't sociable. What could have been the purpose for this quilt?

It occurred to me to compare the signature on this quilt to her writing on the quilt in the upstairs closet. I couldn't run up the stairs fast enough! I got the ladder and proceeded to pull her quilt from the pillowcase. I hoped that Josephine wouldn't mind. She had made it clear to me more than once that she didn't like me showing this quilt. Leaving the ladder in place, I headed back down the stairs.

I placed the quilts side by side. The texture of the black thread certainly didn't compare. In the 1920s, outlining in black thread was a trend. Sunbonnet Sue quilts and appliquéd butterfly quilts frequently seemed to be outlined in black thread. There wasn't a place on her quilt where she had actually signed her name. Some of the letters in the writing seemed to be similar on both quilts, it seemed. Maybe I was wishing too hard.

Looking at the signature quilt, I still didn't think Josephine would actually participate in making anything like that. Yet, I could be wrong. Doc definitely had a brother and sister with families, so it was also possible that this was one of their signatures. I thought that perhaps the church ladies at Concordia could shed some light on my little mystery. I carefully folded up both quilts. I would have to wait for further examination by the church-lady quilters. Even if I could identify it as Josephine's signature, the quilt did not belong to me.

Back in bed, I glanced at the clock which now read three o'clock. Should I get up and start the day? I tried hard to relax and think about something else. Where was Clark sleeping tonight? Was Cole camped out in the woods? Oh, please let sleep come soon!

Chapter 36

Despite sleeping late, I began the day feeling a bit worn out. I leisurely wandered down the stairs to get some coffee. I needed to focus. Cotton was going to deliver my tree today and I needed to clear a path for him as soon as I could. I wanted to call and request an appointment with Rev. Lohmann this morning as well.

I glanced at the answering machine and saw there were two new messages. How had I missed them? One was a request for a shower event and the other was a request for a room. The room request mentioned that they had a baby. I was too tired to respond at the moment. My cell rang.

"Good morning!" Ellie's voice was upbeat and energetic.

"You are cheery today. I just got up. I didn't get much sleep last night."

"It must have been that hot dinner date you had recently," Ellie teased.

"Funny. Actually, I had a lot of things on my mind. What's up with you today?"

"I guess you've heard by now that the O'Brazo Winery

has opened."

"I've heard a little bit about it. Are you concerned?"

"Maybe. I need to check it out. Trout's gone hunting, so I can't count on him to go over there. I wondered if you were game. Can you go with me tonight?"

"Sure, but I think you should stand tall and welcome them to the industry."

"Easy for you to say! I think what gets my goat more than anything is that Carson has helped the owner set up his business."

"That is pretty low." I paused. "Okay, what time?"

"I've got a new girl coming in for Trout at the bar. Because of that, I'd like to go early before it gets too busy here. How about five?"

"I'll be ready!"

I drank my coffee slowly. How betrayed Ellie must feel! At least I didn't have anyone opening a guest house nearby. I'm sure anyone considering that would just have to look at my constantly empty parking lot to make them think twice about that!

Cotton arrived at about eleven, accompanied by a friend to help him with the heavy lifting. It was a big, beautiful tree! I guided them through the front door to the living room. It would be lovely situated right in front of the window. I placed the small tree they brought on my kitchen counter until I made a decision as to where to place it. After they each enjoyed a cup of coffee, they were on their way.

Sticking to my game plan, I called Pastor Lohmann to ask for an appointment. To my surprise, he answered the phone himself. He knew immediately who I was and agreed to meet with me first thing the next morning. I was glad to see him on the same day as the quilting ladies at his church. In the meantime, he promised to check on any records the church might have on Doc and Josephine Paulson.

Throughout the afternoon, I gazed at the bare tree. It smelled heavenly. I certainly wasn't going to bake all those cookies like I did last year. I thought about decorating it with just lights and carefully-placed tinsel. The idea settled well with me.

Later, Aunt Mandy called and reported that Cotton had delivered her Christmas tree. "It's so cute. I wish I would have asked him to cut me one for the sun porch. It would be so nice to look out there and see the lights."

"Consider it done! I happen to have an extra little tree that he left for me. I have no plans for it. I'll drop it off sometime soon."

"That would be delightful. I have plenty of lights. Did you get yours decorated?"

"I guess you can say that. At least I know what I'm planning to do. It's going to be only lights and tinsel for me this year."

"That should be stunning! I can't wait to see it."

Before we hung up, I told her I was going with Ellie to check out a winery that could potentially bring Ellie some unwelcomed competition.

"Stop by when you can and give me some advice on this darling tree I have. It's a beauty!"

Chapter 37

Ellie picked me up and off we went to check out the competition. She was very grateful to have me with her and I was looking forward to a night out with my good friend. It was a good little drive before we got to the O'Brazo Winery. O'Brazo was a tiny little town known for its annual Christmas walk. The few townspeople did a great job decorating the town with white lights on trees and buildings. The winery was centrally located near the town hall, church, and post office.

A warm fire was waiting for us when we walked inside the white framed historic building that housed the winery. There were very few people sitting inside, but it was early. We found a table near the fire and an elderly lady came to our table to wait on us.

"Welcome ladies. Here is our wine list and an assortment of small plates we offer."

"Thank you," I responded.

"Why, you're Ellie Meers!" the waitress exclaimed.

"Yes, I am. I've been hearing about your place and

wanted to see it." Ellie explained with a friendly smile.

"My son will be thrilled. He's the owner. I'm his mother, Irma. I help him out when I can. He'll be in shortly."

"Nice to meet you," Ellie answered. "This is a very charming place."

"Well, he is living his passion," she explained. "Our family had the property and he saw potential in the location. We'll see what happens. His focus is on sweet wines right now."

"I'll have to try some and see!" Ellie said, looking over the menu.

"I'll have the German berry wine and a plate of cheese and sausage," I decided.

"I'll try the English berry," Ellie stated.

Now that we'd ordered, Ellie began to relax. "They have more wines than I thought," Ellie noticed as she looked around. "Right now, they only have wine. That'll be interesting to watch in the future. Did you see this?"

I nodded as she looked at the entertainment listed.

Ellie picked up their brochure and read every word to me pointing out that they had music on Friday night, just like she always does at her winery.

"That's okay," I said.

"Did you notice the gazebo and the large patio outside?"

I nodded. "Now stop comparing," I said, touching her hand. "It's all about charm here in this little town. You have a whole different look up on the hill with an incredible view. He doesn't have that. Not to mention the amazing food you offer. The man is living his dream, for heaven's sake."

"Well, just so he doesn't destroy mine!"

I had to chuckle at her concern. As we sat, we noticed

some familiar faces. One of them gave Ellie a second look. Irma's son did arrive. To my surprise, Ellie left our table and went over to introduce herself. I was pleased to see that. As time passed, I was getting restless and wanted to get home. That's about the time that Chuck walked in the door. He saw me sitting alone and walked directly over to me.

"Well, here alone at your best friend's competition? What's wrong with this picture?"

Although I knew he was teasing, I gave him a stern look. "Hi Chuck, how are you?"

By this time, Ellie had walked back to our table and greeted him. He was taken completely off guard.

"Well, Ellie, I didn't expect to see you here!" he said, surprised.

"We were about to leave, but I wanted to congratulate Curt on his new place," Ellie explained.

"That's mighty nice of you." Chuck scrambled for words.

"Enjoy your evening," Ellie said as she practically pushed me toward the door.

When we got in the car, we laughed about our little adventure.

"I think if Clark would have come in next, I would have had a heart attack," I gasped, giggling. "You handled everything well, Ellie."

"I guess I'd better get used to the idea that there's another sheriff in town," Ellie joked. "This has been an eye opener."

Chapter 38

Pastor Lohmann lived in a charming rectory behind Trinity Church. It must be a very handy arrangement for him. I knocked on his door and a charming elderly woman answered. I assumed that she was his wife.

"Ms. Meyr?" she asked with a smile.

"Yes," I responded.

"Please come in and make yourself at home," she instructed. She led me to a comfortable sitting area that reminded me of an old-fashioned parlor. "The pastor will be here shortly. He just went over to the church to do a quick errand. Can I get you some coffee or tea?"

"Coffee will be fine. That is, only if you have it made."

"Good morning, Ms. Meyr," the pastor said, coming through the doorway.

"Please call me Kate," I insisted.

He nodded. "I've been intrigued by the purpose of your visit. I'll have to admit that the records here leave a lot to be desired. We do indeed have a record of the Paulson's wedding that took place here at our church. Their marriage was announced in church a week before the wedding. Their wedding date was April 16, 1902. What's unique, however, is that they brought in a guest pastor from Frohna to marry them. Perhaps there was a close relationship. It looks like Doc's brother and his sister stood up for them."

"You'd think there would be a wedding picture of them somewhere, but there isn't," I said in frustration.

"We don't have one either. If there had been children, your task would be simpler," the pastor said.

I nodded in agreement.

"If I may interrupt, I asked my mother in the nursing home about the Paulsons," Mrs. Lohmann interjected. "She said she remembered the wedding because she helped with the refreshments in the church basement. She also remembered Josephine as a striking bride and that she and her sister-in law carried yellow roses."

"Yellow roses?"

She nodded and smiled.

"I found yellow roses on Josephine's grave and wondered who put them there," I revealed. "I had no idea that there was a personal connection."

"They married a little later in life compared to most folks around here," Pastor added. "She was 23 and he was 27."

"Did your mother say anything else?"

"She was a young teenager then, so it wasn't like she knew her," Mrs. Lohmann explained. "Mother said they went to church at Concordia."

"That's also where they were buried," the pastor mentioned. "There's no doubt that they were prominent folks. Then they built that beautiful home that you now own."

"We went to Dr. Fisher when I grew up, so I never saw

the inside of that house," Mrs. Lohmann added.

"I've taken up enough of your time today," I said, looking at the clock on the wall. "You both are welcome to visit and have a tour anytime. I understand you have ladies quilting today?"

"Yes, I should be joining them," Mrs. Lohmann noted. "Would you like to walk over with me to meet them?"

"Would you mind?" I asked. "Thank you so much for the coffee."

I followed Mrs. Lohmann across the yard to the church where we then went down the narrow basement stairs. The quilting room was quite nice.

"Good morning, ladies," Mrs. Lohmann greeted everyone cheerfully. The five elderly women were kind enough to look up and smile. Mrs. Lohmann told them who I was and that I quilted at Concordia.

I had so many questions for them. I wanted to know about their quilts. However, more than anything, I wanted to know if anyone knew the Paulsons. When I asked about them, some of the quilters gave me confused looks. One lady's look was rather unfriendly.

"Did any of you go to Dr. Paulson?" I asked.

There was silence. Finally, someone spoke up. "Well, Doc's reputation wasn't the best, I guess you'd say," the lady with the gray bun on her head said.

"Why is that?"

"You never knew just how much liquor he had consumed, for one thing," she mumbled.

The woman next to her nodded, indicating that she agreed.

"You're saying he practiced medicine while he was

drinking?" I asked more plainly.

She nodded.

"How do you think his wife Josephine handled that?"

"Well, she outlived him!" a heavyset lady retorted.

Some giggled at the slight joke.

"Yes, she did," I said in agreement. I suddenly felt badly talking about the deceased in such a way.

Chapter 39

It was obvious I wasn't going to garner any further information about the Paulsons. Learning about the yellow roses was the big prize of the day. Finally, one of the ladies asked if I would like to put a stitch or two in their quilt. I smiled and agreed to stay a little while longer. I went to the end of the frame and looked for some straight lines.

"Why, you do a fine stitch," the lady with the bun said.

"I just don't quilt often enough to do such even, small stitches like you ladies," I explained. "Did you all learn to quilt when you were young?" Most of them nodded.

"We had one of those frames that came down from the ceiling," claimed Mrs. Lohmann. "Come suppertime, we had to pull it up to put food on the table."

"Well, we couldn't see too well when it was nighttime, too," another lady added.

"Most of you have been quilting all your life, right?"

"I wouldn't miss it," said a sweet lady who hadn't spoken before. "As a young mother, it was my only social life. My husband would watch the little ones if I could hitch a ride with the mailman when he came by. If I wasn't ready, I'd feel disappointed the rest of the day."

"Well, that was nice of them to do that for you," I responded.

"I haven't been quilting here as long as Milda, because when I was raising my family, we lived in Unionville. We only got five dollars for quilting a whole quilt back then."

"Goodness!" I responded.

"During the depression, that was a lot of money," stated the bun lady. "If the farmers were having a good year, then we had more quilts that they could pay for."

One woman wasn't talking at all, but continued to give me the sweetest smile as she listened to our conversation. "Have you been quilting here a long time?" I asked her.

She hesitated. "Ja natürlich." She nodded with a smile.

"Ida only speaks German," Mrs. Lohmann explained. "Many others here speak German, so she's comfortable."

It became time for lunch. It looked very tempting. The German chocolate cake certainly caught my eye.

"Please join us," offered Mrs. Lohmann.

"Thank you, but I must get going," I said, getting on my coat. "You all do wonderful work. Thanks for letting me join you."

They all proceeded to the perfectly set lunch table as I headed to the door. I got in my car and felt such admiration for this older generation of women. They were truly hanging on to this pastime as long as their bodies would allow. I'll bet they had shared many joys and sorrows over the years.

I pulled into Imy's parking lot to tell her about J. Paulson's signature showing up on the quilt. There were several vehicles in the lot when I parked. As I was about to enter, I couldn't believe that Clark was coming out! He was laughing. We looked at one another in surprise.

"Oh, hi there!" I felt suddenly awkward. Then I noticed he wasn't the only one laughing. There was a woman hanging onto his arm and following a step behind as they came through the door.

"Hi, Kate," Clark said, bringing his chuckle to a halt.

I couldn't get past him since they were blocking the door.

"How are you?"

I was about to answer when he spoke again.

"Kate, this is Lucy Kilwin. Lucy, this is my friend, Kate Meyr. I told you about her."

She smiled. Her hair was indeed red, just as he had described it. "The guest house lady. Nice to meet you!"

"You, too," I lied. "Did you leave something in there for me to buy?" My question sounded silly even as it left my lips. I quickly managed to move past the two of them and didn't pause to hear their response.

"See you later," I faintly heard Clark say.

Chapter 40

When I got inside the shop, I had to stand still to gather my thoughts and catch my breath.

Imy was watching. “Are you okay?” Imy asked.

“I saw him too late to get away from him,” I responded, my voice shaky. A man passed me on his way out. We were now alone.

“Do you want to sit a bit?” Imy asked, concerned.

I nodded. I sat briefly on a stool near her counter. I couldn’t believe Lucy had made her way to Borna. I couldn’t believe it!

“When did this happen?” Imy asked in disbelief.

“It’s a long story, but if you want to know the gist of it, she’s the mother of Clark’s daughter.”

“Clark has a daughter?”

“Yes, and she’s about to have a baby,” I added.

“Goodness! Did you know all of this?”

“Not until recently. She lives in Nashville. I guess she’s here for a visit.”

“I was so puzzled when they came in. She mentioned

how she loved antiques. They didn't buy anything but she saw lots of things that she hinted to him about."

I took a deep breath and tried to concentrate. "The reason I'm here is that I wanted to tell you that I discovered a name on the quilt that read J. Paulson. Did you happen to notice that?"

"No, but that's cool. Is it Josephine?"

"I figure it could be possible. I just really want to know what the purpose of the quilt was. That would explain a lot."

"Yes, it would."

"I'll take it to quilting with me. Then I'll let you know what they say. I have to go."

"Are you sure you're okay?"

"Sure. Life goes on. I'm happy for him." Even as I said it, I wasn't sure I meant it. The rest of the way home, I felt numb. When I got in the house, I stared at the empty tree. I needed to do something to occupy my mind. With nothing else planned, I decided to decorate the tree. I wanted to call Ellie and tell her about Clark, but I knew she'd be busy without Trout there. Maggie wouldn't be any comfort. She was confused about my men friends and wouldn't understand. I wasn't sure I understood any of it myself! I had been fond of Clark for such a long time. Having Cole for a friend would be a nice distraction. My cell phone rang and it was Ruth Ann.

"I don't know if you have plans, but I have a big pot of beef stroganoff left from a banquet last night and wondered if you wanted to come over for dinner."

"It sounds wonderful, but I have a game plan here to decorate my tree."

"Well, how about I make a delivery? Do you want some help?"

"Wow, do I ever, but you don't have to do that! Ellie always helped me string the lights before, but she's a busy lady these days."

"Let me get some things together and I'll join you."

"Oh, Ruth Ann, that would be great!"

"I'll make a quick salad and be right over."

I hung up. I felt so lucky to have a friend like her. I quickly set the table and got the lights and tinsel organized. The night was turning colder. I decided to make a fire. The plans took my mind off of Clark. A good friend, good wine, good food, and a warm fire. That was all you could ask for! Women were so resourceful without the male species!

Chapter 41

Ruth Ann was as happy as a lark when she arrived. She brought a casserole, some fruit salad, and a pan of fresh dinner rolls. We poured some wine and then the decorating began! I climbed the ladder while Ruth Ann fed me the lights. She loved the idea of just using tinsel. Strand by stand, we carefully adorned the tree. The best part was the conversation as we chatted away.

We took a break to eat our dinner. It smelled divine! It was the perfect time to tell her about my encounter with Clark and his friend. I watched her expression turn to total confusion.

"Okay, I guess I've been out of the loop," she said, shaking her head. "The last I heard was that you had been seen out with Cole Alexander. That came from Harold, so I thought it just might be gossip. His exact words were, 'When someone's away, someone will play,' which I thought was hilarious."

"Is that what Harold thinks of me?"

"Kate, this town is going to talk about something. So fill me in! Did you and Clark break up?"

I took a deep breath. "The answer is no," I said before explaining. "Clark let me go. He was wrapped up in finding his daughter, which I understood. What I didn't know was that he had hooked up with Lucy, the mother. That was the real reason I wasn't hearing from him."

"The redhead that was with him?"

I nodded. "When he came back into town, he showed up drunk at my doorstep late at night to tell me about her. He said he went to visit her and didn't leave until a week later. How about that?"

"That doesn't sound like Clark!"

"That's what I thought."

"So, Kate, what's up with this Cole guy?"

"I accepted a dinner invitation from him. He was so nice to me when we worked out the purchase of my Jeep. Clark had dropped off the planet. I didn't see anything wrong with going to dinner. Clark didn't make any attempt to even ask me about my trip home in that horrible weather. There's no question that Cole's interested in me, but he made it very clear that he isn't interested in interfering with the relationship between me and Clark."

"From what I hear, he and his family are pretty well respected in Jacksonville. He has some bucks, my friend, unlike your artist friend in the woods."

I had to chuckle. "That doesn't impress me, Ruth Ann. I've been there, done that. Clark was just so accepting of me when I moved here."

"He took you for granted is what he did. Any woman would want more attention than he gave you."

"Oh, I don't know. On New Year's Eve, he told me he loved me."

She looked surprised. "He did?"

"Yes, and do you know what I said?"

She anxiously waited for my response.

"Nothing. I was caught off guard, and frankly, as fond as I was of him, I didn't love him. I knew I hurt his feelings, but I just couldn't go there."

"Well, that explains some of this. He's got his old fling back and you've got a new beau!"

"I don't see it quite that way, but I was surprised that he brought her back here."

"Why do you care?"

I shrugged my shoulders.

Ruth Ann suggested, "Let's get this table cleaned up. I need to get home. It's almost midnight."

We did just that. There was a reason Ruth Ann was sent to my house this evening. She helped me not only with my Christmas tree, but helped me process my feelings. Friends like her were priceless.

Chapter 42

The next morning was forecast with an onslaught of sleet mixed with snow. Today was quilting day. Did the ladies typically show up in this kind of weather? I had a good vehicle that would do well in snow. I planned to go. I found the stain remover and put it in my purse for Paula. I then packed a tuna sandwich for lunch and remembered to take the signature quilt with me. I bundled up and made a dash to the garage to warm up Red.

I arrived at the church and saw other familiar cars. Ellen was glad to see me when I walked into the quilt room. We chatted about the weather before we sat down. I wanted another cup of coffee. I knew I had already missed their coffee break, and I didn't dare mess up the routine by pouring a cup. Ruby, our fierce leader, was absent. I wondered how this group would function without her. Esther also arrived later. She seemed content to complain about the roads.

When everyone was seated, I asked for their attention. Thank goodness Ruby was not there to tell me to sit down. "Imy just purchased this quilt from an antique dealer. The dealer originally bought this at a farm sale here in the county. I don't have any more information than that, however, you will all recognize these names. Would you mind taking a look to see if some of these folks are your relatives?"

Everyone got up and looked closer. They mumbled the embroidered names quietly to one another.

"Erna, would you look at this block that has J. Paulson written on it?" I asked. "Do you suppose it could be my Josephine Paulson?"

Erna was the oldest in the group. She moved slowly towards the block and brushed her fingers along the signature. "I suppose it could be," she said.

"Do any of you have any idea why this quilt would have been made with these signatures?" I asked, looking at each of them.

"Well, these two names are actually sisters," Erna revealed.

"They each have a different last name, but you're saying these would be their married names?" I asked.

She nodded.

"Do you think these ladies went to the same church?" I asked, looking at Ellen. She wasn't missing a name as she walked around the quilt.

"I think they were all members here at Concordia," Ellen guessed. "They could have been members of the Women's Missionary League or some other group, I suppose."

"Good morning, ladies!" Pastor Hermann said, coming into the room.

I quickly explained to him about Imy's quilt and that it had a date of 1920 in one block.

"In 1920, there was a pastor here by the name of

Frederick," he recalled.

"I think these women were all members here, but it doesn't explain the purpose of the quilt," Ellen added.

"Pastor, I brought your favorite casserole today. Please don't leave without it," Matilda chirped.

"Why, thank you so much!" he replied.

"I have a plate of your favorite oatmeal cookies," Paula chimed in. "I even included the recipe in case you want to make them yourself sometime."

"Oh, you ladies spoil me," he blushed. "God bless you!" When he went into the kitchen to retrieve his food, I went over to Paula and showed her my spot remover. As the others watched, it worked like a charm! Too bad Ruby wasn't able to see the results. Paula was thrilled and I made a friend for life! I had just gotten into the rhythm of quilting when the pastor came over to me.

"I'll check on who was preaching here in 1920," he assured me. "I figure this could easily have been a special quilt for a pastor who was leaving or who was perhaps celebrating a special anniversary in the congregation. When I left as pastor of Immanuel Lutheran Church in South Haven, Indiana, I was presented with a quilt from all the members. It was a very thoughtful gift!"

"Now, many of us would like to know the story," I acknowledged. "These quilts can document the history at that time."

He nodded. "Yes, many churches have textiles hanging in their foyers with signatures on them from a former occasion," he noted. "We'll see what we can do." The pastor thanked the ladies for everything and they blushed as if he had kissed each one of them on the cheek.

Chapter 43

I had just sat down to put my thimble on again when a woman walked into the room as if she were lost.

"Can I help you?" Matilda asked. It felt as if she were taking over Ruby's leadership role.

"I'm Stella Clifton. I'm here to pick up my quilt." Her voice sounded firm and determined.

"Is it ready for you?" Paula asked innocently. "I'll be happy to get it for you."

"You're quilt isn't here," Matilda said flatly.

"Well, where is it?" the woman asked with a raised voice.

Everyone was speechless until Ellen spoke up. "I'll look in the chest. Let's just make sure." Ellen jumped out of her seat and headed for the chest. "It's locked. Where is the key?"

"Only Ruby has a key, Ellen," Matilda said. There was a certain amount of sarcasm in her tone.

"I'm sorry, Mrs. Clifton," Ellen apologized. "She probably still has it at home to mark."

"Where does she live?" Mrs. Clifton asked sharply. "She's had it over a year now. What kind of operation is this?

My friend had her quilt back within two months. There is no excuse for this!"

"I asked her about it last week," Esther started. "She said it wasn't ready."

"Ruby lives on A," Ellen said calmly. "I'll write down her telephone number so you can call her."

"You can't treat people's belongings like this!"

"We're sorry," Ellen said as kindly as she could. "We'll get your quilt back to you."

Those were the last words spoken as Mrs. Clifton marched out the door.

"This doesn't sound right," I whispered to Ellen when she sat back down.

"We can't let this incident get out," she whispered back.

"What could possibly be the problem?"

"Did you say that Imy is going to sell that signature quilt?" Ellen asked, determined to change the subject.

"I think so."

"Well, I know you may be interested in it because of the Paulson block, but if you don't buy it, I will."

"I'll tell Imy," I said with a chuckle.

After we all ate our lunches, I decided to leave. I had lost my desire to quilt. I made up an excuse about having an appointment. It was a weak one, given the weather conditions. I took my signature quilt and went straight to Imy's shop to report my findings.

Imy was about to leave when I arrived. "Oh, Kate, how did it go?" she asked with anticipation.

"It seemed like nearly all of them could connect to one name or another. Pastor Hermann came by and he said it could have been a quilt made for Pastor Frederick. He was the leader there in 1920. Pastor Hermann said it was very common for the ladies to make a quilt as a going-away present or perhaps for an anniversary."

"That would make sense," Imy said, pulling it out of the bag. "I kept thinking there might be a family connection."

"It is all family around here, remember," I teased. "By the way, if you decide to sell this, you have two interested parties."

"Really?"

"Ellen and me."

She laughed. "Right now, I'm going to hang onto it. It's a nice piece of history. Say, you haven't run into Clark again, have you?"

I shook my head and smiled at her concern.

"I need to run, but I'll let you know if Pastor Hermann has anything else to say about the quilt."

"Thanks, Kate. I'll show it to a few locals, too."

"I'm on my way to Harold's. I'll see you later!"

Chapter 44

It was good to see Harold in person when I visited his hardware store. He was never too busy to say hello and indulge in a little town gossip. "Long time, no see," he teased, issuing his belly laugh. "You haven't been in since you got back from South Haven!"

"You're right. How have you been?" I asked.

He moved a ladder and readied himself to chat. "I'm fit as a fiddle, but if you ask Milly, I'm as sassy as ever! What can I help you with today?"

"Well, I need a couple of extension cords, a three-way light bulb, and I think you can add on three of those pine wreaths you have outside," I recited.

"Those wreaths go fast and they look pretty darn fresh this year," he bragged. "You have a mighty nice Christmas tree again this year, I noticed. It's nice that everyone can enjoy it when they pass by your house."

"Thanks, Harold."

As we walked to the electrical aisle, Harold stopped to say what was on his mind. I wondered how long it would take before he mentioned Clark.

"Kate, I don't know what happened between you and Clark, but no one was more shocked to see him come in here with another woman."

I smiled to show I wasn't surprised. "Did you get to meet her?"

He nodded and had a sad look on his face. "Clark knew I was shocked," he revealed. "I asked her if she was from around these parts and she said she was from Nashville. I know it's none of my business, but I thought you and Clark were the perfect couple. I hated to see that."

"You are sweet to say such a thing, but as you know, Clark travels a lot. Things change and he's had a prior relationship with her."

"You don't say," he said shaking his head in disgust.

"I'm fine with it." I replied, my tone serious. Then I chose to change the subject. "Did you see my new Jeep?"

"You don't have to change the subject around me, Kate," Harold teased.

As I began to check out, Harold commented that his sister-in-law mentioned I was helping out with the quilting at church.

"Yes, those ladies are something!" I bragged. "I'll never be able to quilt as well as they do!"

I left feeling a sense of family protection from Harold. It was a strange feeling to know Clark was taking Lucy around for everyone to meet. I was a little embarrassed, but I sure didn't want him back since I saw how all of this was playing out.

When I returned home, I made a fire and turned on the Christmas tree lights. I had a strong urge to bake something and fill the house with wonderful aromas. I decided it was time to get going on some Christmas cookies. This year, I would make them for me and not for my tree! I got out my favorite baking cookbook. It was one I had used since Clay and I were first married. Tons of cookbooks filled my shelves, but I always went to my favorites. These recipes had memories attached to them. Some pages were stained from dough and stray drops of vanilla. I had marked my favorite cookie recipes, starting with Jack's favorite chocolate chip cookies that used chocolate candies. I would have to send him some. My peanut butter drop cookies were always a hit. I had to chuckle because the first time I made them, I left out the sugar! I thought everyone would never let me live that down. Chocolate crinkles were also a favorite of mine. Which should I start with first?

I loved to arrange all of the ingredients before I started the process, just like they did on the cooking shows. From time to time, I wouldn't have all of the ingredients I needed and this routine helped me avoid making the mistake of mixing things and then finding that I lacked an item.

To my surprise, someone was knocking at my back door. Happily, it was Ellie. This was about the time she went to the winery each day. "Hey, come on in!"

"What smells so good?" she said, coming in the door.

"Christmas cookies! I just put the first batch of chocolate crinkles in the oven."

"You are the bakiest person I know!"

I laughed. "It's therapy! You know there's more snow predicted for tonight, so I'm hunkering down, as they say. I've got the fire and my Christmas tree. Why are you going out in this bad weather?"

"With Trout gone, I have to be there. I'll likely spend the night, so don't worry if you don't see my car come home."

"Thanks for telling me. You know I worry when it gets too

late."

"Yes, I really need a garage, but there are too many other things to spend money on. I guess I should tell you that the real reason I'm here is to tell you Clark stopped by for a couple of drinks last night."

I stopped to wash my hands. I knew there was more news to come. "Did he bring Miss Lucy, the redhead?"

"Yes, he did. It shocked me to see how she was flaunting the relationship."

"It's okay, Ellie. Remember that she bore his child and he wasn't there for her. She's probably putting a guilt trip on him. Plus, the two of them will be grandparents really soon."

"I barely talked to her, but she sure was giving Bev a hard time about mixing drinks. I guess being a bartender is her big claim to fame."

"Who's Bev?"

"She's the new gal I am breaking in while Trout is gone. She's easy on the eyes for the guys and she appreciates the work. I think she'll be good."

"Well, you can use some help. Maybe this will free you up a little more."

"Have you heard from Cole?"

"Not recently. He wants to have dinner when he returns."

"Man, I don't know how you do it. You just have those guys waiting in line! Have you heard from John lately?"

"No, and I miss him. I think I'll text him later. I haven't heard from Carla and Maggie, either. I think they've moved on without me."

"Well, when you snooze, you lose. You made it pretty clear to them that Borna is now home and John knows now he isn't the chosen one, so what do you expect?"

Chapter 45

After Ellie left, I continued baking until about ten forty-five when I took the last sheet of chocolate cookies out of the oven. It was a nice distraction and it kept me from thinking about Clark and Lucy touring the town. I noticed the fire was about out. I took a minute to sit on the floor near the fireplace and send John a text.

Hey, I'm missing you! I'm learning a lot about church ladies' quilts. Interested? K

Well, hello, Ms. Borna! I miss you, too. I just finished an article about a local award-winning quilter here in Michigan. She reminded me of you! J

Hate being replaced! How is Carla? K

She misses you. J

I'll call her. K

I'm leaving for Florida in the morning. Tough assignment! J

I feel bad for you! K

I can feel the love. J

I smiled, feeling his presence. He had taken my rejection really well. I felt a frown on my face, knowing I wasn't sure I had wanted to reject him. Despite the late hour, I called Carla. The guilt I was feeling would not be conducive to falling asleep anytime soon.

"Is everything okay?" Carla asked instead of saying hello.

"Sure. I was just feeling badly that I hadn't touched base with you for some time now."

"I'm fine. However, I can't say the same about Roxy."

"What's wrong?"

"Cancer and old age."

"Seriously?"

"Yeah, the poor thing is really dragging. He's not been his old self. The vet has given him something for his pain. Nothing seems to help his spirit. I may have to put him down. My biggest concern is that you might want to tell Jack before that happens."

"Oh, Carla, you've been so good to him. Jack was always fonder of him than I was. Are you sure there's nothing more they can do? I'm happy to pay for any expenses."

"This isn't something that money can fix. I don't want him to suffer. I'll let you know."

"You can always get another dog."

"There won't ever be another Roxy. He's been great company for me."

"I'm so glad."

"I saw Maggie at the Blueberry Store and she shared with me about becoming a silent partner in the quilt shop. That's great news for Penny and she said Cornelia is already doing some traveling."

"Yes, but I didn't realize the deal had become final. I'm happy South Haven will still have a quilt shop."

We talked for about another fifteen minutes before hanging up. I wondered when Maggie would choose to tell me about closing the deal on the quilt shop. Would Carla have waited to tell me about Roxy after she had put him down if I hadn't called tonight? Did any of this matter? Of course. It all mattered. These were women who were close to me. Yet, I had a sense of missing important things going on with them. I hadn't planned to go back to South Haven until spring when the bridal shower would take place. I needed to be here with Aunt Mandy at Christmas.

It was too late to call Maggie. I would do so first thing in the morning. I had to chuckle to myself about Maggie being a silent owner of the shop. Maggie was never silent about anything! I wondered how long it would be before she'd be telling Penny how to run things!

I crawled under the covers when it was close to midnight. My cell phone on the nightstand rang and scared me. When the phone rang late at night, I always thought about something being wrong with Jack. Even though he was an adult, I suppose I would always react like a normal mother.

"Am I calling too late?"

"I had just fallen asleep," I said to Cole.

"I'm sorry, Kate. I wasn't able to sleep and took a chance that you'd be up. I'll call you tomorrow."

"Okay," I agreed and hung up. I went back to sleep and a dream turned into a nightmare. I watched Cole and Clark get into a fistfight at Marv's place. I tried to make peace between them and that was when Stella Clifton came in and accused me of taking her quilt. By then, I was screaming from all the turmoil. Lucy then came on the scene and told Stella that I am a crook and that's why Clark left me and why he now loves her. While trying to defend myself, I woke up in a cold sweat.

I got up to get a glass of water. I looked at the clock and it was only one. How could that be? I went back to bed. Thankfully, Josephine's warming light enveloped me. I embraced her hug and fell back to sleep under the many covers that made me feel safe.

Chapter 46

I woke up knowing I'd had a horrendous nightmare. Oddly, I couldn't remember any of it. Heading to breakfast, I felt bright and refreshed. I checked my computer for any inquiries. There were none. Well, who would want to come to Borna on a cold day like today anyway? An email confirmed a meeting with the woman who wanted to plan a shower at the guest house. That began my day on a positive note. I was about to devour a hot English muffin when Aunt Mandy called. That was odd because she always slept until nearly ten each morning.

"Well, aren't you up bright and early?"

"There's a good reason, honey," she said, her tone serious. "Barbara called early this morning and said Wilson had a car accident last night."

"Oh, no! Is he okay?"

"He's pretty bruised up. She was quick to tell me that there were no serious injuries. This postpones his knee replacement."

"Well, things could have been a lot worse. Let's be

thankful for that."

"Barbara said he's had too many fender benders in the last six months. I'm sure it's just his eyesight. I think he's a perfectly good driver. He's at home today. I'm going over there to have lunch with them."

"Well, Aunt Mandy, the roads can't be very good today. We got more snow last night. Do you remember how to get to Barbara's? I'll take you if you want."

"Oh, it's supposed to clear up. I think I can find it. I just wanted to let you know in case you dropped by."

"Tell him I'm very sorry and I hope he gets well soon. You be careful!"

"I will."

I didn't like her plans at all! The thought of getting old and losing independence wasn't going to be easy for those two. I took my coffee and muffins to the sun porch. I decided to call Maggie before she left for the day.

"Hi, Kate," Mark answered. "How have you been?"

"Great. How about all of you?"

"We're dealing with the weather."

"I thought I'd catch up with the new quilt shop owner in town."

Mark chuckled. "Don't get me started, Kate," he said, joking. "I told her not to do this and she's already got her nose of out of joint about some changes Penny is making."

"Hey, quit talking about me," Maggie said, taking the phone away from Mark. "He doesn't know what he's talking about."

"I talked to Carla last night and she said everything was settled on the purchase."

"Yes, it's all wrapped up," Maggie confirmed.

"Is Penny doing okay?"

"I'm trying to give her the benefit of the doubt. I do think she's going to regret some of her changes."

"It will all work out. By the way, has there been a date set for Jill's shower?"

"Yes, March 30. You'll be there, right?"

"Of course! Where are you having it?"

"At the club. That way, I can have all the folks I want!"

"Well, you didn't get to have the reception there, so this will be the next best thing."

"I have no idea what to get my own daughter. Isn't that crazy? Sometimes, I feel like I don't know her anymore."

"Jack says she's pretty stressed lately. I'm sure the move to New York has to be worrisome for her."

"I'm sure it is too, but she won't talk to me about it. She is excited about the London honeymoon."

"As she should be," I agreed.

"Have I talked to you since we heard that James got remarried?"

"No, but that doesn't surprise me since he found some rich gal."

"They went off to Las Vegas and I'm told there wasn't a family member present. How are Aunt Mandy and Ellie?"

"They're fine. Aunt Mandy called me this morning about Wilson getting in an accident last night. I think they're both afraid they will take away his driver's license." I paused. "She's getting fonder and fonder of him. Her adjustment to Borna would not have happened so smoothly without him."

"Sort of like Clark was for you, huh? How is he?"

"The short version is that we have both moved on. There is no more us. Maybe there never was."

"Well, that's news! I saw John at the concert hall last week with a date, so I guess he has moved on as well."

"He has, but we still communicate. We have a good friendship and we enjoy each other's senses of humor."

"I'm glad you called, girlfriend."

"Me too. I miss you and Carla."

"You know where to find us. Love you!"

"I love you, too!"

I felt complete again since I had touched base with my school soul mate. We always kept each other grounded and could be completely honest with one another. I knew she took it hard when I moved to Borna, but she also understood my reasons for doing so after my experience with Clay.

I was still in my robe when Cotton knocked at the back door. He put his snow shovel down when I answered the door.

"Good morning, Miss Kate! I won't come in with all this snow on my shoes, but I just wanted you to know that I should have everything clear soon in case you want to get out."

"Don't you want a cup of coffee?"

"I've had plenty, thank you."

"I'm sorry I don't have any muffins this morning. I haven't had any guests."

"Not with this weather! Say, Susie said I should ask when you'd like her to clean again."

"Maybe next week. There's no one getting things messy except me. How are Carly Mae and Amy Sue?"

"They're fine and sassy. I'll be going over to your Aunt Mandy's when I finish here."

"I worry about her going out today. She wants to go see

Wilson."

"I heard he had a little mishap yesterday. Is he okay?"

"I think so, but she may have an accident next if she isn't careful."

"I'll check things out. Maybe I can give her some advice. Call us if you need anything."

I shut the door and Cotton went to work. It was a good reminder of how much Cotton and Susie depended on odd jobs during the winter months. I wrote a check to him each month, but more than ever, I was sure they would appreciate their Christmas check.

Chapter 47

I called Esther to see if I could get a haircut on short notice. She was able to see me first thing. After that, I planned to stop by and visit with Pastor Hermann. The roads were partially clear as I drove out in the country where Esther lived. I was ever so grateful that she had her yellow mailbox. It would easily catch my eye. Once I arrived, she greeted me like an old friend. She had the coffeepot on and had some fresh pound cake to offer me. Before I even sat down, she didn't hesitate to say what was on her mind.

"Kate, we have a real problem on our hands with Ruby and the situation with Stella Clifton's quilt. Matilda called and said that when Stella showed up at Ruby's door, Ruby told her the quilt was locked up in the box at church."

"Really?" I asked, confused.

"Well, Stella was furious and went directly over to the church to speak to Pastor Hermann. She demanded that she be given her quilt! Of course, with Ruby having the only key, they couldn't open it up until he intervened. The pastor got the janitor, Arnie. They all went to the quilt room and Pastor

Hermann instructed the janitor to break the lock!"

"My goodness!"

When they got it open, there were only two quilts inside. One was the next to go in the frame. It belongs to Elsie Ehlers and the other was the wedding quilt Paula had made for her niece."

"Then, where is the quilt?"

"That's a good question!"

Esther still hadn't started on my hair. She was pretty worked up. I was a little afraid for her to pick up scissors until she calmed down a bit.

"It has to be at one of those two places, right?" Esther asked. "She said the pastor became angry and called Ruby to tell her the quilt was not where she said it was. Ruby insisted that's where she put it."

"How in the world does Matilda know all of this?"

"The pastor called her next to see if she might know where the quilt might be."

"Stella must have been livid by this time."

"You bet she was. Matilda thinks Stella will go to the sheriff and make a complaint. That kind of scandal could finish our little fundraiser for the church. No one will trust us with their quilts again."

"You're right about that!"

"I'm sorry. Take a chair, Kate. I didn't mean to get so upset."

I sat down to process it all as Esther fitted a cape around my neck. "Do you think Ruby accidently did something to the quilt and doesn't want to be blamed for it?"

"I guess anything is possible, but she can't hide that forever. Stella's quilts are pretty amazing. Her appliqué takes forever."

"You know we'll all be suspects if that quilt doesn't show up."

"Yes! My husband said there's a rat in the mix and we'd better catch them sooner rather than later."

I had to chuckle inside but I knew it was a serious matter. "Do you think she'll be at quilting this week?"

"She'd better be. The pastor is most unhappy about this."

"If Ruby has the only key, then Ruby has to be responsible."

"That's the way I see it."

"I guess Matilda is enjoying all this blame on Ruby. Why do you suppose they don't get along?"

"I think the story goes way back. One of them married someone the other didn't approve of. That is the simple version."

"That sounds interesting. I sensed their hostility towards one another the first time I went to the quilting group."

"I think Ellen said she thinks they're distantly related to one another."

"That figures!"

"Well, how do you like it?" Esther asked as she swung me round in the chair.

"It feels better," I admitted, smiling. "Thanks for seeing me on such short notice."

"No problem. Do you have your charity shopping done?"

I shook my head. "I did order some clothes online for my three little girls. I chose matching pajamas for them. For the older girls, I chose matching bedrolls and pillows. I will get the mother a few things, but I will also give her a gift card so she can pick out what she needs."

"Lucky you. I have a couple of teenage boys and their mom to buy for. Where are the dads in these families?"

"Beats me! It's sad, isn't it?"

We chatted for a few more minutes and then I excused myself. I wasn't a mile down the road when Aunt Mandy called on my cell.

"Did you make it to Wilson's okay?"

"I did get to Wilson's. Before I left, Cotton convinced me that I shouldn't drive. He drove me there and picked me up."

"Wonderful! I'll bet he was thrilled to do it. How is Wilson?"

"He's recovering slowly. I didn't stay long. I could tell he was tired. I was glad I could join him for lunch. He's so worried about Barbara insisting he not drive anymore."

"That is a tough one to ponder."

"Barbara took me aside and told me about some incidents that I didn't know about. I certainly don't want him getting hurt or putting himself in a place to hurt other innocent people." She paused for a breath. "Can you come by for a cocktail?"

"I can tell you're a bit down. I will be there."

Chapter 48

I pulled into the church parking lot hoping that Pastor Hermann would still be there. I dreaded any conversation about the missing quilt. I honestly hoped he wouldn't bring it up. As I was about to enter the building, I noticed that there was a woman on the cemetery hill at about the place where Josephine's gravesite was located. I went into the pastor's office and caught him as he was putting on his coat to leave.

"Good to see you, Kate. I just got a call from the Homer Koenig family and need to leave. Evidently Homer has taken a turn for the worse."

"Oh, I won't keep you. I'm sorry to hear that."

"Well, I was going to give you a call today to tell you it was Pastor Wengert, who was pastor here in 1920. He came here in 1910 and left in 1924."

"That's good to know. Thanks for taking the time to check."

"That quilt is a wonderful piece of this church's history." He glanced at his watch. "Well, I'd better run." He exited quickly just as Arnie entered the room. He was ready to lock things up. He said hello and gave me a second uncertain glance that made me feel like he wanted to say something to me.

"Sorry to hear about the missing quilt," he murmured, shaking his head.

"Yes, but I'm sure it will turn up somewhere. I heard you had to break the lock since we only have one key."

"I did, by golly. There used to be two keys, but somehow we lost track of the other one. Pastor said to keep the quilting room locked now, just as a precaution."

I followed him out the door and headed toward my car. To my surprise, the car was still parked on top of the hill. My curiosity got the best of me so I decided to approach the person. The hill was still slightly covered with snow, so it was a bit challenging. One of us would have to back out or drive on the grass, which wouldn't be a good idea. As I pulled up, an older, attractive lady got out of her car. She most likely wasn't happy about where I had parked.

"Hello, my name is Kate Meyr and I noticed you seemed to be paying your respects to someone I know who is buried here."

She looked at me strangely.

"Are you here to visit the graves of Doc and Josephine Paulson?"

She stared at me with aggravation on her face. "Is there a problem?"

"No. Not at all! You see, I live in the Paulson's old house that they built on Main Street. I made it into a guest house. If I may ask, are you related to them?"

She shook her head. "I have driven by your place and saw where you named it after Josephine," she said. She spoke in a much softer tone.

It was then that I noticed the yellow roses on Josephine's grave. "You're the one who brings her yellow roses!"

She nodded.

"I wondered who it was that brought them. I just learned recently that Josephine was fond of them and carried them in her wedding bouquet."

She smiled and seemed to relax.

"I leave them here as a remembrance from my grannie."

"Your grandmother? Did she know Josephine?"

"Its' a very long story. I don't get this way very often, so when I do, I pick up some yellow roses in Jacksonville and place them here. I know it sounds crazy, but it was Grannie's wish to remember her. My mother used to do it, but she died in 1983."

"I would love to hear your story if you don't mind sharing it with me. I have been trying to research Josephine's life and it's been very difficult."

"Why don't we sit in my car? It's very cold out here."

"Thank you!"

Her nice SUV still had the heater running. Sitting in the car was a great suggestion.

"To begin with, how did your grandmother know Josephine?"

She took a deep breath. "Grannie became pregnant out of wedlock at a very young age. The family was disgraced. I'm sure that if they did abortions back then, she would have had one. Instead, she was brought to Dr. Paulson who was located out of town. Grannie was told her baby had to be adopted as soon as it was born. That was quite upsetting to her. She said Josephine would visit with her when she came for her exams and felt very sorry for her. As you probably know, the Paulsons didn't have any children, so Josephine begged her husband to adopt Grannie's child. Grannie wanted that as well, especially when she was told she couldn't keep it. She thought it would be comforting to know where her baby was."

"Of course. That makes good sense."

"Well, Doc wouldn't hear of it, which broke Josephine's heart. They took the baby away as soon as it was born. For some time after that, Grannie and Josephine kept in touch."

"Do you know who got the baby?"

She shook her head.

"I'm telling the story as it was told to me. Adoptions were kept very secret back then. I do know my mother said it really affected Grannie the rest of her life and she felt so bad for Josephine. Josephine would have been a wonderful mother. They just kept saying it was all for the best."

"Well, the records can be researched better now, I think."

"Grannie was a very strong woman. Mother said it was from her early experiences in life. She finally married later in 1946 and had my mother. She named her Josephine. She never forgot Mrs. Paulson who had been so kind to her. She would send yellow roses to her on her birthday in October and continued that practice through the years."

"How nice of your grandmother to name your mother after Josephine!"

"As my mother aged, she asked me to continue the tradition of the yellow roses." She shook her head, smiling. "I am seventy years old and am still doing what my mother told me to do. Silly, isn't it?"

"No, not at all," I said. "Do you happen to have a photo

of her?"

She shook her head.

"Did you have children?"

She nodded.

"Yes, a son." She paused and drew a deep breath. "He died five years ago from lung cancer."

"Oh, I'm sorry. Where do you live now?"

"I just sold my home. I'm looking to relocate to Jacksonville. I am looking at an assisted living place that's just been built. I am going there today, as a matter of fact. I have a few relatives there. The nice young couple that bought my house said they would be patient until I find a place to go, but I know they are eager to get settled before the holidays. Folks around here have always been nice and friendly."

Chapter 49

"Thanks so much for sharing this information with me. I didn't get your name."

"Charmin Richards."

"Well, Charmin, it was so nice to meet you. I'd love for you to visit the guest house. I don't know whether you believe in spirits, but Josephine definitely has a presence there."

"Is that so? When I get settled, I'd love a tour. This young couple would like to be in my house by Christmas, so I have a lot to take care of before then. I hope it will work out with Jacksonville Meadows. Since I have no children to help me with this, I have to make a move now while I'm still able. I hate giving up my yard and flowers. Life seems so final when you start giving up the things you love."

I thought of Wilson and his car keys. "Here's my business card. Please keep in touch. If you don't have plans for the holidays, you are welcome to stay at Josephine's Guest House."

"Well, aren't you sweet? I'm pleased that you are paying homage to Josephine. She sure would have made a wonderful mother."

We said our good-byes and I carefully pulled around the side of her car. If anyone should get in trouble, it should be me. My afternoon was nearly shot, but I sure didn't want to miss cocktails with Aunt Mandy. However, I was surprised to see that Imy's car was still at her shop. I decided to make a quick stop. I noticed that Santa's Workshop was open now. I was dying to see inside. "Hello, hello?" I called aloud.

Imy came in behind me saying she had been in the workshop putting out some new merchandise.

"I wanted you to know that Pastor Hermann said a Pastor Wengert was at the church from 1910 to 1924. It doesn't make sense for the quilt to be a going-away present, I guess."

"It could have been presented to him for his nineteenth anniversary with the congregation," Imy said thoughtfully.

"You're right! You know, I've been thinking about making a suggestion, Imy."

"About what?"

"I think you should donate that quilt to the church. The pastor seems to think it's a great piece of history."

She considered the notion. "You know I'm a member of Trinity, not Concordia, right?"

"So what? The ladies' signatures on the quilt are from Concordia. Would you really feel guilty about something like a quilt returning home, so to speak?"

"I see your point. I guess it's better than watching you and Ellen fight over the quilt."

We laughed.

"If I decide to keep it for myself, you two wouldn't approve, I'm sure."

"You do what makes you comfortable. It would be good for business for you to show your community spirit. I'm sure Pastor Hermann would display it where many folks could enjoy it."

"I'll think about it, okay?"

"Deal. I have to get to my aunt's house. I'll have to shop in the workshop another time. Is there anything in there I should have?"

"Probably not. I try to put mostly primitives out there. However, I have something behind the counter here that you would give your eyeteeth for. I haven't unpacked it all yet."

"What?"

Imy went behind the counter and pulled out a charming china teapot that had a Christmas holly motif on it.

"Oh, that is lovely!"

"It's Havilland, late 1800s. It's priced pretty darn high on the web. It has a china tray and cups and saucers with it. I bought it online at a pretty good price, but it wasn't cheap, by any means."

"Where do you suppose it came from?"

"It just said an estate in St. Louis. Wouldn't you love to know who the original owner was and the path this piece traveled to get here?"

"Okay, how much will it be in Imy's Antique Shop?' I asked with a grin.

"I don't know yet. I have to own it myself for a bit."

I nodded and smiled. "My aunt adores pretty china like this. I'd love to buy it for her as a Christmas present."

"I thought she just liked cocktails," Imy teased.

"I can see it on her coffee table right now. I would give it to her early to enjoy through the holidays."

"Now, wait a minute. I haven't even unpacked it yet!"

"You should have known better than to show it to me! My auntie is worth your price, Miss Imy!"

Imy shook her head in disbelief as she giggled. "I'll let you know about the quilt and the tea set as soon as I can decide. Just give me a couple of days or so."

"You've got it! Remember, you said it has my name on it!"

Imy laughed and waved me on.

Chapter 50

Aunt Mandy was watching TV when I arrived. She didn't hear me knock, so I came on in with my key. "Anybody home?" I called.

She perked up and greeting me with a big grin.

"I see you didn't wait for me to join in before you opened your Merry Merlot."

She laughed. "No, but I made some artichoke and spinach dip that's in the oven. It should be ready soon."

"Wonderful. I love that dip. I can make a whole meal of it."

"Your hair looks great. I like that length on you."

"Thanks. Boy, do I have lots of news to share. I'd better fill my wine glass to the top!"

She laughed and used the remote to silence the TV.

I began with the mystery of the missing quilt. I could see that she got more confused as I spoke. She just kept shaking her head in disbelief. "Well, if that doesn't beat all! I'll be very interested to know where the quilt is found."

I went to get the dip out of the oven and switched on the

Christmas lights on her little tree and also the ones on her mantel. I offered to make a fire, but she wasn't interested. "I met an interesting lady on the cemetery hill by Josephine's grave today."

"Kate, I can't believe you're still going there."

"Well, had I not checked it out, I wouldn't know who has been putting the yellow roses on Josephine's grave!"

Her mouth opened in surprise.

"A granddaughter of someone Josephine knew very well."

Aunt Mandy was all ears to hear the story. It took me awhile to explain about the relationships of everyone involved. "I sensed she was pretty lonely after she decided to sell her house. I offered to give her a tour of my place and that seemed to delight her. She said she'd give me a call after she got settled in. I told her she'd be welcomed to share her holiday with us."

"Why sure! The more the merrier!"

"I just can't believe the family was that dedicated to acknowledging Josephine. She also said her grandmother and Josephine corresponded for awhile. I wonder if she has any of those letters."

"What a darn shame that Doc and Josephine didn't adopt that child."

"He sure was an arrogant son of a gun."

"Well, it's a shame. Who knows? With him having a drinking problem, they may not have allowed them to adopt anyway. He evidently didn't care that Josephine had maternal aspirations."

"Good point!"

"What was her name?"

"Charmin Richards."

"Well, I'll look forward to meeting her."

"So, back to Wilson. Did the doctor say when they will reschedule his knee surgery?"

"No. They want to get him feeling better. He had his neck in a brace as a precaution, but that was removed."

"Good."

"Are you going to let him rest up a bit before you go to see him again?"

"I suppose so. He hates having to be waited on. I feel so for Barbara."

"He is lucky to have her."

"As I you, my dear," Aunt Mandy said, blowing me a kiss. "I need a drinking companion right now. Wilson's not supposed to have alcohol."

"Happy to oblige!" I said with a laugh. "I'd better get on home."

"You certainly were full of news. Thanks for stopping by."

"Thanks for the wine and dip."

We hugged briefly and I left. As I got in my car, I was grateful for all the outdoor lighting that had been installed at her recently-built home.

Chapter 51

After a very good night's sleep, I awoke energized by the additional news about Josephine. I decided to order some yellow rosebushes to plant in the spring. Why hadn't I done that sooner? Then, I became concerned about another upcoming event. I was trying to decide what dish to bring to the wrapping party. A casserole would be wiser than a dessert. We typically had too many desserts. My phone rang and I could see that it was Cole.

"How is the great hunter doing? I asked.

He laughed. "We're heading home today. I should arrive in a couple of days. I had little luck in the hunting arena, but we sure had a great time."

"Great, I look forward to hearing more about it."

"That's why I'm calling. Are you free for dinner on Saturday evening?"

I thought for a minute and then replied, "Sure. What do you have in mind?"

"A quiet place where we can talk."

Oh? That caught me a bit off guard. I responded, "I'm

sure you will know the perfect place. I don't get out much."

"That I do!" He sounded confident. "How are things going for you?"

"Good. Today, I plan to meet with a woman who wants to have a shower here. I hope it materializes. I haven't had much business this winter."

"Your time will come. How does seven work for you?"

"I'll be ready."

After I hung up, I sat there smiling. The day was off to good start. He was such a class act. Then, on the heels of that thought, I wondered if Clark and Lucy were still in town. To take my mind off of that, I made some iced tea and prepared a plate of cookies for my potential client, Rhonda Walker. She was right on time. I didn't expect her to be with anyone. "Come on in, ladies," I said to them both, making an effort to make them feel comfortable. "I'm Kate Meyr."

They repeated their names and they turned out to be the mother of the bride and the mother of the groom. I couldn't help but think of Maggie and me.

Rhonda, the bride's mother, took charge of the conversation as they inspected my place. "Now, you won't be having any other guests that day, will you?" Rhonda asked curtly as she eyed me carefully.

"No. That day will be reserved entirely for you," I assured her.

They let me know their list was quite extensive, but in actuality, they did not expect even half of the invitees to attend. I hated when folks did that. It was obvious that they were only looking for a gift. I was rather puzzled by their choice to have the shower in Borna in the first place, but I couldn't get a word in edgewise even if I had wanted to!

"We will bring a sizable cake. I'd like you to prepare finger foods and provide coffee and tea," Rhonda instructed me.

"I can do that," I said with a smile. "Here is a list of charges for each service if it does not extend over thirty people."

"Oh, we won't have that many," the groom's mother assured me.

"Well, there's no guarantee of that, so you need to be prepared," I warned. "You have requested that people let you know whether or not they plan to attend, I presume."

They nodded.

"Do you have enough chairs?" Rhonda asked, her eyes scanning the room.

"I will borrow what I don't have. My friend has a banquet hall down the street."

"Well, Rhonda, why aren't we having it there?" the groom's mother asked, sounding perplexed.

I occurred to me that this meeting was not going very well.

"Because I want the charm of this historic house," Rhonda explained. "It will be so much more personal here."

"I will use china, silver, and crystal," I added. "I'll have the food on the dining room table and we can do a gift table in the living room. Will you be bringing flowers or do you plan to provide something else as a centerpiece?"

"Yes, I will bring flowers," Rhonda nodded. "The colors are lavender and white. Everything will be in those colors."

"It sounds like everything should be covered then," I said, hoping to move things along. "I have a bridal shower coming up myself in South Haven, Michigan. My son is getting married."

"Oh, how nice," the groom's mother exclaimed. "I'll bet that is difficult to plan from so far away."

"The bride's mother has it all under control. I needn't worry," I said with a grin. "Like a good mother-in-law, I'll just show up and keep my mouth closed."

The groom's mother looked shocked by my response. They then got up to leave. It appeared that I had secured the event. I was hoping I wouldn't be sorry later. Seeing the two of them plan this shower made me realize I may be in the safest place here in Borna when it came to planning my son's wedding!

Chapter 52

I dreaded going to the church to quilt today. I wondered if anyone would show up, given the current circumstances. Tonight was also the wrapping party at Ruth Ann's. I wanted to prepare my rice and chicken casserole before I left so I could refrigerate it and it would be ready for later. That done, I left early so I would be in time for the quilter's coffee break. I brought a plate of Christmas cookies.

As I walked in with Esther, I felt like our expressions said it all. Neither one of us knew what to expect. Ellen arrived early as well. It was obvious right away that Ruby was the one that was absent. There was less chatter than usual as everyone settled into their designated spots. Erna was in charge today. That became apparent as she busied herself with arranging the place settings.

"Good morning, ladies!" Pastor Hermann said, entering the room.

"Good morning, Pastor," we said in unison.

"Please, help yourself to some coffee cake," Erna offered. "I think you said once that it was your favorite."

"Thanks, but I have a meeting that starts in just a bit," he said politely. The look on his face was one of concern. "I'm sure you all know by now that we have an embarrassing situation on our hands regarding Stella Clifton's quilt."

The room was completely silent as everyone waited for him to say more. The silence was broken by Matilda. "Well, Pastor, we're sorry we don't have any answers. Ruby was in charge of the quilt." Her tone was curt and dismissive.

Undaunted, the Pastor Hermann explained, "Ruby claims that she brought the quilt here and put it in the chest you use. Now, it would be easy to point fingers at Ruby, but she claims she is telling the truth. So far, I have convinced Stella Clifton not to go to the authorities. I told her that I'm sure that this is a miscommunication. I want you all to pray about this matter."

We exchanged looks with one another without saying a word.

The pastor continued, "I'm keeping the quilt room locked as another precaution. In the meantime, we'll leave the quilt box unlocked."

"Thanks for stopping by, Pastor," Ellen said quietly. "I'm sure it will show up sometime."

He gave us a quick wave and left us to ourselves.

"Has anyone heard from Ruby?" Esther asked as she looked around the room. "She never misses."

"She can't face us, that's what," Matilda quipped.

"Who else goes in and out of this room?" Paula asked, curious.

"The janitor, of course," stated Ellen.

The discussion continued in whispers back and forth between the quilters. When we broke for lunch, Matilda took every opportunity to point fingers at Ruby. I told Ellen that I really felt uncomfortable around all of the gossip; however, I was determined to stay to the very end in case anything happened. Ellen reminded me once again that this situation could not get out to the public and especially should not be discussed at our party tonight.

I came home feeling frustrated. If Ruby stole the quilt or did some kind of damage to it, we needed to be understanding of the situation. To have her falsely accused would be terrible. Regardless, poor Stella Clifton would have to be compensated for this regrettable experience. I wasn't in the mood to party tonight, I decided, but it would be good to get my mind on something else. I wrapped a small hostess gift for Ruth Ann while the casserole was baking.

I chose to wear a red sweater with my jeans in an effort to look a bit festive tonight. After all, it was the Christmas season. Then, I packed everything up and traveled down the street to Ruth Ann's banquet hall.

Chapter 53

Mary Catherine and Ruth Ann were receiving all the potluck donations as we arrived. This was our second annual wrapping party and it was obvious how excited the group was to be gathering together again. After all the members arrived, Ruth Ann got everyone's attention. She said grace and we got in the buffet line. I sat down next to Ellen so I could ask her if she had heard any news since our quilting earlier in the day. She said word had gotten out about the missing quilt and it seemed to have come from Stella Clifton herself.

Ruth Ann once again got our attention and explained how the process would go once we finished eating. First, we would show our gifts to everyone and then we would all start wrapping. As we moved into the show-and-tell portion of the evening, I was amazed at how much money had been spent on this charity effort. Of course, they loved the pajama sets I had purchased for my three little girls. Ruth Ann reminded us that other organizations were also contributing. She also said that after last year's donations, she received many thank-you notes from the recipients.

Ellie had to leave early to check on the winery, but before she left, I asked her if she had seen any more of Clark and Lucy. She said she had not. She thought they may have left town. I reminded her that Trout and Cole were on their way back to town.

I stayed to the very end to help Ruth Ann clean things up. She really appreciated the help. The next day, she had a men's club card tournament booked. After we finished, she convinced me to come upstairs to have a glass of wine.

I loved Ruth Ann's taste in decorating. The arrangement of her living quarters and quilt studio was quite clever and attractive. When she asked me about Cole, I told her I would be having dinner with him after he returned.

"That's great! You'll never guess who I heard from yesterday."

"Who?"

"Chuck."

"My goodness," I exclaimed, genuinely surprised. "What brought that on?"

"I have no idea. He made a lot of small talk and then finally asked me to go to a Christmas party with him. I told him I would, but I have concerns that people will think we are an official couple."

I had to chuckle. "Are you going?"

She nodded. "I told him I would. It's not like anyone else is knocking at my door!"

"I hear you. You'll probably have a great time." We chatted a bit more and I decided to share the story about how I met a new friend at Josephine's gravesite.

She didn't seem to be too impressed. I think many of my

friends were not as fascinated with Josephine as I happened to be.

The conversation died for a few moments and then Ruth Ann caught me off guard by asking, "What's this I hear about a missing quilt at Concordia?"

"Where did you hear about that?"

"I'm not sure, but is it true?"

"Yes, it's true, but I'm sure it's just a misunderstanding."

"I think I may have heard it from Connie Mecker. I'm quilting a quilt for her right now. Her Aunt Matilda quilts at Concordia every week."

"Oh, for heaven's sake. We do have a Matilda quilting there, but she shouldn't be spreading the story. This group takes me back to high school by the way they gossip."

She laughed and nodded. "Well, I can't wait to hear how it turns out. We don't need a quilt thief in Borna," she joked. "You have to admit, it's an odd situation."

"I know. I can only hope that Pastor Hermann has convinced the owner of the quilt to be patient."

Chapter 54

It was Saturday morning and all I could think about was seeing Cole and having dinner with him. However, before I could get very excited about the evening, I knew that most of the day would be spent preparing for the shower the following day. Cotton would be delivering extra chairs from Ruth Ann. There was much to think about! Most of the menu I was making could be refrigerated, so once things were made, the lion's share of the work would be complete.

I planned to use an antique tablecloth that I had purchased from Imy some time back. I cleared a table in the living room for the gifts. I knew this event would be a learning experience for me so that in the future, I would have a better idea of how to do things. The latest RSVP number was only twelve guests, but I also knew I had to prepare for more. I was in the middle of making curry dip when Aunt Mandy called to see if I needed any help. I told her I had gotten up early and was in pretty good shape.

"Are you ready for Mr. Alexander tonight?"

"Not just yet, but I will be! How is Wilson?"

"His daughter is bringing him by here tonight for dinner."

"Did she take away his keys?"

"No, not yet, but really, he is too sore to drive."

"Well, that's very nice of her to bring him over. Now listen, you don't want her picking him up the next morning!"

She gasped at my suggestion. "Kate Meyr, you are a stinker! Do you know that?"

"I'm just sayin'!" We laughed and ended our conversation on that note. It made me feel good that we both had dinner dates with men we were fond of.

After I finished mixing some hummus, I went upstairs to decide what to wear for the evening. It became obvious that I needed to do some serious clothes shopping. After piling a small mountain of clothes on the bed, I eventually decided on black wool slacks with a black sweater. Silver accessories would not be a problem. I showered and put on a robe to do my makeup when I heard the cell phone ring.

"Kate!" a familiar voice said.

"Clark, is that you?" I asked in disbelief.

"Yeah. Am I calling at a bad time?"

"No, what's up?"

"Do you want to talk?"

I paused, thinking it was an odd question for him to ask. "About what?"

"About us."

"There's an—us?" My question was met with silence.

After a long pause in the conversation, Clark explained, "I just got back into town and thought maybe we could go get a drink and talk."

I couldn't believe my ears. "I'm sorry, but I already have

plans tonight. I was just getting dressed. I can't imagine what we have to talk about." I hesitated. "Is something wrong?"

"No, no. I just felt like our meeting at Imy's was rather awkward. I'd like to catch up and see you."

"Look, Clark, I totally understand your new situation. I'm a big girl and have moved on. I don't think your Lucy would appreciate your seeing me anyway, for any reason."

"Okay, okay, I get it. I'm sure Cole Alexander has something to do with your decision."

"I can make my own judgments, thank you. You know that."

"I just felt like we needed to talk."

I could feel Clark's sadness and confusion. Yet, his call came at an exasperating time for me. I couldn't resist asking, "When did you become such a conversationalist?"

"Okay, Kate. I deserved that remark. I'll let you go. Enjoy your evening."

"Good-bye, Clark."

Chapter 55

Ignoring that phone conversation wasn't going to be easy. I worked to push the call out of my mind as I finished dressing. Was he feeling guilty about something? Had things gone south with Lucy? I finally got myself ready and headed downstairs. I was pouring a glass of wine as Cole arrived at the back door.

"Hey, beautiful," he said as he gave me a kiss on the cheek.

"Welcome back, brave hunter!" I responded.

"Well, we put on a good show and had a lot of laughs, that's for sure. The weather here is sure a lot better. Truly, it's even greater being back here at Josephine's Guest House."

I smiled. "Do we have time for a drink?" I asked as I took another sip of wine.

"Probably not. I made reservations in Perry. A friend of mine just opened a cute little Italian restaurant called Cusumano's. It's right outside of town. I like to support him when I can."

"That's great. How do you know him?"

"I know him mostly from real estate, but he's wanted his own restaurant for some time. His sauce is the best. I think I remember you saying you liked Italian food."

"I love it. You don't find much of it here in Germanville."

He laughed and nodded. I got my coat and he helped me put it on. I appreciated his attentiveness. In the car, we chatted about how our Jeeps were doing, tomorrow's upcoming bridal shower, and finally, about my experience of meeting Charmin Richards at Josephine's gravesite.

John Cusumano greeted us with open arms and placed us at a table near the gas fireplace. It was a romantic spot. "Cole has told me a lot about you," John said.

"He's told me about you as well," I responded. "I'm anxious to try one of your specialties."

"Mindy will be your server tonight. I will be busy in the kitchen. It's a control thing I just can't give up quite yet. Anything that comes out of that kitchen has to meet with my approval."

John ordered a good bottle of wine and our dining experience began. There was no question that Cole had instructed John to pull out all the stops! As he brought out various courses, it was fascinating to hear his description about how they were made. In spite of considering myself quite a baker, I had never made cannoli, so when I heard they would be coming out for dessert, I got excited.

After some time, we had finished an entire bottle of wine and were now moving on to coffee. John was able to join us for a little conversation. Cole convinced him to take a seat.

"Before Cole told me about your owning Josephine's Guest House, my wife had already hinted that we should go there for a weekend getaway," John intimated.

"That would be wonderful!" I responded. "We have two wineries in the area that you might enjoy, too."

"With us just opening, it's hard for me to leave," he admitted. "However, we have an anniversary coming up, so I may just have to surprise her."

"I'll be happy to include a dinner. Fine dining is a little hard to find in that area," I lamented.

"If I'm lucky enough to be included, I could be your server, Ms. Meyr," Cole teased.

That would be an interesting sight.

"I can't tell you how pleased I am that Cole has found such a lovely woman," John said, smiling at the two of us. He was the consummate host to the end, ushering us to the door and wishing us a safe drive home. We left having had a wonderful experience. We were full, content, and ready to retire for the evening.

When we arrived at my house, we sat in the car and finished a conversation about the latest development Cole was working on. After that, I asked, "Would you like to come in?"

"I do, but I don't think I should."

"Why is that?"

He paused. "Trout advised me to take my time with this relationship. He said you are very independent and that I shouldn't crowd you or I might lose you."

"I see." Maybe Trout knew me better than I knew myself!

"He also made note of the fact that it hadn't been too long since you and Clark were together."

"Oh, dear. I don't think Clark has anything to do with anything. I'm not sure we were even a couple when I think back over our relationship."

Cole took a deep breath and smiled.

I waited and chose not to say anything else until he spoke.

"Trout told me that Clark screwed up the relationship."

"I think that's a little strong. Clark has a new life with a new daughter. Did Trout explain that?"

"He did, and it's quite a story! Look, if it works out that you two get back together, I'll live through it."

I shot him a questioning look and then forged ahead. "Okay, if you refuse to come in, I'll just have to kiss you out here in the car like I used to do with boys in high school!"

He laughed as I leaned in and pressed my lips gently against his. He was a bit taken aback, but returned the kiss passionately. He murmured, "I guess I'm a little out of practice about how all this works and I don't want to mess this up. Kate, you have lit up my soul in a way I would have never thought possible."

"No one has ever said that to me before," I replied, tenderly kissing him on the neck, his cheeks, and again back to his lips. It was as if time had slowed. While I had been chilly just moments ago, the vehicle now seemed to be steaming with warmth. Cole finally walked me to the door to say good-bye. I thanked him for taking me to Cusumano's. As I watched him leave, I decided that some things turn out to be sweeter than cannoli.

Chapter 56

Sunday morning church had not been the same since Emma passed away. I had felt so comfortable sitting next to her on Sundays. She always made me feel like I belonged. Ellen's family occupied the same pew every Sunday, as did other families who occupied their special pews. I spotted Erna and Paula with their families. There was no sign of Matilda or Ruby.

Before the first hymn, my mind drifted to the wonderful evening Cole and I had shared. I didn't remember him saying whether he belonged to a church. I would have to ask him. I didn't want to think about Clark's phone call, but it kept sneaking into my thoughts. What would Ellie think about that call?

As the service progressed, Pastor Hermann's sermon was a message about treating your neighbor with love and forgiveness. It was good for all of us to hear. I had to wonder if he had been thinking about the church quilters as he prepared his sermon for this particular week.

As I turned to leave, I got a glimpse of Ruby heading out the door. Without thinking, I rushed ahead to get her attention. "Ruby, wait!" I called.

"Good morning, Kate," she said without smiling.

"We missed you at quilting this past week. Are you okay?"

"I've been nursing a cold, but I think the worst is over."

Somehow I didn't think that was the real reason. "I want you to know that we all feel badly about Stella's missing quilt and I can only imagine how you must feel."

She looked to the ground. "I told the pastor the truth. I took the quilt back to the church. If it's not there, I have no explanation as to where it might be."

Out of the corner of my eye, I saw Ellen watching as I conversed with Ruby. "I'm sure there's an explanation. You do such a wonderful job marking and organizing everything. That's a big job."

She looked at me, surprised. "Well, thank you, Kate. No one else seems to realize how much work it is. Whoever took this quilt only wants to make me look bad."

"Try not to worry about it. This will all work itself out."

She smiled and went on her way. I went to my car unsure as to whether I had done the right thing. My gut told me that Ruby was telling the truth. I rushed home to make sure I had everything ready for the bridal shower. Knowing those two mothers, I felt sure they would arrive early in order to micromanage everything.

By one, I was still alone. At one-thirty, the mother of the bride, the bride, and another woman showed up. The other woman was carrying the cake, Rhonda had gifts, and the bride had the bouquet of flowers for the centerpiece.

"This is Marie, my sister," Rhonda said. "And this is my daughter, Jennifer."

I smiled and welcomed them both. While I took their coats, Rhonda walked around the first floor, inspecting everything and making certain it was to her satisfaction.

"Your cake is lovely," I said to Jennifer.

"It certainly looks wonderful with your accessories," Marie noted.

The groom's mother knocked at the door. After she got settled in the room, everyone made small talk, but I could feel the tension building. I was more worried about the poor bride's feelings being hurt. It wasn't long before the conversation between the two mothers started to heat up as they made excuses for there being no guests other than the four of them! I chuckled to myself. It seemed ironic that this shower was experiencing the same problem as my guest house.

"I'm hungry," Jennifer announced, ignoring any protocol. "I'm eating."

By three-thirty, it was painfully clear that the event was a flop. They picked at the food. I made myself scarce in order to avoid any negative conversation. After all, I wasn't an invited guest and it was a relief to be out of the room.

When Jennifer finished her plate, she opened up the few gifts that were displayed on the table. She didn't seem to be the least bit affected about the no-shows. She had an attitude that said this flop was not going to affect her wedding.

When they decided to leave, they failed to take the cake, food, or flowers. Their disappointment with the event caused them to decide to leave it all. They paid a good price for my services and I wasn't about to compromise my fee. It wasn't my fault that they had experienced a poor turnout.

As they put on their coats, I wished Jennifer well. I told her I had a honeymoon suite that I thought she and her new husband might enjoy. She thanked me for all my trouble, which was more than I received from the mothers. No one was speaking to each other by then, and they couldn't leave the house fast enough.

Chapter 57

After they left, I received my Sunday phone call from Jack.

"I miss you so much," I said immediately.

"I know, Mom. I miss you, too. I really hate not seeing you at Christmas. If it is any comfort to you, my future mother-in-law is unhappy about us not being in Michigan for the holidays, either. Who are you having Christmas dinner with this year?"

"It will be small, starting with Aunt Mandy, of course. I need to visit with her about it. Will you try to make it to Jill's shower?"

"I can't say for sure. I'm flying out to Boston this week. We'll have to see how things go."

"I understand."

"Tell Aunt Mandy and Clark that I said hello, okay?"

"Sure," I assured him, neglecting to explain Clark's absence in my life.

After every conversation with Jack, I liked to go over in my mind what we had just talked about. I sometimes wondered how it would have been different if I'd had a daughter versus a son. I also wonder what our relationship will be like when he is a husband. After I finally got everything cleaned up from the shower, I got an unexpected phone call from Charmin Richards.

"Hello, Charmin. How are you?"

"I'm fine. I'm calling to let you know that I did secure a residence at Jacksonville Meadows."

"That's wonderful!"

"I move next week. Another reason I'm calling is that I will be going by your place this evening on my way to Unionville and I wondered if I could stop by for a quick tour."

"Of course! I will be here."

"I can't say an exact time. I'm thinking it will be between seven and eight."

"Good. I'll see you then."

As I looked around the house, it was looking spic and span from my event today. I went to the kitchen to make a platter of goodies in case she had time to have a drink or enjoy some coffee.

An incoming text beeped on my phone. It was John. What a surprise!

How's my neighbor? Lonely in Nashville on assignment. Miss you. J

Nashville? What's the story? Miss you, too! K

Reporting on a restoration effort of a country singer's home. J

Interesting! K

Will you be coming home for Christmas? J

No. I'll be in Borna. K

;-(I'll call you soon. J

I tried to picture him in Nashville. He led such an interesting life. Hearing from him reminded me just how much I thought of him. It was always comforting to know that we still share a building in South Haven.

Chapter 58

I left the front porch light on for Charmin. When she arrived, she was wearing a nicely tailored coat and khakis.

"Kate, thanks for seeing me on such short notice."

"No problem. I'm so glad you called. Let me take your coat. Would you like a glass of wine or some coffee?"

"I really shouldn't."

"Well, why don't I give you a little tour of the house and then we can relax and have some refreshments."

"That would be swell."

We started in the reception room. I imparted the story about it being where Doc's patients waited. I didn't know a lot about the house, really. As we went into each room, I told her what had been told to me and she listened intently. When we got to the second floor, I told her that her grandmother would have most likely been born in one of those two bedrooms since the master bedroom was occupied by the Paulsons. She paused at each room as if she were waiting for a sign of some kind.

When we arrived at the attic suite, she was delighted

with the décor and was amazed that such a barren attic had been turned into such luxury. I told her about my theory of Josephine spending a lot time up there trying to stay out of the way. I then asked if she'd like to see Josephine's quilt that I had found in the hall closet on the second floor. She lit up with interest. I told her to wait where she was while I set up the ladder in the hallway in order to get the quilt. In the back of my mind, I hoped that Josephine wouldn't mind Charmin seeing the quilt! When I arrived with the quilt in hand, Charmin was sitting on the edge of the bed looking like she had seen a ghost.

"Are you okay?" I asked, dropping the quilt on a nearby chair.

"I think I must have imagined something and it just took me a bit by surprise. I'll be fine."

"What do you mean?"

I went to admire the bathroom. When I came out, I could have sworn that a woman was standing by the door. She was smiling at me."

I had to think about my response. I wanted to act like I wasn't surprised at her experience. "Well, what did she look like?"

She thought for a second. "She had a thin frame and had black, pulled-back hair. When I gasped, she disappeared. Am I crazy?"

I shook my head.

"It's her. It is Josephine. I've never seen her, but it's the same description that I have gotten from others. I'm sure she had to be pleased to see you here."

Charmin was truly shaken. I sat next to her on the bed and shared the story of Josephine saving my life when I had an intruder. I wasn't sure if she believed me or not. Perhaps she was still in shock. I was probably giving her too much information. After she had time to gather her wits about her, we took our time going down the stairs. I brought the quilt with me and prepared a cup of tea for her. I was ready for a glass of wine. Charmin remained very quiet.

"Please don't let this upset you. I think Josephine wanted you to see her. Drink some of this tea while I spread out her quilt."

"How can this not faze you, Kate? It isn't normal."

"You know, I felt her presence in this house from the very beginning and I have never been scared. She knows I love the house and she has to be pleased with all of the improvements. I honored her by naming the house after her."

"I see."

Charmin couldn't eat a thing. I did most of the talking so she could get to know me better. When I spread Josephine's quilt on the floor, her face turned even paler. She repeated some of the embroidered sayings and shook her head in disbelief. She said she had no idea that Josephine was so religious. She wanted to take a photograph of the quilt but I discouraged her from doing that.

As a bit of time passed, Charmin began to relax. I could tell that she was feeling a bit lonely after selling her house. I told her to keep in touch and that I would love to include her over the Christmas holidays. I was mentally exhausted after she left. Having another sighting of Josephine in this house left me with mixed feelings.

Chapter 59

As soon as I thought Aunt Mandy was up, I called to say I was dropping by with some leftover food from the shower. I also hoped she could help me firm up my Christmas Eve dinner plans. When I arrived, she was still in her pink bathrobe. Her hair and makeup were perfect, however.

"Goodness, Kate! Are we going to have a party?" she asked when she saw all that I had brought.

"I know that it's a lot. If you don't care for any of it, just get rid of it."

"How many showed up?"

"Four!" I exclaimed, holding up four fingers for emphasis.

"What? Did that include the bride and both mothers?"

I nodded and she shook her head in disbelief. "I inherited a lovely floral centerpiece, too!" I poured each of us a cup of coffee and shared a bit more about the shower. Then I told her that I didn't have time to relax even after I had cleaned up from the event because of the visit from Charmin Richards. I didn't have the heart to tell Aunt Mandy that Charmin had experienced a sighting of Josephine. I knew Aunt Mandy thought I had exaggerated about Josephine and her activities in the guest house.

"I would like to meet Charmin," Aunt Mandy said.

"You would like her. I wondered about inviting her to Christmas Eve dinner. I think she is a bit lonely. What do you think about including her? Besides you and Wilson, I'm hoping that Ellie will come, too."

"That is fine with me. What about inviting your new beau?"

"I don't know. Don't you think he'll be with his daughter?"

"You should ask anyway. I'll bet he'd do everything in his power to come and spend that time with you. How did things go on Saturday evening?"

"It was a great evening. We went into Perry where a friend of his owns an Italian restaurant called Cusumano's. His friend was so gracious and the food was divine."

"It sounds like Cole and Charmin both live alone and would appreciate a dinner invitation. Don't you think that's what Christmas is all about?"

Visiting with Aunt Mandy was just what I needed. Now, I felt I could plan the menu and invite those I wanted to attend. If Susie and Cotton had no plans, I'd invite them as well.

When I got home, my landline was ringing, which was unusual.

"Kate, its Imy."

"Hey, what's up with you?"

"Well, I did some thinking this past weekend and I decided to donate the quilt to Concordia."

"That's wonderful! You might want to bring it on Thursday when we meet to quilt. The pastor is usually around."

"I might do that. I decided something else, too. I decided to part with the Christmas tea set—if you're still interested."

"Seriously? That would be awesome!"

"You may change your mind when you find out the price tag."

"I want it, so hang on to it for me. Aunt Mandy will love it!"

I had barely hung up from Imy when my cell phone rang, showing Cole's name.

"I was wondering how your big event turned out on Sunday," Cole asked, sounding sincerely interested.

"It was a complete flop, but it wasn't my fault."

"Oh, I'm sure it wasn't!"

We laughed together. I realized how good it felt to be able to laugh with him."I'll tell you more at another time. Hey, Christmas is nearly here and you've never said what your plans are."

"Wow, I guess you're right."

"I'm hosting a small dinner party on Christmas Eve and I wondered if you'd like to come."

There was no hesitation before he gave me an answer. "I would be honored. I know my daughter will want me there on Christmas, so it should work out! I didn't even put up a tree this year. This is a year of transition, I guess. Your place is decorated so beautifully and it would be a happy place to enjoy the holiday."

What a sweet thing to say. "Aunt Mandy and Wilson will be here, of course, and I'm hoping Ellie will be free. I've decided to ask my new friend, Charmin. She stopped by for a tour of the house after the shower on Sunday."

"It sounds like a party. Please let me bring something."

"Perhaps I'll think of something as time gets closer."

"I keep thinking about our great night together."

"It was lovely, and I really enjoyed your friend, John."

"We'll go there again—soon!"

Chapter 60

The Christmas House Tour was on everyone's mind in East Perry County. I made a quick recipe of divinity to take to Concordia as my contribution. Last year, there was a snowstorm and I ended up in the ditch on my way to Concordia! It looked like smoother sailing this time around.

I needed to pick up the tea set from Imy if I had time. I also needed to get a little something for Cole this Christmas. I had no idea what to give an avid outdoorsman. Maybe Trout could help me with some suggestions. I wanted to give Charmin a basket of things from East Perry. The Heritage Museum gift shop was the perfect place to get the things I would need for her. I could get a book for Wilson. He loved to read. I had a delivery coming from South Haven that would satisfy Ellie. A phone call from Maggie interrupted my planning.

"Good morning, girlfriend!" she said enthusiastically.

"Good to hear from you, girlfriend," I repeated.

"I'm calling to solicit your help on what to get my future son-in-law for Christmas."

"I was just planning my gift giving, too! Let's see. I know he is so fond of South Haven. Perhaps give him something that is related to the area."

"I also wanted to warn you that I have something for you that I'm working on, but it will not be ready in time for Christmas."

"Wow, that's cool. Mine will arrive in the mail soon. Don't get too excited."

She laughed. "You have to catch me up. How is it going with Cole?"

"Good. I just invited him to join us on Christmas Eve. I hope he doesn't take it the wrong way."

"Wrong way? Why are you so afraid to show your feelings?"

I paused. "I guess it's the commitment thing that is usually attached to it. That was something I never had to worry about with Clark."

"Cole sounds more like your type, to be honest. I wish I could meet him."

"He may be too nice. Also, maybe a little too perfect! I think he's a little vulnerable right now. He hasn't been divorced very long. I don't want to crowd him in any way."

"You need to email me a photo of him. Your Christmas Eve dinner sounds more fun than what we will enjoy at the country club. I will miss Jill, of course."

When we hung up, I realized how lucky I was to have such nice folks to invite to my home on Christmas Eve. I was also thankful that East Perry County didn't have a country club! After we hung up, I bundled up with the intent to attack my list of things I needed to do. I decided to stop by the church and drop off the divinity before I did anything else.

The church doors were open. I called out, but no one responded. I couldn't see anyone. I wandered into the fellowship hall where the refreshments would be served. I placed mine next to a wonderful plate of chocolate chip cookies. It was tempting to take one.

"Hey, Kate," Pastor Hermann said as he was coming out of his office. "I thought I heard someone out here! You're out and about early today."

"I am. I'm on a mission to get some shopping done! By the way, the church's decorations are absolutely beautiful."

"You can always thank Ellen for that."

"Pastor, I am a bit baffled about this missing quilt belonging to Stella Clifton."

"What do you make of it, Kate?" he asked, shaking his head in bewilderment.

"I don't think Ruby is to blame, despite all the clues pointing to her."

"I feel she is being honest, but that makes it all the more mysterious."

"The janitor told me he thought there were two keys to the quilt chest. Did you know that?"

He shook his head. "No, I didn't. I guess I'm a little confused as to why anyone would want this particular quilt."

"I guess because her work is really wonderful. It takes her a long time to complete one of her quilts. Do you think one of the quilters has it in for Stella?"

"Have you heard any of them comment about her?"

"No, but I'm the new kid on the block. I have to say, I'm a bit taken aback about how critical they can be of one another."

He laughed and nodded. "Because they're church ladies,

right?"

"I guess," I said with a chuckle.

"They're no different than any other women's groups I've seen through the years."

"They sure have a love affair with you!"

He blushed. "Let's put it this way. I sure don't want to get on the wrong side of any of them!"

"You've got to convince Ruby to come back to quilting. If not, she will be presumed guilty."

He nodded as he folded his arms across his chest. "I told her at church this morning that we missed her at the quilting group."

"I'm sure that meant a lot. It was the good Christian thing to do. I don't think any of the others want her job of marking all those quilts and then keeping an organized list of what quilt gets done and when. That could alter the group's willingness to quilt for folks, which could then impact your income."

"I can't think about that right now." He shifted his weight and remarked, "It looks like we'll have decent weather for the tour this year."

It was clear that he was ready to change the subject. "I left some pretty good divinity. You may want to sneak a piece for yourself!"

"Thanks, Kate. Speaking of tours, I would still like to take a tour of your guest house. I have relatives who occasionally visit from Iowa. The next time they come, I would like for them to stay there."

"Great. That's what I'm here for!"

Chapter 61

Sharla Lee and Gerard were always happy to see me. The Christmas tree exhibit was up and they were expecting a great crowd because of all the people attending the church tour.

Sharla Lee was eager to help me check things off my gift list. The gift shop always had more merchandise this time of year, which I loved. I put her in charge of collecting things for Charmin's gift basket and she cheerfully reminded me to bring Charmin by so she could tour the museum.

"Kate, those charity families sure were grateful for all their Christmas gifts!" Gerard shared.

"I would have loved to have seen their faces," I replied. "I'm so happy the effort is expanding."

The beautifully decorated Christmas trees drew me into the large gallery. I took my time and enjoyed each colorful tree! I was also curious as to how folks were responding when they came upon my feather tree. When I approached it, Frieda, a member of our quilting group, was standing right in front of it.

"Hello, Frieda!" I said, catching her by surprise.

"Why, Kate. I was just looking at your feather tree. This really brings back memories!"

"Did you use to have one?"

She nodded. "There was one in our family. It eventually got too tattered to display it anymore. I think we had some of these same ornaments!"

"I was hoping the tree would get this kind of reaction." I paused before asking her my next question. "Frieda, what do you make of this missing quilt situation?"

She wouldn't look at me. "It's a shame. I never did think we should take people's quilts to be quilted until it was time for us to quilt them. Goodness knows how many items Ruby has at her house for us to quilt!"

"You make a good point."

She now looked at me and said, "I remember when Stella Clifton brought that top to us. It was over a year ago. She was very precise about how she wanted it quilted. Ruby didn't agree with her, of course."

"Do you think anyone saw Ruby put that quilt top back in the quilt box?"

"I doubt it. She always gets there earlier than the rest of us."

"The janitor said there were originally two keys."

She paused to think. "Now that you say it, I was there when Timmy Petzoldt delivered that storage box to us. He handed one key to Ruby and one to Matilda to give to the pastor."

"Are you saying the pastor should have the second key?"

"Well, he wasn't there that day. Then Matilda gave the key to Arnie who was supposed to give it to the pastor. He was there helping Timmy. Well, Kate, I need to get going. Nice running into you. I certainly enjoyed seeing your tree."

Glancing at the time, I headed to the counter to pay my bill. It was a shocker, but I couldn't think of a better place to spend my money!

"Thank you so much, Kate," Sharla Lee gushed. "Gerard will help you out to the car with these things."

I felt I had accomplished a lot during this visit. Now I needed to digest what Frieda had said about the transition of the second key. Matilda did not have the second key. Why didn't the pastor mention it if he had the second key? This birthed new questions in my mind. I would need to have a conversation with him in order to understand what had transpired.

When I got home, I saw that Ellie's car was still in her driveway. I decided to give her a call and ask to come to my Christmas Eve dinner.

"What's up, neighbor?" she answered energetically.

"I think I just finished my Christmas shopping at the museum today!"

"You're way ahead of me!"

"I was wondering if you had plans on Christmas Eve. If you don't, I'd like to invite you to join us."

"How sweet of you! I do need to see my aunt on Christmas day, so I think I can arrange that. Thanks so much!"

"That makes me really happy. Aunt Mandy and Wilson will be here and I've asked Cole to join us. What do you think about that?"

"I think it's great! Did he accept?"

"Yes, but it was a big step for me to even ask him. It was like asking him to come and meet my parents."

Ellie laughed heartily. "You're nuts, lady!"

"I also asked Charmin Richards. She's new to Jacksonville."

"Who is that again? I can't keep up with you."

"She's the woman whose grandmother knew Josephine. I met her at Josephine's gravesite."

"Oh, the gravesite lady!"

We chuckled again.

"I hope she can come. You would enjoy her."

"I'm sure I will enjoy meeting her. What can I bring?"

"Nothing. Between Aunt Mandy and me, it'll be a feast."

Chapter 62

Aunt Mandy and I decided to visit only a few of the thirty churches on the Christmas Church Tour. She was not only amazed at the natural green beauty of the decorations but delighted in the array of homemade pastries offered at each church. We had fun discussing which treats were our favorites.

When we got to Concordia, I was hoping to see Pastor Hermann. Sadly, he wasn't there. In my mind, questions were mounting about Stella Clifton's missing quilt. I tried to pull myself into the present. It was made easier by the wonderful coffee cake Concordia served every year. It was donated by The Coffee Haus, a local business.

When I took Aunt Mandy home, she asked me to join her for a glass of Merry Merlot. After all the goodies we had consumed at the churches, dinner was not required!

"You should have asked Charmin to join us today. She would have enjoyed it."

"I didn't think about it. She's probably busy getting settled in her new place. If you don't mind, I think I'll give her a call now and invite her to dinner on Christmas Eve."

"Good idea. While you do that, I'm going to change into something more comfortable." With that, Aunt Mandy rose and headed toward her bedroom.

It took a while for Charmin to answer. I could tell that she was very pleased to hear from me. "How do you like your new digs?" I asked, curious to know her experience thus far.

"I really love it. I've surprised myself! The staff is so helpful. They have assisted me in hanging pictures and even moving some things around. I feel much more settled in because of that. Everyone is so friendly."

"That does sound nice. I'll have to visit sometime."

"I would enjoy that, however, give me a few weeks."

"I'm calling to see if you have any plans for Christmas Eve. I'm having a small dinner party and I thought of you."

"Why, Kate, that is so generous and sweet of you! I actually do have an invitation, but it's too far away for me to consider. I don't drive too far at night anymore."

"Well, if you don't want to drive home that night, I have plenty of rooms to spare."

She chuckled. "I'm supposed to have chauffer service within a certain distance. I'll check that out. If you think I won't be intruding, I think I'll accept your offer."

"You belong here more than anyone. Everyone else coming will enjoy meeting you."

"Thanks so much, Kate. We'll talk again soon."

When Aunt Mandy walked back into the room, I told her Charmin had accepted my invitation. "Aunt Mandy, what are you hearing from Wilson these days? I hope he'll be available to join us for dinner."

"Well, I usually speak to him every morning. He's got a

little project he's working on for Oscar. That takes his mind off of his aches and pains."

"Is he driving?"

"Yes, but it's a continuous battle with Barbara. He's promised her that he will stop driving at night."

"If he comes over for dinner, that means he can't drive home until morning, right?" I teased.

She grinned and blushed. "He's been here a night or two."

"Auntie! You have been holding out on me!"

We erupted into laughter.

"The next thing you know, I'll be hearing wedding bells."

"I haven't said anything, Kate, but he would like to be married."

Why was I shocked to hear this? Even so, it did take me by surprise! "How have you responded to him?"

She smiled and chose her words carefully. "Well, I'm too old to be a caretaker, but I love being with him. We have such a good time together. It always feels so relaxed when we are together. I let him think that I don't take him seriously. However, I know he'd move in with me in a flash."

"I'm sure he feels like he is an imposition to Barbara at times."

She nodded.

"You know, in today's world, you don't have to have a license to move in together if you don't want to marry."

"We're both old school, my dear. Wilson would never let me be a kept woman."

We giggled again.

"I'm sure he knows you are thinking about what to do. You are so lucky to have found each other. I'm a little jealous."

"Honey, you have to open up your heart. I've watched you with Clark, John, and now Cole. You only let them in so far. I know it goes back to your unhappy marriage with Clay, but you have a totally new life here in Borna. To have someone care for you is nothing to take for granted. You can't go through life being afraid of getting hurt. It is a gift that can bring you peace and joy. It's my hope that you don't spend the rest of your life alone. Now, I have Wilson to think about instead of only myself. It can be a blessing."

The rest of the evening's conversation remained rather serious. I'd never heard that kind of frank talk from her before. On the way home, and all the way up to my bedroom, I replayed the advice my aunt had given me. It was a lot to consider.

Chapter 63

I was surprised that our quilting gathering wasn't rescheduled since it fell on the day before Christmas Eve. I had so much to prepare! In addition to Christmas Eve dinner, I had decided to invite Cotton and Susie over for breakfast on Christmas Eve. We'd had a special gathering last year and I had determined that I would like to continue that tradition. However, I was not going to miss anything regarding that missing quilt!

When I arrived at church, a light snow was falling. The forecast predicted heavier snow to follow. It appeared that we were going to have a white Christmas. We were likely to have fewer ladies today and I wondered if Imy would show up with her donated quilt.

"Good morning, Matilda!" I said as I walked in with Erna and Esther.

"I have the refreshments today," Esther revealed, displaying a cake carrier.

"Wonderful! I forgot my lunch again, so your cake will have to do," I laughed.

Esther smiled. "I'll be happy to share mine, if you'd like," she offered. "I hope I don't smell up the place with my egg salad."

I laughed.

"Matilda, I heard you make delicious chicken and dumplings for the church picnic every year," I mentioned.

She blushed and nodded.

"That is quite a responsibility." I then looked at Matilda but said to anyone within hearing distance, "Will you all be finishing your quilt today?"

"I think so. I hope there is a marked top inside our quilt chest. It appears as if Ruby is a no-show again."

"Can I visit a moment in private with you, Matilda?" I whispered so no one else could hear.

"About what?" She looked perturbed.

"Let's go into the kitchen."

She didn't look too happy to oblige, but she followed me. The other ladies had started quilting. They couldn't hear us and didn't really seem to notice that we had slipped away.

"Do you remember when Timmy Petzoldt brought in the quilt chest for all of you?"

"I do."

"Do you recall that Timmy gave you a key for you to give to the pastor?"

She looked at me suspiciously, perhaps wondering how I would know all that I knew.

"Yes, but Pastor Hermann wasn't there that day. I gave it to Arnie to give to him."

"So, Arnie took the key?"

She nodded.

"I guess the pastor misplaced or lost it. We should have

had another key made. I never liked the idea of Ruby being the only one with a key."

"I agree. I'm sure it will all work out."

Miltilda walked back and took her seat at the quilt frame.

Why didn't Pastor Hermann say anything about having a key? Maybe Arnie never gave him the key. That would make Arnie a suspect. Esther then joined me in the kitchen and prepared to cut her cake.

"Imy just arrived to donate her quilt," Esther announced.

"Oh, I want to say hello and thank her," I said, leaving Esther.

"Thanks so much, Imy. Was the pastor pleased?" I asked, excited.

"Oh, yes. He knows exactly where he wants to hang it," she added. "By the way, since you haven't gotten by to pick up the tea set, I have it all boxed up and in my car. I was thinking that I might see you this morning."

"Oh, thank you so much!" I responded happily. "Let me get my coat." I told everyone I'd be right back.

Chapter 64

The snow was getting heavier. I put the tea set in my car. I gave Imy a great big hug because her asking price for the set turned out to be very reasonable. I wrote her a check as snowflakes gathered in my hair. I went back inside and decided to make a detour to the pastor's office on the way. His door was closed. I knocked gently.

"Come in," he responded.

"Hello, Kate. What can I do for you? Have a seat."

"As you probably know by now, I have many questions regarding our missing quilt." I smiled, hoping to gain the confidence needed to express myself well.

He nodded. "Anything new in that regard?"

"Yes. I learned that originally, there were two keys left here by Timmy Petzoldt when he delivered the chest."

"Really?"

"Yes. One was given to Ruby. Then, one was given to Matilda. She was to give it to you."

"Oh. Really?"

"When I approached Matilda, she said you weren't here

that day. In your absence, she gave it to Arnie, who was to give it to you."

He looked puzzled.

"Did he give it to you?"

"Not to my knowledge." He paused. "Maybe I just don't remember."

"It's rather important because Ruby and Matilda both deny removing the quilt top from that chest."

"I see," he said, nodding.

You could tell he was trying hard to remember. "Would you ask Arnie about that? I didn't think I should ask him."

"Why, sure. I absolutely will."

"It's odd, because he was the first to casually mention that there were two keys," I explained.

"Well, I'm sure Arnie wouldn't be guilty of taking the quilt," Pastor Hermann said quickly, coming to Arnie's defense.

"Of course not, but it's not fair to the ladies if there are others that could be responsible."

"Sure."

"Word has gotten out in the community about this, which is such a shame. The sooner this gets put to rest, the better. We're fortunate that Stella hasn't taken this issue to the authorities."

"Good advice, Kate. I appreciate your taking this so seriously."

I left his office feeling even more curious. The pastor seemed to dismiss Arnie's role in this, but that quilt had to be somewhere! When I got back to the quilt room, some of the ladies were leaving because of the accumulating snow. I decided to leave as well. It would give me more time to prepare for my upcoming events. "Merry Christmas!" I said as I left. I'm not sure anyone responded. The roads were becoming problematic, even for my little Jeep. I was glad to arrive home, even though the distance was short.

I had presents to wrap and a French bread casserole to refrigerate for tomorrow's breakfast with Cotton and Susie. I set the table and then proceeded to write their Christmas check. I left Amy Sue's doll unwrapped and under the tree. Carly Mae's presents were clothes since she was still so young. It was a happy thought to have children sharing Christmas with me.

By six, I was exhausted. I poured a glass of wine and put my feet up. Aunt Mandy called to say she had made potato and leek soup. She planned to bring it for our dinner tomorrow. I went over the menu with her while she was on the phone. Besides her soup, we'd have Waldorf salad, roast pork, cranberry and apple dressing, creamed onions, and sweet and sour carrots. For dessert, it was my easy raspberry crème brûlée and a platter of Christmas cookies.

When I hung up, I wondered what kind of Christmas Cole was accustomed to. Was it casual, traditional, or kind of crazy? What would Clark be doing this year? Would he be with his daughter and Lucy? Last year, he brought his brother with him and had dinner at my home. I was about to head upstairs to bed when someone knocked at the front door. It startled me at first. I was relieved to see a delivery man through the glass door.

"Kate Meyr?" the young man asked.

I nodded. "Thank you!" I said, accepting a big wrapped plant. "You're working late tonight."

"Yes, I got stuck at a couple of places. Sorry this is

arriving so late."

"Merry Christmas!" I shouted as he ran back to his truck. Who would send me flowers? If it was Cole, why wouldn't he just bring them? Maybe it was sweet John. I uncovered a large, white poinsettia in a gold paper-wrapped pot. It was the largest poinsettia I had ever seen! I couldn't find a card at first, but when I did, it read, "Merry Christmas! Clark."

Clark had never sent me flowers. What was going on? He was always a generous man, but this was unnecessary since we were no longer a couple of any kind. Whatever his motivation, it made me think kindly of him for sending them. I found the perfect spot in the living room, near my all-white lit tree. I couldn't help but smile and tell myself, "Merry Christmas."

Chapter 65

My alarm went off early so I could prepare for my first guests of the day. I kept my robe on while I put the casserole in the oven. I looked out the window to see that more snow had accumulated. I was hopeful that Cotton's pick-up truck would get them here safely. I made a fire and went to open the back door to get more wood from the deck. The wind howled so hard that it nearly pushed me back inside the house! Shelter was indeed a comforting thing! I hurriedly shut the door. I finally made my way upstairs to change. I was nearly finished when I heard Cotton's truck pull into the driveway.

Everyone in the little family was bundled up as if they were coming from the North Pole. As I took their coats, Amy Sue made a direct line to the Christmas tree where she spied her doll. It was fun to see this sweet child experience the joy of Christmas. Carly Mae was sound asleep in her little seat. Susie said Carly Mae had just had her bottle.

I had everything ready to serve, but Amy Sue was too distracted to sit at the table with us. I made a point to talk to

Susie and Cotton about things that were not chore related. Their faces were priceless when they saw the Christmas check. They said they had been having some problems with their furnace so I'm sure some of the money was going to be spent on practical things.

Susie instructed Amy Sue to give me my present. It was a large gift bag that contained a beautiful cream-colored crocheted afghan. Susie mentioned right away that she had made it. I was impressed! When would she have found the time to make this while rearing two small girls? It was a splendid gift!

Susie offered to help me clean up after we finished eating. I wouldn't allow it. At about that time, Carly Sue woke up and was rather fussy. They decided to go on home and they knew I had a lot to do for the upcoming evening meal. I sent the leftover muffins home with them.

In the middle of loading the dishwasher, I received a text. I retrieved my phone from the counter and saw it was John.

Merry Christmas! All this Santa has for you is a big smooch and hug. J

I had to chuckle.

This Borna Santa sends a bigger hug and smooch. K

That was really sloppy. Guess I'd better wait until spring when you come back. J

I sent a big smiley face in response and went back to cleaning up the kitchen and putting another log on the fire. Hearing from John always gave me a pleasant feeling.

I heard something outside the back door. It was Cotton. He had returned and was cleaning off my sidewalks. He was unbelievable! He was so loyal and always took such good care of me. I reset the table with Grandmother's nice linen tablecloth and her lovely china. It looked so festive! I couldn't wait for everyone to arrive. Christmas was in the air!

Cole called and offered to pick up Wilson and Aunt Mandy because of the treacherous weather. The thought was a good one and I became concerned about Charmin. Unless I heard from her, I assumed she would make it here.

Late that afternoon, I changed into black velvet slacks and a sheer, white blouse. I piled my hair on top of my head. I hoped it made me look more festive than on other days. My upswept hair called for pearl drop earrings which I produced. I was happy with the look and headed back downstairs. There, I turned on some Christmas music and set out several trays of appetizers. I was about to add another log to the fire when Charmin knocked at the back door.

"Merry Christmas, Kate! I took advantage of the chauffeur service at the Meadows so I wouldn't have to drive in this awful weather."

I gave her a big hug and sent her to the fire to warm up. Next to arrive was Ellie who showed up on foot! She left her snow-covered boots on the sun porch. Ellie and Charmin hit it off immediately. Ellie had brought wine, so I put her in charge of pouring for everyone. Charmin brought a lovely platter of various nuts. Cole, Aunt Mandy, and Wilson arrived and seemed to be in good spirits. Cole gave me a peck on the cheek and I gave him a hug for picking up Aunt Mandy and Wilson. It was so gratifying to see everyone chatting and entering into the Christmas spirit. After we enjoyed some wine and appetizers, I steered everyone to the table.

I asked Wilson if he would like to lead us in prayer. He nodded and smiled. Everyone took the hand of the person seated next to them and Wilson prayed,"Dear Lord, bless this food and bring Christmas joy as we celebrate Your birth. Bless those who are not with us this day. For those who are traveling, we pray for their safety. We ask this in Jesus name. Amen."

Cole took my hand and kissed it when Wilson was finished. I'll have to admit that I didn't know how Cole would react to the prayer since we had never discussed his religion.

Ellie assisted me with the different courses. Conversation was plentiful and the compliments flowed. Cole tapped on his glass to make a toast. "I'd like to toast our beautiful hostess for this delicious meal." Everyone nodded their heads in agreement and toasted one another while wishing them a very merry Christmas. After dessert, we took our coffee and after-dinner drinks to the living room to unwrap our presents.

"Kate, if you had a piano, I could lead us in some Christmas carols," Charmin observed, looking around the room for a piano.

"Who needs a piano?" quipped Wilson.

"No, no, honey," Aunt Mandy scolded with a giggle.

Interesting. Now, Aunt Mandy was calling Wilson pet names.

Chapter 66

"Cole, I was at a loss as to what to get you," I said, handing him an East Perry coverlet and a blueberry basket from South Haven.

"It's great! I can use both of these things. I really want to make that trip to South Haven someday. Thanks so much!" He leaned over and kissed me on the cheek.

I noticed that he had a small wrapped package for me. The interruptions throughout the evening seemed to impede his ability to give it to me. Charmin went on and on about her East Perry gift basket. The others admired it as well. I'll have to admit that I was quite pleased with Sharla Lee's selections for the basket. Aunt Mandy and Wilson announced they were having their gift exchange tomorrow morning. When Aunt Mandy finally opened her tea set, the entire household cheered in admiration. She said she couldn't believe I had found such a treasure. I waited a bit before I told her I had purchased it from Imy. She quickly said that someday it would be mine, but in the meantime, she intended to enjoy it. Ellie loved her South Haven treat as well. She gave me a silver necklace with matching earrings. The set was very striking. I didn't typically wear much jewelry. This lovely set was something I would have purchased for myself had I seen it in a store. As the others engaged in loud and merry conversation, Cole handed me my gift.

"They say that the best things come in small packages," I joked as I began to open the gift. The only person watching was Aunt Mandy. "Oh, Cole!" I responded when I saw the diamond bracelet he had chosen. It was obviously expensive and the kind of gift I would have received from Clay. As Clay's business transactions had grown, so had my collection of expensive gifts.

"I liked the simplicity of it," Cole stated. "I hope you won't be afraid to wear it with jeans or whatever."

"This is way beyond beautiful," I said, wanting to kiss him in front of everyone. By now, Ellie and Charmin took note of what was happening. Their mouths opened in surprise. There was no doubt that Cole had taken a leap of faith by giving me such an expensive gift. I think it gave him more joy to give me the bracelet than I got from receiving it!

The evening was winding down. Charmin was the first to leave after she called her chauffeur to pick her up. I think she truly enjoyed herself and she said the dinner would be the highlight of her Christmas celebrations. I hoped that Josephine was watching Charmin have a good time.

Wilson then suggested that he and Aunt Mandy be on their way. Cole was happy to take them home. "Oh, Kate, this dinner was lovely and your bracelet is divine!" Aunt Mandy raved as she gave me a hug. She leaned in closer and whispered, "I think he is a keeper. I love my tea set. Thank you again."

"You and Wilson enjoy your little Christmas together," I said as they put on their coats.

"Merry Christmas!" Aunt Mandy and Wilson said in

unison as they left.

"That is so sweet of Cole to take care of them," Ellie pointed out. "What's your take on this very, very nice Christmas gift?"

"Well, he can afford it and that's the world he lives in. Clark would make me something and Cole gets out his credit card. I don't mean that one is better than the other. I'm just afraid that I am falling in love with him."

"I didn't want to ask in front of the others, but who gave you this gorgeous poinsettia?" Ellie asked.

"Clark. Can you believe it?"

"Oh! I thought you were going to say that it was from John."

"It's nice of Clark. Something is going on with that relationship he is in. Did I tell you that he called me some time ago and wanted to know if I wanted to talk?"

"No," Ellie answered in disbelief.

"Who does that when they're in a relationship with someone else?"

"Wow. I'll see if Trout knows anything."

"Frankly, I don't care. Cole is worth my time and energy. Sometime, I'll tell you a little secret about the two of us."

She looked at me strangely.

Cole came in the back door as Ellie was tugging her boots on and getting ready to go home. I hugged and hugged her. She was such a good friend. Cole enjoyed watching our exchange.

"Don't forget to flip your light when you get home," I reminded her.

"Merry Christmas, Cole," Ellie said, blowing him a kiss. "If you can find another guy like yourself, send him my way!"

He laughed. "I'll do that!"

Chapter 67

Cole came up from behind me and said that this was the best Christmas he'd ever had.

"Thanks for taking care of Aunt Mandy and Wilson in this weather. Aren't they the best?"

"Yes. I can tell they truly care for each other."

"I think my aunt is trying to decide whether they should live in sin or get married."

He laughed. "Let me help you get this all cleaned up."

"You know, it's Christmas Eve and this can wait. Let's go in and snuggle by the fire." I took his hand and we walked into the living room.

"I'm not going to argue with that. Would you like another glass of wine?" Cole asked as he poured himself a little more.

"I'd better not. I like the way I'm feeling right now."

He smiled. "And how is that?"

"Content. If Jack would have been here, it would have been a perfect Christmas."

"Maybe we can arrange that next year."

I wondered what he meant.

"You know, Kate, I was pretty touched by the hand holding at the dinner prayer. My wife and I quit attending the Presbyterian Church when our troubles started. I guess I never went back because of my fear that she might be there. I think I may be interested in visiting Concordia sometime. I hear you talk about it so much."

"I think you'd like it," I replied. "You know, I think the roads have to be treacherous by now. Would you like to stay at Josephine's Guest House tonight?"

"It sounds tempting, but I think Black Stallion is up to the mission."

When we got to the door, Cole engulfed me with hugs and more kisses. I dangled my bracelet in front of him as I thanked him one more time. He left, giving me a final wish for a wonderful Christmas.

I extinguished the fire and turned on the alarm, ignoring the mess from dinner. I walked up the stairs feeling pretty happy.

Morning came quickly and I slept too late, almost not leaving enough time to get ready for church. I grabbed a cup of coffee and flew out the door.

The church looked beautiful. There was the sense of anticipation and excitement that only Christmas morning brings. I saw a group of folks gathered. They were looking at something at the end of the hallway. I moved closer to see what was going on. Imy's quilt was hanging on the wall! It looked fabulous and comments were flowing as individuals repeated the family names stitched onto the fabric. Imy would have been pleased to see the joy the quilt was bringing.

The church was crowded, which was not a surprise. I sat in the back where I usually sat. I loved singing traditional Christmas hymns. "Silent Night" was my favorite. Pastor Hermann's sermon was brief, but full of the hope so present in this season. Then, their small bell choir performed. I'm sure I wasn't the only nostalgic one in the congregation as we listened to the angelic tinkling of the bells and thought about Christmases past. The service ended and a sense of gratitude welled up inside of me. I felt truly blessed by the things God had provided in my life.

As we filed out of church, we were invited to enjoy some refreshments in the fellowship hall. There, I approached Ellen who had some family members that she wanted me to meet. She was excitedly telling them about the well-attended church tour. She paused and added, "Kate, your divinity was delicious!"

"Thanks. It's easy to prepare and the only time I make it is at Christmas," I said. She mentioned that she'd like my recipe and I assured her that I would be happy to get it to her soon. I walked out of church and was met by sunshine. However, it was cold and not a flake of snow was melting. It made me wonder if Cole got home safely last night. I made my way home and Jack called just as I was walking in the door.

"Merry Christmas, Mom! Jill and I are both here and have you on speaker."

"Merry Christmas, you two! Just think, this time next year, you will be Mr. and Mrs. Jack Meyr."

There was a pause. "Well, Jill has decided to keep her last name, but yes, we will be husband and wife."

"How do you feel about me keeping my maiden name?"

"It's fine, Jill. Not many people did that when my peers were getting married, but a few did. I am not opposed to it at all."

We talked for another five minutes as I gave them the rundown of last night's lovely dinner. I heard about their plans for the day. Christmas was complete now that I had heard from Jack.

Chapter 68

I cleaned during the afternoon while I waited to call Maggie and Mark. I knew that they would have their Christmas celebration in the morning. She was probably missing her daughter as much as I was missing Jack.

"Merry Christmas!" I greeted them when they answered.

"The same to you," Mark responded. "Your buddy has been moping around all morning. Maybe you can cheer her up."

"Merry Christmas, girlfriend," Maggie said, her tone somber. "Some Christmas without our kids, huh?"

"We'd better get used to it," I warned. "Have you talked to them?"

"Yes. They were thoughtful enough to call."

"What did Santa bring you?" I asked, hoping to move on to a happier subject.

"A new car! I think Mark thought he had to make a big splash since Jill wouldn't be here."

"Wow, I'm impressed."

"And this new guy in your life—what did he give you?

His name is Cole, right?"

"Yes, he was here for dinner last night and he gave me a diamond bracelet."

"Now we're talking my kind of serious, right?"

I laughed.

"It's certainly more impressive than the wooden chopping block Clark gave you one year."

"It's his style. I loved the handmade chopping block. He is a sweetheart."

"They all are, at first," Maggie grumbled.

I didn't respond.

"By the way, Jill said she can only come home for the shower around Valentine's Day. She won't be able to come in the springtime. It would be a good theme for a shower, I'll have to admit."

"Well, whenever you choose have the shower, I will be there. Jill does love red!"

"Sorry, Kate, but we were about to leave for Mark's sister's house, so I need to run. Thanks for calling. Let's talk later. Love you!"

"Love you, too!"

I hung up, realizing I was going to have to make the trip to South Haven in the dead of winter. Aunt Mandy wanted to go as well. I needed to start planning.

Ruth Ann called and said she was having a last-minute gathering if I wanted to come over. I declined. I felt like I had experienced a very full Christmas. Instead, I sat by the fire and made a thank-you note list.

When I awoke the next morning, I felt sad that Christmas was over. I had enjoyed so much of what the holidays offered in Borna. Even though the tea did not bring overnight customers to my guest house, I had thoroughly enjoyed the event. I cherished the time Aunt Mandy and I spent on the tour. And, I got to spend time preparing and hosting my own Christmas celebrations. With so many activities, I now found myself a bit at loose ends. I took my time going downstairs. I looked out the front door and saw that the snow wasn't budging. I was glad that we got to have a white Christmas. As I was making what felt like the hundredth fire in my fireplace, Ellie called.

"Good morning!"

"And what is so good about Christmas being over?" I joked.

"For me, it means getting ready for our annual New Year's Eve party. I'm counting on you to come. Bring a date, if you like."

"Well, I don't have a date and it's not my favorite time of year."

"Remember how you and Clark came last year and it was fun? Ellie reminded me. "Thanks again for such a lovely dinner. You sure know how to entertain! It wouldn't hurt for you to rethink adding that dining component to your guest house."

"I'd better think of something creative. The ongoing vacancies are getting to be embarrassing."

"Cheer up! I'll check back with you," she promised as she hung up.

I slipped on some jeans. A trip to the grocery store was in order. On my way, I called Aunt Mandy to see if she needed anything.

"I'm fine, honey," she responded. "What are you and Cole doing for New Year's Eve?"

"He hasn't asked me to do anything. Ellie is determined that I need to go to her place. I have done that every year since I've been in Borna. What about you and Wilson?"

"He's trying to get a foursome together to play some cards. Too bad you are not a fan of cards."

"You are right! When it comes to playing cards, I'd prefer to just stay at home."

"You sound a bit down," she observed.

"A little bit, but nothing a little chocolate ice cream can't fix! I just put some in my cart!"

She laughed.

Chapter 69

I didn't hear a word from Cole until the next day when he was on his way to Perry. He sounded like he was in an especially good mood. "I told Abbey, my daughter, how much I enjoyed having dinner with you. She really wants to meet you."

"How sweet. Have you been busy?" I asked, curious.

"Yes, very. A lot of things are coming together that I've been working on. It always feels good when that happens."

"I know. I am happy for you."

"I should have asked you this sooner, but do you have any plans for New Year's Eve?"

"It's not my favorite night to be out and about, but Ellie always insists that I have dinner at the winery."

"I'd like to invite you to dinner at my place. If you'd like to stop and have a drink at Ellie's, that would be fine with me. We could do that together."

"I suppose, but I could make it a very quick drink. Are you sure you want to cook?"

"It won't be as grand as your dinner, but I like to cook

every now and then."

After I agreed, I thought about what seeing his house would be like and I wondered what I should bring. Ellie would be happy about us stopping by the winery. In the back of my mind, I thought about Maggie and the usual trip to the country club. I did not miss the ritual of spending most holidays at the country club.

I reluctantly started taking down Christmas decorations. Later in the day, I would have to get over to the museum to take down my exhibit tree. I called Cotton and told him to remove my tree when it suited him. I also said I could use some cleaning help from Susie. Dry pine needles were beginning to show up everywhere! My poinsettia from Clark was still gorgeous. Where might he have spent his Christmas?

Before I went to the museum, I stopped by Marv's for a late lunch. I knew most of the crowd would be gone. I took a seat at the bar and Marv spotted me right away.

"Did you have a nice Christmas, Kate?" Marv asked as he served me a glass of water.

"I did. How about you?"

"With the exception of the flu making its rounds, we did fine," he explained.

I told Marv I wanted his specialty hamburger called Marv's Melta-burger. Just then, Charlene walked in to pick up an order. She said she enjoyed a great Christmas season at the coffee shop. She then mentioned she would be closing on Mondays until spring. I told her I was on my way to the museum where she, too, had a tree on exhibit.

"Yes, I will get by there later," Charlene confirmed. "I thought of you this morning when Clark and two other people I didn't know stopped in for coffee."

"Oh, I guess he was in town for Christmas," I replied, feeling suddenly distracted by Charlene's mention of Clark.

She looked at me oddly.

"I'd imagine so. Well, I've got to get these hamburgers to some hungry folks. I'll see you at the museum," Charlene said before she sped out the door.

There were other people working on their trees when I arrived at the museum. Sharla Lee immediately approached me and asked how the people on my list liked the Christmas gifts that we had chosen from the museum gift shop. I told her that everything had been a big hit and thanked her again.

"Gerard is here to help you if you need him, Kate," Sharla Lee offered.

"Thanks, but these ornaments are so fragile that I wouldn't want anyone else to be responsible for them."

There were still a few people walking around and seeing the trees for the first time. One woman stood and watched me remove the ornaments. She eventually said she owned a feather tree. She added that she hadn't displayed it in years.

"I see that you are from Josephine's Guest House," she stated. "Are you Josephine?"

I smiled and shook my head.

"We passed the guest house on the way here. Is it as nice inside as it looks on the outside?"

"I think so," I said, blushing. "I'm the owner, Kate Meyr."

She seemed pleased to meet me and took one of my cards from the display. She, like so many, stated there would be times when she would need a place like mine. My tree didn't win the grand prize this year, but it was good advertising.

When I had everything packed, Gerard helped me carry

some boxes to the car. I told him that Cotton would be by with his truck to collect the tree so I could keep it all in one piece.

"Have you all found out anything more about the missing quilt at church?" Gerard asked when we got to the car.

"No, I haven't heard anything else about it."

"It sure is a shame. Mrs. Clifton does such fine work. My sister said she wouldn't be taking her tops to be quilted at Concordia any longer."

"That's too bad. I'm sure it'll show up. Thanks for your help, Gerard." I left feeling sorry for everyone concerned in this quilt matter. If Gerard knew about the missing quilt, then the whole town knew.

Chapter 70

The year was about to be over. I hated winter, but the trip back to South Haven would be something to look forward to. I was now counting the days. Today was the regular day to go quilting at church, but because of the holiday, we wouldn't quilt until next week. That was fine by me. Perhaps that gave us more time to discover the quilt. Ellie called before she left for the winery to see if I planned to stop by.

"Cole is preparing dinner for us tonight, but he said we could stop by for a quick glass of wine so we wouldn't hurt your feelings," I teased.

"Well, I'm glad someone cares," she replied. "That sounds like a pretty romantic evening, if you ask me."

"I am more curious about his house and what he may be cooking."

"Yes, there's no telling what he may be cooking up," Ellie teased.

I chuckled.

"You always have a wandering mind, girlfriend," I

teased back.

"What are you going to wear?"

"What I always wear in Borna! I'll be wearing jeans and an outdated sweater." We chuckled again about wearing the same clothes all the time, made some small talk, and then hung up. I went to get dressed after I made a sheet of brownies to take to Cole's house. What man didn't like brownies?

When Cole arrived, I was ready to get out of the house. When he saw the container in my hands, he was anxious to know the contents. I eventually let him peek inside. He threatened to steal a piece before dinner.

I couldn't believe how crowded it was at the winery for this early in the evening. The band wasn't starting until nine. Ellie and Trout were happy to see us. There were many people enjoying the prime rib. It was Kelly's New Year's Eve special.

"Hey, Kate, this menu looks super," Cole exclaimed. "Maybe we should have had dinner here tonight."

"No, it won't be as good as what you're cooking, I'm sure," I added with a grin.

Cole kept his arm around me the whole time we were at the bar. Trout and Ellie were so busy that they barely had time to talk to us as we had our glass of wine.

Suddenly, I heard a familiar voice.

"What'd ya say, Clark?" Trout said from behind the bar. "Happy New Year."

"Happy New Year to you guys!" Clark returned. I took my time turning around.

"Well, if it isn't Kate and Cole!" Clark said. There was unmistakable sarcasm in his voice.

"Happy New Year, Clark," Cole said.

"How are you, Clark?" I ventured. I can't say that I liked the way he stared at me.

"Good! Can I buy you all a drink?" Clark asked. His words came out thickly and awkwardly like he was trying too hard to say them correctly. The evening was early and it was clear that he had been drinking for some time.

"Sorry. We have plans and were about to leave, but Trout, put Clark's beer on our tab," Cole said.

"Well, that's mighty generous of you since you stole my girlfriend here," Clark teased.

I couldn't believe he'd said it, but he had. "Are you ready to go?' I asked, looking at Cole and hoping desperately for a quick exit.

Cole placed two twenty-dollar bills on the counter for Trout and stood up to leave.

"I didn't mean to chase you off!" Clark responded, his voice a bit too loud.

"Happy New Year to you all," Cole said cheerfully as we walked out the door.

I couldn't get out of there fast enough. When we got in the fresh air, I took a deep breath. "I'm sorry about that, Cole."

"Hey, I'd be a little sore too if someone stole my girlfriend."

I laughed. "I don't think any stealing went on. He was the one that came to my house to break up with me, just to set the record straight."

"Kate, I know the whole story. Let's forget this happened and enjoy our evening."

"Thanks," I said, squeezing his hand.

For some reason, I felt completely safe and secure with Cole. Perhaps it was because he had saved my life from that horrible person soon after we'd first met. It also meant something to me that he kept the whole ordeal a secret because I had asked him to.

Wonderful aromas engulfed us when we entered his house. "Oh, Cole, it smells divine! What are we having?"

"Southwestern brisket."

"Wonderful! I don't think I've ever eaten that before. What can I do to help?"

"You can pour us my Mighty Merlot, which will go perfectly with the meal. You may not like it as much as Merry Merlot, but it's good."

I laughed. I walked into the spacious dining room where his table was formally set with gold-rimmed china and matching water goblets on a burgundy tablecloth. A simple centerpiece consisted of several white candles. I wondered if all of these lovely things were left from his former wife. Would she have left them willingly or unwillingly?

Cole pulled a tossed salad out of the refrigerator and began making his own salad dressing. "I'm going to steam some broccoli and cook some rice while you plate those luscious brownies," Cole explained with a smile on his face. "Wait! Let me grab a quick one to go with my wine."

"I don't think so," I said, playfully slapping his outstretched hand.

"I didn't plan a dessert, knowing what a baker you are. I don't know how you keep that sexy figure of yours with all the baking you do."

That was nice to hear, especially since I felt I was getting heavier by the day. The meal was simply wonderful. You could cut the brisket with a fork. Eating by candlelight was a real treat, especially with a handsome chef sitting across the table from me.

Chapter 71

We took our time at dinner and enjoyed every bite. I found out more about his former life, his house, and his recent divorce. His wife left him to live in a high-rise in downtown St. Louis. He said they speak only when they have to.

"You never mentioned Abbey's husband," I mentioned offhandedly.

"It's because they are about to get divorced," he said, shaking his head in disgust. "I'm afraid she's picked up some of her mother's traits about wanting everything to be perfect. Some of the reasons she gives for her divorce are the exact words her mother used."

"Oh."

"Mike, her husband, is a wonderful human being. He has knocked himself out to please her, but it's never going to be enough. I think she's going to regret this divorce one day. I think many young people just don't take their wedding vows very seriously."

"I sure hope Jill and Jack do. They have known each other most of their lives. It would break my heart if something happened between them. I feel your pain."

"Let's leave this unpleasant subject and go in by the fire," Cole suggested as he took my hand to lead me into the living room. In front of the massive wall fireplace were two large pillows on an Oriental rug. I couldn't help but notice the unusual and rare antiques that made up his décor.

"Should I turn on some music?"

"No, I like the sound of the crackle from the fire."

"More wine?"

I nodded. "Didn't you love the combination of the red wine and the chocolate brownies?"

He laughed as we settled ourselves on the pillows and reclined by the warmth of the fire. It felt wonderful to be so close to him.

"Does it feel strange to have another woman sitting here?"

"It's been so long since my ex and I were a real couple in this house that it hadn't crossed my mind. Maybe I've pictured you here before."

"Really?"

"I think so!" He pulled me close to him and gently pressed his lips to mine. Leaving his arm around me, he took a slow, deep breath and let it out. "I haven't been this relaxed in a long time."

"Hey, it's almost midnight, Mr. Alexander," I noticed. "Will your clock chime?"

"Yes, and I feel like we'd better practice another kiss before the big moment."

"Practice makes perfect," I agreed.

The clock struck midnight.

"Happy New Year," we said simultaneously, looking into

each other's eyes. By now, I was practically reclining next to him, which left me feeling a bit vulnerable. Yet, if I were honest about my feelings, it seemed so natural and comfortable.

"I don't want to let go of you," Cole said as he hugged me tightly. "I want as much of you as I can get."

I eased back to catch my breath. The chemistry was undeniable. "You are so loving and caring, Cole. I could lose myself with you rather easily, but I think we need more time." I took another sip of wine. "I think we are in the process of falling in love, and I don't want to do anything to spoil it."

He smiled. "I'm afraid it's too late for me, but I can wait for you forever."

I didn't respond.

We watched the fire dwindle as we talked and talked into the new year. Neither Clay nor Clark would have ever spent this amount of time listening and sharing this type of conversation. I take responsibility for part of that. Sometimes, I think we think so much about what the other person wants that we shelve our own feelings and push our own thoughts aside.

When we arrived back at 6229 Main Street, it was after two in the morning. Cole walked me to the door to say good night. It truly was a good night and I was left with an awfully good feeling at the start of this new year.

Chapter 12

New Year's Day was a day of reflection and phone calls. It was late morning and I was still in my robe when Jack called.

"Happy New Year, Mom! Did you celebrate last night?"

"I had a quiet dinner at Cole's house after we stopped by the winery to see Ellie and Trout. How about you?"

"Ours was low-key as well. Jill had to catch an early flight."

"Maggie tells me that the shower for Jill will be on Valentine's Day. I hope I'll be able to see you, too."

"We'll see. I'm taking a lot of time off for the honeymoon, so I'm not sure that I will make it."

Our conversation was short since Jack got another call that he had to take. While I got comfortable by the fire with my cup of coffee, I decided to call Carla and Maggie. I had to leave a voice mail for Carla, but Maggie answered right away. She was feeling hung over. According to her, she unwisely mixed her choice of wines. I had to laugh because it didn't ever take much to make Maggie drunk. She gave me a report about who was at the club and speculated that James's new wife may have a drinking problem. Finding I had little interest in that particular topic, I asked how the quilt shop was doing.

"I finally gave up on Penny, just as Mark advised me to do all along. She's trying really hard and is making good progress. You wouldn't recognize the place! She's rented the space next door where the nail salon used to be. She's put the quilting machine in there and added antique quilts to sell in the main part of the shop. It's definitely more attractive."

"I can't wait to see it. I'm pleased that you have let her do her own thing. She has learned a lot over the years about what customers want."

"Yes, and we could use a good customer like you," Maggie teased.

"I sure am looking forward to seeing everyone when I come for the shower. Will all the Beach Quilters be able to come?"

"I hope so, but my list is getting pretty long."

Our conversation continued until Ellie's number showed up on my phone. I said a hurried good-bye to Maggie and a friendly hello to Ellie. "Are you enjoying your day off?"

"Yup, still in my robe."

I laughed. "Me too! I may stay this way for the rest of the day!"

"I'm dying to know how the rest of your evening went with Cole! Did you spend the night?"

"No, Miss Nosey, I did not! He fixed a lovely meal, and while I didn't spend the night, I didn't leave there until pretty late—or early, depending on the perspective."

"I thought Clark got rather bold last night, didn't you?"

"I know! I could tell he'd been drinking and I felt embarrassed for Cole. How long did Clark stay there?"

"Longer than usual. He ate there, which is rare, so I guess he didn't have any other plans."

"Did he mention where he was on Christmas?"

"No. Not unless he told Trout. Honestly, we both were so busy that there wasn't much time for conversation."

"How is it going with O'Brazo? Are they really any competition for you?"

"I don't know and I don't ask about how things are going over there. I'm sure they have their regulars, just like we do. We start our down time now, so I hope to do some upgrading around here."

"I hope I get some business from the spring ad we all are doing."

"I hope so, too."

Chapter 13

The next week brought more frigid temperatures and lots of snow flurries. Today was our first quilting day since Christmas and I was anxious to hear whether the pastor had approached Arnie about the key. I remembered to make my lunch and I had prepared a platter of fruit to take that I thought would be a nice change from the usual items. I had to do something to improve my diet.

Cole and Trout had the luxury of going ice fishing up north. The winery was nearly closed considering how customer traffic had slowed. That gave Trout the freedom to be away for a bit. Cole was his own boss so he could take off when he preferred. It was easy to admire their friendship. Hopefully, Cole would call to check on me, unlike someone else I knew.

I went to the church early because I hoped to visit with Pastor Hermann before the others started to arrive. I popped my head into his partially-opened door to wish him a happy New Year.

"Come on in, Kate," he said congenially.

I shut the door behind me. "You probably know what I'm curious about," I stated.

"Sure, and understandably so," he agreed. He took a deep breath. "I did question Arnie about the key and he doesn't recall much about it."

I continued to listen for more.

"When I told him why it was important, he said something to the effect that maybe he had just misplaced it since I wasn't there when he first got it."

"Did you get the feeling he did take the key but felt badly about not getting it to you?"

"Yes, possibly. I think I scared him a little and I also believe he'll think more seriously about it now. Arnie's a good guy. He's not the sharpest knife in the drawer, but he likes his job here and is pretty dependable."

"That means something, I suppose."

"Stella is going to run out of patience. We just have to hope she'll consider it a loss and let us compensate her in some way."

"The top wasn't quilted, but it certainly has value. She also lost the potential income for it, had it been completed. If she has some record of sales, her insurance company will factor that in."

"Whatever they decide to do with the quilt, we have a moral obligation to cooperate since we lost her quilt."

"It's such a shame. The quilt has to be somewhere. Has the church missed anything else?"

"Not that I'm aware of."

"Well, I'd better get back to the quilters. I hope Matilda and Ruby show up. It's terrible to have this kind of tension going on."

"You're right. I'll come down and try to lighten things up a bit."

"That would be a good idea."

"By the way, I wanted to mention that we have some pastors and maybe their wives coming into town for a small conference. I'll pass on your information as a place to stay."

"Thanks so much."

Surprisingly, every chair except mine was filled when I went downstairs. I gave a happy greeting and announced that I had brought some fruit to share. I placed the platter on the dining table.

"Good to see you, Ruby," I remarked.

She sat across the frame from me. "How was your Christmas, Kate?" she asked politely.

"It was good. How was yours?"

"Not bad. I got to see my grandkids from Nebraska."

"Wonderful," I replied. "Ellen, I'm sure your family enjoyed the holidays."

"Oh, yes," she exclaimed. "I think everyone's exhausted."

"We're done!" Esther shouted from the other quilt frame.

"Thank goodness," Paula added. "This one took a long time."

They all stood up and began unpinning the quilt. Paula then went over to the unlocked quilt chest to pull out another quilt.

"Is this bag labeled Lueders the next one, Ruby?" she asked.

Ruby nodded. Ruby quietly got out of her chair and helped her unfold the quilt. It was a stunning rose-and-white Lone Star pattern. Everyone expressed their admiration of the workmanship.

Matilda cooperated with all the others, but began to examine the quilt closer.

Chapter 74

"Look, she missed marking this corner piece," Matilda said, loud enough for Ruby to hear.

"Oh, we can copy this, I think," Erna suggested. "I don't think I've seen this pattern before."

"There's a lot of quilting to do here," Matilda quipped. "We'd better get started."

"Good morning, ladies," Pastor Hermann greeted as he came into the room.

"Good morning," everyone chimed in unison.

"I see we that have a new quilt in the frame today," he observed.

"Do you like it?" Esther asked.

"My wife would love these colors," he said, smiling to avoid his honest answer.

"How is she?" Paula inquired. "I haven't seen her for awhile."

"Well, she's a little distracted these days," he said, grinning. "She's going to have our fourth child in June."

Everyone gasped in surprise.

"My goodness!" Ellen responded as the others reacted. "How is she feeling?"

"She has good and bad days," he admitted. "You ladies know all about that."

Words of congratulations were expressed for the next few minutes and then the pastor excused himself and left the room.

"Well! Four little ones! How about that?" said Paula.

"I think we'd better get busy and make another baby quilt," Ellen suggested. "We didn't do one for the last one they had. I'll look for some embroidery blocks for each of us to stitch."

"That's a great idea, Ellen," I agreed.

"I'll try to have them ready to hand out next week," Ellen stated.

Pastor Hermann's news was just what this group needed to unite us in something positive. The chatter picked up as we ate lunch together. Matilda and Ruby stayed rather quiet. I'm sure they continued to blame one another for the missing quilt.

"Thanks for the fruit today," Erna said as I washed my platter. "That was a nice treat."

"I'll bring fruit again sometime," I said, feeling happy about making a contribution.

"Kate, it will be your turn to bring dessert next week," Ruby announced.

"Very good. I hope I don't forget!"

We quilted for another hour as I listened to topics ranging from the winter weather to the flu that was going around. On my way home, I stopped at Imy's shop. Her winter hours were so irregular. I was surprised to see Ellen's car pull in right behind me.

"Good minds think alike," I said when Ellen got out of the car.

"I haven't been here for awhile and I want to personally thank Imy for giving the church that quilt," Ellen explained.

"I was thinking the same thing."

"The pastor did mention that he had sent her a thank-you note."

I was glad to hear that.

"Well, ladies, what's the occasion here?" Imy asked, surprised.

"Have you had a chance to see your quilt on the wall at church?" Ellen asked.

"No, but I will soon," Imy promised.

"We both want to thank you so much," I expressed. "I wish you could have heard some of the comments from all the people gathered around it on Sunday."

"This is good to hear," Imy said, smiling.

"I see you have a few more quilts that I haven't seen before," I noticed as I picked up a red-and-white Hearts and Gizzards patterned quilt.

"Yes, I bought a few from the daughter of Elsie Mangles," Imy revealed. "She said she had way too many from her mom."

How can you have too many quilts? It perplexed me to think about it!

"I know Elsie," Ellen said, surprised. "I can't believe she would sell these."

"This is a Hearts and Gizzards pattern, in case you didn't know," I revealed. "This has never been washed! It's such a great pattern for a two-color quilt."

"Here's a beautiful Grandmother's Fan," Ellen said. "You both have such knowledge of antique quilts."

"My quilt group in South Haven loved antique quilts," I said, unfolding the red- and-white quilt.

"These quilts in good condition don't last long," Imy shared. "When they're not washed, I can get more money for them."

"I'll take this one," I said without thinking.

Ellen looked shocked.

"My future daughter-in-law loves red and I need a present for her upcoming bridal shower."

"How perfect!" Ellen said. "The heart shape is perfect for romance."

"Kate is such an easy sale, Ellen," Imy teased.

"I can't possibly take anything else home, Imy, but may God bless you for your generosity," Ellen said, smiling.

Chapter 15

"I don't like bringing up a sensitive subject, ladies, but you don't think my quilt is in any danger of being stolen by someone like Stella Clifton's was, do you?" Imy asked in a low voice.

Ellen and I looked at each other.

"Heavens no, Imy," Ellen responded.

"From what I've been hearing, all fingers point to Ruby," Imy claimed. "I can hardly believe she would do that."

"It's a mystery," Ellen said, shaking her head. "Speaking of Ruby, she got wind that the men's club is doing a fish and chicken fry at the church picnic this year, instead of the usual chicken and dumplings. Ruby's been in charge of the dumplings for many years and has not allowed anyone to take that over."

"Why the change?" I asked, feeling a bit sorry for Ruby.

"They feel the change would bring them more money," Ellen explained. "They've got some young men in that group now who are willing to do the work and they feel that a change is needed."

"Who told Ruby?" I inquired. "Is it certain that they're going to do it?"

"I don't know how she knows, but she knows," Ellen confirmed. "She's furious and gave the pastor a piece of her mind. She thinks it was done because they think she stole the quilt. Of course, that's not the case, but you can imagine how she feels."

"Does she have support?" I asked, concerned for her feelings.

"Not that I have heard about." Ellen responded. "I think it is a pretty good idea to change things up once in a while. If the men volunteer to do the work and they feel that they can bring more money into the church, why not let them try?"

"But Ruby has always received so many compliments on her dumplings," Imy recalled.

"Yes, she has," admitted Ellen. "She has controlled that venue just like she does the quilting group."

I left with Ellen and Imy still conversing about the situation. I hugged my quilt, feeling a bit guilty. I stopped by Aunt Mandy's house to show her my purchase. She was pleased to see me, but complained that her arthritis was acting up. She loved the quilt and thought Jack and Jill would as well.

"I sure hope you will come with me to South Haven," I urged.

"We'll just have to see, Kate. I would love to be there, but I'll have to see how Wilson is doing. I feel like he depends on me more and more."

"How do you feel about that?"

"Oh, honey, he's a dear and I want to be there for him in any way I can."

"Of course. You both have been so good for each other."

"What do you suppose I can get Jill for a shower present?"

"I'll have to give that some thought. I'm glad I have my dilemma solved. They will both have good salaries, but in New York, it doesn't go very far."

I went home just as it was getting dusk. I was too tired to start a fire. The house looked so bare with all the Christmas decorations put away. The only remembrance of the holiday was Clark's poinsettia.

I went up to my bedroom to put Jill's quilt away. I draped it over a chair and stretched across my bed. I remained in deep thought. This quilt mystery was getting the best of me. It reminded me of Josephine and how she moved the quilts around when I first moved here.

"I need some help, Josephine," I said out loud. "How can this quilt disappear at church with such lovely folks around?"

I stayed there for quite some time, feeling rather silly about having asked Josephine, but I felt I had nothing to lose. I said a quick prayer for Matilda and Ruby who were both so caught up in all of this. Could Arnie be the culprit? What was he really like? Why would he even want a quilt top? Did he know something and wasn't talking?

Chapter 76

I was jarred from my detective work by the ringing of my cell phone.

"Did I wake you?" Cole asked.

"Almost."

"I'm sorry. This is the first chance I've had to give you a call."

"It's good to hear from you. Are you having a good time?"

"It's quite an experience. I forgot what's it's like to be cold for such a long time."

"That would not be for me!"

"We have this capable assistant who is helping us with the process, but there's still a lot of waiting time."

"I think that's called fishing," I kidded.

He laughed. "How are you?"

"The holidays are over, which is a bit sad, so I'm counting the days until I can go to South Haven."

"It will go quicker than you think. Excuse me, Kate. Trout wants to say hello," Cole announced.

"Hey, Kate! I'll bet you're missing this city fisherman by now, right?" he teased.

"I am!"

"How's Ellie? I feel awful leaving her when they are doing all of that work at the winery."

"She'd want you to have a good time. Your timing is good because things have really slowed down there."

"Thanks, that makes me feel better. Well, Cole is here staring me down, so here he is," Trout said with a chuckle.

"It looks like I'll be home by the weekend. Let's plan on a night out, okay?" Cole asked.

"You know where to find me," I teased. "I'll look forward to it." We hung up and I realized that talking with Cole always seemed to put a smile on my face.

I rolled over in bed and replayed our conversation. It was so sweet of him to call. Should I ask him to come with me to South Haven? Was that idea already on his mind? How would everyone receive him? Would everyone think we were in a serious relationship? What would John think? What would Aunt Mandy think about the idea? I decided to talk with Ellie and Maggie about it. They could help me make a good decision. Having Cole in South Haven would truly be fun. I could show him all the places I talked about and he would love my condo on the lake, even in the dead of winter. By now, I was wide awake. I decided to go downstairs and make some herbal tea.

When I got to the bottom of the stairs, I felt someone watching or following me. It was an odd feeling that I did not like at all. I proceeded to the kitchen slowly and cautiously. Once in the kitchen, I could not shake the feeling, so I decided to take my tea upstairs and read. Going back up the stairs, I felt the same presence. Was it Josephine? Was she going to appear to me like she had to others? I had an uneasy feeling.

When I walked into the bedroom, I was startled to see that the covers on my bed were turned back! Something or someone wanted me to know they were here with me. I was certain the covers were not pulled back before. They were also pulled back differently than the way I typically turned them down. I looked around to see if anything else had changed in the room. What was going on?

I got undressed. The tea seemed to have relaxed me a bit. I pulled the covers up around my neck. A comforting feeling came over me. It was as if someone were giving me a hug. It was different than the usual morning light that Josephine typically did on occasion. Why was it so easy for me to accept these unnatural occurrences?

Sleep took over and I dreamed I was on the beach at Lake Michigan in the summer. I looked into the hot sunshine and someone handed me a frosty cold drink. I reached up to accept it and saw that it was Cole who was offering it to me. I wanted to thank him, but he faded away as the words were coming out of my mouth.

Chapter 77

It was Mary Catherine's turn to have thc Friendship Circle, but Ellen called to say that Mary Catherine had to go out of town on a family matter. Ellen asked if I could fill in for her as hostess. I accepted, knowing I would have to scramble to get a menu together. Ellen offered to bring the food in order to get me to agree to host the meeting, but I insisted that I would have it under control. Mary Catherine had given Ellen the agenda and Ellen was prepared to assume responsibility for that, so I didn't have to conduct the meeting.

Charmin called to see if Aunt Mandy and I could have lunch with her at her new home.

"How sweet of you to ask us, Charmin," I responded. We would love to come over. I'll talk to my aunt. Can I bring anything?"

"No," she replied firmly. "We have such a wonderful chef here that there is no need to bring anything extra. We'll have lunch in one of the private dining rooms."

"That sounds really nice." I hung up, thinking about what

a gracious person she was. It made me feel so good to have a new friend, and especially one that shares the Josephine connection with me.

I went back to the sun porch to complete my menu and shopping list. I decided I would serve my luncheon favorite of baked chicken salad in a shell and a tossed salad with mandarin oranges, blue cheese, bacon bits, and roasted almonds with a red-wine-vinegar dressing. For dessert, I chose a blueberry lemon cake. Everything except the tossed salad could be prepared ahead of time.

Entertaining my Friendship Circle friends was probably a good idea right now. When I called Aunt Mandy, I told her about Charmin's invitation and that I was the new hostess for the club. She offered to help with the luncheon and loved my menu choices.

"Wilson called this morning and said his knee replacement will be within days," she said with concern in her voice.

"Well, that's good news. I certainly will do what I can to be helpful to you and him."

"Thanks so much, sweetie. I don't know what I'd do without you. He is really dreading this surgery because he knows it will slow him down."

"He'll be fine because he's going to want a future dance with you!"

She laughed.

"Do you want me to come get you in the morning before the club starts?"

"Absolutely not, Kate. You have enough to do. I'll see you then."

Next, I was off to the grocery store. I could always plan

on running into someone I knew there. Folks were so friendly around here that if they even knew your face, they would say hello. The food selection was limited in this smaller store, but I always left with way more than I had planned to buy. Not being able to get fresh produce was always my biggest complaint. Once I had checked out, I pushed the cart to my car. I had filled the back seat and was about to squeeze in my last grocery bag when someone asked, "Can I help you with that?" It was Clark.

"Clark! No thanks. I've got it."

"How have you been?"

Clark asked this with such seriousness in his voice that it gave me the impression he had somehow heard that I was ill. "Fine. I had to stock up for the Friendship Circle luncheon tomorrow."

"Do you have time to have a cup of coffee across the street?"

"She closes at eleven," I said flatly.

"We have ten minutes if we hurry," he kidded.

"I'd better not take the time. I'm sure Charlene doesn't like having late customers when she wants to close."

"So you're going to avoid me now?"

I snickered and shook my head. "I have no intention of doing that. I think we have both moved on. By the way, has that grandbaby been born yet?"

He shook his head. "Any day now," he said, grinning.

"Part of me envies you. That has to be such a special time. Well, I'd better go."

He just stood there. "I'm gathering that you must have really fallen for this Alexander guy, huh?"

I smiled. I almost didn't answer. "I do like him. He's a

wonderful person."

Clark nodded. He kept a somber look on his face as I got into Red and closed the door. He tapped on the door as we nodded good-bye to one another. I drove off, and from my rearview mirror, I could see that he was continuing to stand where I had left him. It was hard to figure out what was on his mind. I think he was having a hard time accepting that I had moved on, with or without him.

Chapter 18

The next day was a sunny and beautiful day for a luncheon. I had tea and coffee ready for the guests as they arrived. Several women asked about my beautiful poinsettia and I simply said that a friend had purchased it for me.

"That's a lovely bracelet you're wearing, Kate," Ellen pointed out.

Something told me she already knew who it was from. "I love it, too," I blushed.

"That Cole Alexander certainly has good taste," she said, giving me a wink of approval.

Aunt Mandy was the last to arrive. Although she definitely wasn't a morning person, she looked pretty and was dressed well for the occasion.

Ellen got everyone's attention and thanked me for hosting the luncheon on such short notice. We began eating and I could tell that everyone was pleased with the menu. When Anna asked for my chicken salad recipe, I knew I had hit a home run.

As we were finishing dessert, Ellen tapped on her glass

to get our attention. "I want to start by passing around some of the wonderful thank-you notes we received from our charity gifts," Ellen began. "Some are quite touching."

"I don't know if some of you know that Charlene's mother, Mrs. Grebing, went into the hospital. I'm passing around a get-well card for everyone to sign," Ellen continued. "It's nothing serious, but I thought it would be nice of us to send a card."

"Are you having the plant sale again this spring?" Esther asked.

Ellen smiled and nodded. "I am!" she assured us. "I welcome any plant donations. There will also be a bake sale on the patio this year. I have encouraged Imy to bring some of her antique flower pots to sell that day. They are perfect to have there as folks buy plants."

Leave it to Ellen to plan another nifty event for the local folks to enjoy.

"Ellie, I hear renovations are taking place at the winery," Ellen stated. "Do you want to tell us about them?"

"Yes, it's one of those things that once you start, one thing leads to another," Ellie explained.

Most everyone chuckled and knew what she was talking about.

"The majority of the updates are taking place in the kitchen."

"Ellen, can you tell us if you know anything more about the missing quilt at your church?" Anna asked.

I couldn't believe she asked that so openly.

Ellen took a deep breath, choosing her words carefully as we waited for her response.

"What missing quilt?" Peggy interrupted.

Ignoring Peggy's question, Ellen replied, "Nothing yet. It's just been misplaced. I'm sure it will turn up."

I thought Ellen handled the situation well and I could tell that Peggy was on a mission to find out more.

"Ellen, if I can have the floor, I'd like to announce that the village is opening up earlier this spring," Anna said, understandably excited. "We have a sizable tour coming through and we want them to witness the restoration of the schoolhouse cabin. We have received a nice donation from the Henry Wills estate and it was to only go toward cabin maintenance. We can't do much until the weather gets warmer, however."

"How nice!" Ellen responded. "Keep us posted on your progress."

"I still have Girl Scout cookies to sell for my two granddaughters, by the way," Ellen mentioned before she closed the meeting. I noticed that Aunt Mandy was the first to approach her after the meeting was adjourned. She was developing quite a sweet tooth! Little by little, my circle friends went on their way until only Ellie and Ellen remained.

"Another refill, Ellen?" I offered.

"Sure," she agreed. "I was so busy talking that mine got cold. I could use a warm up."

"Ellen, how well do you know Arnie, the janitor at church?"

My question caught her off guard. "Well, Kate, he's been there quite a few years. I don't know much about his family. I think I heard that his wife is not well. We pay him a pittance for all he does. I think digging graves is the only task he doesn't do."

"Did you know he had possession of a second key to the

quilt chest?" I asked Ellen.

She looked confused. "Really?"

"Timmy Petzoldt left two keys when he delivered the chest," I stated. "One was for Ruby and the other was to be given to the pastor. Matilda accepted the key to give to Pastor. When she went upstairs to give it to him, he wasn't there, so she gave it to Arnie to give to him. Well, as I followed up, the pastor never received the key from Arnie. When the pastor questioned Arnie about it, he didn't recall ever having the key."

Ellie was listening intently.

Ellen replied, "Hmm, I could see Arnie responding that way. He's always worried about getting in trouble and strives to please the pastor. He could have innocently misplaced it. He gets distracted rather easily. I'm sure glad the pastor keeps that quilt room locked now."

"Well, well," Ellie said, grinning. "Who would have thought there would have been any shenanigans going on amongst the church ladies?"

Ellen didn't want to hear that.

Ellie continued, "I guess there are always the good, the bad, and the ugly in any organization."

Ellen didn't like that comment either. "I think that things like this can occur anywhere."

Chapter 79

After Ellen left, I told Ellie about running into Clark in the grocery store parking lot. "Why do you think he wanted to have coffee?" I asked Ellie.

"It's obvious that things have fallen apart with this Lucy gal. I think he's sorry he let you go, but you know Clark, he's not one to say he's sorry. I also think he's torn about still having a relationship with his newly-found daughter."

I nodded in agreement. "He probably didn't realize that his relationship with the daughter came with the mother who was anxious to have him back."

"My feelings exactly. I feel sorry for him, but I don't think he treated you right, Kate. Frankly, his lifestyle will never leave room for a permanent partner in his life. You were a very dear friend that he could trust. He didn't feel threatened by you wanting more from him."

"I think I agree, Ellie."

When he returned from his trip, Cole called. He was eager to know when we could get together. He said that he'd had a good time but also said he was glad to be home.

"Why don't we meet up at the winery tomorrow night for dinner?" I wanted my invitation to be casual and simple.

"Are you sure? We could go into Perry again."

I assured him that the winery would be fine for tomorrow night. "If the weather gets bad, I will rethink my offer. Otherwise, I'll meet you at the winery."We talked a while longer and agreed that it would be great to see each other again.

Ruth Ann called as soon as I hung up from talking with Cole. She wanted to request the attic suite for two women who were coming to take one of her quilting classes. I was delighted to take the reservations after not having any guests for such a long time! She also asked if I could help make desserts for a couple of events she had lined up. I was starting to feel needed again.

I wanted to be careful not to book anything too close to my visit to South Haven. I still could not decide how long I should stay there.

I wondered how I should wrap Jill's shower quilt. I knew Maggie would have invited many of her rich friends. I hoped I wouldn't embarrass Jill with my old- fashioned gift. I looked the quilt over carefully to make sure therc were no spots or stains that would embarrass me. I wanted to give Jill and Jack many of my valuable treasures, but I had to respect their taste and the fact that they wouldn't have room in their small New York apartment. It would have been great if I had made them a quilt, but a project like that would have to come at a later time.

I rolled the quilt and wrapped it in white embossed paper I had purchased for a wedding gift many years ago. I then tied red bows on each end. I had to admit that it looked adorable.

I went downstairs and put a frozen flatbread in the oven for my dinner and poured myself a glass of wine. It was late, so when the phone rang and I saw that it was Aunt Mandy, I was somewhat alarmed.

"Am I interrupting anything?" she asked.

"Not at all. I'm just having a late dinner."

"I have to tell you again how much I enjoyed your luncheon. I'm so glad I brought my dessert home with me. I just finished eating it."

"Thanks! What's on your mind?" I asked, removing my flatbread from the oven.

"Wilson, of course. His surgery is tomorrow. Barb told me not to come, but I want to be there. If you don't have any plans tomorrow, would you mind taking me to the hospital?"

"Of course not. What time would you like to leave?"

"Noon perhaps. That way, I will be there when he gets out of surgery."

"Perfect. I'll pick you up around noon."

"Thanks so much, sweetie. He told me to wait a few days, but I'll not hear of that."

"I understand. Try to get some beauty sleep now, okay?"

She chuckled and we hung up.

Chapter 80

The next day, I rearranged everything so I could be totally devoted to Aunt Mandy. I hoped to convince her to have lunch when we arrived there in order to help pass the time. It was an amazingly beautiful day, which pleased both of us. Aunt Mandy came out of her house wearing a lovely lavender wool suit that I hadn't seen before. It was gorgeous with her white hair. I could tell she was feeling anxious, so I kept our conversation light. I told her I was meeting Cole for dinner and that I had two ladies booked for the guest house.

Wilson's daughter was surprised to see us and she told Aunt Mandy that she could still go in to see him since his surgery had been delayed a bit. I stayed in the waiting room with Barbara. She was such a sweet person. I told her it was going to be difficult to keep those two apart. When Aunt Mandy returned from visiting Wilson, we went to the cafeteria to get a bite to eat. Perry Memorial was a small hospital where everyone seemed to know everyone else.

The afternoon passed by very slowly. I took a break and went down the hall where I found a cute little gift shop. They stocked everything from handmade baby quilts to clothing and jewelry. I picked up a few greeting cards, which included one for Jill and a Valentine card for Cole.

"I hear you're making a trip back to South Haven," Barbara said when I returned.

"Yes, I'm going up next week for my future daughter-in-law's bridal shower. I'm hoping this lady will accompany me on the trip." I winked at Aunt Mandy.

"Kate, I've been thinking about that. I must tell you that I am most uncomfortable about leaving town right now," Aunt Mandy explained.

"You mean because of Wilson?"

"I want to be around to assist Barbara and he would be such a worrywart while I was gone," she blushed.

"He'll be fine," Barbara assured us. "You are right, however. He will indeed worry about you, but don't let that keep you from going to such a joyous event."

"No, I think I've made up my mind," she said. "He would want me here."

"I get it and I totally understand," I said as I patted her hand. "You wouldn't be able to enjoy it the way you should under the circumstances."

"Thanks, sweetie," Aunt Mandy replied. "I hope Jill will understand. I'll try to make that wedding with Wilson on my arm."

We chuckled.

After quite some time, the doctor came out and talked to Barbara and Aunt Mandy. He reported that things had gone very well and that Wilson was currently in recovery. I never saw Wilson, but Barbara and Aunt Mandy were relieved and happy after their visit with him later in the day.

Aunt Mandy was exhausted when we returned to Borna. I was ready to collapse as well! She would sleep well tonight, as would I. I poured myself a glass of wine and checked my emails. When I removed my phone from my purse, I realized I'd had it turned off all day at the hospital. When I turned it on, a text came in from John.

Carla says you'll be coming in for a shower for Jill. Can you squeeze in time for dinner one night? J

I quickly responded.

I can't commit at this point. I'm looking forward to my visit! K

I knew my response was rather cold, but having dinner with John was too much like a date. Knowing I had feelings for Cole and going out with John just didn't seem right to me. Finally, a response came back.

A glass of wine for old time's sake? J

Perhaps. K

John always made me smile. He was so likable and interesting. I was lucky to have him as my neighbor at the lake.

Chapter 81

I was pleased to see only a few cars at the winery when I arrived. Cole's Stallion was nowhere in sight. Trout was glad to see me and said Ellie was in the kitchen.

"I'm supposed to meet Cole here," I informed Trout. "How's it going here tonight?"

"Great!" Trout responded with a wink. "The first drink is on me. What will ya' have?"

"The red wine that I can never remember the name of," I said with a chuckle.

"Got it!" Trout nodded, smiling.

"Hey, neighbor!" Ellie called as she approached me. "Why didn't you tell me you were coming?"

"Cole is meeting me here," I said as I saw him walk in the door. "It was a last- minute plan."

"Nice to see you, Cole," Ellie said, smiling. "Are you guys having dinner?"

"Yes," Cole replied. "I want the most private and romantic table you have. I don't want us being interrupted by someone like we encountered last time."

Ellie knew he was teasing, yet she knew he was hoping not to encounter Clark if he came in. Ellie showed us a nice table close to the fire. When she left us, Cole gave me a hug and a kiss on the cheek. Trout brought our drinks and told us about Kelly's specials of grilled salmon or T-bone steak.

At Cole's request, I brought him up to date on Wilson's surgery, our missing quilt at church, and my plans to leave for South Haven. The way he stared into my eyes made me wonder if he was hearing what I was saying.

"Red is pretty reliable, but I hate to see you make that trip alone, Kate," Cole stated when I paused. "How long will you be gone?"

"Not long, but I want to feel free to stay longer if I choose. I'm going out on a limb here, but you wouldn't have any interest in going with me, would you?" I could tell that the request took him by surprise.

"Are you sure you're comfortable with that idea?" He had a big grin as he asked.

"I've thought about it. Can you get away?"

"Sure, that's not a problem."

"I have two bedrooms and a loft," I volunteered.

"Well that's unfortunate."

We laughed.

"I'm a big girl, and right now, I'm inviting a very good friend to see my wonderful hometown." I wanted to send a clear message of my intentions.

"If you're serious, I'll give it some thought and call you tomorrow."

Hmm, I thought he would jump at the idea.

The crowd was very sparse, which concerned Ellie. There was always country music playing in the background and Cole couldn't resist pulling me onto the empty dance floor. The man could dance and I knew Ellie and Trout were watching. In the end, it was a lovely evening. Since we drove separately, I took the lead by telling him when I was ready to leave. He walked me to my car. After a sweet kiss, told me he'd call me the next day about his decision regarding the trip.

On the way home, I wondered if it had been a mistake to ask Cole to join me. Should I tell John and Maggie ahead of time or should I just let Cole be a surprise to them? I would have to say something, of course.

It was late when I turned on the alarm and went upstairs to bed. There was that feeling again of not being alone when I got to the top of the stairs. I couldn't believe my eyes when I saw the covers of my bed turned down again! Was this supposed to be a friendly gesture or what? No one had been in this house except Josephine. I undressed and was too tired to analyze the situation. I pulled the covers over my head instead!

The next morning before I went down to breakfast, I pulled out my suitcase to begin packing. I wished I had something new to wear. I didn't think I'd have time to shop for something once I got to South Haven. Maggie would remember every piece of clothing I owned. That's the way it always was with the two of us. We used to be very competitive in school. After all these years, I still felt tinges of that competitive spirit between us.

Coming down to breakfast, I started to get excited about the two quilter guests that were coming today. I could make some of the menu ahead of time, which I always enjoyed doing. My cell phone rang at ten-thirty and I saw that it was

Cole.

"Did you have a good night's rest?" he asked.

"I did. Thanks again for dinner. That salmon was delicious."

"I agree, but I didn't get too much sleep, I'm afraid."

"Why not?"

"I was having trouble deciding what to do about the trip."

"So, did the slumber fairy give you some advice?"

"I think so. None of the fairies could tell me why I shouldn't go."

I had to snicker. "Wonderful!"

"Now, there was one request from the slumber fairy."

"What was that?"

"That we travel in Black Stallion."

"I'd love that. I'd have to drive it to the bridal shower though."

"You shouldn't have any problem."

"I can accept your request."

Chapter 62

Well, well, I thought to myself as I hung up. I am going on a trip with a man that I don't know all that well. My level of trust surprised me. Was I fooling myself that this could be a fun, innocent adventure? I surprised myself even more by agreeing that he have control of who would be driving!

Susie and Cotton stopped by to see if I needed anything done. Carly Mae was with them and I couldn't believe how she had changed since Christmas. It made me realize how much I had forgotten about child rearing during those early years.

Susie and I went up to the attic to make sure it was in tip-top shape for my guests. Cotton was restocking the firewood on the deck. I told them before they left that I would be baking muffins in the morning if they wanted to stop by. Somehow, I knew Cotton would not forget that offer.

"Did you notice that with these recent warmer days, you have jonquils popping up in the backyard?" Cotton pointed out.

"I did, and I worry they'll get ruined in a frost before

spring," I lamented.

"We'll look in on the place while you're gone," Cotton assured me. "If I don't see you again, you and Red have a safe trip."

"Well, surprisingly, I am going to have some company on this trip," I announced. "Cole is coming with me and we're driving his SUV."

"Well, if that isn't something," Cotton responded.

"Miss Kate, I'm so happy for you," Susie expressed. "I hope you have a great time."

"Now, just so you know, he's only riding along," I joked. "We're not running off to get married."

They laughed.

"I'll check on Red while you're gone then," Cotton added.

"That would be a good idea," I agreed. "Thanks so much for coming over to help," I said as I waved good-bye to them.

I got busy doing the preparation work for the breakfast casserole and cleaned fresh fruit for a compote. Besides my usual blueberry muffins, I made a quick stollen, which was a favorite of mine and Aunt Mandy's.

My two quilter guests arrived around four that afternoon so they could get settled in their room before going to dinner. It appeared that Ruth Ann was making homemade pizza for them.

The older quilter's name was Lois. Her travel partner was younger and her name was Jane. They were thrilled to be able to spend the night at the guest house. When they saw the attic suite, they couldn't have been more pleased. It sounded like neither of them ventured very far from the small town in which they lived.

"We won't be late," Lois assured me. "We are both

exhausted from our long day and we have another half day of class tomorrow before we go home."

"Well, I'll be here," I assured them. "Just help yourself to anything in case I'm upstairs. I'm glad you're enjoying Ruth Ann's classes."

"Oh, she's wonderful!" Jane praised. "I'm learning so much in addition to the machine quilting class we signed up for."

"She's right," echoed Lois. "In our small town, we'd never be able to attract any good quilt teachers like her. By the way, I took a picture of your guest house quilt with my phone. I hope that was okay."

"Sure! Be sure to tell Ruth Ann how much you like it. I'm so glad I had her make it when I decided to turn this home into a guest house. Guests really get a kick out of it."

Within a few minutes, they were off. The mention of Ruth Ann's pizza made me pull out some frozen lasagna from my freezer. I poured a glass of wine and was determined to stay up until they returned. While I waited for my dinner to heat, I called Aunt Mandy to check on Wilson's progress.

"He'll come home tomorrow. I talked to him this afternoon and he was in a lot of pain, which is to be expected. He's glad it's over."

"Yes, I'm sure. Everyone always says that the key is to follow up with the therapy they suggest."

"Well, how are things going with your quilting guests?

"They are delightful. They just left for dinner. By the way, I want to confess something."

"What did you do now?"

I laughed. "I asked Cole to come with me to South Haven."

"Oh! Did he agree?"

"Not right away, but then he did agree to come and then insisted that he drive his SUV. Another man that has to be in control, you know?"

"Are you okay with that?"

"Sure. It's a drive I don't relish, especially this time of year. I'm happy for him to take that on."

"Do Maggie and Carla know he's coming?"

"No, but I'm more concerned about John."

"Oh, yes. Maybe he'll be out of town."

"No, he's around because he asked me to go to dinner with him one night while I'm there."

"Well, have fun figuring that out! You seem to always manage!"

Was she right?

Chapter 83

It was nine when the ladies got back from Ruth Ann's. I offered them a drink, but they refused. However, they did sit down to chat for a few minutes.

"Kate, I have to show you something," Lois said, getting her cell phone. "Ruth Ann said you'd find this very interesting." She pulled up a photo she had taken of my guest quilt in the hallway.

"Look closely at this," Lois instructed me. "There's a silhouette of a woman standing there. At first, I thought it was my own shadow, but it isn't. See her hairline and the full sleeves covering her arms? I look nothing like that."

I looked closely and there was no doubt that it wasn't Lois. I moved my fingers to enlarge it, but I couldn't seem to get any more detail.

"Well, I don't have an explanation, but it does look like a woman," I said, trying to sound casual.

"Ruth Ann thinks it's your ghost, Josephine," Jane said with a sly grin. "What do you think?"

"I've never seen her and there aren't any photos of her to

compare anything to," I responded.

"Well, this may be a first," Lois bragged. "It's weird!"

"I don't know what to say." I struggled to say the right thing. "I always thought Josephine would feel honored to have this guest quilt in her home."

"We feel honored to have our names on it," Jane said proudly. "I'm going to take another photo with my phone and see if we get the same results."

We watched Jane take a photo in the same spot. When she checked to see the results, the image of a woman was not there.

"Well, maybe it was just a fluke," Lois sighed. "I'm ready for bed, Jane. I may try that fancy tub of yours, Kate. That would be a treat for me."

Jane giggled at the thought.

"Please do," I encouraged her. "Breakfast is at eight, right?"

"Yes. We will certainly look forward to that," responded Lois.

Upstairs they went and I sat down to drink my wine and digest their discovery. From the descriptions given from others who had claimed to see Josephine, I was pretty sure they had gotten a glimpse of her.

I tried to ignore what I couldn't control and aimed to concentrate on what I needed for my trip. Having Cole on this trip was going to influence my wardrobe. I made a note to call Carla to make sure the condo was in good shape.

After I readied the breakfast table for the morning, I set the alarm and went upstairs. I could hear my guests giggling one floor above me. It gave me great pleasure when folks had a good time here.

Entering my bedroom, my bed was turned down again, as if I were ready to retire. I found it almost comical. Maybe if I didn't make my bed, she'd do the opposite! I had to take this as a sign of affection.

I undressed and fell into bed, hoping to fall asleep right away. Instead, I tried to picture Cole in South Haven. It only resulted in a lot of questions for me. Do I contact John about Cole's visit? Do I suggest that we have dinner with Maggie and Mark? Would everyone assume Cole and I were serious? Was I fooling myself to think Cole would remain in Jack's room?

The next morning, I was awakened by noises above me in the attic. I had slept later than planned, so I jumped up and put on my robe. I made a quick dash downstairs to get the coffee going and the oven heated for the muffins.

When I met up with my guests fifteen minutes later, Lois once again said she had something to show me. "Wait until you see this, Kate," she said, holding up her phone. "I took a photo of Jane in her silly Beatles pajamas and this image showed up in the mirror behind her."

I quickly went over to witness the photo. It was like the mirror had captured something it wasn't supposed to see. I was speechless. It was the same woman seen in the earlier photo.

"This is so spooky, don't you think?" giggled Jane.

"I'll say it is," agreed Lois.

"Well, I've never known this to happen before," I said lightly as I put some fruit on the table. "You ladies had better step it up and eat or you're going to be late for class."

"Oh, Kate, these muffins are so delicious!" Lois exclaimed, her mouth full. "You need to do a cookbook so everyone can have your recipes."

"That's what everyone says," I said, pouring more coffee.

"I want to bring my husband next time," Lois said.

"I'd never get David to stay at a B&B," Jane complained. He likes his privacy, a big screen TV, and having a bar close by."

I had to chuckle.

They finally got away, but not without rushing like crazy. I had to admit that I really enjoyed their visit and was certainly intrigued by their sightings of my Josephine.

Cotton knocked at the back door.

"Good timing, Cotton," I greeted as I opened the door. "My guests just left and I have plenty of leftovers."

Cotton smiled, revealing his approval. "Oh, Miss Kate, that is not why I stopped. I was going to offer to take Red for a maintenance checkup, which you had mentioned. I could do that and get it washed at the same time, all while you're gone."

"That would be great! It's past due and dirty as all get out!"

I gave Cotton a set of keys and a nice basket of goodies leftover from breakfast.

Chapter 84

Cole and the fancy Black Stallion arrived sharply at nine. I had butterflies in my stomach when I waved good-bye to Red and Josephine's Guest House. I described my usual route to him and all my favorite scenic places along the way. Cole also had favorites of his own and surprisingly knew many of the owners of some of the farms along the way.

Carla returned my phone call and assured me that everything was in good shape at the condo. "Did you say anything to John about Cole coming with you?" she asked, leaving me in the awkward position of trying to answer with Cole sitting right next to me.

"No, I didn't."

"Well, he's looking forward to your visit. I guess he'll be surprised."

"Yes, I suppose so," I said, ending the conversation.

After I hung up, I explained to Cole that Carla had been my housekeeper for many years and that I had recently gone back to South Haven to be with her when she'd had breast cancer surgery.

"I'm anxious for you to meet Maggie and Mark," I said, excited. "Just so you know, they have tried to unsuccessfully to fix me up during some of my visits."

"Is that right?" Cole said, grinning. "Well, I'm glad they weren't successful."

"They will love you, Cole," I assured him.

"I've done a little research about South Haven and I'm anxious to see the harbor and the Maritime Museum that's right in town."

"Yes, you'll love it. It's too bad we can't take in the beach."

"Another time."

I liked his response.

When we stopped for a late lunch at a little diner along the way, I shared with him about my first trip to Borna. I told him how I gorged myself with a hamburger and fries in defiance of my late husband's healthy eating habits. Cole seemed to get a real kick out of that.

It was six when we crossed the historic drawbridge entering South Haven. Cole was in awe of the sailboats. He really lit up when he saw Lake Michigan ahead of us. When we arrived in the parking lot, I was relieved to see John's lights were out in his condo. We carried our first load of luggage inside.

"Kate, this is a grand little place," Cole said when I turned on all the lights.

"This is my favorite spot," I announced as I pulled the drapes open to reveal a deck that overlooked the lake.

"I can see why!"

"Now, here is where you can camp," I said, showing him Jack's room.

"Wow, look at this lighthouse quilt on the wall!"

"I made it and Jack loves it," I bragged.

"I didn't know you were such an avid quilter. I just thought you were trying to help the church ladies."

I laughed. "I'll have you know that I am a charter member of the Beach Quilters here in South Haven!"

"Well, you think you know someone and then you get a surprise," he teased. "I'll bet you have a lot of surprises to share with me."

I let that remark pass and gave him a complete tour, which included the balcony studio. I had to admit, I felt happy to back home in this little place. It did feel strange to have someone from Borna standing here with me.

"I'm starved!" I shouted from my bedroom where I had begun to unpack. "How would you like to taste the best pizza in town?"

"Sounds great. Where would that be?"

"Tello's. It's right downtown."

"I'm game!"

The tour of South Haven had begun. He loved the dark, cozy atmosphere of Tello's. I had the perfect red wine to suggest as we took a seat at the bar, as I had done so often in the past.

"I'm surprised that the bartender didn't know you by name," Cole teased.

I laughed. "Jack would be so jealous if he knew we were here."

Cole nodded and smiled.

"It's the first food he has to have when he comes home," I explained.

"What time is the shower tomorrow?" Cole asked as he took a sip of wine.

"It's at two, but I'll be going early in case I can help. I've never done this before, but the bride's mother seems to be in charge."

"Is that because you no longer live here, or is the mother a control freak?"

"It's a little of both. The groom's mother just seems to be an accessory."

He laughed. Cole loved the pizza and we finished a bottle of wine. Our bartender was from Italy and was very entertaining, sharing funny stories as we passed the evening away. We left just before they closed at midnight and we were feeling pretty happy.

Chapter 85

Cole and I ended up dozing off on the couch. After we had returned from dinner, we had talked and talked until exhaustion finally took over. Consequently, neither of us felt very well the next morning from the wine we had consumed the night before. I called Maggie to see when she was expecting me at the country club.

"I think all is well," she reported. "Welcome home, by the way! Did Cole come with you?"

"Yes, and we were wondering if you could join us one night for dinner at Hawk's Head."

"I'll check with Mark and see. I can't wait to meet Cole!"

"You know that I'm a little nervous about that."

She laughed and seemed to understand.

"We did close down Tello's last night."

"Then you're making progress as a tour guide. Have you run into John?"

"No, but that could happen today."

She wished me luck.

Cole and I shared some muffins I'd brought from home

and drank several cups of coffee. I told him that I would take him to the Golden Bakery tomorrow, which was always a highlight when I visited the area. There was a knock at the door and the thing I had been avoiding was finally happening.

"Kate!" John said with a big grin. "Welcome home!" He followed up his exclamations with an enthusiastic hug. "I heard something up here, but I didn't see any sign of your Jeep in the parking lot. I thought I'd better come up here and check on things."

"Come on in, John," I said, feeling thoroughly uneasy. "I'd like you to meet my friend, Cole, who accompanied me on this trip." John's look of surprise was priceless.

"Hi, John. I'm Cole Alexander," Cole said kindly. "Kate's told me a lot about you."

"Has she now?" John said.

I could detect the sarcasm in his response and wondered what Cole must be thinking.

"I understand you've been to East Perry County a couple of times," Cole added.

"Yes, I fell in love with it," John stated. "Kate has been very helpful when it comes to my writing." He paused and looked at his feet. "Well, I'm glad I didn't have to chase away any intruders, so I'll leave you two to get on. It has been nice to meet you, Cole. If you two are free for a drink during your stay in South Haven, let me know."

"Thanks, we will," I assured him. I threw him a kiss as he went out the door, thinking it had gone as well as could be expected.

"You just broke that guy's heart," Cole teased.

"We have a great friendship. He knows this gal is too old for him."

Cole shook his head, smiling. "He seems like a really nice guy."

"He is. He is a great writer. You'll find him very interesting."

"You'd better get on your way soon! You look very beautiful for an old gal!"

I chuckled.

"I'll take a walk and take this key with me," Cole said before I left. "If I get bored, I'll have a drink with your neighbor."

"You wouldn't!" I retorted, knowing how Cole loved to tease me.

"Don't forget tomorrow is Valentine's Day. You're supposed to spend it with someone you love and adore!" Cole teased again.

"I hope we can share it with Maggie and Mark. You will love that restaurant overlooking the golf course." I left the condo with my red-and-white wrapped shower gift.

There were people everywhere in the country club parking lot. Maggie's wish for a wedding at the club was working. At least this event would meet her expectations.

"Kate!" Jill greeted me when I entered the ballroom. "You don't know how much it means to me for you to be here. Where's Aunt Mandy?"

"Her significant other had surgery and she told me to convey how sorry she is not to be here," I explained. "She'll be at the wedding and will likely have him come with her."

"Kate, Kate, so glad you're here!" Maggie said, engulfing me in a big hug. She appeared to be on a high from all the excitement. I couldn't believe Maggie knew so many women! The room was filled with round tables decorated in a Valentine theme. It was eye popping. Red roses and petals were everywhere!

Jill immediately took me to meet her wedding party. I knew her maid of honor, but the two bridesmaids, Sarah and Cassandra, were from out of town.

"Here's a photo of the bridesmaids' dresses." Jill showed me an image on her cell phone. Her primary color was a soft yellow and she said the attendants would carry long-stemmed red roses.

"They are beautiful!" I assured her "What are you wearing?"

"It's a surprise," she smiled. "You will love it, and so will Jack."

This shower was not the stereotypical shower experience with games and prizes. Maggie had a video of Jack and Jill. It showed them growing up together up until the time of their engagement. It was well done and brought many of us to tears as we watched.

As always, the club's kitchen staff served food that could only be described as divine. Individual lemon heart-shaped cakes were iced and had fresh raspberries on top. They were perfect for the occasion. If there had been one left, I would have liked to have taken one home to Cole.

Presents were piled high on two tables. I knew we'd be here forever before they would all be opened. I wondered where on earth they would put everything in their tiny apartment! Jill saved my gift and opened it toward the end. She first read the card and looked at me with such affection. When she saw the red-and-white quilt, her mouth opened in surprise.

"I love it!" she exclaimed.

"Oh, Kate, it is so beautiful!" Maggie agreed. "Where on earth did you get it?"

"Imy, of course," I admitted. "I just thought it had Jill's name written all over it, so don't steal it from her."

Jill got out of her chair and gave me a warm hug. I was touched and wished that Jack could have seen our exchange. One of her bridesmaids was using her phone to video much of the proceedings, so perhaps he would. In the end, it was a splendid event. Maggie was getting compliments left and right and I felt very happy for her. "You really outdid yourself, girlfriend," I said, slipping my arm around her.

"I only have one daughter, so I'm entitled," she said, tearing up.

Jill was planning an evening with her friends and Maggie was exhausted. We decided that the next night would be perfect for us to get together for dinner.

Chapter 86

On my way home from the shower, I got a text. It was John.

Why the secret? Is this serious? J

Oh, no. How should I respond? I couldn't deny that I had kept my relationship with Cole from John on purpose. I sure wasn't going to share my feelings because I wasn't sure what I felt myself! I finally answered.

Too many questions. K

There was no response after that. When I walked into the condo, Cole was sleeping on the couch. His face had a sweet, innocent look I had never seen before.

"Hey, sweetheart," Cole said, surprising me. "How was the shower?"

"Marvelous! How was your day?"

"Wonderful. I think I may have worn myself out."

"Since we're both worn out, I have a simple plan. I know a cute little restaurant downtown where we can grab a bite and then walk over to the beach to see the best sunset known to man!"

He grinned and nodded in agreement.

I changed into casual clothes and off we went. Taste was a casual tapas dining experience. We talked nonstop as we enjoyed some unusual foods. There was so much I wanted to share with Cole about the shower and also about South Haven. We made sure to check the time so we wouldn't miss the sunset.

When we got to the beach, we saw an empty bench where we'd have the best view. The last time I saw the sunset, I was with the blind date set up by Maggie and Mark. It was summer then and we had taken advantage of the wonderful snack bar nearby. This evening, silence prevailed as we watched the sun slowly disappear into the water. Even in the dead of winter, folks came out of their beach houses and condos to witness this perfect time of day. We held hands as we walked back to the car. Back at the condo, we were happy to fall into our beds and get some much-needed rest.

The next morning, the excitement of going to the Golden Bakery had me up early. I put the coffee on and peeked into Cole's room, only to find that he wasn't there! On the kitchen bar, there was a note that said he had gone out for a run. Was Cole a runner?

I showered and dressed before Cole returned.

"You're a runner?" I asked when he returned.

"I run at the gym, but I couldn't resist running around the harbor. If I lived here, I'd be doing that every morning. The boats in the dock are amazing."

"Well, it is beautiful. I sometimes take it for granted. I hope you've worked up an appetite."

"Indeed I have. I'll be ready in a flash."

Thank goodness they hadn't sold out of their large blueberry scones that I continually bragged about. When I placed my order, I got some extras to take home.

"Let's sit back here where I usually sit with Carla and Maggie," I said, leading the way.

Cole ordered the full breakfast and claimed the scone as his dessert. I loved watching him devour every bite. While we sat enjoying our coffee, I called Maggie about dinner plans for the evening. We also decided we would head back to Borna the next day. It would mean me skipping lunch with the Beach Quilters, but I had seen most of them at the shower.

When we left the bakery, I drove around town, explaining things to Cole. We also drove to the cemetery where my sister-in-law was buried. I was pleased to see flowers on her grave. They were likely put there by her daughter, Emily.

We then drove into my old neighborhood. Cole was shocked to see its grand appearance. It was an impressive neighborhood. We slowed down and saw a man and two small children get out of a car in the driveway of my former home. It pleased me that a young family occupied the place now.

"That is quite beautiful," Cole remarked. "I can only imagine what a change it was to come to an old house in a small community."

"I needed a dramatic change. I was living a life to benefit someone else only to find out I was being betrayed in the process."

His look was sad, causing me to feel as if he understood. "Had you not found Borna, you wouldn't have found me or Red!" Cole joked, lightening the somber moment.

The last place I wanted to check out was Cornelia's Quilt Shop. I explained to Cole that Maggie was a silent partner and that Penny, a long-time employee, was running the shop. If Maggie hadn't stepped in with some big bucks, our little town would be without a quilt shop. I didn't expect him to understand, but he was listening intently.

When we pulled in front, I realized that the shop wasn't open. I got out of the car and peeked in the windows. It was colorful, had great samples displayed, and had much more fabric than when I was there last. It had every sign of Penny doing a wonderful job. The topic of the shop hadn't even come up with Maggie since she'd had the shower and wedding on her mind. I jumped back into Cole's Jeep feeling confident that things had worked out well.

I knew Cole was absorbing everything he could about South Haven and me. I could have talked and talked about South Haven while we were in Borna, but it was much better for him to see me here in action.

Chapter 67

We headed back to the condo with just enough time to get ready for dinner. I knew tonight was the big test with Cole meeting Maggie and Mark. Their reaction was important to me. So far, I hadn't regretted bringing Cole to South Haven. It was easy for Ellie to approve of Cole because she knew him from coming into the winery to see Trout. I needed the feedback of my lifelong friends.

Cole looked very sharp. He was quite the clothes horse, I noticed. I wore a simple black dress with a paisley shawl. I explained to Cole that this club would be the location of Jack and Jill's wedding. When we arrived, he thought it was quite nice. We found Mark and Maggie waiting for us at the bar. From Cole's very first word, Maggie listened intently to everything he said.

When we went into the dining room, I talked Cole into ordering salmon, which was the signature dish. As we waited for our first course, I motioned for Maggie to come with me to the restroom, just as we had done in high school. It seemed that the men would hardly notice we had gone since they were engaged in a deep conversation about real estate. That part was certainly going well.

Once inside the restroom, Maggie put her hands on my shoulders.

"Do you love this man?" she asked, looking me in the eyes.

She caught me off guard. "I don't know," I blurted out. "We haven't been seeing each other very long. What do you think of him?"

"Girlfriend, he's the cat's meow, and if you don't hold onto him, I'll never forgive you!"

"Really?"

"Really. I can tell he's in love with you."

"He is wonderful. I just get full of doubt when I think what might be ahead."

"You mean marriage?"

"Perhaps. I just cannot make another mistake. I thought I knew Clay. He was nearly perfect, just like Cole. I don't want to lead him on. I think he'll be the type to want to get married again."

"When I said to hold onto him, I didn't exactly mean marriage. I think folks our age really do need to think hard before taking that step again. I don't think I'd marry again if I got divorced or was widowed."

"That's interesting. I guess that's why I felt so safe with Clark. He had no intention of getting married, so he was completely safe."

"Is Clark is the reason you're feeling so unsure of yourself?"

"No! Not at all! We have both moved on." I said that knowing that Clark may not have moved on so completely.

"Good, because this guy will challenge you. Life and love is an adventure. Keeping you safe should not be a reason for you to marry him. I'm not saying he shouldn't be dependable. Goodness knows that at our age, we do require that much."

I chuckled and was amused at Maggie's opinion.

"Oh, Maggie, you know me so well."

"You have always known me. I wouldn't give you this kind of advice if I didn't know you like I do. I do see a wonderful twinkle in your eye when you look at him. I haven't seen that look since the first date you had with Clay."

I shook my head, trying to remember. Then we busied ourselves by reapplying lipstick and checking our reflections in the mirror. We exited the powder room arm in arm like the two best friends we were.

"Well, we thought you two went to the bar, you've been gone so long," Mark teased.

Cole gave me a peck on the cheek when I sat down next to him.

A flurry of chatter flew around the table as we shared our dinner. I could tell that Mark and Maggie were impressed with my new beau. I detected a sense of humor in Cole that I had never seen before. I wondered what Mark and Maggie would have thought if Cole and I would have shared our rescue story with them!

Chapter 88

When we arrived at the condo, we turned on the fireplace and cuddled on the couch in order to warm up. I was anxious to hear what Cole thought about Maggie and Mark. To my surprise, Cole took a valentine out of his suit coat pocket.

"Don't worry, this is not anything gushy for you to worry about," he teased.

"I hope not, because my card is goofy."

He laughed. "I wasn't sure you'd get me a card at all. Right now, Kate, I'm just happy to have you in my life."

"That is so sweet and you said it better than any valentine could have." I handed him the card I had selected for him. It showed a damsel in distress who was tied to a railroad track with a train coming. The message was about a rescue, which of course was our little secret.

"This is pretty funny. I will come and rescue you anytime."

We pecked each other on the cheek and I got up to get us some glasses of wine.

"Are you disappointed that you didn't get a chance to visit with your downstairs neighbor?

"Not really, but I'm glad you both at least met each other. Are you jealous, Mr. Alexander?" I asked sweetly. "I have never seen that side of you."

"I don't think of myself that way. Perhaps that was something my wife would have liked, but frankly, I lost so much respect for her through the years that it didn't matter."

"That's sad."

We talked and talked until late into the night again. I think we could have taken our relationship to the next level, but we both knew it wasn't time. Cole had a good way of reading my mind. I did hope he realized how special I thought he was.

The next morning, we both felt rested and ready for the trip. I requested that we make a quick stop at the Blueberry Store to take goodies back to all of my friends. Cole was amazed at everything they had on the shelves. He bought some blueberry salsa and blueberry tea for himself.

The weather was delightful, making me wonder if we were going to have an early spring. Little by little, I shared with Cole that he was a big hit with Mark and Maggie.

"I like Mark a lot," Cole admitted. "We had a great conversation. I wasn't sure about Maggie at first. Of course, I knew she was sizing me up, big time."

I laughed and nodded.

We arrived in Borna around seven that evening. The trip went by so much faster with having someone to talk to. After we unloaded my things, Cole went on his way. I could tell he knew me so much better after this trip. Maggie's observation about Cole was correct. He was ready for a more serious relationship than I was at this point. I wondered if it was because his divorce had just been finalized. I called Aunt Mandy to see how she and Wilson were doing.

"Oh, I'm so glad you're back. I'm dying to hear how everything went."

"I'll fill you in, but I want to hear how Wilson is doing."

"He's doing great. Barbara picked me up and took me to dinner at their house last night. Wilson had a brother in from Indiana that he wanted me to meet. It was a lovely evening."

"Good. Glad to hear it."

"So, back to you, honey. Did you feel comfortable bringing Cole with you? Did you see John? What did Maggie think of Cole? Oh! And how was the shower?" We burst into giggles before I could answer.

"Slow down, Auntie! It was all good and he fit right in. Jill asked about you and was sorry you couldn't make it. The shower was like a full-blown wedding. It was gorgeous, well attended, and Maggie got the kudos she so deserved."

"Did Jill like the quilt?"

"Oh, yes. She made me feel really special and I think she was completely sincere."

"Now, Wilson is coming for lunch tomorrow and we'd like you to join us. He's going to make his special chili, so we need eaters."

"Well, I have quilting at church in the morning. I'm anxious to see if there is anything new about the missing quilt. I suppose I could skip lunch and join the two of you!"

"Oh, that would be great. We certainly want to hear more about your trip."

"I brought you some blueberry treats, as always."

"Wonderful. I may give Charmin a call to see if she'd like to join us. I feel badly that we had to cancel on her lunch invitation."

"Good idea."

Chapter 89

The next morning, I enjoyed a leisurely breakfast and then went upstairs to unpack from the trip. However, time didn't allow for it if I wanted to get to the church in time for coffee. I was almost skipping as I realized how happy I was to be back in Borna again.

When I got to the church parking lot, I looked up on the cemetery hill and saw Arnie removing wilted funeral flowers and debris that had been left on the graves. The weather was pleasant, so I decided to join him near Josephine's gravesite.

"Well, good morning," Arnie said, surprised to see me approaching him.

"Good morning, Arnie. Were there any yellow roses on Josephine's grave?"

"Not this week," he said, shaking his head. "Funny thing, they're always as fresh as they day they arrived. It's the craziest thing!"

"I just got back into town and was wondering if you'd heard any news about Stella Clifton's missing quilt top."

He paused and scratched his head. "Golly, Kate, when

Pastor asked me about having a key, I felt terrible that I couldn't remember what I did with it. That was such a busy day when Matilda gave it to me. In all the confusion, I must have lost track of it."

"What do you mean about confusion? What was going on?"

"Oh, they were getting ready for the annual Mission Angels' meeting."

"I've never heard of them."

He laughed. "Oh, they're a lively bunch. It is when all the local church women's groups meet in their district. These women can make more loud chatter than a bunch of hens! My Aunt Virginia was in charge this particular time, so I was helping her out with the setup and all. She claims it all turned out great. They gave the pastor a pretty nice donation."

"That's wonderful. I don't think I know your Aunt Virginia. Does she go to church here?"

"No, but she'll come once in a while when there's something special going on. She's a quilter, like you. I've seen pictures of some her quilts and they would make your hair stand on end! I've never seen anything like them. Someday, I hope she'll leave me one of them."

"I bet she will if she knows you like them so much."

"She knows all about the fancy quilts Stella Clifton makes, too."

"She does?"

"Sure. I bragged about the fact that she gets hers quilted right here at Concordia Lutheran Church."

"I'll bet that impressed her."

"Yes it did, because she asked right away if we had any of her quilt tops ready to set up."

"She did?"

"I said I could check because I had a key to the quilt chest to give to the pastor. I told her Miss Ruby would have a fit if I got in the box, but she said she wouldn't say anything."

"So you opened the chest? Was Stella's top in there?"

"Yup, right there on the top, so I didn't have to root around. It had her name on the bag, bright and clear. I got it out for her to see and she couldn't believe what a different kind of pattern it was."

"Arnie, you know you shouldn't have done that. The pastor and the quilters would be very angry with you."

"No harm done, Kate. Aunt Virginia just wanted to take a picture of the pattern so she could make one just like it."

"She took a photo?"

"She took several. No one was around. Like I said, nobody but maybe Ruby would even care."

I couldn't believe what I had just heard.

"What about the key to the chest? Did you put the quilt back in and lock it all up?"

"I had to run because the upstairs alarm was goin' off again. That darn thing is supposed to be fixed. We've had folks come and repair it, but now and then, it still goes off. My aunt said she'd put the quilt back and lock it up when she was finished."

"Are you very sure she put the quilt back and locked the box?"

"She said she would put it back just like we found it. Oh, she locked it because I checked when I returned. She's a Mission Angel member, by golly. She knows we have to keep them quilts safe, like Pastor said."

"The key, Arnie. Did you get the key back from your aunt?"

He thought for a minute. "I imagine I did. I really don't

remember. She probably left it on the table for me. I think that's when I lost track of it."

"That extra key is still missing, Arnie. You were the last one to have it. It is important that you remember where you put it. Ruby said she brought the top back to the church, but then it was gone."

"Oh, it was there, by golly. It was a pretty thing, just like everyone said. My aunt was ever so grateful to see it up close and all."

"You're right, the pastor would be very angry with you for getting that quilt top out of the chest."

"He shouldn't be. Nothing happened to it. We were very careful. When he asked me about the key, I didn't even think to tell him about my Aunt Virginia taking a peek at it."

"I know you meant no harm, Arnie, but the quilt top is missing and so is the key."

"It's a darn shame. I'll keep looking for it. Pastor said the chest will stay unlocked from now on, so maybe we don't need the key back after all. He says now I have to keep your quilt room locked when you all are not there."

I didn't know what else to say. "Well, I've kept you from your work long enough. I need to get to the quilting room for the coffee break."

"Don't you worry none, Kate," he said as I walked down the hill. "You won't snitch on me and Aunt Virginia will you?"

I turned around and thought about what to say before I spoke. "If it's as innocent as you say, no one needs to know. You must never do anything like that again, Arnie."

"No, I won't," he answered, much like a little boy getting caught doing something wrong. I had to ask myself if he really was that naive.

Chapter 90

Joining the quilters in full chatter, I poured myself some coffee. I'd have to digest Arnie's confession at another time.

"I see that Mrs. Schierding brought a sheet to use for her backing after I told her specifically not to," Ruby complained. "Folks just don't realize how hard they are to quilt through."

"It's an easy fix for them, that's why they do it," Esther remarked.

"We won't be able to get to her quilt right away, Ruby. Why don't you have her bring in something else?" Paula suggested.

Ruby shook her head and went into the kitchen.

Watching Ruby's reaction, I decided that I don't think that woman ever smiled or had a happy day!

"Well, at least the blocks match up," Erna noted. "Remember that last top with all the different-sized blocks?"

"Yes, the sampler," Esther remembered. "It needed a lot of canoodling."

"What does that mean?' I asked with a chuckle in my voice.

"It means you have to pull and fudge a bit to get everything to fit in the frame. I hate to say it, but you can only do so much with some of those tops."

It appeared that everyone was in a complaining mood today! I could really throw them into a state of disarray if I told them the news Arnie had just shared with me.

It was Ellen's turn to bring dessert. She chose to bring what she called her family's "German cheesecake." After I voiced enough compliments, she offered to give me the recipe. There! Something positive had occurred!

When I sat down next to Ellen to begin quilting, she immediately asked me about my trip to South Haven. I didn't tell her that Cole had accompanied me or the whole town would know.

"Did you forget your lunch again?" she said, nearly scolding me.

"No, I've been invited to my aunt's for lunch."

"I hear that Wilson is doing better," Ellen commented.

"Yes. Aunt Mandy is ever so grateful that Oscar continues to give him projects to work on."

"Why not? He's a genius," Ellen said. "Oscar said he is lucky to have a man of his caliber and experience. Say, how is that friend of yours that lives in Jacksonville Meadows?"

"She may be joining us for lunch today, as a matter of fact."

"Why don't you see about getting her to join our church, Kate?" If she keeps coming to the gravesite and the church is right here, why not attend church?"

"I can't answer that, but I'll see what I can do," I said to appease her. "She said they have a quilting group at the Meadows, but I guess I don't know if she's even a quilter."

"Well, that would be a bonus if she is." Ellen stated.

"Ellen, do you know Arnie's Aunt Virginia?' I asked, catching her by surprise.

She paused. "I think she comes to church with Arnie every once in a while when we have special services. I've never spoken to her. Why do you ask?"

"He mentioned that she was in charge of the Mission Angel's event when we had it here at our church."

"Oh, yes, that was quite a large group. We didn't start a chapter because we have the Lutheran Missionary League. They do pretty much the same thing."

I didn't feel I could share much more with Ellen. If I shared my news with anyone, it would be with Pastor Hermann. When the ladies took their break for lunch, I actually observed a conversation between Ruby and Matilda. That had to be interesting. I got Esther's attention before I left to see when I could set up another hair appointment.

"Any time, Kate," she said happily. "I'm anxious to hear about your trip. I heard a handsome man went with you this time."

"Goodness, will I ever be able to have any secrets around here?" I said, shaking my head and smiling.

"You know better than to try," she teased. "I know Cole. He was involved in the sale of my parents' farm in Perry when they built that nursing home. He is a mighty nice fellow."

"Thanks, I think so, too."

Chapter 91

Aunt Mandy and Wilson were anxiously waiting for me when I arrived. I looked for Charmin's car, but I didn't see it. "Something smells good," I said as I came in the door.

"Wilson's outdone himself again," my aunt bragged. "You probably smell the cornbread that we just took out of the oven."

We sat down to a lovely table. Aunt Mandy had also outdone herself.

"Oh, Charmin had other plans today," Aunt Mandy explained when I asked about her absence. "She really wants us to visit soon. I feel badly that we had to cancel. I really am anxious to see her new place."

"Yes, we need to do that," I agreed. "This chili is delicious, Wilson. What makes it so different?"

"My secret is that I use brisket instead of ground beef," he revealed.

"What a good idea! I'm going to have to try that."

Wilson asked about my Michigan trip and listened intently to my response before he got to the real reason for my invitation to have lunch with them today.

"Kate, you probably know how fond I am of your aunt," he began. "We are so fortunate to have found one another, thanks to you and Oscar."

I waited for more.

"Mandy and I are not getting any younger," he pointed out while they both chuckled and exchanged knowing looks. "My point is that I have asked for your aunt's hand in marriage and we would like your blessing."

I smiled while wondering what to say. Then, as the happy news hit me, I exclaimed, "I couldn't be happier for the two of you!" I took Aunt Mandy's hand in mine and said, "It gives me such joy that the two of you have found each other. You have my blessing, but it's certainly not needed. This announcement doesn't surprise me, but I am so grateful that you included me."

"Oh, honey, thank you for those kind words," Aunt Mandy responded. "I know Wilson could move in here with me, but we're both old school and want the whole commitment to each other."

I smiled. "When is the big day?" I asked with anticipation.

"We want a small and private ceremony, of course," she assured me. "Pastor Hermann said he could do a morning ceremony as early as next week."

"Next week?" I asked, surprised by the short time frame.

"Well, sweetie, it's not like we have to plan anything much," she explained.

"I don't care how private you want this to be, Auntie, but we have to celebrate! I'll do a brunch at my place after the ceremony if that would suit the two of you."

They looked at each other and smiled.

"I think we can agree to that," Wilson said.

"I'd like for you to stand up for me, Kate," Aunt Mandy requested, suddenly looking a bit shy.

"I plan to ask Oscar to stand up for me," Wilson added. "After all, he is responsible for introducing me to Mandy after she decided to build a home here in Borna and needed an architect."

"I'd be honored." I said, giving her a little hug.

"Have you told Barbara?" I inquired.

"Barbara has known my intentions for some time and she wholeheartedly approves," Wilson reported.

We toasted the news with glasses of iced tea. As we started to eat, so many things were going through my mind. I realized that there was nothing that was going to keep these two apart. Before I left, Wilson said he hoped next week would give me enough time to plan the brunch. It looked like there wouldn't be any long engagement for this couple!

I left with a smile on my face. There would now be two occupants on my land, which gave me much better satisfaction regarding Aunt Mandy's security. Little did Wilson know when he designed this house that he would be living in it someday! My mind was full of plans for next week's celebration. Cotton and I arrived at my driveway at the same time.

"Welcome home, Miss Kate," he shouted as he got out of his truck. "I brought you the paperwork on your vehicle. It was in good shape. No repairs needed."

"Great. Thanks for doing that for me. I brought you some blueberry treats from South Haven."

"Oh, Susie will love that. Thanks so much. Did you and Cole have a good time?"

"We did, but it went very quickly."

"I'll be back to do more of a spring clean-up. We can start trimming some of these bushes and clean out your flower beds then."

His plan was a good one since there would be a wedding brunch here next week. I didn't want to discuss the event with him just now. I got his goody basket, gave it to him, and off he went. I was about to go into the house when Ellie pulled into the driveway on her way to the winery. Living on Main Street, it seemed that every move I made was viewed by the whole community!

Chapter 92

"Good to have you back," Ellie called from her car window. "Is it too early or too bold to ask for my South Haven treat?"

We chuckled.

"Why don't you come on in?"

"Perhaps for a minute or two. I have to meet up with a salesman."

"Yeah, I remember how that went," I teased. "You'd better be careful!"

"Not fair, Kate," she retorted, feigning offense.

"Speaking of Carson, have you seen him anywhere?"

"No. I wonder if he even has the same job."

Ellie came inside and I handed her the blueberry treats.

"I have a day-old blueberry scone if you'd like it."

"I wouldn't think of it. I know how you cherish those. I'm sure everyone adored Cole, but I want to know how you handled John."

"He knocked on my door like he always does, so of course, he was shocked to see a man inside my place. I introduced them to each other and that was that."

"John had something to say about that, I'm sure."

"He did, but I let it go and didn't respond."

"Did the trip bring you and Cole closer together or pull you further apart?"

I knew what she was getting at. "If you're asking what I think you're asking, the answer is no. If you're asking if it helped us get to know one another, the answer is yes. Seeing Cole in South Haven was pretty cool. Maggie and Mark really liked him, which made me feel good."

She was staring at me with an odd look on her face.

"What?"

"I've never met anyone like you. I know taking him to South Haven was a big step, but I see you holding back again, like you did with Clark."

"Perhaps, but he's not going anywhere and neither am I. Cole's divorce was only recently declared final and I want him to have lots of space and time to discover what he wants. I don't want to be a desperate replacement for someone else."

Ellie chuckled. "You may not want to be, but that's what happens when a new romance is started."

"How did you become such an expert, Ms. Meers?"

"Okay, you have me there. You won't get any more flak from me. You seem to be the type that is fine with or without a man."

"Thanks, Ellie. I'd like to think so, anyway. You know, I think we are in the process of falling in love with each other."

"That's all you could want. I envy you."

"Ellie, you meet new men every day at your winery. I don't want to hear any excuses from you!"

We laughed as Ellie left the guest house and headed to work.

I should have told her about Aunt Mandy's wedding because I might need Kelly's help with the menu. I had time to start a list of all that needed to be done. Besides a menu, I would need lots of flowers. What a happy thing to think about! It was sad to think that they wanted to keep it so plain and simple.

Before I realized it, the day was nearly over. My mind wandered to Cole and what he might be doing. I think I missed him after spending so much time with him for several days. I wanted to contact him, but I knew he must be terribly busy after missing work and spending those days in Michigan. When I got into the shower that evening, I dismissed any thought of contacting Cole. I decided instead to analyze what I had learned from Arnie.

Arnie was truly naive and wasn't well educated. He had no idea how foolish it was to let his aunt look at the quilt top and take photos. If Arnie left the room before she put the quilt back, she could have kept the quilt top for herself. If I asked Arnie directly about my suspicion, it would anger him. I supposed it would be best to approach the pastor with my information and let him take it from there. If his aunt truly put the quilt back, we were back to square one again.

I was in the shower way too long trying to figure out the disappearance of the quilt. The water was not as hot as it was at first. In fact, it was cooling off pretty fast! I was forced to get out and select a towel from inside my towel warmer, a luxury I truly cherished. The shower had totally relaxed me and I was sure I would fall asleep instantly when my head hit the pillow. That didn't happen, of course. My mind flitted between weddings and the crime committed in the quilt room at church.

Chapter 93

My cell phone rang, jarring me into the present.

"Kate, are you asleep?" Cole asked.

"No. Unfortunately, I can't seem to fall asleep. It's one of those nights when I have too much on my mind."

"You're not alone. I never have this problem. Would it be too forward of me to admit that I miss you very much?"

"Not at all! I miss you, too. I was going to call, but I knew you were busy catching up on things. So much has happened since I've been home, too."

"Nothing bad, I hope."

"No. When I went over for lunch today, Aunt Mandy and Wilson announced their plans to get married."

"That is big news! Good for them!"

"It's great, of course, but I offered to host a brunch after their morning wedding at the church. The ceremony is next week, so I don't have much time."

"You can handle it. No wonder you're not sleeping, though."

"Thanks. It's just going to be a small group, but I want it

to be perfect."

"Of course, and they expect nothing less from you."

We chucked.

"I'm also trying to play quilt detective with a little problem at the church. I won't bother you with the details, but it has me puzzled."

"At that rate, you'll never get any sleep! I have enough on my plate as well. You know, I didn't officially thank you for the wonderful trip to South Haven. I really enjoyed meeting Mark and Maggie and seeing where you lived."

"It was special for me to have you there."

"My dad wanted to know all about my trip. He's anxious to meet you."

"That would be nice."

"When can I see you again?"

"I don't know. I have a ton of things to do before the brunch. Maybe my aunt will invite you to the wedding."

"I'm busy as well. I have to go into Perry tomorrow."

"Well, why don't you stop by on your way home and I'll grill some steaks for us."

"That would be great. You provide the grill and I'll bring the steaks."

"That's a deal."

"If I can do anything to help you out with the brunch, let me know."

"Thanks, but right now, we both need some sleep."

"I agree, but it's more fun talking to you."

"Goodnight, Cole Alexander. Sweet dreams."

I hung up, knowing that we both shared some of the same feelings. It made me wonder if Aunt Mandy would invite him to the wedding despite his not being family. Perhaps Cole could just bartend for me that day. I'd just have to wait and see, I supposed. Cole coming for dinner gave me something else to think about. Did I need more to think about? Yes, I needed that to think about.

The next morning, I felt groggy from lack of sleep, but I knew I had no business sleeping late. I put on a robe and checked emails before getting some coffee. My landline rang, which made me jump.

"Good morning!" a chirpy voice rang out. "This is Sharla Lee. I couldn't find your cell number, so I hoped you'd be at home."

"Oh, I'm up but really not at 'em, so to speak," I responded with a yawn.

"We've got a big tour coming through today so I'm here at the museum early. I'm calling to see if you would consider volunteering for us once in a while. We lost Elsie to bad health and we already use Carolyn more than we should. Gerard thought you might enjoy it and remarked about how he thought you would be very good at this."

"Oh, Sharla Lee, I sure couldn't commit to anything like that right now, especially if I have guests. I'm very flattered and will give it some thought when I have some time."

"Alright then, sweetie, but please give it some serious thought."

"I will. Good luck with the tour today."

That was a call I wasn't expecting! As I poured my desperately-needed coffee, I pondered the idea for a moment or two. I loved everyone at the museum, but my better sense said to say no, no, no!

Chapter 94

Cole arrived for dinner and brought two steaks that could have passed for two chuck roasts. He was truly a meat-and-potatoes guy. It was pretty chilly outside, but we wore our jackets as we hung out on the deck preparing dinner. My salad and baked potatoes would do nicely to round out a great meal.

Cole mentioned he was worried about his dad's declining health. He felt badly that his daughter was doing more to help his father than he was. I mostly listened because, for a change, Cole was the one doing most of the talking.

He also shared that his former wife, Shirley, was having second thoughts about wanting some of their furnishings that she was so eager to leave behind previously. I didn't have to ask what his response was before he stated that he told her he had changed the locks and that she needed to get on with her life. I remained silent because I realized that I only knew one side of the story.

It was eight before we sat down to eat our delicious meal. I told Cole about Sharla Lee calling and her surprising request. He just said he thought I would enjoy it. He also said he had been asked to do various things by non-profits and that he had learned to be careful and made sure to set boundaries for himself.

While we cleared the table, my cell phone rang. It was Ruth Ann.

"Could you meet me at the Coffee Haus in the morning if you don't have guests? I need to talk to you about something." It sounded urgent.

"Sure, I'm free. How about nine?"

"Great. I'll see you then."

Well, that was to the point!

Cole was doing a good job cleaning up from dinner and seemed enormously impressed by my efficient kitchen. "I feel like taking a walk, how about you?" Cole asked when he was finished.

"That would be nice, I suppose, but walking on the street at night is just asking for an accident."

"Oh, I was thinking we'd walk on the gravel road that goes to your aunt's house."

"It's very, very dark. Trust me."

His face beamed. "I'm counting on that. Let's give it a try."

I put on a warmer coat. I had never walked to Aunt Mandy's before, even in the daylight. We went hand in hand as the full moon led our way. It was so peaceful. So far, only one car had passed and they saw us in plenty of time.

When we got to Aunt Mandy's, it was past ten and her lights were out. I told Cole we shouldn't get too close or we would trigger her dusk-to-dawn light and it may frighten her. As it began to get colder and the wind picked up, we turned around and headed home. I was anxious to get warm again. When we approached my house, we saw an SUV that looked like Clark's parked on the side of the road. As we got closer, I saw Clark sitting inside. What on earth was he doing? We stopped walking when I told Cole who it was.

"Does he stalk you?"

I shook my head. "Not that I know of, anyway. I guess he saw your SUV parked at my place and wanted to see if he noticed anything. We can't let him see us. If we walk around this way, we'll come out by Ellie's house and can enter through the front door." I sighed. "I can't believe this."

"Listen, we do strange stuff when things don't go our way. Let's not embarrass him. Let's go the way you suggested."

So, off we went into a more thickly grown part of the property. I almost stumbled as we hiked through a span of woods. I hung on tighter and tighter to Cole.

"Your key also opens up the front door, right? If not, we're in trouble."

I chuckled and nodded. "We're good. Let's hope Ellie doesn't think we're stalking her!"

Our excitement turned into giggles. There was little traffic on Main Street, so we were able to get in the front door without anyone seeing us. We tiptoed into the house like two little kids, neglecting to turn on any lights.

"You know he's out there wondering if I'm going to spend the night here," Cole stated. "I feel for him, but stalking is never a good idea."

"You've got that right. I had an old guy stalk me for a while after I put his buddy in jail. It was just to frighten me, but one day, he had a heart attack in his truck right in front of my house!"

"I remember you mentioning that. Look, as much as I'd like to make this guy really jealous, I think I need to get on home. He'll be very relieved to see me pull away, and hopefully, he'll do the same. If he does not, or if he comes to the door, you call me right away on your cell, okay?"

"Oh, I don't think he'll do that."

"You never know. You didn't think he was capable of stalking you either."

"Okay, I'll call you if something happens."

With that, he gave me a hug and a kiss in the totally dark house. "I liked that walk a lot. It was pretty romantic and even exciting." He chuckled. "You are a peach, Kate," he said, kissing me on the forehead before he walked outside to his vehicle.

I went upstairs to look out the window so I could see whether Clark had driven away or not. Sure enough, after Cole pulled out of my driveway, Clark left. That was a relief. What was he thinking? That wasn't the Clark I knew. I sent Cole a quick text to say that all was clear.

Chapter 95

I loved the idea of meeting Ruth Ann at Charlene's Coffee Haus. She was already chatting with Charlene and Gerard when I arrived. They were both glad to see me. Gerard quickly reminded me that Sharla Lee was waiting for an answer about me becoming a volunteer. I acknowledged his comment without providing a response and met Ruth Ann at a table in front of the window.

I chose the blackberry crumb coffee cake and ordered a cherry crumb cake to take back to Aunt Mandy. Ruth Ann started the conversation about a family reunion that had taken place at her venue over the weekend. She said it was a German fest like no other!

"Food is the pride and joy around here," I added.

"This is just a little gossip I wanted to pass on to you, Kate," Ruth Ann said in a hushed tone. "I know you have been concerned about Stella Clifton's missing quilt, so I thought you'd be interested to know that something odd happened at this reunion."

"What?"

"Well, there was a gathering of women talking while the men were playing cards. They were talking about quilting," she began. "One older lady was bragging about a quilt she had made and was showing the other ladies a photo of it on her cell phone. I was filling their water glasses, so I asked if I could see it. Everyone gave her lots of compliments on it, so I was dying to see what it looked like."

"So?"

"When I saw the quilt, it was just like the quilt everyone had described that Stella made! How many quilts have a large tree in the center? She said it was called the Tree of Life."

"Well, Ruby said Stella did her own version of the pattern and made it so unique that I'm not sure that means anything."

"She said she was going to quilt it herself. Evidentially, this lady makes gorgeous quilts all the time, judging from their remarks."

"I guess there weren't any church ladies there or someone would have said something."

"Most of these folks weren't from here. A cousin from Dresden made all of the arrangements for the reunion."

"Did you get the quilter's name?"

"No, but I have the cousin's name. What are you thinking? I just thought it was odd. The quilt top hasn't been found, right?"

"No, it hasn't. If you could call your contact person, maybe you could say you were interested in the lady who made the quilt because you might ask her to make one for you. He may know who you're talking about."

"I could do that, but then what?"

"Well, Arnie, the janitor, said his Aunt Virginia took a

picture of Stella's quilt top and he doesn't know if she put it back in the quilt chest or not because he left the room."

Ruth Ann was trying hard to digest what I was saying. "I see. Well, it sounds like a long shot. But, it's the least I could do if it'll help. She didn't commit a crime by taking a picture though." Ruth Ann was teasing me.

"Please don't pass on what I've shared in this conversation," I requested.

"Okay. I'll let you know if I can track down a name."

"Thanks." I took a drink and then asked, "You haven't seen Clark lately, have you?"

"No, why?"

"Since you're practically next door, maybe you've noticed something. Do you ever see his SUV at my place?"

She looked at me strangely. "I'm not sure, but maybe I have. Why?"

"He's seemed to have taken an interest in my activities and I don't know why."

"As in stalking you? It wouldn't surprise me. I'm sure he's not happy about your relationship with Cole Alexander."

"I don't know why he'd care. Something must have happened between Clark and Lucy."

"Who's Lucy?"

"She's an old girlfriend with whom he had a child. He's only recently found out about having a daughter who lives in Nashville. It's too complicated to go into."

"My lands, girl!" Ruth Ann gasped in surprise.

We chatted another half hour before we left. Charlene knew we were into some heavy gossip and left us alone, which was perceptive of her.

Chapter 96

After I left the coffee shop, I went to Esther's to get my hair cut. I mulled over the report given by Ruth Ann and wondered if there was any merit to it. Most likely, nothing would come of the incident.

Esther was the only person in East Perry County that had a yellow mailbox. It was the landmark I always looked for to make the correct turn to her place out in the country. It was starting to drizzle and the cool air seemed to go right through me. By the time I ran from my car to her breezeway door, I had gotten pretty wet.

"Thanks for seeing me, Esther," I said, trying to dry myself off.

"Well, it looks like we won't have to wash your hair first," she teased. Like always, she offered me refreshments before we got started. It was the German way around here. As soon as Esther had the cape around me, she brought up the subject of Stella's quilt.

"You know, Ruby said that no one has called to be on the quilt list since the news came out about this missing quilt top," Esther shared.

"It is so unfortunate that news of this got out. I think it's just been misplaced. That's what I'm telling people if they ask."

"Good luck with that," Esther said as she twirled me away from the mirror. "How much do you want cut off today?"

"I want something different, so surprise me."

"Seriously?"

"Seriously."

She began to get scissor happy and I couldn't see a thing. She said it was her turn to have the next Friendship Circle meeting. I asked if I could bring my friend Charmin, just as a guest and not as a prospective member. She was pleased that I asked. I explained Charmin's circumstances.

"I guess I can announce Aunt Mandy's plans to get married to Wilson Schumacher." I said, clearly shocking her.

"Well, that's pretty cool. She doesn't mess around like some people I know," Esther teased.

"I didn't hear that," I said, smiling. "It's just a simple ceremony at church and then a small brunch at my place."

"No wonder you want to look sharp," she said as she began to use the hair dryer. "They make such a sophisticated couple."

"He'll be moving in with her, of course. I have no idea what to get them for a wedding present. They have everything and are trying to downsize."

"I know. I think that you giving them the brunch is enough of a present. Have you decided on your menu?"

"Not totally. My aunt has her favorite foods that I make for my guest house. I don't want it too fancy, but we'll have champagne, of course."

"Okay, I'm going to turn you around now and I'll keep my fingers crossed."

That she did, and it was a pretty sharp look that she had created! It was a bob and she had tucked one side behind my ear. She showed me how to blow-dry it so it would be a good summer look for me.

"Do you think Cole will like it?" she asked.

"I hope so. I like it, and that's all that counts."

I stayed a little while longer while she showed me an early kitchen garden she had planted. She also gave me some apple butter that she was known for making. The rain had stopped, but I had to dodge the chickens that were running around on my way to the car.

I stopped by Aunt Mandy's to give her the cherry crumb coffee cake.

"Well, aren't you looking smart!" she exclaimed.

"You like it?"

"I do! Oh my, what have you there?"

"Something you love," I said, handing her the cake.

"Thank you, sweetie,"

"Can we take a minute to go over the menu for the brunch?"

"I'd just as soon leave it up to you, Kate. You know Wilson has to watch his sugar, but this is a special occasion, right?"

Chapter 97

The next day was quilting at Concordia and I had to decide what to tell Pastor Hermann when I saw him. I sure didn't want to get Arnie in trouble. As I sat having my morning coffee, I got a text from John.

Good morning, beautiful! Sorry we didn't meet. Leave the Mr. at home the next time you come. J

I smiled, knowing he was teasing me. I responded with a smiley face.

You need to check on Carla. She says she's been sick but won't say what's wrong. I'm worried about her. J

I'll do it right away. Thanks. K

I didn't waste any time giving Carla a call. She took a while to answer.

"What's up, my friend?" I asked when she answered.

"What do you mean?"

"Is your health okay?"

"Why do you ask?"

"John is worried about you and told me you were sick."

I could hear her sigh. "No problem," she mumbled. "I don't want to go into detail, but I've been dumped big time by a man I thought really cared for me."

I breathed a sigh of relief. "Oh, Carla, I'm so sorry. That must really hurt."

"It's my fault for being so naive. Who would want anyone like me when there are so many women to choose from?"

"Carla, that is crazy talk. You are an amazing woman with so much love to give. It sounds like this guy didn't deserve you in the first place."

"I can't eat or sleep. I hate myself. How can I feel like a schoolgirl at sixty years of age?"

I thought she was going to start crying. "Stop. I don't want to hear anymore. I love you like a sister. You have given the Meyr family so much love for so many years. John has even fallen in love with you."

She snickered.

"What can I do to cheer you up?"

"Your phone call helps. I've been feeling so helpless."

"I'm going to send you some of that sinful chocolate cake you love from the Golden Bakery. There's nothing like chocolate to heal a broken heart. They can deliver it to you right away. Cheer up. We all love you!"

As soon as I hung up, I ordered the cake from the bakery.

I was relieved that her problem wasn't cancer related. Poor Carla finally succumbed to letting a man get close to her, and he cut out on her. He not only destroyed a relationship, but damaged her self-esteem. Glancing at the time, I could see that I was going to be late for the coffee break at quilting. While on the way there, I remembered I had forgotten my lunch once again! I guess I needed to diet, anyway. I was pleased to see the pastor's car in the parking lot. I rushed in the door just as he was coming out of his office.

"Kate, I was just going downstairs to share some really sad news with the quilters," he reported.

"Is it concerning the quilt?"

He shook his head. "Step into my office," he instructed.

"What's wrong? I was going to share some new information about the quilt with you."

"Kate, we lost Paula last night to a heart attack."

"Our Paula?" I asked, dumbstruck.

"It was a shock to many. She was at home and her husband called me before they even called an ambulance. They knew she was gone. As soon as I tell the quilters, I'm going to meet up with the family again about the arrangements."

"Paula was the sweetheart of our group. I can't believe it."

"She had a houseful of grandchildren most of the time, too. Everyone is taking it pretty hard."

I wanted to break down and cry right there, but I had to think of the other ladies. "They will take this very hard. She's been with this group for so many years."

"Yes, I know. I'd like you to stay with them. I worry about Erna because she has a heart condition, too."

"I sure will," I said, my voice breaking.

"Then let's do this," Pastor Hermann said, leading the way.

Chapter 98

The ladies were busy chatting and quilting when Pastor Hermann and I walked in the room.

"Good morning, Pastor," they said in unison, just like always.

"Ladies, I'd like to have your attention, if I may," he directed. Everyone stopped quilting as the pastor took a deep breath. "Paula passed away last night from a heart attack at her home," he stated clearly.

"What?" Ellen gasped. Everyone looked shocked.

"I know this is unexpected. I was with the family and I will see them again when I leave here. I ask you to pray for them. Paula was a good Christian woman and we can rest assured that she is with our Lord in heaven."

"I can't believe it," Frieda said with disbelief in her voice. "I just saw her yesterday at Harold's. Oh, Paula is his sister. He must be beside himself!"

"Paula touched a lot of folks around here," Ellen added. "That family is quite large."

The pastor nodded in agreement.

"I must go now," Pastor Hermann said, going towards the door. "This group can discuss how you want to remember her."

"Well, this chair will remain empty, just like we have done for Emma," Ruby stated with watery eyes.

When the pastor left, there was silence and a few sniffles.

"I had no idea that she had a heart condition," Erna murmured to herself. Her face was etched with sadness.

I was still standing as I watched the quilters react in their own ways. "Ladies, you know how touched I was by Paula," I started, holding back tears. "I keep thinking of all her little grandchildren who are going to be without her now."

"Oh," Esther said. "I know her daughter really well. I need to go see her."

"That would be nice, Esther," I said, smiling. "I know we have all been uneasy about the missing quilt top, but somehow that doesn't seem as important right now. Losing a friend like Paula puts things in perspective."

"That's right, Kate," Ellen nodded. "I'd like to lead us in prayer, if I may."

"Please do," Esther said.

"Let's hold hands," Ellen suggested as she reached for mine. I reached across the frame to clasp Helen's hand.

"Lord, help us as we grieve the passing of our dear friend, Paula," Ellen began. "We will miss her very much and hope You keep her in your care until we join her one day in heaven. Amen"

"Amen," we said in unison.

By now, we were all in tears. Some reached for tissues and some dug in their purses, looking for their handkerchiefs.

"Ruby, I think we need to dismiss our quilting for today,"

Ellen suggested.

"I'll second that," Matilda agreed.

No one said a word as we put our thimbles away and got our coats. I was so sad when I got in my car. Paula and I weren't close, but she was the first one to be friendly to me when I joined the group. When I brought the stain remover to help get her out of hot water with Ruby, her gratitude was evident. I'll never forget her smile of relief when it worked. Her sudden passing reminded me that she and Aunt Mandy were the same age. How we take everyone that we love for granted! Since Aunt Mandy came to mind, I decided to stop by and see her.

Aunt Mandy wasn't expecting me, so it took her a while to answer the door. She was dressed, but her makeup wasn't on. When I looked into her eyes, I immediately gave her a big hug. She saw the tears in my eyes. We went into the kitchen and sat down at the table where I shared what I had learned at church. Aunt Mandy hadn't met Paula, but I saw the sadness in her eyes.

"I know what's going through your mind, honey," she said, patting my hand. "You mustn't worry about things you cannot control. When it's your time, it's your time. As a child of God, she was prepared."

I nodded, still sniffling. I wiped my eyes and decided that I needed to focus on something else as a distraction. "Okay, so do you and the pastor have everything worked out for the wedding?"

"Wilson has taken charge of that."

"Good. Do you have any special requests for the brunch?"

"Keep it simple. Barbara's husband will be in town and we're pleased about that. I want you to extend an invitation to Cole."

"You do? He's not family."

"It wouldn't be right for him not to be there. Wilson said Pastor Hermann and his wife will be coming, and so will Oscar and Ellen. Oscar was quite touched when Wilson asked him to stand up for him as best man."

"I'll bet. Okay, I'll ask Cole. That makes around ten people. Do you know what you're going to wear?"

She nodded and smiled. "It's the bride's secret," she teased.

"That's what Jill said when I asked her. Well, I'm wearing a suit I've only worn once."

"When was that?"

"At Clay's funeral."

Aunt Mandy gave me a funny look.

"I loved it when I bought it. I hated feeling guilty about wearing it after that. This is a happy occasion and I think it's time to bring it out of the closet."

She nodded and smiled.

Chapter 99

Ellen called the next day to tell me about Paula's funeral arrangements. It seemed that I was going to have a funeral and a wedding back to back! The Friendship Circle was called off at Esther's because of lack of attendance. I was sure Esther was relieved, and of course, Aunt Mandy and I had the wedding to attend. We were grateful for the cancellation.

On my way to the grocery store, I stopped to pay my respects to Harold on the loss of his sister. Both Milly and Harold happened to be there when I arrived. I offered my sympathy and told them how much I had enjoyed knowing Paula. I assured them that I would be at the funeral service. They were touched by my good thoughts on their behalf.

"A little bird told me there's going to be a wedding the same week," Harold teased.

"It's pretty special," I admitted. I'm so happy for my aunt and Wilson. They are a well-matched couple."

"I should say so," Milly chimed in.

"Maybe some of that wedding potion will rub off on her niece someday," Harold chided in a playful way.

"Enough, you guys!" I protested, teasing them.

"You know we love to give you a hard time, Kate," Harold said, grinning.

"Well, I need to get some groceries. I'm so glad I got to talk to the two of you in case I didn't get to at the funeral."

"Thanks, Kate. It means a lot," Milly said as she gave me a hug.

I got what I needed at the grocery store. The drive took me by the Heritage Museum, but I had no time to stop and visit. They would just twist my arm into helping them out. I did decide to make a quick stop at Imy's . She was outdoors lining up some metal antique lawn chairs.

"Are you getting ready for spring?" I asked, getting out of the car.

"Yes, this is the time of year that people want these chairs. I had to repaint some of them. They sell in every color, but folks especially love the bright colors."

"They are so comfortable," I added. "We had them growing up, but I'm not tempted! Sorry."

She laughed. "I sure hated to hear about Paula Schilling."

"It is shocking."

"Schillings are all over this county. You can bet there will be a lot of folks at that funeral."

I went inside to take a quick look around. I felt guilty taking too much time when I had other things to do. "Have you gotten any new quilts in?"

"No, but I heard they are going to have an estate sale after Paula's funeral," Imy shared. "You probably already know that she made quilts all her life and I'll bet there will be many antique quilts from the family as well."

"But surely the family members will want to take them."

"You'd be surprised. It sometimes is all about the money they can get for them. I used to feel badly bidding against family members at auctions, but I don't anymore. My quilts end up in the hands of folks who are willing to pay good money for them and take care of them. With family, that isn't always the case. I don't suppose Stella's quilt top has shown up anywhere?"

"No, it hasn't."

"I just hope the signature quilt remains safe on the church hall wall."

"Not to worry. You really did a good turn there." Then, off I went, empty-handed for a change. I called Susie to confirm that she could help at the brunch. That would allow me to participate in the meal.

Charlene was known to make wonderful wedding cakes, so she was pleased to make a small one for the occasion. I took the liberty of ordering flowers for the church, Wilson and Aunt Mandy, as well as selecting a nice centerpiece for my brunch table. At the same time, I sent flowers for Paula's funeral, not really knowing what the other church ladies would do. Planning a little wedding was kind of fun. I had the perfect place to hold such an affair. I would have been a good mother of the bride if I'd had a daughter. I now understood the pride Maggie took in planning the wedding shower for Jill.

Ellen called near the end of the day and asked if I could possibly help out with serving coffee at Paula's funeral luncheon after the service. She said they were shorthanded because Etta Mueller had to cancel due to a death in her family.

"Well, I guess so," I said with hesitation. Why does Ellen

always get me into everything?

"You have a nice apron, don't you?" Ellen asked to make sure. "Be sure you bring it because you'll need one for serving coffee and tea. I have plenty if you need me to bring one for you."

"I guess you'd better bring one, if you don't mind. My aprons are pretty stained and utilitarian."

"No problem. I'll see you in church."

"Sure," I said, hanging up. I guess I was now one of the servers for what some called the "dead spread."

Chapter 100

When I woke up, I dreaded the activities ahead of me today. Thinking about Paula's funeral reminded me too much of losing Emma. However, I had to get moving because the service was scheduled for ten. I put on black slacks and a sweater, thinking old school about wearing black for funerals. Peering out of the window, I could see that it was sprinkling and that the skies were cloudy. It had all the makings of a sad day.

Ruby was the first to see me arrive at the church. It was as if she were waiting for me. She said most of the quilters were sitting together and she invited me to join them. That was fine by me since I didn't have anyone to sit with anyway. Ellen walked in with Oscar and I followed behind them in order to sit with the quilters. I sat down next to Erna. Frieda, Matilda, Helen, and Ruby were sitting together. As I looked around for Esther, I saw Imy in the back row.

The funeral procession started with Pastor Hermann entering the sanctuary, followed by Paula's casket, and then all of her many family members. They numbered so many that they filled up pew after pew. The church was full. Paula would have loved seeing everyone together.

The 23rd Psalm was read and we sang "Amazing Grace." The pairing of those two things was enough to make me feel pretty emotional. The pastor's homily was short. He mentioned how much Paula looked forward to her weekly quilting meeting at the church. He claimed he knew that her faith was strong and that she was with God in heaven. I could just see Paula smiling in approval.

Her oldest son was the only other person to speak. He reminisced about her love of family. There were five children, twenty-three grandchildren, and two great-grandchildren. He closed by saying her family and friends would always remember her generous hugs and her love of quilts. He said there would be a display of Paula's quilts in the fellowship hall and that everyone was invited to have lunch together after the graveside service.

I really had to fight the urge to cry because it was gut-wrenching as the church bells rang, one ring followed by another, and then again as the family proceeded out of church at the end of the service. Seeing the sad faces of Paula's family members would break anyone's heart.

I didn't take time to express my condolences to the family since I had to hurry and report for funeral duty and retrieve an apron. Ellen was quick to show me a sheer pink embroidered half apron that was trimmed with tiny lace. It was not my taste, but a fairy princess somewhere would have loved it!

"Thanks Ellen, but what if I get coffee or tea on this?" I worried.

"It won't matter a bit," she said as she tied a big fancy

bow behind me. “This looks very nice with your black outfit.”

“Where do you even get aprons like this?” I asked with a chuckle in my voice.

“Didn’t you have an apron drawer growing up?” Ellen asked in a serious tone. “I have drawers of aprons for all occasions. My mother prided herself on wearing some of the prettiest aprons around. They got handed down to me and I use them.”

“I know I’ve seen some of these for sale at Imy’s shop, but I’ve never checked the prices.”

“Well, we need to get started,” Ellen instructed. “They will be here right after the burial and they’ll be hungry.” Ellen was not shy about taking charge. “Go ahead and fill all the water glasses on the tables, and then when they arrive, start pouring coffee for them. It’s all decaf, in case they ask. Cream and sugar are on the tables.”

“Okay,” I said, nodding.

The fellowship hall was set up with wall-to-wall tables and chairs and they were all surrounded by Paula’s colorful quilts. The aroma of the delicious food was tantalizing. Those of us volunteering were clearly instructed that we would eat with the other helpers after all of the family had been served. In the meantime, the aromas were driving me crazy and my stomach was growling.

Thank goodness we had time to prepare before the family and friends returned from the cemetery hill where Paula was buried. I pictured her there with Emma and Josephine. I would pay my respects at another time.

There was the combination of chatter, crying, and laughter as the crowd entered the fellowship hall. Their appetites compelled them to find their seats in a hurry. I put on a smile as I poured my first cup of coffee. This wasn't my first rodeo, serving coffee to folks. Surprisingly, I enjoyed greeting everyone and providing something that made them happy today. I was proud to know Paula and was honored to serve her family. The event had turned into a celebration of her life as everyone shared stories about Paula and admired her beautiful quilts.

This family wasn't going to grieve very long before the events of life propelled them forward. Grandchildren were running everywhere and hugs and kisses were freely given to one another. That is the way it should be.

Chapter 101

I returned my apron without having put a spot on it. Chances are, Ellen went home and immediately washed and ironed it. I loved wearing the apron. I felt special and even received many compliments on it. I knew my grandmother wore aprons, but I could not recall my mother ever wearing one. I loved the apron stories that some of the people shared with me today. I reflected on the practice of the funeral brigade in these small churches and how they were so instrumental in bringing comfort to families during their time of loss. Many folks at the luncheon today commented that it seemed they only got together at funerals and weddings anymore.

When I got home at three, I was mentally and physically drained. Tomorrow was Aunt Mandy's big day and I had a lot to do! I got a text that all the flowers would be delivered before six this evening. It would be reassuring to know I had the flowers in place.

I was stuffed from overeating at the luncheon so I knew I could easily skip dinner. I was looking forward to relaxing with a glass of wine later. I kept seeing visions of all the jello salads, casseroles, and coffee cakes people had brought to the church for the funeral meal. It had been like a county fair competition! Ellen had said you could always count on folks bringing the same dishes to these church functions each time they were needed.

As I sat on the sun porch with my wine, I realized that I felt rather melancholy, so I decided to check on Aunt Mandy. She had to be nervous about tomorrow. The phone rang and rang but no one answered. For a moment, I thought perhaps they had decided to elope instead. That would be a story! Next, I wanted to call Cole.

"Well, this is a nice surprise," Cole responded.

"I knew you would think so. You know I don't make it a habit to call men," I joked.

He laughed.

"What are you up to?"

"I'm sitting at my kitchen table with a cup of coffee and going over a contract that needs my approval. How about you?"

"I'm recovering from playing waitress at Paula's funeral luncheon today. I'm relaxing with some wine and waiting for the wedding flowers to arrive. That's a contrast, isn't it?"

"I'll bet you are tired. Are you getting a second wind for all that is about to happen tomorrow?"

"My Merry Merlot and I are working on it," I said with a chuckle.

"I'll bet you're missing me, aren't you?"

"I might be. Would that be okay?"

"Absolutely! I'm looking forward to the time when you are not able to live without me."

"I won't promise that."

"I thought so, but time will tell."

We continued to chat for a few more minutes. I told him I was looking forward to seeing him dressed up for the wedding. Then I realized someone was at the door. "Cole, the flower delivery man is here. I need to go."

"See you tomorrow!" Cole said, ending the conversation.

I was extremely pleased at the creative floral arrangements. I was so glad I had ordered flowers for the church and wedding party as well. I chose silver and white as the color scheme. I loved weddings, despite the fact that my own marriage had had so many challenges. The innocence of love and hope was refreshing.

I prepared a few things in the kitchen before going to bed. I had gone over list after list to make sure I'd thought of everything. After all, this was my first wedding reception!

I crawled into bed with thoughts of both sorrow and joy. When I said my prayers, I first thought of Paula's family who were without her tonight. Then a smile came to my face when I thought of Aunt Mandy and Wilson starting a whole new chapter of their lives together. I remembered when Wilson first walked in my living room to meet Aunt Mandy. It was almost love at first sight between the two of them. Their friendship was a godsend for them since they had both just moved to East Perry County and knew so few people here.

As I thought about the wedding, I had to admit that I felt some apprehension about not having Aunt Mandy to myself anymore. Wilson now was part of the package. I remained positive as I floated off to sleep.

Chapter 102

Having enjoyed a good night's sleep, I jumped out of bed looking forward to what the day would bring. After I got my coffee, I called Aunt Mandy to make sure everything was okay. She typically slept late, but something told me she would be up early today.

"Are you having any second thoughts, Auntie?" I teased.

"Heavens, Kate, I hardly got a wink of sleep!"

"It's a big day. Where were you last night when I called to check on you?"

"We went to meet with Pastor Hermann and then got a bite to eat."

"Is there anything you want me to do? After all, I'm the maid of honor."

"I should be asking you that question. All I have to do is get dressed and show up."

"I know I didn't get your permission, but I ordered flowers for the church and for the two of you."

"That was very thoughtful. I suppose I should have done that myself, but I just wanted it to be very simple."

"There is nothing simple about getting married!"

She chuckled.

"I'll pick you up at nine-thirty if that's okay. When you come home, you'll be Mrs. Schumacher."

"I'm ready," she said, sounding happy.

Susie arrived, looking very nice. She was wearing a white starched apron over her blue dress. I gave her a thorough list of instructions. She seemed eager to do a good job.

I began getting dressed and was very pleased that, despite a few extra pounds, my suit still fit. It was navy blue. The white corsage would look quite nice, especially when I added some pearl accessories.

With good luck wishes from Susie, I was off to pick up the bride. She looked breathtaking in her winter white suit, an outfit I had not seen before. She must have gotten into her safe and pulled out all those diamonds she was wearing! A white matching hat was just the right touch. My aunt still had it, by golly. I suddenly felt like crying because of how lovely she looked today. Brides can be beautiful at any age.

Wilson and Oscar were waiting for us in the sanctuary. The look on Wilson's face when he saw his bride was priceless. It was a magical moment when they saw one another.

"Good morning, Kate," Oscar greeted me kindly. "You look lovely."

"Thanks, Oscar," I said, smiling. "I see you found the flowers."

"My corsage is lovely, Kate," Aunt Mandy said as I pinned it on her.

"Leave it to you to think of everything, Kate," Wilson said. "Thanks so much."

Ellen walked in and was followed by Barbara and her husband. I looked around the room and kept my eye on the door.

Where was Cole?

Pastor Hermann came out of his office and asked the bride and groom if they were ready for the ceremony to begin. It seemed a bit awkward without any music. We took our places at the front of the sanctuary. As I stood next to Aunt Mandy, I turned around to see Cole coming down the aisle. Seeing him put me at ease and I gave him a big smile. He joined Ellen in the front pew.

Pastor Hermann began with a simple welcome. I was nervous, but the bride and groom were calm and their eyes never left each other's. Short and sweet best described the message. I suspected that Pastor Hermann was instructed to keep it brief. Oscar had the rings, as the best man would. In the span of two quick questions, they had become man and wife. Pastor Hermann told Wilson that he could now kiss the bride. How special and adorable that moment was!

I approached them with misty eyes and excitement for their future. This union was meant to be. Barbara gave me a hug. It was clear that she was truly happy for the two of them. I told Barbara to take the altar flowers home with her and announced that everyone was invited back to my house for brunch. Cole fit right in and stayed by my side as we visited with everyone following the beautiful ceremony.

Cole and I arrived back at the guest house only minutes before everyone else. Cole said he would be in charge of getting guests a beverage when they arrived. The kitchen aromas permeated the guest house and Susie had done everything she was supposed to do and more in anticipation of our arrival.

Wilson's daughter and son-in-law were the first to arrive and were totally taken with the house. I promised them a tour before the day's end.

Pastor Hermann came alone. He was not able to bring his wife. It seemed that she had to attend an event with their son. He, too, was interested in a tour and had a lot of questions about the history of the guesthouse.

Finally, the bride and groom arrived in Wilson's car. They were beaming from ear to ear and cheerfully declared that they were famished. With that, we gathered around the table. I had place cards on the table so everyone easily found their seat. I asked the pastor to say the blessing. Then the toasts began, starting with Wilson who toasted his beautiful bride. Smart man! Aunt Mandy blushed and kissed him on the cheek. Barbara was the next to toast the happy couple and even made a toast to me. Susie busied herself by taking photos, something I had requested.

When it was my turn, I swallowed hard. "I was going to try to do this without any tears, but I can't promise," I began. "Wilson and Aunt Mandy, you are a match made in heaven. Wilson, welcome to the family. May you both have many healthy years together. I love both of you."

"Hear, hear," everyone said in unison as they lifted their glasses in celebration. Aunt Mandy had tears brimming in her eyes, as did I, as we struggled to keep ourselves from becoming too emotional.

"If I may," Cole said, tapping his glass with a spoon to get our attention. "I would like to say how honored I am to be included in this lovely occasion. May your lives continue to be blessed with every happiness."

Everyone cheered again.

"We don't want the food to get cold, so let's begin," I suggested. "Susie, you have been so helpful to me and we are all grateful for your help."

Susie blushed as she began to pour cups of coffee.

Chapter 103

It was a good thing I had enlisted Susie's help. There was lots of chatter and everyone had certainly come with a big appetite! She seemed to be able to anticipate what was needed and did a wonderful job. When we were nearly finished, I announced that a few gifts had arrived for the special couple. Wilson and Aunt Mandy seemed to be taken aback by the thought.

We moved to the living room where I had the gifts displayed on a side table. Cole insisted on helping Susie clean up while the others huddled around the bride and groom. As much as Wilson had tried to keep their wedding plans somewhat quiet, word had spread throughout the county. People had sent cards to my address knowing that I would see that the happy couple received them.

To my surprise, Ellen presented them with a gift from the Friendship Circle ladies. Aunt Mandy was overwhelmed since she was the newest member of the group and the gesture took her completely by surprise. Other gifts were from Oscar and Ellen, Cole, Jack and Jill, and a few of

Wilson's family members.

It was nearly three before anyone mentioned leaving. It was time to give the promised tour. Pastor Hermann, Martin, Barbara, Cole, and even Ellen followed me through the rooms of the house. I prayed that Josephine would behave herself. I explained all about the guest house quilt. Ellen's curiosity had her looking and looking at the names of all who had stayed here.

As I made it up to the attic suite, I realized that the only time Cole had been upstairs was when I instructed him to go up and get my cell phone after my attack. Cole's comments focused on how large the suite was and how the room was so functional. When the group returned to the first floor, Wilson and Aunt Mandy were sitting close together on the couch and holding hands. This was their day!

Pastor Hermann, Ellen, Oscar, Barbara, and Martin said their good-byes. That only left five of us. Around five, Wilson suggested that the two of them be on their way. I knew my aunt was exhausted, especially since she had gone through the day's activities with little sleep from the night before. It was soothing to know that their home was close by.

"Oh, honey, one more thing," Aunt Mandy said as they walked to the door.

"Sure, what is it?" I asked, thinking she may ask me to deliver their gifts at a later time.

"Catch!" she shouted. To the sound of everyone's cheers, I caught her corsage!

"You know what that means," Wilson laughed.

Cole was laughing hysterically while I shook my head in disbelief. I couldn't believe my sly little aunt! Her mischief surprised me!

Then we walked out onto the deck where Wilson got a little surprise of his own. Oscar had tied tin cans to Wilson's back bumper! Everyone laughed and Wilson insisted that they remain there for the drive home. Aunt Mandy was enjoying every moment of this old-fashioned prank. We continued to laugh as they drove noisily down the driveway.

"You have to be happy with the way this day went, Kate." Cole said as he put his arm around me.

I nodded. "I am pleased, but it's also very emotional," I admitted, my eyes beginning to fill with tears.

"I know, I know," Cole comforted me. "I say we let Susie get on home and we relax and enjoy the evening."

I agreed. I heaped lots of praise on Susie for her tremendous help.

"Miss Kate, this was all so special," she blushed.

"I couldn't have done it without you. I'm going to remember this when I have to do a dinner party or another event like this. Thank you so much. Please take home any leftovers that you would like. Here is a check, too."

"Thank you so much," she said shyly. "This was fun."

After she left, I told Cole I was going to change into jeans before we did anything else.

"Do you want me to make a fire?"

"No, it's way too warm outside. I think spring is in the air." Upstairs, my cell phone rang. It was Jack and Jill.

"Hey, we don't want to interrupt, but we wanted to tell Aunt Mandy and Wilson congratulations," Jack said.

"Sorry, Jack. They just left. Call her at home at some point. Everything went well and they are both as happy as can be."

"That's wonderful," Jill added. "We should have called

sooner."

"When you talk to them, try to get a firm commitment from them about whether they are coming to your wedding."

"We will,"' Jack confirmed.

"Thanks for calling!' I said as they hung up. It would have been so special if Jack and Jill could have been here today. I went downstairs to join Cole. He had taken off his tie and suit coat. He was rattling around in the kitchen and had occupied himself by washing the crystal stemware.

"What's this? You don't need to do that."

"It was the only thing left to do and I know from experience that these have to be washed by hand."

"Yes, you're correct."

"It won't take us long," he said, tossing me a dish towel.

It wasn't late when Cole left for the evening. It sure was nice to discuss the day's details with him as we washed the stemware. I was totally drained and went to bed feeling blessed.

Chapter 104

The next morning, the early sunrise was a sign that spring was here and summer was not far behind. At this time of year, I wanted to run to Harold's and see all of his new annuals and get ideas for my gardens. But today, I wondered what the honeymooners were up to. I spent a few minutes reminiscing about yesterday's events as I ate a slice of banana bread.

My plan for the day was to stop by the cemetery and then head to Jacksonville, where I hoped to find a dress for the wedding. Being in Jacksonville, I could also meet Charmin for lunch. It sounded like a good, ambitious plan. Unfortunately, after I called her, I learned that Charmin already had plans for the day. That left me more time to pick out the perfect outfit. I looked at my watch and hurried to get dressed.

The grass was still very wet when I got out of my car at the cemetery. I parked near Josephine's grave and put a few of the wedding flowers on her grave that I had brought from home. Paula's grave was easy to identify. It was the freshly dug grave piled high with wilting flowers. I walked up the hill to get a closer look. It seemed so wasteful to see those beautiful flowers decaying. Among them, I saw the red and yellow roses I had sent. I often wondered why funeral flower arrangements weren't given to a nursing home so others might enjoy them. I guess that old tradition of piling a grave high with fresh flowers would never change.

When I returned to my car, I noticed that there were a few cars in the church parking lot. I wondered if Pastor Hermann had a meeting or something. Curious, I walked into the church and saw him talking to a woman. I didn't want to interrupt. When he saw me, he said, "Good morning, Kate. Is there something I can help you with?"

"Oh, it can wait."

"Kate, this is Virginia Popp," he said. "Virginia, this is Kate Meyr from the guest house here in Borna."

"Nice to meet you," I said, shaking her hand.

"Virginia is Arnie's aunt. She is the fierce leader of the Mission Angels. She conducted a very successful event here recently. They are having a wrap-up meeting downstairs."

"Yes, Arnie has mentioned you," I replied.

She gave me a quizzical look and then turned back to Pastor Hermann. "Well, I mustn't keep the others waiting. Thanks again for being so generous and providing us this meeting space. It's been very helpful for those who live nearby."

"Don't mention it, Virginia," Pastor said with a friendly grin. "Your group does good work."

When she left, the pastor looked at me. He also had a quizzical look on his face. I am sure he wondered about the purpose of my visit. "What's on your mind, Kate?"

"Funny you should ask, but it's about the lady you just introduced me to. Virginia asked Arnie about Stella Clifton's quilts when she was here for a meeting some time ago. Arnie had bragged about how they are quilted here by our own church ladies. She asked him if there were any ready to be quilted and he said he would check."

"Really?"

"So Arnie unlocks the chest with the key he had in his procession and gets out Stella's quilt, which he said he found right on top of the other quilts."

"So it was here! Just like Ruby claimed!" the pastor said.

"Yes, indeed! So then she told Arnie she wanted to take a photograph of the quilt with her phone so she could make a pattern from it. You know Arnie. He was happy to let her take the picture."

"That shouldn't have happened," Pastor Hermann said, shaking his head.

"I know, but then the alarm went off, so while Arnie ran upstairs to turn it off, he trusted Virginia to put the quilt back in the chest and lock it."

"So did she?"

"He says she did. He told me he even made sure the chest was locked when he returned."

"Well, that's good."

"Perhaps, but what if she didn't put the quilt back? He didn't see her do it and he doesn't remember what he did with the key after that. He said he must have just misplaced it, like he told you."

"Oh, I see. He is getting forgetful about a lot of things lately and that bothers me. He is the last person to leave here on many occasions."

"Arnie's heart is in the right place, but I'm not sure about his aunt's heart. Ruth Ann from the banquet hall said she had a woman showing off a photo of a quilt that looked just like Stella Clifton's. Ruth Ann didn't know her, but she thought it was quite strange after all the talk in town about this quilt. Stella's Tree of Life design is original."

"Are you saying she may have taken the quilt with her?"

"I think she could have taken that quilt top with her and Arnie would have never suspected."

Pastor Hermann scratched his head and asked, "Should we confront her?"

"I'm not afraid to speak with her, although I don't really know her. If I did speak with her, I would want a witness."

Chapter 105

I said a silent prayer for wisdom as Pastor Hermann and I walked down the stairs. Virginia was chatting with some women. They looked up, surprised to see us.

"Virginia, I'm sorry to interrupt, but Kate and I would like to have a word with you in private."

Virginia wore the same quizzical look I had seen just moments before. "Well, we are in the middle of something here," she said curtly. "Can this wait until we're finished?"

"Perhaps, but I think if you just come up to my office, this will only take a second," he explained.

Virginia took a deep breath, shook her head in disgust, and followed us up the stairs to Pastor Hermann's office. I could tell that he didn't know where to start. Knowing I had the least to lose, I began. "Virginia, this has to do with you photographing Stella Clifton's quilt top."

You could tell she was trying to figure out what was coming next. "Photographing her quilt top?" she repeated with her voice louder than I knew she meant it to be. "Well, that's nonsense. Why would I want to do that?"

"Arnie said you asked to see if the church had any of Stella's tops and he found one in the chest, which you photographed," I reported.

"Oh, for heaven's sake!" she said angrily. "I did take one on my phone. She is a wonderful quilt maker. So what? I would think she'd be flattered. There was no harm done."

"Well, Arnie had no business allowing you to do that," Pastor Hermann began. "You took advantage of him and you took a photograph of something that wasn't yours. You may not be aware, but that quilt top is missing."

"Well, don't look at me!" she warned. "Arnie was with me the whole time. Just ask him. How dare you accuse me of such a thing! What kind of church is this?"

"Did you put the quilt back into the box?" Pastor Hermann asked.

"Of course!" she fired back.

"Arnie said he had to turn off the church alarm and left you alone with the quilt with the responsibility to return it to the box," I said.

"That's nonsense," she said, shaking her head. "Look, you have a lot of hands in the pot around here, so don't go looking for a scapegoat from another church to blame. Are you finished now? I'm going to tell my friends that we're leaving. If this is how you treat folks, we'll go elsewhere."

To my surprise, the pastor didn't make an attempt to convince her to stay. She marched out of the room and back down the stairs. Within a short time, everyone from the group had exited Concordia Church.

"Kate, you're right. Something is not right here. Arnie used extremely poor judgment and she took advantage of it. You try to believe and hope for the best in people, but sometimes you're disappointed."

"Pastor, I have a hunch about something," I replied. "Let's go back downstairs." He followed me to the meeting room and I went straight to the unlocked quilt box and opened it up. There, right on top, was Stella's quilt bag with her name on it!

"She planned to bring it back. That's why they met here. She probably got scared, knowing that word of the missing quilt had gotten out into the community," Pastor Hermann surmised.

"She probably heard about it from more than one source," I agreed. "She got to make her pattern, which may have been her first goal. She may have been jealous of Stella. Arnie said Virginia's quilts are admired by many, just like Stella's are thought very highly of by so many people."

"I'm just glad it's here," Pastor Hermann said, relieved. "I'm taking this to my office and locking it up until Stella comes over here to pick it up in person."

"I feel so badly for Ruby and Matilda," I remarked. "They have both been suspects through this whole series of events."

"It's human nature to judge others rather quickly. Kate, thanks for going with your instincts and being so observant."

"Well, Ruby would have been shocked to have found it in the quilt box this week when we came to quilt."

"It could have made her look bad again if everyone thought she had put it back," the pastor pointed out.

"You're right," I agreed. "Get that quilt top upstairs and call Stella before anything else happens!"

The Pastor put the bag under his arm and went straight to his office. I couldn't help but wonder what he would tell Stella. I didn't need to know. I'm sure he was used to smoothing over conflicts between people and would convince Stella it was just misplaced. All's well that ends well, I hoped.

Chapter 106

Before I went home, I went to Marv's to get something to eat. His hamburger special was on my mind and I found an empty seat at the bar.

"Good to see you, Kate," Marv greeted me cheerfully. "How are the newlyweds?"

"Great, I suppose. I haven't heard otherwise," I answered with a smile. "How did you know about their wedding?"

"Now, your place is maybe a hundred feet from here," Marv teased. "How do you think? It's a real nice thing, if you ask me."

"I am happy for them. I think they are a perfect match."

"Well, you've become a real regular here, haven't you?" Chuck's voice said as he sat down next to me. "How come I wasn't invited to that weddin' I just heard about?" Chuck teased. "After all, I built the house they're livin' in. I think the world of those two."

I smiled.

"It was just family. They just wanted a really small celebration."

"Since when did Cole Alexander become family? Did I miss somethin'?"

I had to laugh. Chuck's sense of humor was entertaining.

"Is this gettin' serious?"

"I like him a lot, and I like his red Jeep even better."

"How's Clark takin' all of this?" he asked as Marv handed him a beer.

"I don't know. I haven't seen him. Have you?"

"I thought I saw his SUV at your house recently, but I guess I was mistaken."

That was not what I wanted to hear. I decided to change the subject. "Have you seen Ruth Ann lately?"

"Nah, she's not interested in seein' me," he said, shaking his head. "Ya' know, I have it pretty good without a woman hangin' around my neck."

I laughed. We talked and I let him buy me a beer. He said his business was good and he liked his life just the way it was, despite pressure from family and friends to find a special someone. I had to respect that.

When I arrived home, I called Esther to tell her about Stella Clifton's quilt. She hoped the pastor would handle the situation well when he told the other quilters. I thought about calling Aunt Mandy, but then remembered that she was officially still on honeymoon time and thought better of it. I checked my phone messages and Internet for any chance that someone was interested in booking a room. There was nothing. My business was turning into a big disappointment for me. My phone chimed, indicating that I had a text message.

All is well with Carla. I thought you'd want to know. J

Wonderful! How are you? K

In Pensacola on business. J

I'll bet you are. Is she cute? K

I got a smiley face in return. If that was his answer, it must be true. When I go back for Jack's wedding, I will make sure that Cole and John get to know each other.

Tomorrow, I will definitely go to Jacksonville to get my dress for the wedding. On the spur of the moment, I called Ellie to see if she would accompany me. Surprisingly, she said yes! She said that she desperately needed some time off. We agreed to meet at Charlene's coffee shop before our shopping adventure began.

Chapter 107

The next morning, Charlene was tickled to see us. I said hello to Gerard and his cronies who enjoyed their morning coffee there every single day. It was noisy and busy, so it was hard for Ellie and me to talk. Ruth Ann also came by and joined us for a few minutes. We tried to get her to join us for the upcoming shopping extravaganza, but she had to make a trip to Perry to buy a new refrigerator for the banquet hall. With so many people around, I didn't dare tell either of them about Stella's quilt top.

"Clark has been coming to the winery more frequently and drinking at the bar," Ellie confided. "He's not very talkative. He drinks pretty heavily before he leaves, which worries me about his ability to drive home. I've even told him so."

"I'm sorry to hear that."

"I'm sure he misses you, Kate. He seems depressed. I hope it's nothing more than that."

"I do, too. I loved having him as a friend, but as far as having a relationship, I felt like I was in it by myself."

Ellie nodded in agreement. "I say that if you're not moving ahead, you're dying. That goes for business as well. It's risky when you don't do anything."

"That's right, my wise friend," I teased.

After filling ourselves with breakfast goodies and coffee, we were off to shop, going in and out of the usual dress shops. Unfortunately, after having trolled the usual stores, I still had not found a suitable outfit.

"Why didn't you go to a bridal shop and order a dress while there was still time?" Ellie inquired, curious.

"Because I didn't want to look like every mother of the groom," I said with a chuckle. "Let's try this new shop. I cut their ad from the newspaper and brought it with me.

We did just that. It was tastefully done and the young sales girl seemed to know exactly what I wanted. While I worked with her, Ellie went to find a pair of new jeans. After trying on three possibilities, I found the perfect one! It was a taupe formfitting linen dress that nearly matched the color of my hair. I knew I had shoes that would be perfect with it. Ellie seemed to like it a lot, or maybe she was just ready to go home! I saw the total look as classic and the color would go with any flowers they chose. I was excited to have the dress purchased and off my list.

We then went into the flower shop next door. I am a real sucker for all types of garden accessories. I fell in love with a birdbath that I felt my backyard needed. I knew exactly where it would fit and how I would landscape around it. The weight was tremendous, but the young salesman handled it with ease and put it in the back of my Jeep. Ellie found a concrete frog that she said would join the others in her collection. I didn't know that she had actually given names to every frog in her collection! We were pretty happy when we left. We grabbed a quick bite at a deli, but then wished we had gone somewhere where we could have had a glass of wine. When we got back to Ellie's house, I finally told her about Stella Clifton's quilt being found.

"So you're convinced she put it back?"

"You had to be there. She had guilt written all over her face."

"Do you think that's the end of it?"

"I think Pastor Hermann will know how to handle it from here."

"There was a lot of finger-pointing going on. I'm not sure it will be that simple."

"They hang onto his every word, as if whatever he says is gospel. He'll handle it. Thanks for going with me, Ellie. You are a true friend. I wish you could be at the wedding."

"I do, too. Cole will adore you in that dress!"

We hugged each other before she left to go inside. She warned me about not hurting myself trying to get the bird bath out of the Jeep. I told her I would call Cotton so he could help me get it out safely.

Chapter 108

The following day, Cotton was more than happy to come over and unload the birdbath. I had purchased bedding plants that were ready to be put into the ground. I could picture them surrounding my birdbath. I also wanted to plant yellow rosebushes at the side of the house in honor of Josephine. Cotton suggested that I get a stone marker to place nearby. That way, everyone would be aware that they had been planted in her honor. I agreed that it was a wonderful suggestion.

"Your guests would love seeing the marker with the roses," Cotton said.

"If I ever get more guests," I complained. "You probably miss those muffins, don't you?"

He laughed.

"I'll make us a sandwich while you finish up out here," I suggested.

Before I got to the door, Aunt Mandy and Wilson pulled into my driveway.

"Welcome, honeymooners," I called from the deck.

They got out of the car looking quite happy. "My, this is going to be lovely back here, Kate," Aunt Mandy observed. "Where did you get this pretty birdbath? Cotton, I have a few gardening ideas of my own when you have some time."

"Sure! Congratulations, first of all," Cotton offered. "Miss Kate here manages to find things to keep me busy."

"Thanks, Cotton" said Wilson. "I wish I could help more outside, but even with my new knee, I'm not ready for gardening yet."

"Have you two had lunch?" I asked.

"Yes, we stopped at a cute little place in Jacksonville that's owned by three sisters." Aunt Mandy replied. "We need to go there for lunch sometime, Kate."

"What's the name of it?" I asked.

"Oh, darn, something with birds," Wilson said.

"Pie Bird Café, I think," added Aunt Mandy.

"Well, we need our nap, so you youngsters get on with your work," Wilson said as they got back in their car.

Cotton and I shared tomato soup and grilled cheese sandwiches. It was always a quick go-to lunch. While I had Cotton's attention, I discussed my trip to South Haven and how I needed him to keep a close eye out for anything unusual while I was gone. Of course, he agreed to do so. We continued the outdoor work until we were exhausted. When I fell into bed that night, I hurt everywhere in my body. Cole's call before I fell asleep was comforting.

"Just checking in on you," he said. "I hope I'm not calling too late. I just got in from a dinner meeting."

I explained that I was always glad to hear from him. I told him that Cotton and I experienced a fulfilling but exhausting day outdoors. He was also pleased to hear that

I had found a dress for the wedding. I quickly gave him the short version of how the church quilt top had been returned. He applauded my efforts to bring this stressful situation to a close. A good hour passed before we finally said good-bye.

Now, I was wide awake. I got out of bed and decided to drink some herbal tea to help me relax. When I got downstairs, I turned the alarm off. I walked into the dining room and thought I saw Clark's SUV pull out of my driveway. Surely he had to see that my house was dark and that I had gone to bed. Was he checking on me? I took my tea to the living room. What was on Clark's mind? Should I call him and find out? Perhaps I was inconsiderate not to talk to him as he had requested. I was curious about his new family. I wondered if he had become a grandfather. Clark was not a phone person, so I would ask to see him if it came to that. I had to ask myself some pretty hard questions before that could happen. Did I miss him? Did I have more feelings for him than I was willing to admit? Would I give Cole up for him? All the answers were a resounding no. Our time was over, but I did still care what happened to him.

Chapter 109

I was glad to get Maggie's phone call the next day. I had a lot of questions regarding the wedding, which was getting closer. Maggie was nice enough to book the country club for the rehearsal dinner, something I was responsible for. She still had the connections and the discount, of course. Her update sounded wonderful.

I informed her that Cole had agreed to come to the wedding with me and that Aunt Mandy and Wilson were coming only if their health allowed. Maggie said she kept the list to two hundred in attendance as requested but it had been hard. Since I didn't have many names, it allowed her to invite more of her family and friends. I'm glad she insisted on including the Beach Quilters, which Jill gave her grief about. I would enjoy having them there as well. I had told Jack to invite any of the Meyr family that he was comfortable inviting.

Maggie was thrilled when I told her the color of my dress. She was wearing a color she described as blush, so neither one of us would stand out. She said wedding gifts were already arriving. Jill maintained that the gifts would not be opened until she and Jack returned from their honeymoon. That did not sit well with Maggie. She was anxious to see their contents and thought the delay would be inconsiderate. This time, I agreed with Jill.

When she got back to the subject of Cole, she asked how our relationship was progressing. I was keenly aware that she wanted to know if we had made any kind of commitment. I simply said that things were going fine with us.

After we hung up, I realized that I was growing very excited about taking Cole to the ceremony. I knew tongues would be wagging when everyone saw me with him. I tried to call Cole to give him a wedding update, but the call went straight to voicemail. He was probably in a meeting. Five minutes later, he called back.

"I'm looking forward to the trip as well," he assured me. "We can stay as long as you like. Can you give me any suggestions about what to get the happy couple?"

"I'll think about it. Fortunately, they have requested that the parents help with the expense of the honeymoon, so that's what I'm doing."

"I can do the same. You can't have too much of that green stuff on your honeymoon."

"That would be very generous, Cole. Thank you."

"I'm on my way to St. Louis, so if it's not too late tomorrow night when I return, I'll stop by."

"I would like that."

"Because you miss me, right?"

"Right," I said quickly. "Aunt Mandy and Wilson stopped by today. They look so happy."

"That's the way it should be. They really bring out the

best in each other."

"Wise observation. They're very lucky."

"I think it's more than luck. They recognized their needs and wants and didn't play games with one another. They were honest about their feelings. That's what made them want to spend the rest of their lives together."

"So true. I'm so happy they will be living in her house."

"It's a wonderful spot, and made even more special by the fact that he designed it. It's a very special love story. Hey, has Oscar pressed you lately to sell any of your ground?"

"No, and he'd better not. I'm not interested in selling."

"It's getting harder and harder to justify me keeping this house with all the acreage that comes with it. I think that if my ex-wife makes me a good enough offer, I may sell it back to her."

"You would?"

I need a simpler place. I'm gone so much. They're doing some upscale condos in Jacksonville that I'm keeping my eye on. I know the developer. He'd probably give me a good deal."

"That's big news," I responded with interest.

We hung up with me pondering all the thoughts and opinions Cole had expressed in our conversation. I liked what he said about marriage and being honest about what each person wants in the relationship. Clark wouldn't have admitted to any of that.

Chapter 110

The night was still young. I decided to bake something. What did I have in the house? What would taste good right now? I took several of my favorite cookbooks off the shelf and eventually spotted a simple peach cake. That would work! I had fresh peaches ripening on the counter. The recipe said I needed to mix the batter, place the sliced peaches on top, and then sprinkle sugar and cinnamon over everything. There was no need for icing. That pleased me. This would be a good treat for Cole tomorrow, and perhaps for Aunt Mandy and Wilson.

As I was cleaning up the mess, there was a knock on my back door. I immediately jumped. It was eight and I wasn't expecting anyone. I looked out the window and saw Clark's SUV.

"Hey," I said as I opened the door.

"Hey. Why does this kitchen smell so good all the time?"

I laughed. "I'm baking a cake. You know me!"

"I hope you don't mind me stopping by like this. Were you about to leave or anything?"

"Not with a cake in the oven," I pointed out. "Come on in. Do you want a beer?"

"Sure," he nodded, looking more relaxed.

"How have you been?" I asked as we took a seat on the sun porch.

"Good. I'm as busy as always. What about you?"

"Busy, but not with guests. I suppose the warmer season will help. I'm getting some inquiries here and there."

"I heard all about your aunt's wedding," he said with a big grin.

"It's really great to see them both so happy." I ventured into new territory by asking, "Are you a grandfather yet?"

He grinned and nodded.

"Really?"

"It was a boy and she named him Clark followed by Andrew, the name of the other grandfather."

"Oh, I'm so happy for you. Does he look like you?"

"Nah, but he hollers like me. He's a big boy. He weighed almost ten pounds!"

"Oh! You and Lucy must be very proud."

At the mention of Lucy, his expression changed immediately. "About me and Lucy. We couldn't make a go of it."

"I'm sorry."

"I don't know what I was thinking. I overacted after finding out about having a daughter. In the meantime, I treated you poorly. I want you to know I'm embarrassed and I'm very sorry."

I had to think about how to respond. After a moment, I

said, "You don't owe me an apology. You had every reason to pursue that relationship again. The news of finding a daughter and now having a grandson is awesome!"

"Somehow, I knew you'd say that."

"I mean it."

"You were the best friend I ever had and I let you go."

"Clark, I've moved on. I've missed our friendship, and to be honest, I guess I did need more attention."

"It appears as though you've found some happiness with Cole Alexander," he said with an unmistakable hint of anger.

I nodded. "We have a good relationship. He's a very good man. You are a good man as well, Clark."

"You deserve a good man."

"And you deserve a good woman. There is room for both of us to find happiness, Clark."

He grinned. "I guess I got what I needed to hear, so I'm going to get on my way. Thanks for the beer."

"Don't be upset with me, Clark. I think of the world of you and always will. I will always be thankful for your helping me after my arrival here. I was scared and confused."

"I'll settle for gratitude. I think the world of you, too."

At the door, I gave him a big hug, which clearly took him by surprise. I was afraid he wouldn't let me go. I pulled away and he walked into the night.

I closed the door with tears stinging my eyes. The timer went off in the kitchen, jarring me back to reality. I pulled the hot cake out of the oven. The smell was heavenly.

I got out the Merry Merlot and poured myself a drink. The encounter with Clark had gone well. I was pleased that we'd finally had that talk. I think Clark's guilt was why he couldn't move on before. Perhaps now, he could.

Chapter 111

I couldn't wait to get to Concordia for quilting the next day. I hadn't slept well following Clark's visit. I welcomed the distraction provided by the chatter of the ladies and the pending news of the quilt's reappearance. I walked in with Esther and reminded her not to say anything about what I had told her. Erna carried in hot sticky buns so we followed her to the kitchen where we also gravitated toward the coffeemaker.

After that, I sat down next to Ellen at the quilting frame and inwardly gloated that I finally knew a secret that she didn't know! Paula's chair was empty, as was Emma's. It was sobering. Ruby seemed friendlier than usual. It didn't take long for Pastor Hermann to join us.

"Good morning, ladies."

"Good morning, Pastor," they repeated.

"What smells so good?" he asked with a big grin.

"It's Erna's sticky buns," Frieda answered. "Help yourself!"

"I'll do that, but first, I want to share some good news

with you," he announced.

"I just got word that the men's club is going to do a special appreciation dinner, and the dinner will feature Ruby's wonderful chicken and dumplings."

Everyone gasped with delight and Ruby's face turned red.

"Oh, that's wonderful!" I exclaimed. "I've heard so much about her specialty. I'll be sure to be there."

"I have some other news, too," he continued.

"What's that?" asked Ellen.

"We've located Stella Clifton's quilt top," he revealed.

"What?" Ellen nearly shouted. "Where on earth was it?"

The room went quiet and Pastor Hermann began, "There was a misunderstanding. I won't go into details, but we owe Ruby an apology because Ruby did bring the top to the church to be quilted, just as she said."

Ruby looked like she wanted to faint. Matilda looked directly at her.

"Stella has the quilt top in her possession," he continued. "She said that she plans to quilt this particular quilt herself. She did add that her next one would be coming back to Concordia, however."

There were all sorts of responses to the news from Pastor Hermann. I suppose his brief explanation left a lot to their imaginations. I think the pastor's explanation satisfied everyone except Ellen. I said a little prayer of thanks to God for bringing this mystery to a close.

As we quilted along, everyone seemed happier. Gossip and chatter got back to normal. We were now back to discussing the weather forecasts, who'd had a baby, Erna's sticky bun recipe, the upcoming church picnic, and whose quilt would be coming up next for us to quilt. I left before Ellen so she couldn't question me about the quilt top or discuss it with me.

I planned to drop off some peach cake at Aunt Mandy's. When I arrived, I found Aunt Mandy and Wilson relaxing on the porch. Wilson appeared to be dozing off while Aunt Mandy was knitting. Both of them perked up when they saw the peach cake.

"What are you knitting?"

"It's an afghan that I started years ago," she explained, holding it up. "Do you think Jill and Jack would like this for a wedding present? It's almost done."

"Yes!" I exclaimed. "It will mean so much that you made it yourself. It gets pretty cold in New York. Are you both set to make that trip to South Haven? You can go with Cole and me or drive up yourselves."

"Kate, I think we'll make the trip up there a little honeymoon," Wilson said. "We'll take our time and I have already booked the Carriage Guest House that you recommended."

"Kate, that B&B looks wonderful," Aunt Mandy exclaimed. "It's got the harbor and the lake right there, just like you said."

"They will take good care of you and you can stay as long as you like," I concurred. "My condo is just right down the street from there. Wait until you see the wonderful breakfasts they serve."

"Hey, Mrs. Schumacher, how about a cup of coffee to go with this lovely cake?" Wilson teased good-naturedly.

Chapter 112

Cole arrived that night around nine, which was later than I had hoped. He looked exhausted from the drive.

"Have you been baking again?" he asked with a big grin.

"I have. Would you like some dinner, or perhaps a piece of cake?"

"I've had dinner, but I'm not going to pass on the cake," he said, rubbing his stomach.

"Coffee or something else?"

"Coffee. I need to wake up before I go home."

I brought his coffee and cake to the living room. Before he tasted it, he pulled me onto his lap.

"You are so sweet, Ms. Meyr," he said, giving me a kiss on the cheek.

"You're pretty sweet yourself, Mr. Alexander," I said as I kissed him on the lips. "Let me know how you like my cake."

We talked for about two hours, starting with my day at the church. I told him about Aunt Mandy's and Wilson's plans for their trip to South Haven. He was more attentive as I kept refilling his coffee cup. Our conversation was going so well that I didn't want to tell him about Clark stopping by. At midnight, Cole suggested that he'd better be on his way.

"It's getting harder and harder to send you out the door," I admitted.

"I keep hoping that there will come a time when I won't have to leave at night," he said, holding me close to him. "Do you ever get lonely living here?"

His question caught me off guard. "No, but I feel guilty having it all to myself instead of sharing it with guests. Thanks for not expecting more from me right now."

"You're not going anywhere. I'll see to that. I've fallen in love with the perfect woman for me."

"I love you, too," I said while embracing him. I could tell they were the words he was ready to hear. I was surprised at how easily the words slipped from my lips. How could I say those words so easily when I struggled with them so during my relationship with Clark?

When I got into bed, I was hoping to go right to sleep. Instead, I mulled over the day's events, starting with the pastor's announcement at church. I was pleased with Cole's visit and my willingness to admit that I had fallen in love with him. My cell phone rang. It was one in the morning! I looked at the phone and saw that it was Cole. Had something bad happened? "Cole, are you okay?"

"I'm just calling to ask whether you had changed your mind about how you feel."

I chuckled. "You're crazy. Go to sleep."

"I think I've had too much caffeine."

"I'm having the same problem. It's been quite a day!"

"I think I could go to sleep if you repeated those magic words," he teased.

"I love you! I love you! I love you!"

With that, he did agree to hang up. I was pleased and I knew I had made him happy. I wanted to share my discovery with Ellie and Maggie, but I couldn't. What would Jack think?

It was now two in the morning. I got up and began making a list of things to take to South Haven. I also started a reminder list for Susie and Cotton.

It was now four and I had not even yawned once! How could this be? I scrolled down my cell phone and even answered a few emails. One was from Carla saying she had bought a new dress for the wedding. Would she be bringing her new beau? Another email was from Emily Meyr, the daughter of James and Sandra. I had emailed her to ask whether she would be at the wedding and she replied that she planned to be there. She hinted that by this time next year, she might be married as well!

It was five. Should I just get up and start the day? It was getting light and trucks from East Perry Lumber were starting to drive by. I loved the sounds of Main Street. It made me feel like I was right in the middle of this little community.

Chapter 113

Giving up on sleep, I convinced myself to start the day at six. Cotton would be arriving soon, so I brewed coffee and put in a load of laundry. So far, I felt no sign of fatigue. Ellie called at eight.

"Good morning!" she greeted.

"Same to you, neighbor," I responded. "What's up?"

"Just making sure you are coming to the Friendship Circle today. I'm having it at the winery."

"What? How did I not know about that?"

"It was in an email. You seem to have a lot on your mind."

"Would you believe that I didn't sleep one wink last night?"

"What's the problem?"

"Caffeine, for one. Cole stopped by late and we had too much coffee. I wonder if he got any sleep."

"Next time, do it my way and have too much wine. You'll sleep a whole lot better," she joked.

"If you can make the meeting, I'm warning you that Anna is announcing you as chairman of the quilt show at the Fall Festival. I remember the meeting when you said you would help and Ellen decided you should chair it. Do you remember?"

"Holy cow! I guess I remember," I had to admit.

"You'd better remind your aunt to come," Ellie suggested.

"I will. See you there."

I gave my aunt a call and discovered that they were going to a doctor's appointment that Wilson had scheduled. I rushed around, got dressed, and managed to appear energetic. I went outside to say hello to Cotton who was mowing the lawn. I had to stop and admire my beautiful new flower bed.

The drive to the winery was lovely. I loved this time of year. I wondered if Ellie would have us set up on her patio. I didn't have to wonder very long. As I drove up the hill, I could see a very long table covered with red checkered tablecloths. Four centerpieces of yellow sunflowers were perfectly spaced on the tabletop. Trout was filling water glasses when I approached him.

"Good to see you, Kate." He took a moment to pause and gave me a big smile. "It's been too long. Cole should bring you around here more often. I hear you're going to South Haven together."

"Yes, it's my son's wedding," I bragged.

"Congratulations," he said, going back into the winery.

Everyone was there except Charlene and Aunt Mandy. Charlene had gotten held up at the coffee shop.

"Welcome to Red Creek!" Ellie shouted above the chatty crowd. "We have a light agenda, so we'll begin with lunch. As you can probably tell from the tantalizing aroma, Kelly has been barbecuing this morning and you can choose either pork tenderloin or hamburgers." Trout and Kelly brought out a family-style smorgasbord of potato salad, corn on the cob, coleslaw, baked beans, and watermelon slices. What a sight! Some of us took pictures with our phones.

I chose to sit at a distance from Ellen because I didn't want to discuss the quilt's reappearance. I sat next to Esther who had already made a quick comment about how smoothly Pastor Hermann handled the quilt top discovery.

When we got to dessert, we were full, but it didn't stop anyone from choosing either a slice of apple or cherry pie. There was ice cream ready to put on top. By now, my lack of sleep was catching up with me. I was terribly tired and longed for a nap.

Before Ellie began the meeting, we made a toast to her and the staff in appreciation of the wonderful meal. They took a gracious, silly bow. Then Ellie began, "The first thing, ladies, is a reminder that Ellen's garden sale is going on this weekend and it benefits a couple of worthy causes."

"We have lowered some of the prices, too," Ellen added.

"Great," Ellie said. "Next, we received a wonderful thank-you note from the Schumachers for the wedding gift we sent to them."

"That was so sweet of the group to do that," I expressed. "It meant a lot to them. Aunt Mandy would be here, but they had a doctor's appointment to go to. They are also getting ready to travel to South Haven to attend my son's wedding."

Everyone smiled. "That said, Kate, congratulations on getting a daughter-in-law," Ellie remarked. "I hope you have a wonderful trip."

"Thanks so much, everyone," I said, gratified by their positive responses.

"Now, Anna, you have the floor," Ellie announced.

"As you may recall, I promised a quilt show at the village, along with the other festivities in September. Kate has agreed to chair that activity. The way I figure it, we will need at least fifty quilts to make a splash. My sweet hubby has already arranged some places where we can put up clotheslines, but they will also be placed on some of the cabins and fences. It should be very colorful."

"What a sight that will be," said Mary Catherine.

"Kate will need our help to gather quilts," Anna pointed out. "I think I have my daughter's Girl Scout troop lined up to help hang the quilts and take them down. The men will have to hang a few of them in the higher areas. Kate, I'm sure you'll have your own committee. I know that your aunt offered to help."

"I'll help you, Kate," Ellen offered.

"Me too," said Esther.

"Okay, thanks," I replied. "Anna, it sounds like you have done some major work to make this job easier, and I certainly appreciate it. I should be able to get quilts from my Beach Quilters group in South Haven. Remember, they're the group that provided us with Christmas quilts my first year here."

Everyone nodded and smiled. "Oh Kate, that would be such a help," Anna agreed.

I couldn't leave the lunch fast enough because I had developed a stress headache. How do I get myself into these situations? Right now, I just wanted to go home and get some sleep. And sleep I did!

Chapter 114

It was the day before our trip and I must have called Aunt Mandy several times with questions and details, not to mention calls to Maggie, who did not need my interruptions. Jill was driving her crazy and she was upset about her new haircut. I felt for her. It was stressful to be the mother of the bride.

Cole had promised to pick me up at eight sharp. I knew he had a lot of work to do before he left, so I tried not to bother him. I looked forward to spending the time in the car with him.

I asked Cotton and Susie to stop by in the afternoon to go over some of my concerns. Between their two little ones, who were seemingly everywhere, I'm not sure they heard a word I said! Cotton also mentioned that he would check on Aunt Mandy's place. Thank goodness for Cotton and Susie.

I called Carla and confirmed our arrival time. Cole would love sitting on the deck that overlooked the lake. The weather would be divine compared to his last trip to South Haven. I bravely packed a swimsuit just in case we spent any time on the beach.

Jack finally returned my call. I asked if he was nervous, but he just laughed off my question. He was pleased that he would be seeing Aunt Mandy and Wilson. He then asked how I would feel about seeing some of the Meyr family. I told him I would be fine seeing anyone he felt comfortable enough to invite. I hoped he was pleased that I was bringing Cole. I knew he would miss his father on this special day.

Even though it had gotten late, I decided to make some blueberry muffins. Cole, Jack, and Carla would appreciate them, even if they were a day old. I was almost under the covers when a text appeared on my telephone. To my surprise, it was John.

Hey there, mother of the groom! When do you arrive? J

Tomorrow evening. K

Are you coming alone? J

No. K

Damn. J

That's for me to know and you to find out. K

What's the deal? J

Sorry. K

Cruel! J

Poor John. I needed to make some time for him when I got there, but it had to include Cole. I knew they would like each other. Cole had the confidence to forge a friendship, but I wasn't sure about John.

The grandfather clock struck midnight. It was time to get some sleep in preparation for a long day. Somehow, I was feeling Josephine's presence. I hugged my pillow and felt her warm light of comfort.

Chapter 115

Our travel weather was a bit dreary, but Cole showed up on time and all was well. "I think you packed enough for the whole wedding party," Cole teased, laughing at me.

"Don't laugh. I know what I'm doing."

"I brought you some coffee for the trip," he said, handing me a cup of greatness.

"Thanks. Let me check the locks one more time," I said before getting in his Jeep.

Then off we went, catching up with one another about our week's activities. Cole had a lot of questions about the schedule for the wedding. He asked if I thought we would still catch the sunset this evening, and I assured him that we would, unless we ran into difficulty with the weather or traffic. I was pleased that he thought it was as special as I did and wanted to enjoy it together.

I called Aunt Mandy to see how they were progressing on their trip. It sounded as if they would be arriving later than us.

We finally crossed the drawbridge at about six that

evening. It was a welcomed sight. When we pulled into the parking lot, it felt as if I had never left. I unlocked the condo while Cole carried the luggage. John's condo was dark, thank goodness.

"Hungry?" I asked Cole when he had brought in the last suitcase.

"Sure! Why don't we grab some grub and take it to the beach to watch the sunset?" Cole suggested.

"Great. I know a little place on the way to grab some sandwiches and the best dill pickles known to man. We can have a concession-stand dessert after we eat supper."

Cole laughed.

I opened the double doors to the deck to let in some fresh air. Cole teased me about wanting to sleep there. I grabbed a bottle of Merry Merlot, two wine glasses, and off we went.

The beach was rather crowded, but Cole was equipped with a large beach blanket and we situated ourselves away from the crowds. We finally relaxed as we poured our first glass of wine and got out our take-out picnic. This was a nice quiet time. I knew that the next few days would be filled with family and friends.

Cole claimed the last dill pickle and I went to the concession stand to get some dessert. Cole was surprised when he saw me return with an extra-large banana split for us to share.

"This is quite an occasion!" Cole said, sitting up. "How are we going to eat all of that?"

"Not to worry!" I teased.

We made a dent in the ice cream and then put it aside when we had enjoyed our fill. We relaxed on the blanket as we watched the sun close in on the horizon. It was heaven.

Cole kissed me gently and then sat up to reposition himself.

"I want to ask you something before the sun totally disappears," he said with a grin.

"You'd better hurry!"

Cole took a ring box out of his pocket and opened it, revealing the largest diamond ring I had ever seen. "Kate Meyr, will you have my hand in marriage? I want to spend the rest of my life with you."

I couldn't speak. My thoughts were coming too fast. "Are you asking me to marry you?" I asked in disbelief.

"I am doing exactly that and I wanted it to be at this special moment with this special sunset." He took the ring out of the box and reached for my hand.

I thought I was going to faint. "Cole, I'm just so surprised."

"You have a few more seconds to answer before that sun totally disappears," Cole teased. "Your answer, please."

I took a deep breath and said a little prayer. "Yes," I said shakily. "Yes, I will be happy to be your bride and wife."

Cole beamed with happiness. "I love you, Kate," he said, embracing me and moving closer to give me a soft kiss. He effortlessly slipped the ring on my finger.

"I love you, too," I said, as tears began to roll down my face.

Cole gently used his hand to brush them away. "Let's have a toast to us!" Cole said as we touched our wine glasses together.

We sat there and absorbed what had just taken place. The sunset here was always a magical moment, but this memory would make it unforgettable. I was so lucky to have found someone like Cole after such a disappointing marriage to Clay. We stayed on the beach until we were out of wine.

When we arrived back at the condo, we headed straight to the deck to relax. We sat on the floor like two little children.

"You know, it will be up to you as to when to announce our news," Cole said in a serious tone.

"Thanks. I appreciate you saying that because I don't want to do it this weekend. We don't want to take anything away from Jack and Jill."

That night, we fell asleep in each other's arms on the deck. We woke up in the morning with wine headaches and sore bodies from the hard deck floor. It didn't hurt our spirits any, however, as we got up and about.

I brought us coffee and we enjoyed it out on the deck. The weather was going to be beautiful, just like the wedding. Below us, I heard John leave his apartment. Since we were sitting on the deck, I couldn't avoid saying good morning to him.

Chapter 116

"Good morning, John!" I said as he approached the sidewalk.

"Welcome home, neighbor!" he responded. Rather than stopping to exchange a few words, he kept walking.

I couldn't blame him.

Cole remained silent.

"Well, Jack should be arriving anytime," I said, smiling. "The rehearsal dinner is at six."

"Does this mean that you get to share your bed with me?" he kidded.

"No, it means that you will sleep on the couch tonight. Remember, this trip is not about us."

He laughed. "That depends on who you ask," he teased.

We munched on blueberry muffins and fruit on the deck while we waited for Jack's arrival. When he got there, I thought he had become even more handsome. I couldn't stop hugging him. He was more than pleasant to Cole and they immediately engaged in conversation.

Before we knew it, it was time to get dressed for the big

dinner. Cole wore a black suit and I chose a black dress with a white satin collar. I thought we made a handsome couple. Jack was dressed more casually in a white shirt and khakis. He was not looking forward to having to wear a tuxedo the next day.

Elegant was the best way to describe all that Maggie had arranged at the country club. Maggie and Mark were great hosts, even though I was the one paying the bill. From what I saw on the menu, it was going to cost me plenty, but it would be worth it.

Aunt Mandy and Wilson were quite pleased with their accommodations at the Carriage House. "I think we could make a habit of staying there," Wilson commented. "They offered quite a breakfast, just like you said."

"Of course, I had to brag about my niece's breakfasts as well," Aunt Mandy remarked.

I swelled with pride. "We went to watch the sunset last night after we arrived," I informed them. "Be sure to see at least one while you are here."

Little did they know why it was an extra-special sunset. I wish I could have worn my ring, but it would have been noticed within minutes. The dinner and all the toasts went smoothly. Some of the toasts were quite humorous. There was plenty of emotion when Jack mentioned his father. Cole's social skills put him at ease with all the strangers. He fit right in and I was proud to show him off.

After dinner, Jack left to spend some time with his guy friends and Jill left with her bridesmaids. This was their last night to be single. Cole and I said our good-byes, I thanked Maggie, and we went back to the condo. Jack returned home quite late after an evening of celebrating as Cole slept soundly on the couch. I barely heard Jack when he came home. However, I was able to fall into a deeper sleep just knowing he was safe and settled in for the night.

When I awoke the next morning, I tiptoed into the kitchen to make coffee. Still in my robe, Cole pulled me toward the couch as I walked by. He gave me a kiss and threatened to keep me there until Jack woke up.

I couldn't believe the day had finally come for my son to be married! His life would never be the same, nor would mine. Jack confessed to having a great time with the guys as he put on his jacket. He looked so handsome. Cole told Jack how pleased he was to be included in all the festivities.

"My mom sure has been pretty happy lately," Jack joked as he adjusted his bow tie in the hall mirror. "I'll bet you have had something to do with that."

"I hope so," Cole responded. "She's made my life a lot happier!"

It would have been the perfect time to have told Jack our news, but I just couldn't do that just a few hours before his own wedding. When I came out of the bedroom in my new dress, the guys whistled.

"Mom, you look fantastic!" Jack praised.

"She's a knockout," Cole chimed in.

"Thanks guys! Are we ready?"

Maggie greeted us when we got to the church. She looked frantic, but beautiful. We both wanted to jump for joy at the excitement of our children marrying each other. The music had started, and Cole and I were ushered to the front pew on the groom's side of the aisle. My stomach was filled with pure nervousness.

Chapter 117

Walking down the aisle, I saw many members of the Meyr family. I'm sure they wondered about the handsome man following me as I was escorted to my seat. Jack was standing at the altar with his best man and groomsmen. He looked both excited and nervous. The music changed to the familiar "Here Comes the Bride."

Jill resembled a snow queen. She looked radiant in her formfitting white gown. There was no lace, just pure satin with a flowing train. She chose to wear only pearls and looked as elegant as any bride could. I had never seen her hair swirled to the back, but it was a perfect style to match the simplicity of the dress. Jack's eyes were on her alone as she approached him. Mark was clearly choked up as he gave his daughter away. I glanced over to Maggie and she was already mopping tears from her cheeks. I took one minute at a time, hoping to enjoy the entire experience.

I liked the pastor's short message. Cole and I held hands as we listened to each word. When they exchanged vows, I couldn't control my emotions. My son was taking a big step in his life. I had to admit that there was some part of me that wanted Clay with me at this very moment. Their first kiss as man and wife closed the ceremony. They exchanged looks of relief and then walked quickly back down the aisle.

It was now time to celebrate! Cole gave me a quick squeeze to comfort me. We finally got to give the bride and groom our love and best wishes for the future before we left for the reception.

Hawk's Point's landscape looked extra lush and beautiful. Cole felt it would be a great place to play golf. It was the perfect setting for wedding photos. I asked the photographer to be sure to get one of Cole and me in front of the dogwood tree before he left. I told Cole it would be a perfect engagement photo and he agreed.

The inside of the venue looked divine, decorated in soft yellows with touches of red roses here and there. A string quartet played beautiful music.

I was so pleased to see Emily. She hugged me tightly and seemed delighted to meet Cole.

"Have you talked to my father and his obnoxious wife?" Emily asked with a giggle.

"No, I haven't."

We sat down to a delicious four-course meal that was tastefully done. The wedding cake was several layers high with butter-yellow icing. Since the reception was in the afternoon, there was only one wedding dance announced, and that was for the bride and groom. That came as a relief to me. Maggie caught my eye and gave me a signal to accompany her to the restroom, just as we had done many times before. We hugged as we tried to hold back our tears. We were beyond happy. I thanked her for a perfectly planned wedding, even though I knew Jill had done most of it.

"I'm so glad you brought Cole with you," Maggie said, hugging me. "The two of you make such a great couple."

"We're engaged," I whispered in her ear.

She screamed, causing heads to turn toward us. "Goodness, I can't believe you finally did it!" she whispered back as she jumped up and down.

"Don't you dare tell a soul," I threatened, wagging my finger at her for emphasis. "I mean it. Not until they leave for their honeymoon."

"Okay, okay," she said, calming down.

We curled our little fingers together, making a pact. It meant that we had our own shared secret.

Aunt Mandy and Wilson were talking to Cole when I returned.

"Would the two of you like to come to the condo for a cocktail?" I asked.

"Oh, honey, we'd love to see your place, wouldn't we sweetie?" she said, nudging Wilson.

"I'm game," Wilson agreed. "We'll follow you out."

We said our good-byes, including wishing the wedded couple well. At this point, their eyes and attention were only on each other, not on any of the parents. In the car, I told Cole that we should tell Aunt Mandy and Wilson about our engagement. Cole agreed, and we knew they would be pleased.

Chapter 118

"Oh, Kate, this is lovely," Aunt Mandy said as she walked into my condo.

"Look at this view, Mandy," Wilson said as he walked onto the deck. "I can't believe you don't spend more time here in South Haven!"

"Is Merry Merlot okay with the two of you?" I offered.

"I'm ready," Wilson said with a jolly voice.

"We have a special announcement and toast to make with the two of you," I announced. Cole and I had broad smiles on our faces.

"I have never had so many toasts in one weekend," Wilson joked.

"We are toasting the engagement of Kate Meyr and Cole Alexander," I stated.

"What?" Aunt Mandy was clearly surprised. "You've got to be joking!"

"That's no surprise to me," claimed Wilson.

"Oh, honey, this is too much in one day," said my aunt as she sat down. "Now, I can finally be at peace, knowing that my dear niece will not be alone. I'm so happy for the two of you."

"Auntie, you're too much," I said, going over and giving her a big hug.

"Well, here's to the next bride and groom," Wilson toasted. "May you be as happy as me and Mandy."

"Hear, hear!" we cheered.

"Thank you," Cole said as he put his arm around me. "I'm a lucky man."

"This is the day that the Lord hath made, so let us rejoice and be glad in it," Aunt Mandy recited as we cheered again.

Cole looked into my eyes and asked, "Are you happy, sweetheart?"

"Yes, I'm very happy!"

With the blessing of our friends and family, the next six months were busy as we planned our wedding. Cole knew how much I would enjoy the process, so he relished watching me go crazy! I decided I wanted to get married in a private ceremony at the guest house so I could walk down the beautiful stairway. It was my way of sharing our big day with Josephine. I wanted a large reception at Ruth Ann's banquet hall. I told my good friend to pull out all the stops for a gala affair.

While I planned our wedding, Cole was busy planning our new home that was to be built on my property near Wilson and Aunt Mandy. It would be nestled in the woods and would have a picturesque view.

Josephine's Guest House would continue to operate and would have an additional room for more guests. I couldn't imagine ever giving up the real prize that brought me here to Borna. I wanted to live the rest of my life in this wonderful community with my new husband. I thought my married name, Kate Meyr Alexander, sounded pretty wonderful. Don't you agree?

Afterword

Once again, I have to say good-bye to a fictional community that I created with so much love and affection. The characters became very real to me, as I hope they did to you.

It was very easy to bring my love of East Perry County into a fictional series. My respect and admiration for its people and traditions made it a real pleasure to do so.

I like to leave my characters in a happy place, where I can envision them in the future. Thank you for reading, and I hope you continue to take this fictional journey with me in my next series, Wine Country Quilts.

Ann Hazelwood

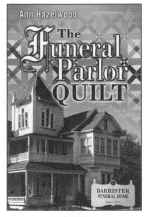

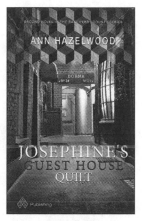

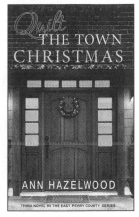

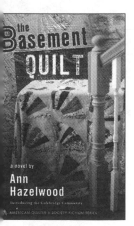